CODE WORD—GOLDEN FLEECE

Many people have written to Dennis Wheatley asking him what has happened to The Indomitable Four—those Modern Musketeers, the Duke de Richleau, Simon Aron, Rex van Ryn and Richard Eaton—during the Second World War. Apart from a perilous adventure in which they were called upon to checkmate espionage by the use of occult means, related in *Strange Conflict*, their doings have, up to now, remained unchronicled. However, in that book a passing mention was made of the fact that the Duke and his friends had been in Poland when the war broke out.

Here is the story of how they came to be there and found themselves, even before the outbreak of hostilities, involved in a most damnable conspiracy. The scenes of intrigue, violence and escape in Warsaw are exceeded only by those which follow in Bucharest—whence the friends are carried in a desperate attempt to sabotage Hitler's war economy and force Germany to ask for peace before she can muster her full might for an assault on Western Europe.

Old friends of this gallant band will renew their acquaintance with two of the most beautiful women in Europe: that pocket Venus, the Princess Marie Lou, and Lucretia José, Contesa Cordoba y Coralles, known for her exploits in the Spanish Civil War as "The Golden Spaniard"; while new readers will embark on a fresh but chequered love affair, of which a courageous Polish airman is the hero.

This is a down-to-earth story of human love, courage, devotion to duty and high adventure, which young and old will alike enjoy.

DENNIS WHEATLEY

DENNIS WHEATLEY'S WORK

has also been published in

THE UNITED STATES:

FRANCE

GERMANY

ITALY

SWEDEN

HOLLAND

SPAIN

HUNGARY

BELGIUM

POLAND

CZECHOSLOVAKIA

DENMARK

FINLAND

PORTUGAL

NORWAY

RUMANIA

BRAZIL

———

RUSSIAN

SERBIAN

ARMENIAN

ARABIC

The titles of his books are :

FICTION
The Man Who Missed the War
The Scarlet Impostor
Faked Passports
The Black Baroness
V for Vengeance
Three Inquisitive People
The Forbidden Territory
The Devil Rides Out
The Golden Spaniard
Strange Conflict
The Quest of Julian Day
The Sword of Fate
Black August
Contraband
The Eunuch of Stamboul
The Secret War
The Fabulous Valley
Sixty Days to Live
Such Power is Dangerous
Uncharted Seas
They Found Atlantis

SHORT STORIES
Mediterranean Nights
Gunmen, Gallants and Ghosts

NON-FICTION
Total War

HISTORICAL
A Private Life of Charles II
 (Illustrated by Frank C. Papé)
Red Eagle (Illustrated)
 (The Story of the Russian Revolution)

*CRIME DOSSIERS WITH
J. G. LINKS*
Murder off Miami
Who Killed Robert Prentice?
The Malinsay Massacre
Herewith the Clues

In Preparation :
Come Into My Parlour
 (A new adventure of Gregory Sallust)

DENNIS WHEATLEY

CODEWORD— GOLDEN FLEECE

A Novel

HUTCHINSON & CO. (Publishers), LTD.

LONDON : NEW YORK : MELBOURNE : SYDNEY

PRINTED IN
GREAT BRITAIN,
AT THE ANCHOR
PRESS, TIPTREE,
::   ESSEX   ::

CONTENTS

Chapter I

THE summer night was warm and still. Laughter came faintly on the air from a house at the top end of Curzon Street, Mayfair, where a dance was just beginning. Débutantes, dowagers and their escorts were driving up in a stream of luxury cars; the girls looking their loveliest in gay silks, satins and brocades, the men in their peace-time uniform of pleasure—white tie, buttonhole and tails. The lights of London were still burning.

Further down the street in one of the first-floor flats at Errol House, a small dinner party was in progress. The Duke de Richleau and his guests had gone in to dinner at eight o'clock, but coffee was not served until after ten.

This party on the night of Friday, the 28th of July, 1939, was at the same time a reunion and a farewell. Rex Mackintosh van Ryn, the great hulking American with the ugly face and the enormous sense of fun, had, as usual, been in London for the season; but now all his world was about to depart with rod or bathing-suit or gun. He was leaving next morning for Biarritz to take part in the International Tennis Championship, and the frailest of their company, little, stooping, bird-faced Simon Aron, was to accompany him as far as Paris. But there their ways would divide, as in August Simon could never be persuaded to forgo the attractions of his spiritual home—the Casinos, beaches and terraced restaurants of the South of France.

Richard Eaton and the Princess Marie Lou, that pocket Venus with the heart-shaped face and deep violet eyes, whom he had brought out of Russia to be his wife, were to make a leisurely progress up the Rhine and so on into Austria.

De Richleau himself was going to Poland, and with him he was taking the remaining member of the party : the beautiful Lucretia José, whose magnificent burnished hair had caused her to become that almost legendary figure in the power politics behind the Spanish Civil War known as "The Golden Spaniard".

The long Hoyo de Monterrey cigars which were the Duke's special pride had just been handed round, and as he exhaled the first cloud of fragrant blue smoke Simon's dark, nervously flickering eyes came to rest affectionately on his host. It flashed through his quick mind how little the older man had aged in appearance since he had first met him, six years before.

His hair and "devil's" eyebrows were no greyer; his eyes, which at times could become so piercing, had lost none of their brilliance, and there was still

7

no sign of age or weakness in the fine distinguished face, with its broad fore-head and beautifully moulded mouth. He was, as usual on these intimate occasions, wearing a claret-coloured vicuna smoking suit with braided fasten-ings; and Simon thought—as he had often done before—how the touch of colour emphasized the Duke's resemblance to the portrait of a Cavalier by Van Dyck, which was one of the four old masters on the panelled walls of the richly furnished dining-room.

The Duke took up the medium-sized balloon glass which held some of his priceless old brandy, and swivelled it gently for a moment below his aquiline nose to enjoy the rare ethers, before he raised it, saying:

"It's good to see you all gathered again about my table, but 'the best of friends . . .' eh—you know the rest. Here's good hunting to us all, and may we yet be spared for many another merry meeting."

Simon lifted the glass of golden Yquem with which he was still toying. "Wish you were both coming South with me," he said jerkily. "So much more—er—civilized than Poland."

"But Poland has its attractions," de Richleau murmured with a smile.

"I'll say it has," boomed Rex; "the best snipe-shooting in Europe and real hospitable folk to do the honours."

Richard ran a hand over the smooth brown hair brushed so neatly back from the "widow's peak" in the centre of his forehead. "But the call of the snipe is only half the story," he said quickly. "The main reason for the trip is to see again the haunts of his boyhood. Isn't that so, Greyeyes?"

The Duke nodded. "Yes, my mother was a Plackoff, and in the Czar's day her family had vast estates in Poland. I recently met Baron Lubieszow, who now owns a small portion of them, and his invitation to visit him was much too tempting for me to think of refusing."

"All right for you," Simon's full-lipped mouth broke into a wide grin, "but how about Lucretia? Not much fun for her."

"How like you, Simon dear," she smiled; "always so thoughtful for all of us. I don't want to go a bit really. I ought to go back to Spain. There are such thousands of our poor people who need someone to look after them."

"Nonsense!" laughed the Duke. "You came back to us more dead than alive barely two months ago, and, though staying at Cardinal's Folly with Richard and Marie Lou has already made a different woman of you, you are far from being your old self yet; and I have no intention of letting you return to those scenes of horror for many months to come. The war is over. You played your part in it most gallantly, but that chapter of your life is finished."

She sadly shook her golden head. "You are wrong, dearest. The war is over but there is more misery in Spain than there has ever been before. As the last of the Cordoba y Coralles it is my job to help lead my people towards better times. All of you here helped me save my millions when they were in jeopardy; now is the time when I must use them to the best advantage."

"But not yet," pleaded Marie Lou. "A few months can make little difference, and the longer rest will make you so much fitter to tackle your task when you do get back there." She was pleading not only for Lucretia herself but also for the Duke, since, although it was never openly admitted, they all knew that the Spaniard was his illegitimate daughter, born of a great romance in the distant days before Spain lost her King, and that her well-being meant far more to him than his own.

Lucretia shrugged the beautiful shoulders which rose bare above a corsage of white sequined satin. "Anyhow, I have agreed to go to Poland for a month or so. After that—we will see."

De Richleau waved the slender hand that held his long cigar in a faintly foreign gesture. "In a month much may happen. If I am not careful I shall lose you to one of those handsome Poles, who, if my memory serves me, are terrific lovers!"

For a moment there was silence round the highly polished table, the rich surface of which set off so splendidly the Georgian silver, big bowls of fruit and fine glass. They all knew that Lucretia had never fully recovered from the tragic ending of her love affair with Cristoval Ventura, but they also knew that Monseigneur le Duc de Richleau was as wily an old fox as any that had ever stalked a chicken-run, and that he would never have made such an apparent gaffe had he not deliberately intended to plant the idea in Lucretia's mind with that half-humorous lightness which can only be achieved when other people are present.

Simon, the quick-brained, was as ever first into the breach. With a little nervous gesture that he often affected, he stooped his bird-like head and tittered into his hand, as he uttered the curious negative which was habitual to him.

"Ner, it's much more likely we'll lose you to some Polish beauty."

Almost simultaneously Marie Lou had caught Lucretia's eye, and as they stood up the men rose with them.

"Five minutes—no more," Marie Lou smiled. "Then you can bring your drinks into the other room, as I'm certain you won't have finished them."

"Never a truer word spoken in jest," grinned Rex, as he held open the door.

When the men were seated again, Simon's dark eyes flickered towards the Duke. "Happy about going to Poland at the present time?" he enquired.

"Why shouldn't I be?"

"Oh, just wondered, that's all."

"Simon, what do you know?" de Richleau asked quietly.

"Nothing much. Money market's in a queer state these days and er—well, it might be difficult to get home."

"You think Hitler is really out for trouble?"

"Hitler my foot!" Rex cut in. "He may have the guns, but he's got no

A*

butter. It was the blockade that brought Germany to her knees last time, and now she couldn't hold out against it for three months."

"You don't believe in the theory of the Blitzkrieg then?" Richard smiled.

"No." The big American shook his dark, curly head. "I lay four to one that if it ever comes to a showdown and Britain antes up to see Hitler's hand it'll be found that he's been bluffing."

"Taken in hundreds, if that suits you!" said the Duke quietly.

"O.K.!" laughed Rex. "And make it pounds, not dollars, if you like."

Richard sat forward quickly, his brown eyes suddenly alert as he addressed the Duke. "You really think we're in for another war, then?"

"Yes, sooner or later we've got to face up to this thing and kill it. Chamberlain got us a year to prepare at Munich, but the sands are running out. Hitler is well served by his intelligence. He knows that behind the scenes our Government is now straining every nerve to make up for these years of ostrich-like complacency, and that if he leaves his bid for world power much longer he will find a Britain, at least partially rearmed, barring his path. He cannot afford to risk that, so unless he is prepared to throw all his most cherished ambitions overboard he must strike soon."

Simon nodded his head up and down like a china mandarin, then shot out: "Why're you going to Poland, in that case?"

De Richleau shrugged. "Because my appreciation of the situation is that we have at least another month, and I should like to travel in Europe again before all that remains of the cultured and leisured ease which was customary among the upper classes in my youth is blotted out, perhaps for ever."

The five minutes that Marie Lou had given them had already lengthened into ten, and she was a martinet in such matters. Max, the Duke's man, appeared soft-footed behind his master and murmured: "Excellency, the ladies request the pleasure of your company."

Still a little awed by de Richleau's last words, they rose silently from the table and, carrying their glasses, moved into the big library.

It was not so much its size or decoration which made this room in the Curzon Street flat so memorable to those who had visited it as the unique collection of rare and beautiful objects that it contained: a Tibetan Buddha seated on the Lotus; bronze figurines from ancient Greece; beautifully chased rapiers of Toledo steel and Moorish pistols inlaid with turquoise and gold; ikons from Holy Russia set with semi-precious stones; and curiously carved ivories from the East. And these were not merely the properties of a wealthy collector, purchased in auction rooms and shops. Every one had a story behind it connected with some exploit in de Richleau's long career as soldier, traveller and adventurer. The walls were lined shoulder-high with books, but above them hung fine old colour prints and maps.

Lucretia was looking very regal as she sat in a straight Jacobean elbow chair, but the diminutive Marie Lou had curled herself up like a Persian kitten in a corner of the big sofa.

As the men came into the room she stiffened slightly, her quick instinct telling her at once that something was amiss.

"What have you four been plotting?" she asked, striving to conceal the agitation she already felt.

De Richleau took her small hand and, stooping, kissed it, as he murmured with a smile: "Nothing, Princess, perish the thought in your bewitching head."

"You haven't got yourselves mixed up in some crazy business in which you'll all have to risk your lives again?"

"No, no. We haven't as much as a fragment of a map of a 'Forbidden Territory' between us, or a sniff of the Devil's brimstone."

"You swear that, Greyeyes?"

"I do indeed. We are all, as ever, the playthings of the Gods, and none of us can say what our tomorrows may bring; but tonight there's not a thing to prevent us from giving our thoughts to how best we can enjoy our holidays."

Richard had come up behind his wife, and gazing down fondly on her chestnut curls he placed his two hands on her bare shoulders, as he said: "Just think of it, my sweet. In three weeks' time we'll be in Vienna again. Vienna—where I first showed you what luxury and gaiety and love could mean."

"Richard, my love!" She quickly clasped one of his hands and turned her face up to him. "Of course, it was stupid of me. Just a silly feeling like someone walking over my grave. Forget it, please."

Rex had turned on the radio and twiddled the knob until he got a band. Then he pulled Lucretia up out of her chair and made her dance a few turns with him in the middle of the big room.

Soon they were all laughing again as gaily as they had during dinner. De Richleau ordered up two magnums of champagne. They were all connoisseurs enough to know that the wine was exceptionally mature and fine, but only Simon noticed that it was Veuve Cliquot, Dry England, 1906, a wine that would almost certainly have been dead from its great age had it been in bottles; and he knew it to be the Duke's very finest, of which he had only half a dozen magnums left.

It was one o'clock before they broke up, Rex and Simon leaving together, and Richard, Marie Lou and Lucretia, who were staying with the Duke, going to their rooms.

When they had left him de Richleau drew wide the curtains of one of the windows, opened it and stepped out on to the shallow balcony. The dance was still in progress further up the street. The music of the band came faintly to him. The street lamps shone with a warm friendly glow on the pavements, where a few young couples, who had left the ballroom for a breath of air, were strolling up and down.

For a few moments he remained there, looking down upon those young, carefree people, yet with unseeing eyes. He had laughed as gaily as any of his guests all the evening, but now he was a sober and sadly troubled man. He was wondering desperately if all six of them would ever meet again. For a second he had an absurd impulse to rush downstairs, and out into the street after Rex and Simon; to call them back so that he might at least make certain of looking upon their well-loved faces just once more. But it was too late now, even for that.

With a little sigh he turned back into the room and put out the lights, still heavy with the grim foreboding that, if they ever did come together again, it could only be in a world gone mad. In what circumstances of distress, and perhaps terror and despair, they might meet, he knew that time alone could show.

Chapter II

THE SECRET RENDEZVOUS

LUBIESZOW was a long, low house set in a clearing of the forest. It had no garden as the English think of gardens, but shady walks wound among the trees and flowering shrubs bordered its drive, while, at the back, a wide terrace with a pleasant view looked out over the meadows to a great lake into which ran the river Stachod.

It was very peaceful there as the countryside of Russian Poland is sparsely populated, and Pinsk, the only town of any size, lay a good thirty-five miles away to the north-eastward across the desolate Pripet Marshes.

De Richleau was enjoying his stay with the fat, jovial Baron Lubieszow, mainly because it was such a contrast to his normal life of a round of engagements among his many friends in the great cities and fashionable holiday resorts. The placid, orderly life of the Polish landowner, with its talk of crops, livestock and horses, carried him back to those more restful and contented days when he had often made one of a house-party on some great estate. The Baron's conversation was strictly limited, but he was shrewd enough in a way that is common among those whose life is devoted to the soil. His table groaned under the good, plain, succulent fare that came from his farms; his cellar was adequate; and if one wished to talk politics or literature there was always his wife, Clotilde.

She was a thin, ailing woman with a sardonic humour, who took little interest in her husband's activities and spent most of her time with Count Ignac Krasinski, their nearest neighbour and a daily visitor to the house. De Richleau suspected that the Count either was or had been her lover. In any case, he was her constant companion and supplied her with the gossip for which she was so avid, about the international situation, which the Count got from Warsaw, with which he seemed able to keep in remarkably close touch through his own channels.

Nearly a month had passed since the Duke and Lucretia had left London. On their way they had spent a few nights in Prague, and a week in Warsaw; the remaining fifteen days at Lubieszow had gone all too quickly, and soon they would be returning to England.

While showing little more than polite interest, de Richleau took in all that the Baroness and Count Ignac had to say about the dispute that was already raging over Danzig. He knew that Europe was a seething pot, on which a few weak, inept statesmen were vainly trying to hold down the lid, in spite of their awareness that the scalding Nazi steam inside must soon blow it off. But, like a condemned man lingering over his last meal, the Duke was determined to savour to the full such little time as might remain far from the excited, propaganda-maddened crowds which waited breathless for each radio bulletin and scare headline.

Besides, Lucretia was enjoying herself, and that meant a great deal to him. Her golden hair had become brighter from the August sun, there was more colour in her cheeks, and she no longer checked her impulses to laugh in the half-guilty, nervous way she had done when fresh from the horrors that she had witnessed in Spain.

Young Stanislas, the son of the house, was largely responsible for that. He was a nineteen-year-old subaltern in a crack regiment of Polish Lancers, now spending some weeks of his summer leave with his parents. No gayer, more irresponsible young blackguard had ever thrown a leg over a horse. Although Lucretia was considerably older than himself, he had fallen for her at once and made open love to her on every possible occasion. She refused to treat him seriously, but his laughing, tempestuous wooing was just the elixir of life she needed to restore her temporarily lost youth; and, as they both adored riding, they spent a good part of each day together cantering through the forest glades on the higher land to the south of the house.

Jan Lubieszow, the Baron's nephew, who had arrived in his own plane some six days before, had also had some share in taking Lucretia's mind off her own problems. He was a thickset, square-faced, determined-looking fellow in his early thirties, and, although he lacked the carefree charm of his young cousin, he could talk well upon a great variety of subjects, and possessed a most melodious voice in which he could croon the latest American torch songs or, with equal ease, sing the old hunting songs of his beloved Poland. The Duke suspected that he, too, was considerably attracted by

Lucretia, but, if so, he hid it with some skill, and in any case Stanislas left him little opportunity of being alone with her.

Four other guests had come and gone in the past fortnight, and more were expected that evening, so there was little excuse for any member of the party becoming bored from lack of congenial companionship. The Baron had said little to the Duke about the newcomers he was expecting, except that one of them was called General Mack and that he and the brother officers he was bringing were really friends of Count Ignac, who lived in too small a house to entertain them and had asked that they should be put up.

De Richleau was so used to such hospitality being extended to the friends of a friend by the old-world nobility of Central Europe that it did not even occur to him to speculate about Count Ignac's possible motive in arranging the visit. But he was a little surprised when about six o'clock four large cars drew up in front of the house and disgorged no less than seven new arrivals with their servants. He was even more surprised when, just before dinner, in the big main living-room of the house, where hunting trophies decorated the walls and bearskin rugs lay scattered over the polished parquet of the floor, he was introduced to General Mack, and realized at the first glance that "General Mack" was only the *nom-de-guerre* of one of Poland's most famous statesmen.

Without batting an eyelid the Duke shook hands, but his curiosity was instantly aroused, and he asked himself: "What the devil is this fellow doing here while Hitler's puppet is creating merry hell for the Polish citizens of Danzig and half the Chancelleries of Europe are in a ferment?"

Next moment he was shaking hands with a portly, grey-haired man who was introduced as Colonel Moninszko, but the Duke felt certain that he had seen his face also somewhere before, and a second later he was convinced that he was exchanging smiling platitudes with a soldier who ranked far senior to Colonel and was, in fact, one of the highest officers in the Polish Army.

The newcomers had brought no women with them, so Lucretia, the Baroness and buxom Anna Lubieszow, a middle-aged cousin who kept house for the Baron because his clever wife was either too frail or too lazy to burden herself with such matters, enjoyed more than a normal share of male attention.

De Richleau noted with interest that the European crisis was barely mentioned and, when it was, General Mack brushed it aside with the light assertion that, though the Government would never give way to these cursed Nazis, the matter would soon be settled, because Hitler was only bluffing.

When the ladies had retired after dinner the men sat for a little over their wine, and the Duke waited with interest to see if they would now discuss the international situation, having perhaps refrained from doing so before from the fear that its gravity might alarm the women. But he was not at all surprised when they continued to confine themselves to light gossip about their acquaintances and casual talk of the season's shooting. He had been involved in too many conspiracies himself to fail to recognize the faint but unmistakable atmosphere of excitement which pervaded the party. The laughter of General Mack and his companions came just a shade too readily, and their silences were just a shade too sudden. Whatever the real reason for their visit, the Duke was soon convinced that they did not intend to disclose it to their unsuspecting host or to himself.

On leaving the table they went upstairs to the Baroness' drawing-room, a large, ornate apartment resplendent with the gold, ormolu and brocades of the French Empire period, so typical of Russia under the nineteenth-century Czars. But she only allowed them to stay there for about ten minutes before, beckoning General Mack and Count Ignac over to her, she packed the remainder of the party off to play cards.

De Richleau was a great devotee of the tables, and on occasion had been known to skin professional poker players on trans-Atlantic runs, but it was one of his principles never to play round games for anything more than token stakes with his friends; and "country house" bridge, with its uncertainties of partners and certainties of recriminations, he normally avoided like the plague. But tonight, that " 'satiable curiosity", which he shared with the Elephant's Child, being roused, he decided to play a few rubbers in order to learn a little more of the Baron's mysterious guests.

The six members of General Mack's party, the Baron and the Duke made up two tables, so Lucretia, Jan and Stanislas were left standing by. Stanislas, determined to lose no chance of being alone with Lucretia, remarked lightly to Jan:

"I know you'd like to cut in, old chap, so don't you worry about us. I'll take Lucretia for a stroll down to the lake to watch the fish rise in the moonlight."

But he had reckoned without his normally indulgent papa, who looked up and said with unusual firmness: "Tonight I should prefer you to remain here, Stanislas. As the son of the house it is your place to look after the comfort of our guests."

A faint twinkle came into Jan's grey eyes as he smiled at Lucretia. "In that case, may I offer myself as a substitute to take you to see the fish?"

She hesitated. "Are you sure you wouldn't rather stay here to cut in if anyone wishes to be relieved of their hand?"

"No, no," he laughed. "Tonight that pleasure is reserved for my accomplished young cousin, and he is welcome to it. Come, let's go."

De Richleau had watched the little comedy with amusement, and was now engaged in a comedy of his own. As a courtesy to the non-Polish guests, French had always been the language spoken during their stay at Lubieszow. Most educated Poles spoke French quite naturally as a second language, but one of the officers at the Duke's table, a square, chunky-faced man, evidently of peasant stock, was having considerable trouble with his bidding. De Richleau was half-Russian by birth and, as a boy, had spent many happy weeks on that very estate, so he could both understand Polish and speak it fairly fluently. However, he had often found that it paid a handsome dividend not to disclose his linguistic gifts without good reason, and now he was very glad that none of the household or guests at Lubieszow knew that he talked their language. While the chunky-faced officer muttered angry asides to his friends in Polish about having been landed with "this blasted foreigner" as a partner, the Duke smiled the rather apologetic, uncomprehending smile of one who has not the faintest idea about what his companions are talking.

Lucretia had previously thought Jan rather a silent man, but she soon discovered that he was nothing of the kind, and it was only then she realized that this was the first time she had been alone with him for more than a few minutes.

She discovered, too, that, like most of the Polish "*Sylachta*", as the nobility were termed, he was passionately fond of his country, knew its history intimately, and dwelt much in the past. He spoke of the battle that had changed the course of European history, in which, with only a handful of men, the Polish hero, Jan Sobieski, had defeated the Turks under the walls of Vienna in 1683 ; and of how Tadeusz Kosciuszko, another Polish paladin, more than a century later had led the Poles against the combined might of Russia and Prussia, as though these events had occurred only a few months ago.

But, as Lucretia knew, Kosciuszko's valour had proved in vain. After two previous disastrous wars, in both of which great areas of Polish territory had been acquired by Russia, Prussia and Austria, in 1795 the final partitioning of the country by her three powerful and greedy neighbours had taken place. Then for over a hundred and twenty years the Polish race had groaned in slavery until, after the First World War, they had at last regained their territories and become an independent nation once more.

What Lucretia did not know was that Poland had been the first country in Europe to adopt a democratic form of government, since in 1791 her nobles had voluntarily relinquished many of their privileges and recognized the right of the people to a voice in the running of their State.

The night was calm, warm and moonlit. By the lakeside they found a dry, grassy bank and sat down upon it. Some young women might have been bored by a man talking of the past to them, but Lucretia had for long been interested in European politics, and the dry bones of history took on new flesh and blood when Jan spoke so enthusiastically of the old Kings and almost forgotten wars. He gave her, too, swift, vivid glimpses into the lives of many of his countrymen who had contributed so much to Europe's civilization: Copernicus, the great astronomer; the painters, Juljusz Kossak,

Artur Grottger and Jan Metizko; the musical geniuses, Chopin and Pader-
ewski, and that outstanding scientist, Madame Curie.

Quite suddenly Jan asked if Lucretia would like him to sing to her.

Hiding her surprise she agreed at once, and, lifting his square, strong face
to the moon, he began, softly at first then with increasing abandon, until the
night was filled with his clear, tuneful tenor.

When he stopped she clapped her hands in applause, and he went straight
on to sing another half-dozen songs. As he was singing in Polish she could
not understand the words, but his rich tones conveyed, as well as any words
could have done, at one time all the sadness of an oppressed people, at another the courage with which they had striven to regain their independence
in many a bloody insurrection, at a third the gay valour of Poniatowski's
Lancers as they fought their way under Napoleon from one end of Europe
to the other, and at a fourth the hearty revelry of a peasant people at a village
merrymaking.

At last he paused, breathless; taking her hand he laughed and said:
"See what you let yourself in for, coming out here alone with me! But I
love to sing, and never have I had a more charming audience."

She let her hand remain in his for a moment, then gently withdrew it as
she replied: "I loved it, and you must sing for me again another night, but
it's getting late. We must go in, or they will be wondering what has happened
to us."

He hesitated only a second. "All right, if that is a promise I'll let you go
this time, otherwise I'd be tempted to . . ."

"To what?" she smiled, scrambling to her feet.

"Why, carry you off, of course."

"But there's nowhere to carry me, except into the woods, and I'm far
too fastidious a person to prove a willing victim in such surroundings!"

"No, no. My aeroplane is in the big field to the west of the house. I
should put you in that and fly you over the hills and far away. Do you like
flying? I simply live for it, and by night, with the land all moonlit below,
it is glorious."

"Yes, it must be fun."

"What about it, then? Let's go up now!"

"No, not tonight. Some other time, perhaps."

"You really mean that?"

She laughed. "I said perhaps. Come now, I'm going in."

"When a lady says 'no', she means 'perhaps', and when she says 'perhaps'
she means 'yes'," he said quickly.

"And if she says 'yes' she's no lady!" Lucretia completed the ancient
jest for him. "But I'm no lady in that sense, and when I say 'perhaps' I
mean just 'perhaps'."

"In any case, you are a most remarkable and lovely woman," he said with sudden seriousness. "I've been wanting to get you to myself for days; but that young devil Stanislas monopolizes every moment of your time."

"Perhaps—once more perhaps!—I won't let him do so quite so much in future. We'll see. Anyhow, I've enjoyed this evening."

He took her arm with an easy, friendly gesture and drew it through his own as they started to walk back to the house together.

She let it remain there until they reached the terrace, and when she got into bed half an hour later she confessed to herself that it really was a very long time since she had enjoyed an evening so much.

De Richleau spent a profitless, or almost profitless, evening, his net gains being forty-five *zloties*, won on the last rubber, and the information that yet more guests were expected at Lubieszow the following day, deduced from a remark which he overheard General Mack make to the Baroness just as the party was breaking up for the night.

Upstairs in his room, having got out of his clothes and into a gorgeous mandarin's robe which he used as a dressing-gown, he began to pace softly up and down like some large, lithe, grey cat. For once in his life he was frankly puzzled. At such a time, when international relations were strained almost to breaking point and Poland the very centre of the vortex, what could one of her principal Ministers and a group of officers, who, he now felt certain, were key-men on her General Staff, be doing at Lubieszow? Why had they left the capital at this hour of crisis? Why had they chosen this remote estate where even their host was a stranger to them? Why had the self-styled General and Colonel taken the names of "Mack" and "Moninszko", instead of using their own?

There could be only one answer, of that the Duke was already convinced; they were here to meet someone whom it would have been highly dangerous for them to receive openly in Warsaw; someone who was so well known that he would almost certainly be recognized in a big city, and, in the present state of tension, press comment on his presence in the Polish capital might prove little short of disastrous.

Half a dozen possibilities as to the identity of the men who were to join the party next day flitted through the Duke's swift brain.

Voroshilov and Molotov, the Commissar for Defence and Foreign Minister of the Soviet Union? But no, Poland had a blood feud with Russia which went back into the dark ages. However crystal clear it might appear to outsiders that Poland's only chance of survival if attacked by Germany lay in an alliance with Russia, de Richleau knew that the Poles would never agree to it—until it was too late.

Daladier and Marshal Weygand, perhaps? France had been Poland's champion for centuries, and it was Weygand's brilliant generalship which had resulted in the "Miracle of the Vistula" in 1920. He had flown from France to advise Marshal Pilsudski and, changing the Polish strategy at the eleventh hour, inflicted an overwhelming defeat upon the Bolsheviks when it had seemed that nothing could stop their victorious armies from sweeping right across Europe. But France was no longer Poland's ally. She had given her guarantee to the Czechs and, finding herself incapable of honouring it when the crisis came, called on Britain, who at that time had given the Czechs no guarantee, to get her out of her mess. Britain had done so, pledging herself to the Czechs in a new treaty which, in turn, she found herself incapable of implementing when a few months later Hitler again turned on the heat and marched into Czechoslovakia. Then Britain had voluntarily guaranteed Poland, but not so France. If it came to a showdown this was Britain's mess.

So perhaps the man who was travelling through the night towards Lubieszow was Mr. Neville Chamberlain? After all, he had flown to Bad Godesberg; why not to Lubieszow?

Then again, it might be Mussolini or Count Ciano. The Italian Dictator had put a check on German schemes of aggression more than once and played the part of mediator at Munich. If ever there were a time when powerful mediation could save the peace of Europe, it was now.

But, on the whole, de Richleau considered Chamberlain the best bet. Britain had been rearming feverishly for the last few months, but many months were required to make up for the criminal negligence of the slothful and irresponsible Governments that had held power for so many years. In the Duke's view, Britain had been right to eat the food of humiliation at the time of Munich. At least it meant that the people would have air-raid shelters if the clash came now; and, if only this new crisis could be tided over, Britain might even have a few modern tanks and a thousand or so automatic rifles when the great showdown came, as come it must. Perhaps Chamberlain was coming to tell the unfortunate Poles that, if they could not see their way to meeting Hitler's demands concerning Danzig, their blood would be upon their own heads. By no conceivable means could Britain give one iota of military support to Poland, if she were attacked, and the Duke, being a realist to his fingertips, believed that no statesman should allow sentiment to jeopardize the safety of his country. Sorry as he was for the Poles, he hoped that Chamberlain would decide that discretion was once more the better part of valour and gain Britain just a little more time.

Next morning the Duke woke to the noise of an aeroplane droning overhead, and, when it ceased suddenly, he left his bed with unusual alacrity. Looking out of the window he saw that the plane had landed a few hundred yards away, and that two men were just climbing out of it. One was tall and thin, the other somewhat shorter, with square shoulders and a slight limp. They were still too far off for him to make out the details of their features, but he knew at once that neither of them was Chamberlain, Daladier, Molotov or Mussolini.

As they approached the house he saw that the square-shouldered fellow was about thirty years of age, and had a strong, almost brutal, face, with a jutting chin and thick, fleshy mouth. The other was much older, grey-haired, distinguished-looking, with a mouth like a rat-trap and a thin, aristocratic, aquiline nose not unlike the Duke's own.

Neither of the two bore the least resemblance to any well-known states-man, although the Duke had an idea that he had seen the taller man some-where before. But they passed round the side of the house before he could verify the impression.

It was still only seven o'clock, and as de Richleau always had his breakfast served in bed he had to restrain his impatience to learn more of the new arrivals until his normal time of appearing downstairs, which was round about half past ten.

As he came down the broad stairway into the big lounge-hall, with its antler-hung walls, he saw a little group of men gathered at its far end; General Mack and the two strangers were among them. They were talking in low voices, but a few sentences floated up to the approaching Duke. As he caught them he stiffened slightly. They had acted as a key to unlock a cell in his brain, and he remembered now the identity of the tall, aristocratic man whom he had seen arriving a few hours earlier.

The new guest was General Count von Geisenheim, a Prussian officer of the old school, who was high in the councils of the German General Staff.

Chapter III

COFFIN FOR "UNCLE"

THE shock of learning that the men responsible for Poland's destiny were secretly negotiating with Poland's potential enemies, the Germans, was enough to make even de Richleau catch his breath, but after a barely percep-tible pause he proceeded onward down the stairs.

General Mack turned and saw him and, with a wave of his hand, intro-duced the two Germans. He made no attempt to conceal their identity, and the younger, coarse-faced man proved to be a Major Bauer. Both men bowed sharply from the waist, then relaxed into smiling affability, von Geisenheim remarking that he recalled meeting the Duke some years before at a shooting party in the Schwartzwald.

Europe was still at peace. No one could question the Poles' right to entertain Germans privately or officially if they chose to do so. There were probably several hundred Germans still freely walking about London, and certainly several thousand Britons enjoying the August sunshine on their summer holidays in Germany. The Duke's amiability rivalled that of the Count as he enquired after mutual friends, but behind his smile his mind was seriously perturbed.

His perturbation was not lessened when, after luncheon, the plump little Baron led him out on to the terrace and, with obvious embarrassment, began to talk about his guests.

"I do hope," he said anxiously, "that the arrival of all these people will not spoil the pleasure of your visit to Lubieszow."

De Richleau raised his grey devil's eyebrows in feigned surprise. "But of course not, my dear fellow. Why should it?"

"Well, only that we are now such a crowd, and Ignac Krasinski said he felt sure you had come here for peace and quiet, so would hate that. As a matter of fact, he suggested that I should find an excuse to terminate your visit before these people arrived, but naturally I would not hear of such a thing."

"But please!" exclaimed the Duke. "I understand perfectly and should have thought of it myself this morning. Your generous hospitality has led you to overcrowd your house. Lucretia and I will go this afternoon."

Actually, he had no intention whatever of leaving for the present and knew quite well that to the simple-minded landowner the laws of hospitality would forbid the acceptance of his glib offer. The Baron reacted even more quickly than he expected.

"No, no. Now that they have arrived and you have met them you must stay, of course. Besides, the house is not overcrowded in the least. For weddings and family celebrations here we have often put up double the number of people."

"In that case . . ." murmured the Duke.

"Say no more," begged the Baron. "I am sorry now that I even mentioned the matter. I would not have done so but for the fact that I have a request to make of you."

"Go ahead, my dear fellow, go ahead."

"You will have realized, of course, that Mack and his friends are not—er—just ordinary guests who have come for the shooting."

"Indeed!" De Richleau's grey eyes opened a little, conveying mild interest.

"Well, yes. They are people of some consequence; friends of Ignac's, not of my own, and they wanted to meet these damned Germans, who arrived this morning, at some place where there would be no risk of any newspaper men getting wind of the meeting. Clotilde, as you may have gathered, is greatly interested in politics, and it was to please her that I agreed to place Lubieszow at their disposal as a meeting-place."

"I see, I see," muttered the Duke, who had "seen" the situation perfectly clearly all along. "And this request that you wished to make of me?"

"It's only that, should you decide to leave Lubieszow before the meeting has concluded, Mack has asked me to request you not to mention this meeting to anyone whatsoever, and not to mention it in the letters that you may write while you are here."

"But of course, I would not dream of doing so," de Richleau assured him blandly.

"Good! That's settled then!" the Baron exclaimed, with obvious relief at having got this unpleasant duty of infringing the freedom of his guest off his mind. "I'm very grateful. You'll forgive me if I leave you now. I've got to see my bailiff about some new cowsheds I'm having built."

Left on his own, the Duke sauntered on along the terrace, enjoying the fragrance of his after-lunch cigar. Lucretia, Stanislas and Jan had gone off riding, and General Mack's party was evidently holding its first conference, as it had shut itself up in the big drawing-room on the first floor.

The room was at the back of the house, overlooking the terrace, and its windows were open. As the Duke strolled slowly up and down, the sound of voices came faintly to him, although, to his regret, not loud enough for him to make any sense of the conversation that was proceeding above. He noted, however, with considerable interest that after a little time the discussion began to grow heated. The voices were raised, and Major Bauer's guttural tones could be heard with particular distinctness, as he endeavoured to ram home some point with true German assertiveness. At a little after four o'clock the meeting broke up, and when the men who had attended it trooped downstairs to drink their afternoon coffee, de Richleau observed that there was a definite atmosphere of strain between the Poles and the two Germans.

That evening, having changed for dinner a little earlier than usual, the Duke quietly walked along to Lucretia's room. She was dressed but still smoothing and coiling her golden hair on the top of her small, beautifully shaped head. Perching himself on the bed just behind her, so that he could see her face in the mirror, he said:

"What do you make of all this?"

"You mean the arrival of the two Germans?"

"Yes. Mack and Co. came here specially to meet them."

"I guessed as much. Von Geisenheim is nice. In a way he reminds me of you; but the Major is just a nasty, common tough."

The Duke smiled a trifle sardonically. "Permit me to undeceive you, darling. Von Geisenheim is a cultured aristocrat, long trained in military diplomacy, and therefore easily capable of disguising his true feelings."

Lucretia laughed into her mirror. "Didn't I just say that in a way he reminds me of you?"

"*Touché!*" de Richleau laughed back. "However, I meant that he is more dangerous than fifty Major Bauers, and that I am much perturbed to find that he has been sent on a secret mission to the Poles. Bauer is posing as von Geisenheim's adjutant, but I haven't a doubt that he is something much more than that. He's a Hitler man: one of those guttersnipe Nazis who have climbed to power by sheer unscrupulous brutality; he's been sent to keep an eye on his General and see that he does his stuff. But the Prussian nobility, who become members of the German General Staff almost by hereditary right, have never bent the knee to Hitler. He has been useful to them, and they will give him their support as long as it suits their book to do so. Von Geisenheim represents the real power behind the throne in Germany, and Bauer represents the throne itself. Together they form a damnably dangerous combination, and I've no doubt at all that they are working hand in glove."

Turning slowly, Lucretia looked at him. "D'you think the Poles are being tempted to sell out?"

"That's about it," the Duke assented. "Mind you, Mack and his cronies are not representative of the Polish nation, but they have the power to do a deal."

"How would that affect Britain?"

"Very well. If the Poles give way war will be averted and Britain will not be called on to honour her guarantee. That would give her a few more months' grace to rush on her rearmament programme before Hitler makes another of his positively last demands."

"You consider that he is absolutely insatiable?"

"Absolutely. If the Poles give him Danzig he will discover that some Germans are being ill-treated in the Corridor; and, before the autumn is out, he will threaten to march in unless they give him that."

"Is there nothing that can be done to stop it?"

"Nothing, I'm afraid. We can only hope for a postponement, provided the price is not too high."

Lucretia's tapering eyebrows drew together in a puzzled frown. "What do you mean by that?"

"Simply that, if Hitler will be content with Danzig, well and good; but he may be asking for a rectification of Poland's western frontier as well. If Mack agrees to that, the Poles will lose their forward defence lines, thus making themselves much more vulnerable to invasion later on."

"Just as the Czechs were deprived of their Sudeten line before they had even a chance to strike a blow?"

"Exactly. And, in consequence, Britain lost a staunch and powerful ally. She will need all the help she can get when the great showdown does come, and I don't want to see the Polish Eagle shorn of her talons before she has dipped them deep in German blood."

"Surely the object lesson of Czechoslovakia is far too recent for the Poles to allow themselves to be tricked into a situation where they may wake up one morning to find their country a German province?"

"I hope so, but that is what worries me about von Geisenheim's presence here. The question of Danzig can be handled perfectly well by the German diplomats, so his visit cannot have been made on that account. He is a professional soldier, and a very brilliant one. All of Mack's people are soldiers, too, so they can only be negotiating on some question which would affect future military operations. However, thanks be to God, the Germans are not getting it all their own way at the moment."

Lucretia looked round again. "How d'you know that?"

De Richleau smiled at her. "Because their meeting lasted less than an hour this afternoon and then broke up after a stormy scene. I have given the Baron my word that I will let no one know that I am aware that these secret talks are taking place; but we shall see about that, since I place the interests of Britain above even my personal honour."

He stood up and added slowly: "Should you chance to overhear any fragments of their conversation which seem of interest, I should be glad if you would let me know. It was that which I came along to say."

Stooping, he took her hand and kissed it, then left the room as silently as he had come.

That evening Stanislas was again detained by his father to keep a watchful eye on the comfort of their guests, so for the second time Jan had Lucretia to himself for the best part of two hours.

The Poles, while outwardly polite to the two Germans, now seemed slightly embarrassed by their presence, particularly when Major Bauer insisted on dragging Hitler into the conversation and talking of him as though he were a Messiah. With consummate tact von Geisenheim again and again tided over awkward pauses in the conversation that arose on this account; yet it was obvious that, despite his rank, he was in no position even covertly to reprimand the fanatical Nazi. Fortunately, by half past nine, Bauer declared himself tired and, with an abrupt good night to his hostess, limped off to bed. After that the atmosphere grew easier, and de Richleau talked amiably with the German General for an hour and a half while the others enjoyed their bridge.

Wednesday the 23rd of August dawned fine and clear, but it was a day which brought a sudden deepening from grey to black of the war clouds that were gathering over Europe. By midday everyone at Lubieszow knew that Joachim von Ribbentrop, the ex-traveller in champagne who had become Hitler's mouthpiece in power politics, had pulled off the greatest *coup* of his career. The Soviet, up to then a staunch supporter of the League of Nations and a great factor in maintaining the balance of power in Europe, had suddenly signed a non-aggression pact with the Nazis.

Oblivious to all but his own pleasure, young Stanislas succeeded in getting free of the duties that his father had imposed upon him and gaily whirled Lucretia off for a ride with him after lunch. General Mack's party and the Germans went into conference upstairs. Jan endeavoured to settle down to a book, but, finding that he could not do so, wandered out on to the terrace, and, looking slightly distrait, joined the Duke.

"What the devil does this new move mean?" he asked, as he plumped himself down in a basket chair.

"It means," replied the Duke, with a cynical little smile, "that Hitler has succeeded in securing his eastern flank. With Russia out of the game, Poland alone can be no serious menace to him; and once he has dealt with her he will be free to launch his armies and air fleets against Western Europe."

"But why?" exclaimed Jan. "Why should Stalin have made this pact, which practically amounts to an alliance with the Germans, when for years past they have openly proclaimed that the Bolsheviks are the scum of the earth and that Stalin himself is a blood-stained murderer?"

"It's quite simple, my dear fellow," de Richleau shrugged. "The basic situation has not changed one iota. Hitler still loathes Stalin and all he stands for, and will destroy him utterly if he ever gets a chance. But he wrote for all to read in *Mein Kampf* that Germany would never again be called on to wage a war on two fronts simultaneously. That is one of the few wise conclusions which occasionally emerge from the spate of lies and gibberish that he utters. He is now ensuring against such an eventuality."

"Yes, I see that," muttered Jan; "but what about Stalin? Why should he enter into a pact with his avowed arch-enemy? What the hell has he to gain?"

"A very great deal. Stalin is just as clever as Hitler, and considerably more far-sighted. Britain, France, Italy, the United States and even Japan are not any serious menace to Russia; they either have ample territories already or are too far away. But Germany, only separated from Russia by Poland, with her obsession for more *lebensraum* and her need for grainlands and oil, constitutes a perpetual threat to the steady reconstruction of the Soviet Union. Stalin is well aware of that and never loses sight of it. He knows that, if Hitler wins his war in the west, after a pause of a year or two to digest his kill, he will direct his victorious armies to march east against Russia; and that, should Hitler lose his war in the west and disappear, some other German warmonger will arise, who in due course will decide that, having waged two wars against the western democracies unsuccessfully, Germany's best hope of gaining empire is to turn her back on the west and make a bid for the conquest of Asia, overrunning Russia in her march."

"But, if you're right, it seems that Russia will have to face up to Germany anyhow, sooner or later, so why not now? Surely Stalin has a better chance of coming out on top if he throws in his lot with France and Britain, and all three of them tackle Hitler together?"

De Richleau shook his head. "No. That, I believe, is where Stalin is proving himself such a master of statecraft. Remember, Bolshevik Russia owes nothing whatever to France or Britain. They would not come to her aid if she were attacked; so why should she come to theirs? If she did Hitler might quite well unleash the first fury of his assault against her. Hitler could sit tight behind his Siegfried Line in the west and go all out to eliminate Poland and Russia; then, having secured his rear, turn his attention to the others later. If he did that, what help could Russia's Western Allies give her? For all practical purposes, none. She would have to bear the whole weight of the German war machine with only Poland to aid her. Could she stand up to that? I doubt it."

"Poland will fight to the death!" Jan announced grimly.

"No one has ever doubted the gallantry of your people"—the Duke bowed slightly—"but, unfortunately, you are lamentably short of modern aircraft, and, believe me, air power will be the deciding factor in this coming war."

Jan sighed. "I fear you are right. In fact, as an airman myself I know it."

"All right then. Why should Stalin deliberately challenge the might of the Luftwaffe? To do so would almost certainly be to lay open the Russian cities to devastation. There will be time enough for him to enter on a trial of strength with Hitler—if he must—later on."

"But if he allows Poland, Britain and France to be beaten first, he will have to fight alone."

"Perhaps, but Germany will not be able to conquer three such great nations without enormous cost to herself. If they succumb—and it is by no means certain that they will—the flower of the German Army and Air Force will be dead before Hitler can proclaim his victory. In the meantime, you can be sure that the wily Georgian, who now occupies the seat of the Czars of all the Russias, will see to it that not a moment is lost in increasing Russia's output of tanks, aircraft and guns. So when he does have to fight the odds will probably be somewhat in his favour."

"And," Jan looked up quickly, "if you are right, he may not wait until the Western Powers are defeated, but come in to turn the tide against Germany after they have taken the first shock of the fighting."

"Exactly," agreed the Duke. "That is by no means unlikely, and we can but hope that it will prove the case. Only one thing is certain. If he can possibly avoid it, he will not come in until it suits him. And, personally, I for one cannot see any reason why he should."

"No, I suppose you are right. Still, this non-aggression pact has given Hitler a free hand so far as Eastern Europe is concerned, and I fear now more than ever for my dear country."

The Duke did not reply. There was nothing that he could say, nothing that he could do to turn aside the evil fate which now seemed to be advancing so inexorably upon unfortunate Poland.

Half an hour later, when Jan had left him, he took a turn along the terrace. The windows of the big room on the first floor were again open, but no raised, angry voices issued from them this afternoon. Instead, there drifted out a low, steady buzz of earnest conversation. That alone was enough to tell him that the German trump card played that morning was having its due effect. The Poles, de Richleau felt sure, were giving way, and he wondered anxiously how much of their frontier territories they would have to sacrifice, in addition to Danzig, in order to buy what could only be a worthless and uneasy peace for just a few months longer.

The conference did not break up until seven o'clock and was resumed immediately after dinner. Over the meal most of the guests had proved unusually silent and preoccupied. The Baron was never a great conversationalist. The thoughts of Major Bauer and most of General Mack's party were obviously concentrated on the work in hand. Lucretia, Stanislas and Jan made an effort which petered out by the time the entrée was served, and, apart from occasional remarks thrown out with some effort, de Richleau and von Geisenheim were the only members of the party who continued to keep the ball rolling with smooth urbanity until the Baroness gave the signal to rise, as soon as she decently could after the appearance of the savoury.

For the third night in succession Stanislas was unlucky, as, to his intense annoyance, he found that Lucretia and Jan had slipped out of the house while he was still busy in the lounge ensuring that his father's guests had ample rations of Cognac or Kümmel with their coffee.

De Richleau retired early, cudgelling his brains as to whether there was any useful action which he might take in connection with the conference. But he saw none, since there could be little point in his letting his friends in Whitehall know that it was proceeding unless he could also supply information on the lines it was taking, and the extent of the demands which the Germans had evidently come to make.

When he came downstairs next morning the conferees were already in session, and an atmosphere of uneasy gloom seemed to pervade the house. His instincts were rarely wrong, and he felt it in his bones that Mack was now selling Poland out; yet he knew that he was powerless to prevent it.

By the second post that Thursday afternoon he received a letter. It was handwritten on a single sheet of paper with a Bayswater address, and, as he read it, his mouth tightened into a hard, grim line.

Putting it in his pocket he went in search of Lucretia, but, although he found her picking plums with Stanislas and Jan in the orchard, he could not get her alone until she went up to change for dinner; and, allowing a few moments to elapse, he followed her up to her room.

"What is it, Greyeyes?" she asked a trifle apprehensively, as he failed to give her his usual smiling greeting. "I haven't found out anything yet. With these two young men ready to cut each other's throats for the pleasure of my society I simply haven't had a chance to talk to either of the Germans or any of General Mack's entourage. Have you discovered a stack of dynamite all ready to be detonated in the cellar?"

He acknowledged her jest with no more than a faint smile and silently handed her the letter, which simply said:

I'm sorry to tell you that Uncle has taken a turn for the worse, and I doubt if he'll last over the week-end. If you want to see him while there is still time you had better return to England immediately.

I hope that you have been enjoying a pleasant holiday, and I'm sorry to drag you back, but I feel sure you would like to be with us when poor Uncle finally expires.

"What does it mean?" Lucretia asked, with a puzzled frown.

"It is from a friend of mine in Whitehall who promised to give me the tip when the time came," replied the Duke. "By 'Uncle' he means the Peace of Europe."

Chapter IV

A TRAITOR'S PRICE

"HELL!" exclaimed Lucretia.

"Yes, it will be hell indeed," de Richleau agreed soberly.

She shook her head impatiently. "I wasn't thinking of the war."

"Indeed!" he remarked with an asperity which he rarely used towards her. "At the moment when one learns pretty definitely that no more can be done to stop several million innocent people from being murdered or maimed by high explosives, I find it difficult to think of anything else."

"I was thinking of Jan."

The Duke's face softened. "Yes, Poland will need every man she has who can fly a plane; so Jan will be in it. Tell me—have you fallen in love with him?"

"I—I don't really know."

He laid his hand gently on her arm. "Had things been otherwise I could wish that you had. You're still young yet, darling, and incredibly lovely. I've prayed for years that you wouldn't let that tragic affair in Spain ruin your whole life. Jan's a good fellow with a lot more in him than appears at first sight. But, as things are, perhaps it's just as well that you're still uncertain."

"But I *want* to be certain," she burst out suddenly. "I thought I'd never love again. Cristoval's face always seemed to come between mine and that of every man who attracted me. Yet, I wanted love. I've been so desperately lonely. And Jan is the first man who has ever succeeded in banishing my ghosts when I'm with him. The awful thing is that in a few more days I would have known one way or the other."

"Why should you think that?"

"Because tonight I agreed to go off on a trip with him. He was going to fly me down to Wieliezka. It's near Cracow, and there are wonderful salt mines there. Huge caves of glittering crystal that have been worked on ever since the twelfth century."

De Richleau nodded. "Yes, I was taken there several times as a boy. Twenty or thirty generations of miners have hewn ballrooms, chapels, altars and sanctuaries out of the rock salt, and the caves are like a fairy palace hidden under a mountain. It is one of the show places of Poland. But why should a visit to Wieliezka provide you with the answer as to whether you love Jan or not?"

"We were going to stay the week-end in Cracow, at the palace of one of his friends. I should have had him for three days almost entirely to myself; and I'm sure I would have known after that."

"All right," said the Duke, with sudden decision. "You had better go then."

Her face lit up, then quickly fell again. "But how about getting back to England? If war does break out over the week-end we might get caught here."

De Richleau had been doing some very swift thinking. He had no desire at all to find himself stranded at the other end of Europe once Hitler had unleashed his legions; but Lucretia's happiness was of immense importance to him. Now that the icy hand which for so long had gripped her heart had at last begun to thaw he knew that he could not bring himself to deprive her of this chance to break the spell for good, even if she must be separated afterwards from the man who had wrought the miracle, by this accursed war which now menaced the happiness of countless thousands.

"Don't worry," he smiled. "But I would like to leave first thing on Monday morning, so you must be back here on Sunday night. That will still give you your three days with Jan. Then on Monday he can fly us into Warsaw and we'll get the plane on to Budapest. If war has already been declared and the air service is cancelled, there will still be plenty of trains, and we'll get home somehow, either via the Balkans or Scandinavia."

Lucretia suddenly put her arms round his neck and kissed him on both cheeks. "Oh, darling," she sighed, "this means so much to me, and no one but you would understand."

"Bless you," he murmured. "Try to put the thought of war out of your lovely head for the next three days. Have a good time, and may the gods bring you back happy."

De Richleau had intended to leave the following morning and go via Vienna, so that he could pick up Richard Eaton and Marie Lou, since he felt reasonably certain that they would have had no special warning that the danger was now so close at hand. Vienna, where he had spent so many happy times as a young man, was now a Nazi city, and it was imperative that the Eatons should not get caught there; but Lucretia's project forced him to change his plans.

Having considered the matter carefully, he took the first opportunity that offered after dinner to have a word with the Baroness. Knowing that it was hopeless to wait for her to be alone, he kept a watchful eye upon the corner of the salon where she held her court, until the officers who were exchanging witticisms with her excused themselves to join General Mack, leaving the faithful Count Ignac as her sole companion.

As de Richleau approached she smiled up at him and, patting the empty chair at her side, cried gaily: "Come and sit down, Duke. I have hardly seen you these last few days. You should be ashamed of yourself for neglecting me so."

Taking her hand, he kissed it gallantly, then made a little foreign gesture of mock distress. "But it is you, Madame, who have neglected me. I am an old man, so how can I compete with all these handsome fellows whom you are now entertaining in your house?"

"Nonsense, Duke," she protested, but her thin, clever face lit up at the compliment. "You are more handsome and distinguished-looking than the lot of them."

"I wish I could believe you really thought that," he said half-seriously.

"Be careful now," she warned him, with a swift, mocking glance from her small, black eyes, "or you will be making Ignac jealous."

The Count's face broke into a lazy smile. "I am told that you are far too good a shot to challenge, Duke, so I would have to console myself with the old saying that you have in England: 'He who laughs last laughs longest.' In due course you will be leaving Poland, whereas I shall remain."

"It was of that which I intended to speak to Madame," said de Richleau with sudden seriousness. "Lucretia and I have enjoyed our stay at Lubieszow more than I can say, but I fear that we must start on our way homeward in a few days now."

"That is sad indeed." The Baroness' ugly face took on an appropriate look, but he noted that she did not press him to stay on.

"Yes," he agreed, "I am most loth to go. The peace and beauty of Lubieszow have made an indelible impression upon me, and if only the troubles which threaten us all can be avoided I greatly hope that you will ask me to stay again."

"But of course. We should be enchanted. Lubieszow is at your disposal whenever you wish."

"You are too good," he smiled; "but if you mean that also to apply to the present I wonder if I may really take you at your word?"

Count Ignac could hardly conceal the suspicion which was dawning in his glance, but the Baroness said quietly: "Please go on, Duke."

"It is this way," de Richleau purred. "I had intended to go home via Vienna in order to pick up two friends of mine—a Mr. and Mrs. Eaton, who are staying there; but I have so much enjoyed Lubieszow that, if it were at all possible, I would like them to see it too. I was wondering if it would be asking too much for you to extend your hospitality to them for the week-end, then we could all go home together via Warsaw."

He saw her hesitation and, out of the corner of his eye, caught the swift, almost imperceptible, negative that Count Ignac flashed towards her by a sudden tightening of the muscles of his face. The Duke had known that they would be most unwilling to have additional strangers in the house while the conference was in progress, but he also knew that the Baroness was a snob; so, before she had time to reply, he went on smoothly:

"She was a Princess de Blanqufort de Cantizanc Schulinoff before her marriage, and he is a Member of the British Parliament."

The latter part of the statement was a flat lie, as not only had Richard never entered Parliament, he had never even stood for it, and everything to do with politics bored him to tears. But de Richleau was a wily man, and he felt certain that the chance of entertaining a British M.P. would intrigue the Baroness, even if extending hospitality to a Russian Princess did not.

As he expected, Count Ignac's signals were ignored, and the Baroness smiled assent. "But, of course, I should be delighted to put your friends up for the week-end, or for as long as they care to stay. Arrange it, please, Duke, and I shall look forward to their visit."

"A thousand thanks, Madame." He kissed her hand again. "If you will permit me I will go now and put through a call to Vienna."

It was barely half past nine, and the Duke put in a personal call for Richard at Sacher's Hotel, where he knew the Eatons would be staying. The exchange could give him no information about delays, and, knowing that the lines must be greatly congested owing to the international crisis, he feared that he might not be able to get in touch with them that night; but at a quarter to eleven the call came through.

De Richleau wasted no time on idle pleasantries, in case he was prematurely cut off; but, having made certain that Richard realized who had rung him up, and could hear clearly, he went straight to the point.

"Uncle has taken a turn for the worse, and we doubt if he'll last over the week-end. He's been——"

"Uncle!" muttered Richard, having not the faintest idea what the Duke was talking about.

"Yes," de Richleau hurried on. "He's been asking for you and Marie Lou, and if you want to make certain of seeing him again you had better do your utmost to join us here by tomorrow night. I've looked up Bradshaw, and there is a train leaving Vienna at twenty minutes past midnight. It will get you into Warsaw at nine-thirty tomorrow morning. I'll make arrangements to have a car meet you at the station, which will bring you out to Lubieszow. Then we'll all return to England together on Monday. Is that all right?"

As far as Richard was concerned it was anything but all right. He and Marie Lou had dined at "*Die Drei Hussaren*" on *scampi*—those delicious Lilliputian river lobsters—cooked in cream, roast saddle of hare and *omelette au Kirsch*, washed down by a peach bola made from a bottle each of sparkling and still Hock; so they were feeling very well indeed and just going on to dance at Vienna's most amusing "*Nacht Lokal*"—"The Crooked Lantern".

Only the discovery that he was a little short of money had caused him to stop at Sacher's for more on their way to the night club, and it had been the merest fluke that he had been at the hotel *caisse* when the Duke's call came through. He was not unnaturally annoyed at being asked to abandon his pleasant evening for a hasty packing and a rush for a night express on which he had not even had a chance to reserve sleepers, but since the international crisis over Danzig was now agitating everybody's mind he had soon tumbled to what the Duke meant by "Uncle not being expected to last over the week-end", and in any case such a summons from his old friend could not be ignored, so he replied at once:

"Right oh! We'll make the night train for Warsaw somehow."

"Good!" said the Duke. "If there is any hitch over the car, hire one yourself and get out here as soon as you can. The place is spelt L-U-B-I-E-S-Z-O-W, and it is in the province of Polesie. See you tomorrow. Bless you both." Then, with a sigh of relief, he hung up the receiver.

The following day passed without episode. It was again a pleasant, sunny morning, and about half past ten the Lubieszow family and the Duke saw Lucretia and Jan off in his aeroplane, which, having circled twice, headed south for Cracow, where they planned to arrive in good time for lunch. General Mack's people and the Germans were already in conference, and with a short break for lunch they kept at it until half past five.

De Richleau did a round of the stables with his host and spent the best part of the rest of the day listening to a variety of stations on the radio. He was by no means a wireless fan, since he maintained that casual listening, far from stimulating thought, dulled it, and he was mildly contemptuous of people who allowed themselves to become enslaved by its facile entertainment, instead of employing it deliberately on occasions when special concerts or items of real interest were being broadcast. But today he wanted to know how people all over Europe were reacting to the crisis, and to learn any hard news that was available.

As he spoke several languages with great fluency and could converse quite well in a number of others, he was able to switch from station to station as each news bulletin came on, and there was very little in them that he did not catch.

All that he heard confirmed his worst forebodings. The German propagandists had wrought themselves up to a fever pitch over Danzig. The Poles were hardly less belligerent in their determination not to give way. Italy was advocating Germany's right to the Free City. The Czech and Austrian stations were muzzled, already harnessed by Dr. Goebbels' propaganda machine. The rest were endeavouring to report the facts objectively, pleading for calmness, time, further arbitration; none of them openly daring to defy Hitler and use the only weapon they had—united opposition—which might have given him reason to pause.

The Duke remembered so well the 1914 crisis. If only Britain had told the Kaiser then that she meant to fight, should he invade France, instead of waiting until the German armies were already shooting and burning their way across Belgian soil, war could have been averted. But Britain made clear the position she intended to take up—too late. It would be the same this time. If only the League States had had the courage to stand up to Hitler and tell him plainly : "If you attack Poland you must fight us all," unprepared as they were individually, he would not have dared to take on so many nations controlling among them the potential resources of half the world. But each was hoping to escape the *débâcle*, and de Richleau felt instinctively that humanity would do nothing to save itself. Only the purge of war could bring true vision and courageous statesmanship back to the pampered, effete democracies—and the sands of Time were fast running out.

About six o'clock he was listening with cynical despair to Radio Paris when he caught the sound of a motor horn. Switching off the wireless, he hurried outside and found, as he had hoped, that the car he had ordered in Warsaw early that morning to meet Richard and Marie Lou had just drawn up.

With a tired smile Richard climbed out. He was unshaven and a little bleary-eyed, but Marie Lou appeared to have survived the eighteen-hour journey somewhat better. Her small, beautifully proportioned figure was as neat as ever in smart travelling tweeds, and somehow she had managed to conceal the disorder of her chestnut hair under a round, flattish fur hat, which she wore over one ear at a rakish angle.

"No need to ask if you had a good journey," laughed the Duke. "I can see you haven't. I imagine it proved impossible to get sleepers at the last moment ?"

"You're right there," Richard grunted. "We had to sit on the floor in the corridor most of the way, and were lucky to be able to do that. Half Vienna seemed to be wanting to get away on the trains last night."

Marie Lou sighed. "We felt terribly guilty about taking places on the train at all. We shouldn't even have been able to squeeze in if it hadn't been for a gang of Nazi bullies who arrived on the platform about five minutes before the train was due to start. They went through every carriage and wherever they found Jews—men, women, or children—they flung them off. I shall never forget the faces of those poor people. It was probably their last chance to get out to Poland. Of course, we were allowed to travel because we are English, and those Nazi bullies couldn't have been more polite, clicking their heels and saluting after they had examined our passports ; and, as Richard said, if we hadn't pushed into the corner from which an old Jewess had been ejected, there were plenty of other Aryans behind us who would. But it was really pretty ghastly."

"I can imagine it," the Duke nodded. "Once war is declared, and the Nazis have to tighten their own belts, God help the Jews who are left inside the Reich! But come along! After a hot bath and a couple of cocktails you'll both feel new people. I know the rooms you've been given, so I'll take you straight up to them, then when you're changed and rested I'll present you to your hostess."

Unlike the Duke, Richard was neither inquisitive nor suspicious by nature ; in fact, so blind was he to everything which did not personally concern him that Marie Lou used sometimes to relate that for fun she had once walked him three times round the same London square before he woke up to the fact that they had twice passed the house to which she had asked him to accompany her. In consequence, the fact that war now appeared imminent seemed a perfectly adequate explanation for the urgent summons which had caused him to leave Vienna overnight, and it never even occurred to him that there might be anything odd about the house-party of which he had so unexpectedly become a member. He did notice vaguely at dinner that there seemed to be a somewhat undue preponderance of males, but his hostess left him little time to speculate on the reason for that.

De Richleau had warned him before dinner that, as an inducement to the Baroness to issue her invitation, he had falsely described him as an English M.P. ; and now he required all his wits to avoid making a complete fool of himself as she cross-questioned him regarding the British political scene.

Both the Baroness and von Geisenheim, who was seated on her other side, knew far more about British politics than he did, yet both made the cardinal error of believing that British foreign policy was really controlled by the so-called "Cliveden set", and that its members were so strongly anti-Communist that they would never allow Britain to become involved in a war against the Axis. Richard, who until then had believed that the "Cliveden set" had some connection with professional bridge, heartily agreed with them as the easiest way out, and then managed to switch the conversation to personalities, for, although he took little interest in politics, he had a slight acquaintance with Lord Halifax, Lord Lloyd, Anthony Eden, Oliver Stanley, L. S. Amery, and a number of the younger Conservative members.

Marie Lou, on the other hand, was quick to perceive that no normal country house-party would have brought such a number of womanless men together, and she felt at once that the gathering must have something to do with the imminence of war. The scenes in Vienna the night before and the excited, news-hungry crowds that she had seen in Warsaw that morning were still fresh in her memory.

The Polish officers on either side of her and Major Bauer opposite were all striving to secure her attention. She was polite to the German and to all appearances enjoying a mild flirtation with the other two, but actually her smiling acceptances of their compliments were almost automatic. She had long since learned that men love to show off before a beautiful woman, and that an occasional exclamation of apparent interest will keep them talking endlessly about themselves and any field of endeavour in which they have achieved personal success. Jaljusz, the tall, fair man on her right, was a famous horseman who had won cups for jumping at half a dozen international horse-shows; Josef, a smaller, dark-haired man on her left, who said he came from Southern Poland, was an Air Force officer and one of the crack airmen of his country. In competition with their gay, rather boyish boastings, the stolid German opposite seemed to have no personal triumphs to offer, so he confined himself to occasional aggressive pronouncements about the greatness of Adolf Hitler and the reflected glory which shone on all who were privileged to work for him.

But all three might have saved their breath as far as making an impression on Marie Lou was concerned. Twenty-four hours earlier she had been dining alone with her dear Richard at "*Der Drei Hussaren*" in Gay Vienna, carefree and happy, hardly conscious of the clashing wills of great sections of the human race which now threatened to engulf them all in one vast maelstrom of blood, tears and death.

The position had not perceptibly worsened since, and around her were a score of people all chattering unconcernedly, intent only upon the rich dishes placed before them and the contents of the tall flagons of cool wine. Yet, now she was terribly conscious that all of them and every soul she knew and cared for were standing on the edge of the abyss.

If war came, how would it affect her nearest and dearest? Everyone said this would be a young man's war, so Richard would not be involved, at all events to begin with; besides, food would be important, and he would be needed at home to get every possible ounce out of the estate. Fleur was still only a schoolgirl. How Marie Lou thanked God now that she had never had a son. Greyeyes was too old to be accepted in any fighting service, and Simon would never pass the doctors. The United States would almost certainly remain neutral, so that let Rex out. She heaved a mental sigh of relief as she thought how incredibly lucky she was at this time when nine out of ten women all over Europe stood in grave danger of having to part with a husband, a lover, a son, or at least some man they loved dearly.

But was she really going to be so lucky after all? None of these men she loved were stay-at-homes by nature. Not even Simon, who always pretended that he was a born coward. Not even Richard, although he often swore that he would rather spend the rest of his life at home than anywhere else in the world. No question of neutrality would ever stop Rex from fighting for England in a struggle such as this, if he could possibly find a way to do it. And Greyeyes? Would he be content to work for the Red Cross and take cigarettes to wounded men in hospital? Of course not. She knew well that he spent an hour every morning of his life practising special exercises, taught him long ago by a Japanese, which kept his slender limbs as flexible and strong as steel, and he was still one of the finest shots in Europe. Age would prove no bar to him, and before the war was a week old he would be in it. Not in uniform perhaps, but engaged in some secret, deadly, dangerous business where subtle trickery, high courage and quick wits could serve Britain better than bayonets and guns. And the others would become his willing helpers, just as so often in the past.

She sighed again, this time almost audibly, although she knew in her heart that if England were to face grave peril she could never wish that the swords of her four Modern Musketeers should lie rusting in their scabbards. The blond Jaljusz had just concluded an anecdote at which she knew instinctively she was expected to laugh, so she turned the dazzling battery of her big, violet eyes up to his face, and converted the sigh into a little moue of amusement. A moment later the Baroness caught her glance and the long double line of men stood up as she left the table with her hostess and the buxom Anna Lubieszow.

Half an hour later, as the men began to make up tables for cards in the big lounge, de Richleau tapped Richard on the arm and, presenting him with one of his long Hoyo de Monterreys, said softly:

"I've quite a lot I want to talk to you about, and the night is fine. Let's smoke a cigar together while we take a stroll in the garden."

"And I've plenty to say to you," Richard replied in a low but aggrieved voice. "You let me in for a pretty party by saying I was a British M.P. That black-haired, monkey-faced harridan nearly caught me out a dozen times."

"Nearly, but not quite." The Duke smiled. "Fortunately, my dear fellow, I happen to know that you are not such a fool as you like your friends to believe, and that I can always count on you to pull through somehow when a little harmless duplicity is required."

Richard, whose natural good nature never remained ruffled for long, grinned back, completely mollified, and the two old friends passed out on to the terrace.

The night was warm but dark, as the moon was not yet up, and patches of cloud veiled all but a few clusters of stars. When their cigars were lit de Richleau turned and led the way along the terrace towards the wild garden to the left of the house. He did not speak until they were well away from the buildings and pacing slowly down one of the twisting walks which zigzagged through the best part of an acre of flowering shrubberies, then he said:

"I told you before dinner that the outbreak of hostilities is now virtually certain and that it will take place within a few days—if not hours; but what I did not dare to tell you then, for fear of walls having ears, is that the result of the first round, and, as a consequence of it, possibly the fate of the whole civilized world for hundreds of years to come, is being secretly arbitrated upon and will, I fear, be definitely 'rigged' in Hitler's favour by that bunch of crooks with whom we have just been dining."

"The devil!" exclaimed Richard, after emitting a low whistle. "But, if that's really so, why on earth aren't you on your way to London, to let your friends in Whitehall know what's going on?"

"Because I might make matters even worse if I gave them the wrong impression, and I still have no definite proof that Mack and Co. are actually prepared to sell us out."

"But you know beyond all question that they are negotiating with our potential enemies behind our backs—surely it's up to us to get that information to our own Government at the earliest possible moment?"

The Duke took a long pull at his evenly burning cigar, then said slowly: "I'm not altogether certain of that, Richard. Chamberlain is an honest man, but he's a fool; also, I'm convinced that he would seize on any straw which would be just enough to satisfy his conscience in an attempt to do another deal with Hitler. It's not that he's a coward, but that he believes himself to be a man with a mission—the preservation of world peace. If he were told that the Poles were trying to do a deal with the Nazis he would probably consider that let us out of our obligation to go to the Poles' assistance in the event of war, and would tell them so in the hope that they would then give in over Danzig."

"Well, perhaps that might not be so bad as it sounds. If ever anyone had a good case, Hitler has it over Danzig. A new deal on those lines would give us another six months at least, perhaps a year, to prepare; and by that time we'd be in a far better state to face the real showdown."

"I entirely agree, but the devil of it is that we don't know how far Mack is prepared to give way to the Germans. If it's only Danzig, well and good, but if this deal involves the Corridor as well and other frontier rectifications in Silesia, that will be a very different matter. We know what happened to the Czechs, and we dare not allow the same thing to happen here. The Poles are a nation of thirty-five million people, and first-class fighters at that. If it is a choice of another few months to rearm, against Poland's becoming a German province, like Czechoslovakia, before the party even starts, we had far better face the music now."

"Yes, I quite see that," Richard agreed; "but you haven't told me yet what you've found out up to now."

For the next few minutes de Richleau gave a short résumé of events since the arrival of General Mack and his friends at Lubieszow, then Richard said:

"It doesn't look too good, does it? From what you say I haven't a doubt that Mack is prepared to sell us out, but if nothing is definitely settled yet there's still a chance that Hitler may refuse to pay his price and that he'll decide to dig in his toes and fight. And if that happened after you had tipped off Whitehall and Chamberlain had decided that he was justified in ratting on the Poles there would be a ghastly mess."

"Yes, even a few days' delay in our coming in, if the Poles do fight, might prove disastrous; because, if we failed to declare war on Germany at once, they might feel that it was hopeless to try to fight the Nazis on their own and throw in their hand after the initial clashes on the frontier. Then Hitler would have Poland in the bag with scarcely a shot fired."

"If only we could find out how far Mack is prepared to go," Richard mused.

For a further ten minutes they talked on round the subject, then suddenly the Duke laid his hand on Richard's arm, bringing him to a halt.

As they stood there in the close, warm darkness between two groups of high bushes, they could hear the approach of footsteps and the murmur of voices. A moment later they could distinguish the clear, precise voice of General Count von Geisenheim, speaking in German, and then the rather high-pitched voice of General Mack.

With a little grimace of regret, de Richleau dropped his cigar and put his foot on it; then he swiftly turned up the silk lapels of his dinner-jacket so that they should hide his white dress shirt. Richard quickly followed suit, and they stood there straining their ears to catch the words of the slowly approaching couple on the far side of the bushes.

"I know that, but I cannot help it," von Geisenheim was saying.

"The Luftwaffe absolutely insist?" demurred General Mack.

"Absolutely. Air power will be the dominant factor in all future wars, and, if the campaign is to be rendered as short and bloodless as possible, it is essential that your air force should be grounded from the very beginning. All the other matters which we have discussed openly in conference these past days are of comparatively small importance compared with this. And, after all, what are the lives of a few score airmen weighed against the thousands of troops you would lose if we were compelled to inflict a major defeat upon your army before you could decently advise your Cabinet to ask for an armistice?"

Mack grunted. "There is much truth in that. All right, then, say that I agree to give you the order of battle and dispositions of our air force, will the Fuehrer give a definite undertaking that he will maintain me in office, by force of arms if need be, and allow me, as *Grossgauleiter* of the new Protectorate of Poland, to select my own Cabinet, consisting entirely of Poles?"

"He will make you *Grossgauleiter*, yes. But whether he would agree to your Cabinet being exclusively composed of Poles, I do not know. I think he would at least require German representation."

"That I will not have." Mack's voice was harsh and determined. "With even one Nazi in my Cabinet I should not be the master—and on that I insist."

"We have little time, but if you are absolutely adamant on this point . . ." Von Geisenheim's voice faded away as the two men passed out of earshot.

"Well, now we know," murmured Richard.

De Richleau nodded. "It is clear now that Mack is placing his personal ambition before all else. He evidently realizes that, if his Government gave way to the Nazis, it would fall, so he does not even intend that they should climb down over Danzig. Instead, he is planning to pose as one of Poland's heroes by defying Hitler, while secretly stabbing his country in the back; his price being supreme power as Hitler's Viceroy directly the war with Poland is over."

"In other words, he means to eat his cake and keep it too. The swine! Just think of those poor devils of Polish airmen!"

"Yes, if he is prepared to see his own air force annihilated before they have even had a chance to give battle he is capable of anything. Having sunk to that, he will make a deal with the Nazis anyhow—even if Hitler refuses to agree to his having the Polish Cabinet for which he asks."

"Hitler will agree," said Richard with sudden bitterness. "He'd be mad not to. What is a promise to Hitler? Of course he'll agree, knowing perfectly well that Mack will be in no position to do a damn' thing if he chooses to change his mind afterwards. The thing is, what the hell are we to do?"

"Now we know where we are one of us must get this information back to London at the earliest possible moment."

"It shouldn't be difficult to pinch a car. I can easily collect Marie Lou. We'd have to leave the baggage, but we'd be in Warsaw before morning."

The Duke shook his head. "No good, my friend. If any or all of us did a moonlight flitting, Mack and Co. would immediately smell a rat. Every policeman in Poland would be turned on to hunt for us, and we'd never get out of the country. Besides, Lucretia is not due back till Sunday night, and we can't leave her stranded here. No, at the moment, none of them suspects that we are on to their game, and our only chance is to use that. Somehow, you and Marie Lou have got to leave here first thing tomorrow morning, perfectly naturally. But we have to produce a thumping good excuse for this sudden curtailment of your visit, and this is not the sort of place where you can walk down to the village and send yourself a telegram."

For a few moments they stood in silence, each striving to think of a pretext which would be even remotely plausible; but the problem seemed entirely beyond them, as who, in their senses, would undertake a ten-hour train journey followed by an eight-hour car drive for the purpose of joining a country house-party, and then, having arrived at six o'clock in the evening, evince a desire to rush off again early the following morning?

Suddenly Richard snapped his fingers. "I've got it—at least, I think I have."

"Go on," said the Duke.

"It's Fleur's birthday on the 5th of September, that's Monday week. We could say it's this Monday and we simply must get back for it—our only child and all·that."

"But you'd have known about that before you left Vienna."

"Of course, and if we had left Vienna by plane today, as we can say we had planned to do, we should have been back in ample time for it."

"True. Yet, if you had meant to get back anyhow, you would hardly have agreed to come all this far out of your way to Lubieszow, for the sake of spending a single evening here."

"Wait a minute," Richard parried. "How were we to know that Lubieszow was right out here in Eastern Poland? All you said on the telephone was to get on the night train for Warsaw, and you'd have a car to meet us at the station. Marie Lou and I might quite well have assumed that Lubieszow was only half an hour's drive from the capital. If it had been we would have had the best part of the day here today and all tomorrow as well, and still have been able to catch the train out of Warsaw that we hope to take tomorrow night. Two days and a night is not an unreasonable visit to people one has never met before, particularly when one's visit is proposed by a third party solely on account of the place being considered something of a beauty spot."

De Richleau nodded. "I believe you've hit it, Richard. Anyhow, we might rack our brains all night and not think of anything better. You can say, too, that the line to Vienna was bad last night, and when I said that I meant to leave here on Monday you *thought* I said that I meant to get home by Monday, so you were under the impression that we should all be travelling together."

"That's it; and naturally I thought that if you could make it we could too, without curtailing our visit to a point that must now seem almost rudeness. It's just an unfortunate mix-up which we couldn't regret more, but we're sure our monkey-faced hostess will understand how impossible it is for us to disappoint Fleur by not being home in time to spend her birthday evening with her."

"Exactly," purred the Duke. "And the sooner you get hold of Marie Lou the better. She can tell the Baroness that she knew there must have been some mistake directly she realized this morning that she was in for a full day's car run, but she didn't like to say anything immediately on her arrival or make you both look foolish by mentioning it at dinner. Directly she has made her excuses, I will arrange with the Baron's man for a car to be ready to take you back to Warsaw tomorrow morning. You must see our Ambassador there and tell him the whole story, then he will pass it on to London by high-grade cipher. He may be able to arrange seats on a plane for you, too, which will get you home via Stockholm or Copenhagen. It's too late to risk going via Germany, but, in any case, once you have handed in your stuff to our Embassy there will be no violent hurry, and, if you like to wait in Warsaw till Monday evening, Lucretia and I will join you there."

"That's what we'll do then," Richard agreed, as they turned to walk back to the house.

Returning to the lounge through the french windows which gave on to the terrace, de Richleau mixed himself a drink and walked over to show a feigned interest in the card-players, while Richard went in search of Marie Lou.

He found her in the company of the tall, fair Pole, Jaljusz, and young Stanislas; and it took all his tact plus half an hour of playful badinage before he succeeded in getting his wife to admit that she was really tired after her long day and ought to go to bed. With obvious reluctance the two Poles accepted their dismissal, and Richard led Marie Lou off into another room, where he explained as swiftly as he could that it was necessary for them to leave Lubieszow early next morning, and the excuse he was proposing to make for doing so.

Marie Lou asked no questions. She had already sensed that something abnormal was going on, and guessed that the Duke was behind this sudden decision that they should leave earlier than they had planned. She agreed at once, and they went to look for their hostess.

A quarter of an hour later they joined de Richleau in the lounge. He moved away from the card tables at their approach, and his grey "devil's" eyebrows lifted slightly in interrogation.

Richard gave an almost indiscernible nod, and Marie Lou said softly: "It's all right, Greyeyes. The Baroness was naturally surprised at first, but when I explained about Fleur's birthday she couldn't have been more charming."

"It went off better than I expected," Richard confessed. "That fellow Ignac gave us rather a suspicious look, but she sent him away to fetch something for her, so he wasn't in on the latter part of the conversation and had no chance to ask awkward questions."

"Quiet!" breathed the Duke through unmoving lips. "Here he comes."

Next moment Count Ignac joined them. A pale smile lit up his thin face as he addressed the Duke:

"General Mack has sent me to ask you if you would be kind enough to join him for a few moments in the library."

"Certainly." The Duke smiled back, and leaving his friends he followed the Count out of the lounge through a curtained entrance that gave on to a square, booklined room. In one corner of it there was a large, ornate porcelain stove, and in front of this General Mack was standing, his hands clasped behind his back. As soon as the curtains had fallen into place he began in his suave, slightly high-pitched voice:

"I am told, Duke, that your friends, Mr. and Mrs. Eaton, are thinking of leaving Lubieszow tomorrow morning?"

"That is so," de Richleau agreed amiably.

Mack nodded his high, semi-bald head, which, with his long nose, gave him a faint resemblance to a bird of prey. "I see. Well, much as I regret to inconvenience them, I fear that I cannot agree to their departure."

The Duke drew himself up. "Really, General! Even from our host such a statement would border on impertinence. By what right——"

Raising a hand, Mack cut him short. "This is no question of hosts or guests, and it is best we should not mince matters any further. I have no intention of permitting either you or your friends to leave this house; and to ensure that I am placing all three of you under arrest."

Chapter V

PISTOLS ARE DRAWN

"But this is fantastic!" exclaimed the Duke.

"It is nothing of the kind," snapped Mack. "It is an elementary precaution."

"Against what?"

"Against you or your friends prejudicing the safety of the State."

"Indeed!" De Richleau's eyebrows lifted. "I had always believed that Poland was a properly constituted democracy in which it was illegal for army officers arbitrarily to arrest law-abiding citizens."

Mack's sallow face paled a little. "That is true; but you must know perfectly well that my authority far exceeds that of any ordinary army officer."

The Duke had realized within a minute of entering the room that the game was up, and that nothing he could say would persuade or intimidate Mack into letting the Eatons go; but the best policy to allay suspicion was obviously to continue the pretence that he had no idea what lay behind the General's apparently strange behaviour. Accordingly, he now burst out in well-simulated anger:

"A general naturally has more authority than a lieutenant, but that still does not entitle him to override the civil law. In any case, how can the Eatons' departure prejudice the safety of the State? Either you are under some complete misapprehension regarding us or you have been drinking. This talk of 'authority' and 'arrests' does not make sense, and I demand a proper explanation."

"D'you mean . . . ?" Mack hesitated and frowned slightly. "Can it possibly be that you don't know who I am?"

"Since you were introduced to me as General Mack," the Duke began with some asperity, "I naturally assumed . . ." His voice suddenly tailed off, his eyes widened, and he exclaimed: "Good heavens! When we first met I had a feeling that I had seen you somewhere before, but as your name was not familiar I dismissed it. Of course, it was your photograph I had seen in the newspapers. You are——"

"My dear Duke!" Mack interrupted. He was smiling now. "I fear I have been very stupid, and I can hardly wonder at your resenting my apparently arbitrary conduct."

"Well, frankly," the Duke smiled back, "I am still most puzzled about that. I can't for the life of me think what I or my friends have done to incur your Excellency's displeasure."

"I would much prefer to continue to be known as 'General' while I'm at Lubieszow," said Mack hurriedly; then, taking out his cigarette-case and offering it, he went on: "But sit down, Duke, sit down, and I will explain matters."

"Thanks." De Richleau accepted one of the thin, gold-tipped cigarettes and made himself comfortable in an arm-chair as the Polish statesman continued, with a slightly self-conscious laugh:

"You see, it's like this. I'm afraid I flattered myself by assuming that you would know my face at once; then when the Germans arrived here I felt you might begin to get ideas. When one sees only half a picture it is so easy to jump to wrong conclusions."

"Actually, I hardly gave the matter a thought," lied the Duke blandly. "The Baron requested me not to mention in any letters I might write that he was entertaining a party of high Polish officers and two Germans here; but it was none of my business, so I dismissed the whole thing from my mind."

"Of course, Duke, of course. But you realize, I am sure, how disastrous it might be for Poland if it became known that I had been conferring in secret with von Geisenheim?"

"No, to be absolutely frank, I don't," replied the Duke with assumed innocence. "Surely it is your job to save your country from being plunged into war if you possibly can, without loss of honour, and your best chance of achieving that was obviously by having a quiet off-the-record talk with the Germans."

"True! Absolutely true!" Mack exclaimed, with evident relief. "But some people might not take that view. You pay me the compliment of assuming my integrity to be as impeccable as your own, and I am happy to think that your confidence is not misplaced; but others . . . well? Few statesmen are without enemies who are only too eager to put a malicious interpretation on their actions, and I am no exception. That is why I dare not risk its becoming known that von Geisenheim and I have been staying here together."

"Richard Eaton would not dream of mentioning the matter to the press, or to anyone else who is likely to do so, once I have had a word with him. I will go guarantor for that."

"It's not only the press," replied Mack, swiftly evading the Duke's pretty little trap. "He is a politician, and directly he gets back to England he will come in contact with his fellow M.P.s. With Poland so much in the news it is almost certain that the Foreign Secretary will send for him to learn his impressions of the state of feeling in the country. How can he be expected to refrain from any mention of the people whom he met here in Lubieszow?"

De Richleau smiled a little ruefully, realizing that, through having falsely represented Richard as an M.P., he had quite unexpectedly hoisted himself with his own petard. But he also realized that he must keep up his rôle of the transparently honest dilettante, so he said:

"But since Poland and Britain are allies, surely you would have no objection to our Foreign Secretary's knowing about these talks?"

"No, no, of course not. At least, not if he could be told the whole story. But that is just the trouble. As I have not yet reported the result of these conversations to my colleagues in the Government, I cannot possibly take either you or Mr. Eaton into my confidence concerning the way they have progressed. I am very sorry, Duke, but I really see no alternative but for you and your friends to remain at Lubieszow for the time being."

"I see," said the Duke gravely, standing up. "I appreciate the difficulty of the position in which you find yourself, but it is only fair to warn you that Richard Eaton may not accept your decision so calmly; and you must know yourself that there will be extremely strong reactions from the British Foreign Office if you persist in your intention to arrest a Member of Parliament without the faintest legal grounds for such an act."

Mack spread out his hands deprecatingly. "Let us not use the unpleasant word 'arrest'. You will all continue entirely free to go and come in the house and grounds as you wish; but I must ask you not to go beyond them and to send no more letters or telegrams while you are here."

"A thorn by any other name is still a thorn," remarked the Duke with his cynical smile. "And for how long, may I ask, do you propose to detain us?"

"A few days only. Von Geisenheim is returning to Germany tomorrow for fresh instructions. He should be back by Monday, or Tuesday at the latest. One final talk should settle matters. I shall then return to Warsaw, and, if you and your friends care to accompany me, I will gladly do what I can to make up for the inconvenience I have caused you, by seeing that you get the highest priorities to expedite your journey home."

"Thank you—General. May I assume that you will let our hostess know the reason why the Eatons will not be departing, after all, tomorrow morning?"

"Certainly, my dear Duke, and please convey to them my sincerest apologies."

"By all means," agreed de Richleau, slightly inclining his handsome head, as he moved towards the door.

He found Richard and Marie Lou where he had left them. They had felt at once that the summoning of the Duke boded no good for their plans, and now, as he approached, they both shot him a swift glance of interrogation.

"We're stymied," he told them in a low voice. "Mack believed that we were already on to his little game. I think I managed to bluff him that we hadn't even guessed who he was. But, all the same, he is taking no chances. All three of us are more or less under house arrest."

"I'll pinch a car and make a bolt for it tonight, then," Richard murmured. "Only thing to do."

"You'll do nothing of the kind," the Duke countered softly. "I inferred that I accepted the situation and would do my best to persuade you to do the same; but I warned him that you might quite possibly resent his interference with your plans most strongly and make trouble for him later. I want you to play up to that rôle. I think the two of you had better go off to bed in a huff, right away, without saying good-night to anyone; and tomorrow Richard can make a formal protest to our poor little host."

"But we've got to agree on a plan for getting away from here," Richard objected. "Let's go out into the garden again and talk it over."

De Richleau shook his head. "It's no good trying to rush things. Mack will almost certainly use the chauffeurs to form a guard for the garage tonight; and, even if you could get a car, as I said an hour ago, they would catch you long before you could cross the frontier. You play your part of showing natural resentment by going off to bed while I play mine of having accepted the situation under protest by staying down here for a bit. That's the best way to lull their suspicions; and if we can do that we'll stand a much better chance of getting away later on."

"What *is* all this about?" Marie Lou asked with a puzzled frown. "Neither of you has told me a thing yet, except about pretending that Fleur's birthday is next Monday and using that as an excuse for leaving here tomorrow."

"I'm sorry, Princess," the Duke said contritely, "but I want to avoid giving the impression that we three are conspiring. Please be a darling and take Richard upstairs, then he can tell you all about it."

"All right, Greyeyes." She turned to Richard. "Come along, my sweet, and remember that we've both got to look thoroughly sulky."

When they had gone the Duke carried on a desultory conversation with some of the Poles, at the same time listening with half an ear to the wireless; but he did not wait up to hear the midnight news, as he knew already that Hitler would not, after all, make his bid for world power that week-end, as Whitehall anticipated. "Uncle" would survive at least until von Geisenheim had made his trip to Germany and returned with the final terms of the secret treaty that the Nazis were well on their way to concluding with General Mack; so it looked as if the helpless millions of Europe were to be given a respite until the end of the month.

After breakfasting in bed next morning, de Richleau sent a message to the Eatons inviting them to ride with him, and on receiving a reply that they would be delighted to do so he ordered horses.

When he came downstairs about an hour later he found Marie Lou seated near the great wood fire that burned summer and winter in the lounge, with the two Poles who had fallen for her the night before in attendance and Richard in the far corner of the big room holding what appeared to be a most acrimonious conversation with their host.

Having said good morning to the group by the fire, de Richleau walked over to Richard and the Baron. The unfortunate Lubieszow was obviously most distressed. Never before had he found himself compelled to detain a guest against his will, yet he could do little but reiterate apologies. Richard was playing his part of an indignant M.P. well, but the Duke thought that matters had gone far enough, so he began to pour oil on the troubled waters. Having ordered the horses he found it comparatively easy, as horseflesh was the Baron's ruling passion. Directly he heard that they were about to ride, he hurried them outside where the grooms were walking the horses up and down, and began to expatiate upon their beauties.

For the Duke a big black, which he had ridden several times before, had been saddled; Richard was to be mounted on a strawberry roan, and Marie Lou on a bright chestnut mare. To the Baron's relief, Richard abandoned the vexed question of his return home to his Parliamentary duties to enthuse about the graceful chestnut, and a few minutes later their host had the satisfaction of seeing them trot away along a drive that led into the nearby woods.

After cantering for a mile over the soft pine needles, they entered a wide glade in which there was a deserted forester's hut; at a word from the Duke they drew rein.

"I thought this the best plan to ensure us a talk with no likelihood of being overheard," he said at once.

"Good scheme," Richard agreed; "but I must confess that I haven't a single idea to offer."

"We talked for hours last night," volunteered Marie Lou, "and again this morning; yet neither of us could think of any way of escaping from this place except by stealing a car. It's such miles from anywhere."

De Richleau lit a cigarette. "True; and I'm afraid we shall have to reconcile ourselves to remaining here until Mack lets us go."

Marie Lou turned towards him; her violet eyes were troubled. "That doesn't sound like you, Greyeyes."

He gave a rather rueful laugh. "It's nice of you, Princess, to be so concerned because it appears that I'm losing my grip."

"Well—er . . ." Richard hesitated. "I'd hardly liked to say so, but since you put it that way yourself . . . Hang it all, you agreed last night how vital it was that we should get word to London now we know for certain that this Polish crook is selling us out; yet you won't let me take a sporting chance, and you actually suggest that we should sit twiddling our thumbs while——"

"Steady on!" the Duke cut in. "It's you two who are getting rusty. I told you that our tactics last night were solely to allay suspicion. I reasoned that, if you went off to bed in a temper, Mack would give you the lion's share of his attention and probably put a servant on to you to see that you did not leave your room with the idea of putting a midnight telephone call through to London; whereas, since I appeared reconciled, he might not bother about me at all. And I proved correct. When everyone else had gone to bed I did a little quiet snooping. The pimply-faced fellow who acts as Mack's secretary had been posted to watch your corridor; he was sitting on that shallow flight of stairs that leads up to it."

"Sorry, Greyeyes," Marie Lou blew him a kiss. "We ought to have known better than to think for a moment that you would fall down on a thing like this."

"That goes for me, too," Richard added with feeling.

"Bless you both!" smiled the Duke. "Don't give it another thought. But, to continue. You know that I am pretty light on my feet and can see fairly well in the dark?"

"Then you managed to get downstairs and telephone," said Marie Lou.

"I went downstairs, but I didn't attempt to telephone in the house. I thought it too risky. I went round to the garage and found, as I had antici-pated, that it was guarded. But that didn't worry me; the starting of a car would have made too much noise at night, anyway. I continued my ghost-like progress to the stables, got this good fellow out of his box and saddled him up."

Patting his horse's neck, the Duke went on: "It's about five miles to the village and back, and I saw no point in walking all that way, if I could ride. Of course, I muffled the horse's hooves so that the sentry by the garage should not hear the clatter on the cobbles as I led my mount out. The rest was easy."

"Then you succeeded in telephoning from the village?" Richard put in quickly.

"That's it. The local postmaster was somewhat irritable at being roused from his bed at three o'clock in the morning, but he was easily mollified when I produced my note-case. The fellow was scarcely better than a peasant, and he probably made more out of my nocturnal visit than he earns normally in a month. We parted the best of friends, and I don't think he's likely to talk."

"Did you actually manage to get through to the person you wanted in London?" Richard asked.

"Yes. It took over an hour, and I spoilt poor Pellinore Gwain-Cust's beauty sleep, but I talked to him for the best part of ten minutes. Of course, I couldn't refer openly to what has been happening here, for fear someone in Brest-Litovsk or Warsaw who might have been listening in should cut me off; but Pellinore is remarkably quick in the uptake, and I am satisfied that, by the time we had finished, he fully understood what lay behind my some-what cryptic utterances."

"Good work!" laughed Richard. "In that case, there is no point in either of us trying to make a breakaway now."

"Not for the moment. Pellinore will inform the F.O. that a deal is in progress, the terms of which are virtually agreed. It only remains for us to let him know when it is actually completed."

"Then we can resign ourselves to remaining here for a few days?"

"I do hope it's not longer," said Marie Lou. "Fleur would be terribly disappointed if we weren't home for her real birthday on Monday week. We arranged, too, for Simon to come down the week-end before that and stay over for it. He'll be arriving at Cardinal's Folly the Friday before—Septem-ber the 1st."

"I think you should just make it," de Richleau reassured her. "With luck we'll get away from here on Tuesday. But, in any case, you need not concern yourselves unduly if you're not back in time to receive Simon next Friday. I was afraid that with all these rumours both he and Rex might become worried by the thought of you two being in Nazi-occupied Vienna so I asked old Pellinore to get hold of one or both of them and tell them that you had joined me here, and the reason why we might all be detained for some little time at Lubieszow."

The horses were moving restively under them, and for the moment there seemed no more to say, so by mutual consent they turned into another ride and set off down it at a canter.

Throughout the rest of Saturday and the Sunday that followed they played the parts they had decided. The Duke remained as amiable as ever to the Lubieszows and their guests and appeared in no hurry whatsoever to depart; but the Eatons, while showing every politeness towards their hosts, treated General Mack and his officers with a frigidity which plainly demonstrated their resentment at being detained against their will.

It was on Sunday evening, just as the light was beginning to fail, that Marie Lou noticed that the Duke had suddenly become quite restless. As he walked out on to the terrace for the third time in half an hour, she followed him.

"What is it, Greyeyes?" she wanted to know, taking his arm.

"Lucretia," he confessed. "Before you arrived, or Mack had forbidden our departure, Lucretia and I had arranged to leave for home tomorrow morning. She promised to be back here tonight; but she hasn't turned up, and in another quarter of an hour it will be too dark for Jan to bring his plane down in that open field without landing lights. I'm beginning to be afraid that they may have met with an accident."

"Surely that's most unlikely?" Marie Lou strove to reassure him. "You told me that Jan was an ace-pilot."

"So he is, my dear. I believe that at times he even acts as a test pilot; but that is no guarantee against engine trouble."

"From what you've said I gather that Lucretia takes quite a good view of that young man?"

"Yes. She went on this trip to make up her mind whether she had really fallen in love with him."

"Then hasn't it occurred to you that, having left these friends of his with whom they've been staying at Cracow, they might have decided to spend a night together on their own, on the way back?"

He turned to smile at her. "What an idea to put into my grey and sober head!"

"Nonsense, Greyeyes!" she admonished him. "You must have been about his age when you seduced her mother and——"

"Really, Princess!"

"You can't deny it. You've probably forgotten, but you told us the story years ago, before we ever met her. And, after all, it's quite time that Lucretia threw her shoes over the moon again."

"Yes, I agree about that. Her affair with Cristoval went so deep that I was beginning to fear that she would never get over it. I'd give a great deal to see her happily married, and anything would be to the good which will free her from this awful inhibition that has been robbing her of the best years of her life. All the same, I don't think your theory is the cause of their non-appearance tonight. Lucretia knew what was going on here and how anxious I was to get back to England before war actually broke out.''

"Poor Greyeyes." Marie Lou squeezed his arm affectionately. "How little you really know about women ! We all hate wars, because they take our men away from us, but we never allow them to interfere with our private lives if we can possibly help it. Love means so much more to us than frontiers and nationalities or having the right to vote for some silly man to talk in a Chamber of Deputies. If Lucretia really has fallen in love again she'll be so excited at the discovery that she is not made of stone after all that a little thing like the possibility of a European war breaking out, and delaying your journey home, will not even enter her head."

"Perhaps you're right," laughed the Duke. "I certainly hope so, and in any case we can't leave here yet even if she does turn up."

It was after dinner that night that Jan telephoned; but to the Duke's fury he received the message second hand, and a very garbled version of what Jan had been attempting to convey. Anna Lubieszow had taken the call; the line had been very bad, and she had not heard clearly. Apparently, although no order of general mobilization had yet been issued, the Polish War Office was taking steps to muster certain key personnel, particularly reserve air force pilots, of which Jan was one. The friend with whom he had been staying in Cracow was another, so they had gone off that morning together to report, but before leaving had made arrangements for Lucretia to return from Cracow by train.

At this point, unfortunately, the supply of information broke down. The nearest stations to Lubieszow were Pinsk, on the line from Warsaw, about twenty-five miles to the north-east, and Kowel, which lay fifty miles to the south-west, on the Lublin line. Lucretia's shortest route lay through Jaroslaw and Lublin, but she would have to change trains at both junctions, so it might prove quicker if she caught an express to Warsaw and came on the northern line from there. Added to this uncertainty, they had no idea at what time she had left Cracow, so they could not even make a guess about when to send a car in to either station.

De Richleau was somewhat concerned as Lucretia knew no Polish; but reference to the railway time-tables showed that, even if she had left Cracow quite early in the day, there was no chance of her getting in that night.

After breakfast next morning they telephoned the station-masters at both Pinsk and Kowel, requesting that a look-out should be kept for a young foreign lady with golden hair, aquiline nose and grey eyes, and that if she arrived she should be made comfortable in the station hotel until a car could be sent to pick her up.

In the absence of von Geisenheim and Major Bauer, the Polish Staff officers had no conference to occupy them, so, having sat about reading or sleeping most of the week-end, they had arranged a snipe-shoot for the Monday. De Richleau went out with them and would have thoroughly enjoyed his day had he not been vaguely troubled about Lucretia. When they got back in the late afternoon he learned to his dismay that not only had she not yet arrived but there was no further news of her.

He spent a good part of the evening ringing up hotels in Warsaw on the chance that she might have stayed at one of them the previous night; but the war scare had now become so general that people all over Europe were curtailing their holidays and making emergency arrangements, which resulted in the lines becoming so congested that his efforts proved both exasperating and useless.

First thing on the Tuesday morning the most urgent enquiries at both stations still failed to produce any information about the missing Countess, and the Duke's friends had all their work cut out to persuade him that a serious accident was much less likely to be the cause of her disappearance than a misunderstanding of Jan's garbled message, or the generally unsettled state of things; and, indeed, from the news bulletins it seemed that Europe was on the very brink of catastrophe.

The Polish Government evidently knew nothing of the secret negotiations which were proceeding so well at Lubieszow, and the German Government gave no appearance of doing so. Each was accusing the other with ever-growing bitterness of injustices and persecution towards its nationals and it looked as though the street clashes which were already occurring in Danzig might at any time be made the excuse by one side or the other for an open declaration of hostilities.

Just after five o'clock an aircraft circled over the house and came down in the fields behind it. Two minutes later the guests, who were drinking their afternoon coffee in the terrace, saw the tall, grey General Count von Geisenheim and his lame, brutal-faced Nazi adjutant approaching. As soon as the new arrivals had been given refreshments Mack muttered a few words to the Count, upon which all the officers present left the terrace to go into immediate conference.

"If only Lucretia turns up it looks now as though we'll be able to get away from here tomorrow," murmured Richard.

"Yes—if only she does," de Richleau agreed. "I got on to the police in Warsaw about her this afternoon, but they could tell me nothing, and they are so busy with emergency measures that I fear they will prove of little help. However, I have no doubt you're right about tonight seeing the end of the conferences here. The war is three days overdue already, and even Hitler

will not be able to restrain those young blackguards of his in Danzig much
longer. It is only a question now of whether he will pay Mack's price for an
easy victory, and to that von Geisenheim will have brought the answer."

For a little time they paced moodily up and down the terrace, then in
due course went up to change for dinner.

During the meal they were conscious of a suppressed excitement, yet
nothing was said to indicate how the negotiations were proceeding, and the
Duke guessed the reason. The full limit of Mack's contemplated treachery
was not known to his companions. To him alone would von Geisenheim
give Hitler's answer, and it was probable that the German had not yet done
so.

As soon as dinner was finished the two of them went out on to the terrace
together. When they returned, after only a few minutes, Mack was smiling.

Richard's hazel eyes met the Duke's grey ones. Their faces remained
impassive, and they glanced with seeming casualness towards Marie Lou.
Her face, too, was completely expressionless ; but all three of them knew that
the Polish pass had been sold.

Mack suddenly addressed his officers : "Gentlemen ! The *Herr General*
has just told me that he wishes to leave again at first light for Berlin. One
final session tonight should conclude our business. Let us go upstairs."

With von Geisenheim beside him he walked straight towards the broad
staircase ; his staff and Major Bauer quickly drank up their liqueurs and
followed.

Shortly afterwards, the rest of the party accompanied the Baroness up to
her drawing-room. Somehow they managed to maintain an apparently
normal conversation about trivialities, but all of them, except old Anna
Lubieszow and the phlegmatic Baron, were secretly engaged in wondering
what was going on in the big room across the landing, so it was not surprising
that occasional short silences occurred.

During one of them the sound of a car driving up to the front of the house
could be heard quite clearly, and everyone looked round startled, wondering
whom it could be. Two minutes later, Jan, now in the uniform of a Polish
Air Force officer, came hurrying into the room.

He laughed at their exclamations, kissed his aunt's hand, was introduced
to the Eatons, then gave the Duke a cheerful but puzzled look, as he said
"I expected that you would have left here days ago for Warsaw, sir ?"

"And I," replied the Duke coldly, "expected that you would have returned
here days ago with my ward. Is Lucretia with you ?"

"Of course not. I——"

"Then where the devil is she ?"

"But didn't you get my message ?"

"Yes. To say that you were reporting to your unit and that she was
returning by train."

Jan spread out his hands. "I am most sorry—terribly so. The line was very bad. Anna could not have heard properly what I said. I knew you had planned to leave here for England on Monday morning, and as I could not fly her back on the Sunday afternoon it looked as if you must be delayed a whole day. To avoid that I put her on the train for Warsaw and telephoned my housekeeper to expect her. My idea was that she could sleep there Sunday night and that you could pick her up in Warsaw on Monday."

"I see," murmured the Duke. "Your intentions were certainly of the best, Jan; but we have been terribly worried about her. And why, I wonder, as I failed to appear, has she not telephoned?"

With a slightly uneasy smile, Jan shrugged his broad shoulders. He did not like to say in front of them that his own duties had taken him to Warsaw, where he had arrived only a few hours after Lucretia, and that they had since been hitting up the town together without giving a thought to the Duke. Instead, he said:

"Believing that you knew where she was, I think she has been content to wait there until it suited you to pick her up."

Clotilde nodded her dark head. "That must be it. All your worries are over, Duke, and we have been alarmed for nothing. But you, Jan," she went on, shaking a reproving finger at her nephew, "you are a very naughty boy not to have made quite certain that Anna understood your plan. And now, tell us how it is that you have been able to get back here after all."

"That was sheer luck," he grinned, "and this is only a flying visit. Owing to the non-aggression pact between Russia and Germany, many of our air force dispositions have had to be changed. We can no longer afford to leave our eastern frontier altogether unguarded, and a number of our best Reserve Squadrons are being sent there. Mine is one of them, and as I was motoring to my new station I thought I would break my journey here for the night."

"Forgive me, Madame," the Duke addressed Clotilde, "but I would like to get through to Lucretia, and I'm sure Jan could help me by getting his own Warsaw number and asking for her to be brought to the telephone."

"But certainly!" the Baroness and Jan agreed almost simultaneously, and the two men left the room.

On the way downstairs Jan said quickly: "You've no need at all to worry about her. As a matter of fact, I've come straight from Warsaw, and she was in grand form when we lunched together just before I set out."

De Richleau gave him a sharp glance. "Am I to conclude that the story of your being called up last week is actually a fairy tale, or is it that you have been neglecting your duties to entertain my ward?"

"Neither," replied Jan, a little stiffly. "I had to report to the local head-quarters in Cracow on Sunday, and I had no idea that I should be ordered to the Central Depot in Warsaw until some hours after Lucretia had left. We Poles are not the people to neglect our duty at a time like this; but once

I got to Warsaw I was simply waiting to be posted, so I was able to devote myself to showing Lucretia the city with a perfectly clear conscience."

"I fear I deserved that," de Richleau admitted with a smile. "I'm sorry, Jan, and I'm very glad that you were able to give Lucretia such a pleasant time. It's a great relief to know that she is safe, though, and as there is almost certain to be a long delay in getting through to Warsaw we won't bother to telephone now. I really do expect to leave here tomorrow morning, so I should be with her again later in the day."

"I'd like to telephone all the same ; just to—er—wish her good-night. But, you know, Lucretia thought that you might decide to stay on here a few days longer. That's why she wasn't at all worried when you did not turn up."

"Did she give any reason why I might stay on ?" de Richleau probed with assumed casualness.

"No, and it was none of my business, so I did not press her."

The Duke hesitated only for a second. He thought that Mack would keep his word and allow the Eatons and himself to leave the following day, but he was by no means certain of that. The arch-traitor might well believe that they had guessed too much and go back on his promise. Now that the Duke knew the final outcome of the secret talks the urgency of getting home to report in person had increased a thousandfold. Whatever Mack might intend, the Duke meant to leave within the next twenty-four hours. If Mack did prove obstructive, and it came to making a bolt for it, Jan, who was unquestionably an honest fellow, might become a very valuable ally to the escapers. As these thoughts flashed through his brain, the Duke said :

"It's rather a long story, Jan, and I would prefer not to talk about it in the house. Put in your Warsaw call and while we are waiting for it to come through we will take a stroll in the garden."

While Jan was talking to the exchange, the Duke considered carefully just how much he should tell him. He felt that the whole story would be far too strong meat for a fanatically patriotic Polish airman, and he did not wish Jan to put a spark to the powder magazine by some premature and ill-advised action ; so when they were well away from the house he talked for a little of the obvious importance of the secret conference with the Germans, and then disclosed the fact that Mack had placed Baron Lubieszow's English guests under arrest and was detaining them against their will.

Had he been able to foresee the frightful repercussions which were to result from his disclosure before he was an hour older, he would never have made it ; but beneath Jan's cheerful, easy manner there lurked a highly explosive nature, and Polish traditions meant much more to him than his career or personal safety.

Having listened with growing astonishment and impatience to what the Duke had to say, he suddenly burst out :

"But this is fantastic—unthinkable ! You and your friends are our guests.

Naturally, you are free to go whenever you wish. My uncle cannot possibly be aware of this conversation you had with Mack. He would never agree to such an outrageous abuse of hospitality by one of his guests towards another."

"I am sure the Baron doesn't approve of what is going on," murmured the Duke, "but all the same I am quite certain that he knows about it."

"Have you spoken to him about it yourself?"

"No, I was reluctant to embarrass him."

"Then you have no proof at all that he is a party to Mack's disgraceful behaviour. I will speak to my uncle at once, and Mack shall be forced to apologize."

Jan had already turned back towards the house, and the Duke, who now had some difficulty in keeping up with the young Pole's impetuous pace, said quickly: "Listen, my friend. I would much rather that you did not make a scene about this. If Mack goes back on his promise to let us go tomorrow, well—we can discuss the matter again. But, as long as the conference has been in progress, he has no doubt felt that he had adequate grounds for detaining us."

"I disagree entirely. What grounds could he have? Britain and Poland are allies. Why should he object to your Government learning that he has been holding talks with the Germans in an eleventh-hour attempt to avert war? No one but a lunatic could want war, with all the misery that it brings. What could he have said to them at these conferences that he would be unwilling that the British Government should know? Obviously nothing. Therefore, his prohibition on your departure is not only a flagrant breach of courtesy, but also entirely pointless."

"True enough! True enough!" de Richleau agreed a little breathlessly, as he wondered what on earth would have happened had he told this volcanic young man the whole truth about General Mack and his nefarious machinations.

As they emerged from a screen of flowering shrubs they saw that the big lounge on the ground floor, which had been in semi-darkness when they left it, was now a blaze of light. On drawing nearer, they could hear the babel of many voices, and when they entered it through the terrace window they saw that the whole house-party had now gathered in the long, antler-hung room.

The last meeting of the conference was over, the Baroness had come down from her sanctum to join her military guests, and the Baron had ordered up champagne that a toast might be drunk on the successful conclusion of the negotiations; the black-clad butler and his more colourfully garbed henchmen, who still wore the local, gaily embroidered costume, were already handing round trays of tall-stemmed glasses.

Without a second's hesitation Jan walked straight up to the Baron. "I'm sorry if I've chosen an awkward moment, Uncle," he said firmly; "but for the

honour of our family the matter permits of no delay. Are you aware that—
er—General Mack has so far forgotten himself as to tell your English guests
that they may not leave without his permission?"

The poor, slow-witted Baron began uncomfortably: "My dear boy, I
was most upset. I—er—well, I protested myself, but—er—reasons of
State . . ." he broke off miserably with an appealing look towards his wife.

A sudden hush had fallen on the whole assembly. The Baroness stepped
forward, and her voice, which she strove to keep calm and pleasant, came
clearly to every listening ear.

"My dear Jan, control yourself, please. There is nothing to get excited
about. General Mack simply asked the Duke and his friends not to leave
until the conference was over."

"It was not a request but an order," Jan stormed. "As a member of the
family, I demand that he should apologize at once."

Mack had paled slightly at this unwelcome scene. His natural instinct
was to pacify the outraged dignity of his troublesome countryman, but he
dared not display such weakness before the Germans. His dark eyes glisten-
ing, he snapped:

"You forget yourself! You must be quite well aware who I am. How
dare you question the wisdom of my decisions?"

"I know who you are, and I don't give a damn!" retorted Jan. "As a
Polish nobleman, I refuse to stand by and see Polish hospitality shamed
before our English allies."

The room was now so silent that as the lame Major Bauer clumped forward, his game leg dragging slightly, each footfall of his heavy boots rang
hollowly upon the polished parquet. Advancing to within a foot of Jan, he
said with studied insolence:

"Your—English allies!" and spat contemptuously on the floor.

The blood drained from Jan's cheeks. He would have hit the German
but for the fact that he, too, was Poland's guest. With an effort he turned to
the Baron and cried:

"Uncle! How can you permit this? For God's sake tell His Excellency,
the Minister, and his German friends to go and cheapen themselves
elsewhere."

Before the Baron had a chance to reply, Major Bauer, his coarse face lit
up with fanatical excitement, spoke again:

"*Dumbkopff!* You question the right of your superior to give orders as
a Polish Cabinet Minister, eh? All right! Let me tell you! He is something
a thousand times greater than that now. He has today been appointed
Grossgauleiter of Poland."

Jan's eyes seemed to start from his head. He raised a hand as though
to ward off a blow, and gasped: "I don't believe it! No Pole would ever
surrender Poland's independence without a fight."

In that tense moment General Mack caught the expressions on the faces of his Staff. That of the elderly, very senior officer to whom they always referred as "Colonel" was calm, but with a faintly cynical twist of the lips. The rest showed either amazement or anger. Mack saw that, if he were to retain his authority, he must take a bold line, and, banging his fist on a nearby table, he cried :

"Listen ! I have entered into certain undertakings for the sake of humanity. War is unavoidable. We all know that. I have simply arranged that, so far as Poland is concerned, the war shall be short."

"By God ! You've betrayed us then !" Jan almost screamed. "You've sold us to the Nazis before we've had a chance to fire a shot ! You filthy traitor ! I'll kill you for this, if it's the last thing I ever do !"

"Not sold you, but saved you !" Bauer shouted. "Don't you understand ? Your forces will put up a token resistance only, and your casualties will be few. Then, immediately they lay down their arms our glorious Fuehrer has consented to do Poland the honour of permitting her to become a Protectorate of the Reich."

His eyes gleaming with frenzied ardour, the Nazi Major ended his pronouncement by shooting up his right arm to its fullest extent, bawling : "*Heil Hitler !*"

Losing all control, Jan hit him a resounding slap across the face.

Marie Lou was standing between Richard and the Duke, right opposite the broad staircase and near the main doorway of the lounge, which led out into the front hall. As, wide-eyed with apprehension, she surveyed the scene, she realized that every face now portrayed fear, anger, or excitement, except for two—those of de Richleau and von Geisenheim. Their faces remained grey masks, betraying nothing.

She saw Bauer, his cheek still white with the imprint of the blow and his features distorted with rage, wrench an automatic from his pocket.

She saw that von Geisenheim had already produced a pistol and was holding it levelled as steady as a rock ; but she could not tell from where she stood if it were aimed at Jan or at Bauer's back.

She saw Jan grasp the butt of the heavy-calibre service weapon at his belt and tug it out.

At the same moment, out of the corner of her eye, she saw de Richleau's right hand suddenly flick up the double row of electric light switches at his elbow, which controlled the lighting of the room.

The Duke beat the guns by the fraction of a second. The room was plunged in darkness the flicker of an eyelid before the shooting started.

Chapter VI

THE HOLD-UP

RICHARD flung himself in front of Marie Lou ; the Duke grabbed her arm and pulled her back through the doorway.

Two shots rang out almost simultaneously. The flashes from the guns stabbed the darkness, each for an instant revealing the scene in the long room by a startling contrast of highlights and shadows.

Mack was disclosed half-crouching behind the heavy refectory table. Bauer was standing squarely, his chin and the hand which held the gun thrust aggressively forward. Jan had side-stepped and seemed to have collided with Anna Lubieszow, who had evidently run towards him. De Richleau glimpsed her face. It was that of a mother who sees her only child in danger, and he remembered then that this poor relation of the Lubieszows was Jan's spinster aunt.

Neither shot had, apparently, taken effect ; but other weapons were about to be brought into play. Mack's staff were closing round him, evidently determined to protect their Chief from Jan's threatened attack, and several of them had produced pistols.

Bauer fired again. Anna Lubieszow screamed. De Richleau shouted : "Run for it, Jan ! Run for it or they'll kill you !" Then came a burst of shots.

Marie Lou, even hemmed in as she was between Richard and the Duke and pressed back in the doorway, could glimpse enough by the light of the recurrent flashes to see Bauer fling up an arm before he crashed headlong to the floor, and Jan leap over his body in a dash towards the french windows ; but she did not see Anna, after a few faltering steps, collapse limply in a nearby chair.

"Stop him !" yelled Mack, and two of his officers sprang forward in pursuit of Jan. Richard knocked over a chair, which slithered across the parquet, catching the nearest officer sideways as he ran. Darkness blacked out his fall, but they heard the sharp snap of one of the chair-legs and the heavy bump of his body.

A gun flashed again, this time from the window. It was Jan's parting shot, fired almost at random towards Mack in a last attempt to carry out his threat to kill the traitor statesman. By its light they saw that the officer who had tripped over the chair had cannoned into his companion as he fell, and that they were sprawled in a cursing heap together.

By the same flash de Richleau and his friends saw something else. Right opposite them, halfway up the broad staircase at the far end of the lounge, two men were now standing; both had guns in their hands, and from their point of vantage they dominated the whole room.

Marie Lou's heart missed a beat; Richard stifled a cry of surprise; the Duke's satanic eyebrows shot up in amazement. An instant later, as darkness blotted out the scene again, all three of them momentarily rejected the evidence of their senses, believing that their eyesight had played them a trick. It seemed unbelievable that those two familiar figures, the big man, who gripped his gun so confidently, and the little one, whose obvious distaste for his made him hold it with such awkwardness, could have arrived unsummoned in Poland and found their way undiscovered to the upper floor of the Lubieszow château.

"Did—did you see what I did?" gasped Richard in de Richleau's ear.

"*Mon Dieu*, yes!" breathed the Duke, flashing on the lights, which revealed to the whole startled company the silent, watchful figures of Rex Van Ryn and Simon Aron.

"That'll be enough shooting for the present," Rex boomed, giving his big automatic a swift, threatening sweep from side to side across the crowd of astonished, upturned faces below him. "Drop your guns on the floor, all of you. Quick now! I'm in a mood to take a little target practice on any character who disobeys me."

Although he spoke in English his tone and gesture were quite enough to convey his meaning to those who did not understand his actual words. Von Geisenheim, as shrewd a judge as anyone there of when a situation warranted taking chances, quietly laid his pistol on a nearby table. But the sullen-faced Pole that de Richleau had partnered at bridge half-turned and made to raise his weapon.

Instantly Rex's automatic cracked, the Pole's pistol clattered to the floor, and with a gasp of pain he clutched a shattered wrist.

"I warned you," said Rex, this time speaking in French. "Put your guns on the floor, or next time I'll shoot to kill."

With scowling looks but making no further protest, the antagonists hastened to obey him, as he added: "Go to it, Simon. Collect the arsenal."

De Richleau stepped forward. "One moment, Rex. Stay where you are, Simon, and keep the terrace door covered, in case any of them tries to get away. I'll attend to their disarmament." Even as he spoke he had relieved "Colonel Moninszko" of his automatic and passed it to Richard with the words: "Stay by the door and see that we're not interrupted from the hall."

Quietly but swiftly he collected all the weapons and, keeping one for himself, deposited the rest on a small table just outside on the terrace. Stepping back into the room, he addressed the two newcomers with a smile.

"I need hardly say how delighted I am to see you both. Your arrival could not possibly have been more opportune, and I can scarcely wait to hear how you accomplished it. Now that you, Rex, with Richard's help, can easily control the situation, perhaps Simon can come down and help me round up the remainder of the servants." Turning towards Marie Lou, he added: "It's not the first time that you've handled a gun, Princess, so perhaps you would give us your assistance by guarding these windows on to the terrace while Simon and I are away."

As Simon and Marie Lou crossed the room, Mack suddenly stepped forward and spoke with swift acidity. "It seems, Duke, that you are in control here now. Need I remind you that several people have been wounded? Surely you will allow us to give them immediate attention?"

These swift interchanges had occupied barely two minutes, and, although it seemed much longer, it was less than five since the shooting had started. De Richleau's quick ear had caught the sound of cautiously approaching feet. He guessed that some of the chauffeurs must have been wakened by the shots and that the bolder of them were coming to see what had happened. As most of them were soldiers, they might be carrying arms, so, if this unexpected *coup* were not to fail through a turning of the tables, swift action was necessary.

He gave a quick glance round the casualties of the recent fracas. Anna Lubieszow lay still, slumped in the chair where she had fallen. The Duke had seen too many dead bodies in his time to be mistaken as to the meaning of her lolling head and loosely huddled limbs. Bauer had been knocked out by a bullet that had seared his bristling scalp, but he was now groaning loudly and evidently about to come to. The Pole whose wrist Rex had shattered was cursing under his breath and sweating with pain, while one of his companions was already staunching the flow of blood from the wound with a napkin from the silver salver upon which stood the bottles of champagne.

"I fear that Madame Anna is past our aid," de Richleau replied sharply, "and the other two will come to no harm through waiting. Stay where you are, everyone. Come on, Simon."

As Marie Lou snatched up the smallest pistol from the collection on the little table, the Duke and Simon hurried away in the direction of the now clearly audible footsteps.

The chauffeurs proved easier to deal with than they had anticipated. There were only three men in the little party that they came on at the end of the terrace, and none of them was carrying a gun. De Richleau spoke to them in Polish and promptly marched them back whence they had come.

At the stable gates they found seven still less courageous spirits who had also been roused at the sound of the shots, but remained there, half-dressed, conjecturing in anxious whispers on the possible cause of the shooting. Under the threat of the guns the whole party was herded back to the house, taken down to an inner cellar and locked in there.

"Stay here, Simon," said the Duke, "and put a bullet through the door if they attempt to break out; I am going in search of some female companionship for them."

A quarter of an hour later he returned, shepherding a dozen scared women servants in front of him, including the old cook, whom he had terrified into collecting all the others, under pain of the direst penalties if he learned later that she had overlooked even the humblest scullery-maid.

The women were locked in with the chauffeurs and grooms; then their captors rolled a great cider barrel, of which there were a number in the outer cellar, against the door, and, having wedged it there, went upstairs again.

"I think that's the lot," murmured the Duke. "All the indoor men servants appear to have been rounded up by the Baron just as they were about to go to bed, to serve the champagne; so they are still with the rest of the party in the lounge."

As they hurried back to the terrace, he went on:

"The next thing is for us to let you and Rex know what has been going on here and to hold a council of war. That won't be any too easy, as two of our party will have to keep the prisoners covered all the time, but I think I know how to arrange matters."

In the lounge the scene remained unaltered, except that Major Bauer was now sitting scowling in a chair, and Rex had seated himself for greater comfort on the top step of the stairs.

"We've collected all the servants and locked them in the cellar," the Duke announced, glancing up at Rex. "All well here?"

"Yep. Not a crack out of any of 'em."

"Good. Now, I'm going to have a short talk with Simon out here on the terrace, but we'll both be with you if there's the least sign of trouble." Turning to Marie Lou, he went on: "We'll take over the french windows now, Princess. I want you to go upstairs and sit down behind Rex, so as not to interfere with his freedom of movement. Then tell him as briefly as you can what led up to the shooting. If you keep your voice low they won't hear much you say down here—and, in any case, they know most of the story already. Richard, you had better remain where you are for the time being."

Moving a few paces away from the window and perching himself on the stone balustrade, from which he could still see most of the well-lit room, he said to Simon in a low voice:

"Now, my son. Tell me how you managed to arrive here so opportunely."

Simon stooped his bird-like head and half-smothered a chuckle with the palm of his hand. "Quite simple, really. Seeing the way things were moving, I cut short my holiday and got back to England last Wednesday. Very fond of Monte, but not fond enough to want to get caught there when war breaks out. Old Pellinore 'phoned me Saturday morning; made me cut an engagement to lunch with him. He seemed to think you were in a muddle. You know how I hate muddles. Didn't want to be mixed up in it a bit. But I dined with Rex that evening. He'd cut short his holiday to get back to London, too, and he seemed to think we ought to take a trip to Poland—just to see what was going on."

"Which, being interpreted," smiled the Duke, "means that you got hold of Rex just as soon as you could, and the two of you came dashing to our rescue in his plane?"

"Well, more or less," Simon admitted with a jerky nod. "Pellinore didn't say much about what the Poles were up to, but he was definite enough that you'd got on to something pretty big and—er—hinted that you'd got into a bit of a spot in consequence. Even with Pellinore behind us we couldn't get visas till Monday afternoon; but since then we've flown half round Europe to avoid coming down in German territory, and we landed at Pinsk about six o'clock this evening. Soon as we could hire a car we came on here. That's all there is to it."

"So the explanation is really quite simple. I might have guessed it. But how on earth did you manage to get into this house and upstairs, unseen?"

"Well, I'll tell you. Pellinore seemed to think you were more or less under arrest, so we—er—decided not to announce ourselves. Left the car in the woods half a mile away, waited till dark, then walked up to the house with the idea of snooping round a bit. We saw through the lighted windows that the Baron was throwing a party, but couldn't see you. Didn't like to risk coming too close before we'd found out a bit more how the form was."

"As a matter of fact, I must have been out in the garden myself just then," interjected the Duke. "I was in the shrubbery talking to Jan Lubieszow."

"I see. Anyhow, we thought they'd probably got you locked up somewhere. Went round to the front of the house, found the door unbolted and no one about—so we slipped in. Seemed a good opportunity to have a look round upstairs while the party was in full swing. Back stairs creaked enough to wake the dead, but it brought us out on the main landing, and just at that moment the fireworks began. Now let's have your end of the story."

De Richleau briefly outlined the events that had led up to the recent affray. When he had done Simon nodded.

"Seems you're pretty well through here, then. Next thing's to get out of the country. 'Fraid we'll have to abandon Rex's plane—not big enough to take us all; and anyhow, when we landed he had to turn her in for a minor repair, so he couldn't even fly Marie Lou out till after tomorrow. Luckily the car we've got is a big one, though—easily hold five. Best thing would be for me to go and get it. Then Rex and I will take care of the crowd while you others pack. When you're ready we'll take Mack and his friends down to the cellar, lock them in with the servants and beat it for the frontier. Hungary's the best place to make for. Had a good look at the map on the way here. It's all of three hundred miles, but with four of us driving in turns we should get there well before midday tomorrow."

De Richleau shook his head. "I'm afraid it's not going to be quite as easy as all that. Lucretia is still in Warsaw, and we daren't risk leaving her behind. Mack is quite capable of arresting her and holding her as a hostage, then we'd be in a pretty mess. No, one of us must go to Warsaw and fetch her back here before we make our break for the frontier."

"I say! That's a nasty one!" Simon exclaimed. "Hadn't thought of that. It's a good eight hours' drive to Warsaw—sixteen there and back. Couldn't get her here till tomorrow afternoon, and we can hardly hope to keep all these people under the counter without interference till then. There'll be telephone calls, postmen, village people turning up with stuff for the kitchen, and goodness knows what."

"No, but we could hold them till morning, and whoever goes to fetch Lucretia should have got her and be well out of Warsaw on their way back by then."

"We'll have to fix a secret rendezvous—some place where the Warsaw party can join the rest of us tomorrow afternoon."

"That's the idea," agreed the Duke.

"Save time if the Warsaw party headed south instead of coming back here. Whoever stays could pinch a car from the garage, and leave at dawn, also heading south. The two parties could rendezvous in Lwow tomorrow night —or even nearer the Hungarian border."

De Richleau considered for a moment, then spoke softly again. "No, Simon. I don't like it. The hunt will be up pretty soon after our party leaves here tomorrow morning. Two cars would mean a double chance of some of us being captured, especially those in the stolen car, because a description will be issued of that. Again, their first guess will be that we're making for Hungary, so for the next few days a sharper watch will be kept for us in the Lwow area than anywhere else. The one thing they will never expect is that any of us would remain in the neighbourhood of Lubieszow or, when they learn that Lucretia has left Warsaw, that she is on her way back here."

"You're for lying up somewhere in the woods near here, then?"

"Yes. There's a forester's hut only about two miles away that Richard, Marie Lou and I passed when we were out riding on Saturday. It is on the opposite side of the house to the village, and well away from either of the roads that run through the estate, so it would serve excellently."

"Then either Richard or you will have to go to Warsaw. Neither Rex nor I would ever be able to find it."

"True. I had better go, and Richard can guide the rest of you to the forester's hut tomorrow. About holding this crowd, though. These people have much more initiative than the servants, and might try breaking out of the cellar by forcing up the floorboards of one of the ground-floor rooms.

Much better keep them here in sight at the point of a gun for the night, then lock them in the cellar just before leaving in the morning. You go in now and take his place while I have a word with him."

The exchange was quickly made, and, having told Richard how Rex and Simon had succeeded in arriving at such a lucky moment, de Richleau outlined his proposal.

"It sounds as good a bet as any," said Richard thoughtfully, "except for one thing. You must stay here while I go to Warsaw and collect Lucretia."

With a quick gesture he forestalled the protest the Duke would have made and went on: "Surely you realize that, as you're the only one of us who speaks Polish, it's essential for you to stay here? Otherwise, who is to deal with any early bird that happens to come up on business from the village, or answer the telephone if an emergency call comes through for Mack in the middle of the night?"

"Yes, I hadn't thought of that," admitted the Duke. "But how about Marie Lou? Naturally, neither of you would wish to be separated at a time like this if it can possibly be avoided. Shall you take her with you?"

"No, I don't think so," Richard replied, after only a momentary hesitation. "It will be the devil of a long drive, and there is no point in tiring her unnecessarily."

De Richleau did not press the point, as he knew quite well what was at the back of Richard's mind. Although neither of them had mentioned it, both realized that whoever went to Warsaw would be in much more immediate danger during the journey back than those who had already hidden themselves in the forester's hut.

"I tell you what, though," Richard continued. "I'd like to take one of the others, if you can spare him. With two of us driving alternately we'll make the trip much faster than I could alone, and an hour gained on the run in might make all the difference in getting clear of the city again before the police are warned to keep a look-out for us."

"I agree entirely. Take whomever you like."

"I'll take Simon. He's been in Warsaw before, so he'll be more use in helping me find the way to Jan's house."

De Richleau's grey eyes twinkled. Rex was a far finer driver, but Richard was leaving him deliberately, because he would also be of much more use at Lubieszow than Simon if the captives mutinied and attempted to break out during the night. Again, however, he did not argue, as he knew that it would be no light undertaking to keep some twenty people, exclusive of the servants who were locked in the cellar, under control for seven or eight hours.

"Thanks, Richard," he said quietly. "I can certainly do with Rex here. Now, you mustn't waste a moment. If we lock the door leading into the hall we shan't need a guard on it, and I can remain here at the terrace entrance."

As they entered the room again, Mack stepped forward. "How long do you propose to keep up this farce?" he snapped at the Duke.

"Just as long as it suits us to do so," de Richleau replied imperturbably.

"It's an outrage!" went on the Polish statesman with rising anger. "How dare you hold us up like this! I demand that you should restore our liberty of action immediately."

"Your Excellency has only yourself to blame. Your present situation differs little from that in which you placed me and my friends a few nights ago." The Duke's glance shifted to the Germans. "I have an idea, too, that in due course certain other people will also learn that in the long run it does not pay to set the example of assuming the arbitrary powers of a dictator."

Major Bauer's face turned scarlet, and jumping to his feet he bellowed: "You insult the *Fuehrer*! You shall die for that!"

"You'll be dead yourself if you don't sit down," snapped Simon with unusual venom, thrusting his pistol towards the German. "Don't like shooting people, myself, but I'd get quite a kick out of killing you."

Bauer shot one look at Simon's long, curved Semitic nose, and knew that he meant what he said. With a shrug which was meant to convey contempt, he subsided in his chair again.

Ten minutes later the new dispositions were completed. Richard led Marie Lou out on to the terrace to tell her of the plan that had been agreed on. They took a swift farewell of each other, and he set off with Simon. Then, at the Duke's suggestion, she went upstairs to pack for him and Lucretia, as well as for herself and Richard.

Rex collected a couple of cushions and made himself comfortable in his old position halfway up the stairs. De Richleau covered Anna Lubieszow's face with an antimacassar, drew a chair into the centre of the terrace doorway, and settling himself in it addressed the company.

"I fear it will be necessary for us all to remain here until the morning. Please make yourselves as comfortable as you can. You may read, if you wish, and I am sure the Baron will have no objection to your helping yourselves to the drinks and other refreshments which are already on the side-tables; but if you talk it must be in your normal voices and in English or French, so that both my friend and I can understand you. I will tolerate no whispering, and not more than one of you is to leave your seat at one time."

At the idea of spending the night where they were there was some sporadic grumbling, but the tension eased, and, in relays, under the Duke's watchful eye, the party sorted itself out. The Baroness lay down on a sofa, the men servants, who all this while had remained fascinated spectators, now congregated in one corner of the big room on a row of upright chairs which they collected there, and the others arranged themselves in the armchairs and sofas.

There was little talking, and the vigil soon became monotonous. Some of the party began to doze as well as they could in the brightly lighted room, others settled down to read; occasionally one of them got up to get a drink or a sandwich. Von Geisenheim had drawn a chair up to the refectory table, and taking a sheaf of papers from his pocket began to work upon them.

After about twenty minutes, finding that de Richleau did not attempt to interfere with his writing, he wrote the following note on a small piece of paper:

Presently I shall ask to be allowed to go to the lavatory. As the door to the hall is now locked the chances are that the American will be detailed to take me to the one on the landing at the top of the stairs. If so, there may be a chance for you to rush the Duke while he is alone.

Concealing this note in his hand, he got up, walked over to one of the console tables and poured himself a glass of champagne, asking casually over his shoulder as he did so:

"Want a drink, Bauer?"

"*Bitte, Herr General,*" replied the Nazi.

Pouring out a second glass, von Geisenheim took it over to his adjutant and, as he handed it to him, skilfully passed him the slip of paper without being observed by either Rex or the Duke. He then returned to the table and continued making his notes.

After working away diligently for a further twenty minutes, he collected his papers, put them in his pocket and moved over to a more comfortable chair; but after a little he began to show signs of restlessness and eventually, standing up, addressed the Duke in English.

"My apologies. It is necessary that I should leave the room. It is for circumstances over which I have no control. I have your permission, yes?"

"Very well," agreed the Duke, who had foreseen that among such a numerous company a request of this kind was almost certain to be made by someone during the night. "You had better go upstairs. Rex, will you escort the General across the landing? If he attempts anything, or you hear the least sound of a commotion down here, shoot him. If he has locked himself in put three or four bullets through the door and hurry back here immediately."

Von Geisenheim bowed stiffly and walked across the room with a firm tread; but as he mounted the stairs he realized that for him they might prove the equivalent of the steps of a scaffold. It struck him as grimly humorous that by his own action he had quite possibly condemned himself to death. If Bauer did start anything in his absence, the confined space of a lavatory would give him little chance of escaping a spate of bullets sent crashing through the panels of the door, and he noted with additional concern the heavy calibre of Rex's weapon. But the German *Junker*, once having initiated a plan, was not the man to abandon it through any thought of his own safety, and with unhurried gait he preceded Rex across the rug-strewn polished floor at the head of the stairs.

For two minutes everything remained still in the lounge below, then Bauer slowly got to his feet.

"Sit down!" snapped the Duke.

Bauer held up his empty glass. "I have finished my wine. I would the glass on the tray put back."

"Sit down!" repeated the Duke, still more sharply.

The two men were about twelve feet apart; Bauer standing and de Richleau still seated. Suddenly, with a flick of his wrist, the German hurled the cut-glass goblet at the Duke's head.

De Richleau ducked, and an instant later fired from his waist. With amazing agility, considering his lameness and weight, Bauer sprang aside. At the same time he thrust out his left hand to grasp the back of the chair in front of which he had been standing. As he regained his balance he heaved with all his might upon the chair, half-jerking and half-throwing it towards the Duke.

The goblet landed with a crash out on the terrace. The Duke's bullet missed Bauer by inches and thudded into the wall. The chair came hurtling across the floor. The Baroness screamed. Everyone else in the room had now sprung to their feet, and while the Nazi was occupying the Duke's attention they were grabbing up missiles and weapons with which to join in the attack on him.

He alone was still seated, and had deliberately remained so from the knowledge that every second was precious and that to fire again while in the act of coming to his feet would interfere with the certainty of his aim.

Putting out his foot to stop the chair from crashing into his knees, he raised his pistol to send a bullet through Bauer's head. As he did so two of the lights went out. Two more followed almost instantly.

The Duke felt confident that once he had killed the Nazi Major he would be able to cow the rest, provided that he could still see. But if one of them succeeded in playing his own trick and plunging the room in darkness, he would be at the mercy of the pack.

With instant decision he switched his aim and fired at Jaljusz—who was now snapping off the electric light switches as hard as he could go.

Two more lights went out, and now only one wall bracket was left burning at the far end of the room, half-hidden by the stairs. Almost simultaneously, the Duke's pistol cracked, and with a loud cry the Pole collapsed, falling across a table and sending the glasses upon it crashing to the floor.

Three more shots rang out in quick succession from upstairs, and de Richleau realized with grim satisfaction that von Geisenheim was paying a heavy price for this outbreak, which there were fair grounds for suspecting that he had somehow managed to engineer.

Seizing the brief respite gained him by Jaljusz, Bauer had flung himself at the Duke. Again de Richleau fired, but he had no time to take proper aim, and the shot tore through the shoulder of the German's coat.

The chair that Bauer had himself flung forward now proved his temporary undoing. Tripping against it, he lost his footing and fell heavily; but in falling he managed to grab the Duke's arm and drag him down.

The room was now in semi-darkness. Shouts, cries, the crashing of furniture, and the screams of the Baroness created a positive pandemonium. The Nazi and the Duke were struggling fiercely together in the terrace entrance. The German was far the stronger of the two and had got his adversary by the throat with one hand, while he strove to seize his gun with the other. But de Richleau, despite his age, was still wiry and agile; moreover, his cool, calculating brain was an asset which did much to offset the brute force of the Nazi. Forcing down his chin, he ignored the agonizing grip on his windpipe and concentrated on keeping his gun arm free.

Rex's stentorian bellow from the staircase now added to the din. "Stand back all of you! Stand back, or I'll blow the guts out of you!"

His shout checked the ugly rush of the crowd that was surging forward to aid Bauer, but it was of no immediate assistance to the Duke. He knew, too, that, if Rex left his position on the stairs to aid him, he would perforce expose himself to being attacked and overwhelmed from behind.

As de Richleau squirmed and struggled in the German's grip the sounds in the room grew vague and blurred. There was a rushing noise like the sound of surf beating on a shore in his ears. His eyes were bulging in his head, and his sight grew dim. But he had managed to wriggle his gun hand down beneath the Nazi's body. Thrusting up the barrel, he pulled the trigger.

Bauer jerked spasmodically, gave a sudden groan and relaxed his grip. De Richleau fired again and heaved himself upward; the German went limp, and with another heave the Duke rolled from beneath him.

Slowly, he picked himself up. Bauer now lay on his back; a little patch of blood that was rapidly increasing welled from his chest.

"All right, Rex," the Duke shouted. "I'm not hurt. Keep the rest of them covered while I get the lights on." Still gasping for breath, he walked across the room and turned down the switches. Then he returned to his old position by the terrace door.

The big room now presented a grim spectacle. Anna Lubieszow dead in her chair; Jaljusz lying still in a pool of his own blood, his head shattered, the glasses he had knocked over in his fall and the spilt wine scattered about him; Bauer groaning and twisting as he lay in the terrace entrance.

As de Richleau's glance swept the sullen, angry faces of the others he missed one. Count Ignac was no longer among them. Then the Duke saw that the curtain masking a small door that led to the library, where Mack had placed him under arrest four nights before, had been partly pulled back.

It was the curtain that had caused him to overlook this possible means of exit, and with grim foreboding it now flashed upon his mind that the Count must have slipped out unobserved that way during the recent confusion. It was no good giving chase. He would be well on his way to the village by this time, to raise the alarm. Their plan to hold the house until morning had been frustrated. They must act on fresh lines and act at once, or within half an hour at most Count Ignac would bring a hornets' nest about their ears.

Chapter VII

NIGHT IN THE QUIET FOREST

IN vain de Richleau cursed himself for having neglected to secure the small library door. True, the portière, which, when drawn, concealed it, formed in itself a barrier that none of the captives could have got by quickly enough to escape a bullet in the back, so long as they were under the eye of their captors ; but the Duke felt that he had been unforgivably remiss in not taking the precaution of locking the door against just such an eventuality as had occurred.

Ignac's escape now jeopardized their whole plan. If the Duke and Rex had been able to hold the occupants of Lubieszow until morning, Richard and Simon would have reached Warsaw, collected Lucretia and got clear of the city unmolested ; but, now that Ignac was free, police headquarters in the capital would be fully informed of the situation as soon as he could reach a telephone. Police or troops would be rushed from the nearest post to Lubieszow, and a description of Richard and Simon issued. It was not yet midnight, and they had been gone barely an hour ; so they might well be caught long before they reached Warsaw. As for Rex, Marie Lou and himself, if they remained where they were they would certainly be rounded up, and their margin of safety was now decreasing every minute.

One thing was clear : with a single bird gone from the net no purpose could be served by continuing to hold up the rest of the flock. Richard and Simon could not now be helped by their friends remaining at Lubieszow to be captured ; and, if they were captured themselves, they would stand a much better chance of regaining their freedom if their friends remained at liberty to plan their rescue.

Knowing that it was beyond his powers to warn the pair who were driving hell-for-leather through the night, de Richleau was not the man to waste further time crying over spilt milk.

The sound of the shooting had brought Marie Lou running back from her packing to the head of the stairs, where she was now standing behind Rex.

Looking up at them, the Duke said: "While Bauer had me on the floor Count Ignac got away. He'll be back shortly with the gendarmes. We must get out—and quickly."

"I've finished packing!" exclaimed Marie Lou, a trifle breathlessly. "All but a few things. I can't manage Lucretia's wardrobe trunk on my own, but I could bring down the suitcases. I left my own trunk in Warsaw."

"Good! We'll collect that when we get there."

"But——" Rex began.

"I've changed my plan," de Richleau interrupted. "The best thing we can do now is to make for Warsaw and place ourselves under the protection of the British Embassy. We must borrow a car. You go out to the garage, Rex, and bring the most powerful one you can find round to the front door, while Marie Lou brings down the luggage. We shall have to leave Lucretia's trunk behind, but that can't be helped."

As he finished speaking, the Duke began to herd all the unwounded members of the company into the far corner of the lounge where the men servants were standing. When they were bunched together there he said to them: "If any of you starts any more trouble I'll shoot to kill first, then empty the remaining contents of my pistol into the rest of you indiscriminately. My friends and I will be leaving in a few moments, and you can do your best for the poor fellow whom I shot while he was putting out the lights directly we've gone. If Major Bauer dies I don't think any of us will count that a great loss."

Glancing at Baron Lubieszow, he went on: "I'm terribly sorry, Baron, that our visit to you should have ended like this; but you must blame Count Ignac and these intriguers whom he introduced under your hospitable roof. That they do not represent the true spirit of Poland I am well aware. No doubt some of them are already heartily ashamed of the part they have been forced to play, but felt in duty bound to stand by their leader when my friends appeared so unexpectedly tonight and held you all up. That's why I feel deep regret at having had to wound two of them—one perhaps fatally— when they might yet have fought gallantly for Poland in the struggle that now seems inevitable. But they, too, must blame Count Ignac and the treacherous Minister on whose staff they have the misfortune to find themselves."

There were tears in the Baron's eyes as he looked first at the Duke, then across at his dead cousin, Anna. "I cannot blame you," he said slowly. "You were to us all that a good guest should be, and we detained you here against your will. It was not you who brought tragedy to my house; and, if I had gained knowledge of such a conspiracy in England as you have found here, I should have done all that lay in my power to defeat it. I thank God that you do not leave us with the belief that all Poles are like His Excellency.

Jan, at least, has saved our honour; but he will be in grave danger for a time, and if opportunity offers I beg you to do what you can for him."

"Thank you, Baron." De Richleau bowed gravely. "As soon as I can communicate with the British Government I will ask them to interest themselves in Jan and, provided the Anglo-Polish alliance continues, I feel confident they will find means to ensure that he is not victimized on account of the gallantry he displayed tonight."

While they had been talking little Marie Lou had been gamely dragging downstairs the Duke's heavy pigskin suitcases and the other baggage. The engine of a powerful car could now be heard purring outside the house and a moment later Rex came hurrying in. Taking the bags, he carried them out. As he grabbed up the last and Marie Lou followed him to the door, de Richleau spoke again, this time to "General Mack".

"I must now request Your Excellency to come with me."

Mack took an instinctive step backwards, treading on the foot of the man behind him.

"I refuse!" he exclaimed. "You and your friends have shown yourselves to be completely unscrupulous. You are saboteurs—brigands—you mean to murder me."

The Duke shrugged. "If you maintain your refusal to come with me your blood will be on your own head—as I give you my word that I shall shoot you where you stand."

"You—you——" Mack's face had suddenly gone grey and old. "Do you promise that—that if I do as you wish no harm will come to me?"

"I promise nothing. I simply propose to take you with us as a hostage. If these gentlemen remain quietly here, the odds are that you will still be alive tomorrow morning. On the other hand, should they make any attempt to follow us, I warn them now that at the first sign of pursuit I shall put a bullet into you. If you reject my proposal I shall put several bullets into you before I leave this room. And, with or without you, I intend to leave in sixty seconds' time."

"I won't go! I won't!" Mack almost whimpered.

De Richleau raised his gun. His steel-grey eyes, which at times could flash with such brilliance, were as hard as agate.

Mack threw out a protesting hand. "Stop!" he cried. "Stop! I'll come if I must." Dabbing at the beads of sweat that had suddenly started out of his forehead, he stepped out from the crowd.

As he reached the door the Duke gave a slight nod to the others, then turned to follow him with an inaudible sigh of relief. Ignac's escape was an irreparable mishap, but the game was not yet entirely in his hands. By having secured Mack's person the Duke felt that he had at least one trump still left to play.

Rex was already seated at the wheel of the car with Marie Lou beside him, and neither of them asked any questions as de Richleau motioned Mack into the back before getting in himself. Rex slid in the clutch, the headlights carved a gleaming arc across the larch trees that bordered the curving drive, and the big car gathered speed for its dash through the still August night.

When they had passed the lodge and turned on to the main road, Rex threw back over his shoulder: "Say, d'you really mean us to go to Warsaw?"

"Yes," chimed in Marie Lou, "what about our rendezvous with the others?"

"Of course not," replied the Duke. "I only said that in the hope of throwing a little dust in their eyes. We'd be caught long before we got there, and even if we succeeded I doubt if the British Ambassador could afford us much protection, seeing the dead and dying we've left behind us at Lubieszow. Still, there is a chance that they may think us fools enough to make for the capital, and, if so, the hunt will be less strenuous for us locally."

"You meant to ditch the car then, and stick to our original plan?"

"I would prefer to hide it somewhere, if we can find a suitable spot. It might be useful later."

"How about our being followed?"

The Duke laughed grimly. "I think the General here is our guarantee against that. I told them before I left that any attempt of that kind would result in his being shot out of hand."

"I don't mean by the Lubieszow boys," said Rex quickly. "I put all their other flivvers out of action before I naturalized this beauty. I had in mind Ignac and the cops. They'll sure trace our tyre-tracks in the dust."

"Let's try a double bluff then. Drive up the next ride on the left for half a mile. I know it well, and it's quite broad enough for you to get back on to the road again thirty yards further on."

Rex slowed down a little and, after a mile, at the Duke's warning, reduced his speed still more. The moon was up and gave ample light to see the long grassy opening between two belts of trees. The car bumped a little on the grass and ran on until it reached a patch of higher ground on which, assuming that it would be dryer than the lower levels, Rex turned and, hugging the further belt of trees, brought them back on to the road.

"Won't having turned in there make them think that we've decided to hide up in the woods, as we really mean to do?" remarked Marie Lou doubtfully.

"No, Princess. I don't think so. That ride comes out on another road about three miles further south. We have ridden and shot quite a bit round here in the past month, so Ignac will know that I should know that, and, I trust, assume that we have endeavoured to fox them while still heading for Warsaw."

"Good work," murmured Rex. "I was wondering where the double bluff came in."

"Then I should have said triple bluff," the Duke replied. "In a minute we shall come to a cross-roads. To reach the hut we should turn to the right, but I want you to turn left. When we are some way along the side road we will turn back across country at an angle of forty-five degrees. That will bring us back to the main road again about half a mile beyond the cross-roads."

"Make a sort of triangle, eh? But how in heck am I to do that through these woods?"

"The forest ends just before the cross-roads. Beyond it is open pasture-land, so you should be able to drive us over it without getting stuck. When we reach the main road we shall cross it, turn half-right again and cut off another triangle, so that we strike the right-hand side-road in due course. We shall cross that, too, and re-enter the wood at a place that cannot be much more than a mile from the forester's hut. Having hidden the car, we shall do the last mile or two on foot."

"I get you," Rex laughed. "But it sounds like a quintuple bluff!"

"No, when they see the tracks going into the ride they'll think at first that we've taken to the woods, but Ignac will go one better and deduce that we've gone right through it to get on to the road to the south. But there is so little traffic in these parts that someone is sure to spot the tyre-marks where we came back on to this road. They'll realize then that we've tried to bluff them. When they reach the cross-roads they'll see the tracks going south again, and when they find that they turn on to the grass they'll jump to it that we've laid a second false trail. After that I hope they'll decide to waste no more time poking about, but go all out along the Warsaw road in the belief that we really are making for the capital."

While they had been talking they had reached the cross-roads, and Rex carefully followed the Duke's directions. In that part of Poland most land is still held in common by the village communities or forms part of great estates, so there are few hedges, and the pasture often runs unbroken except by belts of woodland for many miles. Once off the road the going was in places extremely rough, and the big car lurched heavily from side to side as they bumped their way along; but they reached the main road without accident and, having crossed it, bumped on again until they struck the side-road to the north.

On its far side the forest loomed up black and mysterious in the moonlight; but, having entered it, they found that the bare tree-trunks would give little cover to the car when daylight came. Rex edged it in as far as he could through the ever narrowing gaps until he was finally compelled to stop some three hundred yards from the road.

"Not too bad," muttered the Duke. "We are quite a way from the village here, and the odds are all against the car being found for some days unless a gamekeeper happens to come this way."

"They'll be even better if we cover her up with branches," added Rex,

c*

and, getting out, he set about breaking off the lower branches here and there among the trees.

All this while their captive had remained a silent and gloomy spectator. The Duke now made him leave the car and put Marie Lou in charge of him with instructions to shoot him if he showed the first sign of making a bolt for it. He then turned his attention to the baggage.

It was impossible for them to carry all the cases, so the Duke undid them and, after frequent consultations with the others, repacked two with the more valuable items and things which were likely to prove of the most immediate use.

By the time he had done Rex had screened the car with foliage so that from the distance it would look like a big patch of undergrowth. As he picked up one of the suitcases de Richleau handed the other to their prisoner, remarking pleasantly :

"As you are a considerably younger man than I, Excellency, I will not deny you the privilege of relieving me of this small burden."

For a moment Mack hesitated, then he took the case, growling : "By God, you'll pay for this !"

"Perhaps," smiled the Duke ; "but I rather doubt if you will be there to receipt the bill."

They then set off in single file, de Richleau leading, Marie Lou next, the prisoner third and Rex bringing up the rear. Having never before approached the forester's hut from this direction, the Duke was a little uneasy as to whether he could find it ; but he said nothing of this to the others, putting his trust in the fact that at one time or another he had shot on dozens of estates, and in nearly every country in Europe, so he was no mean woodsman. His only anxiety was that the moon might be down before he could definitely locate their destination. In consequence, he set a quicker pace than he would otherwise have done, the only sufferer as a result being his conscript porter, who sweated, cursed and stumbled, not being accustomed to carrying heavy luggage.

When they had been walking for the best part of an hour the Duke came to the conclusion that they had overshot the mark, so, after a short rest, they turned back, inclining somewhat to the east. The moon was sinking now, but, after a further quarter of an hour, they came to a big tree that had been struck by lightning. Recognizing it, the Duke altered course again, and ten minutes later brought them safely to the small clearing in which lay the abandoned hut.

It was a ramshackle affair, consisting of two rooms only, in one of which the starlit sky could be seen through a gap where the roof had caved in ; but the floor of beaten earth was dry, the front room still housed a rough wooden table, and a fixed bench ran down one of its walls.

Mack was put in the inner room, and his hands were tied firmly behind him to prevent his climbing out through the hole in the ceiling, then the others unpacked and made themselves as comfortable as they could in the small living-room. They had brought all their rugs, and the night was not cold, but it was now getting on for three o'clock in the morning, and they all felt very tired after the hours of acute tension through which they had passed ; so, in spite of the roughness of their quarters, they had hardly settled down before they fell sound asleep.

When they woke the sun was shining. The clean forest air scented with pine was good to drink in for a few moments, but they soon decided that it was a poor substitute for coffee, and they were all ravenously hungry.

The night before, just as they were leaving Lubieszow, the thought that they ought to take food with them had flashed through de Richleau's mind, as also the idea that it would be a good thing to disconnect the telephones and smash the receivers. But he had done neither. As Ignac's escape had forced their departure, it had seemed to the Duke imperative that every moment should be used to get as good a lead as possible before the pursuit started. Mack's friends could benefit by the telephone only to let the police know what they would learn for themselves within half an hour of their arrival at Lubieszow, and, fond as the Duke was of good food, nothing short of sheer necessity would have induced him to prejudice their safety for it. Yet, he thought a little sadly now of the excellent breakfast trays, bearing cold ham or snipe, as well as eggs, fruit and jam, which had always been sent up to him during his holiday in Poland.

At the time of the previous night's crisis the practical Marie Lou had also thought of food and, not being as fully occupied as the Duke, had seized the opportunity while Rex was carrying out the bags to snatch up a napkin and tip into it a trayful of little pastries. She now produced them, much broken and with the sardines, caviare, smoked salmon and so on, with which they had been covered, crushed together ; but they were still edible.

Rex contributed a half-pound slab of chocolate, but knowing that it would be many hours before they saw another square meal they decided to put it by for the time being.

They found their sullen prisoner sitting uncomfortably in a corner of the inner room and, untying him, gave him a share of their strange breakfast ; after which there seemed nothing to do but to wait and hope that Richard, Simon and Lucretia would succeed in rejoining them.

For a little they whiled away the time by discussing the events of the previous night, and the Duke enquired of Rex what had happened to von Geisenheim.

"He had locked himself into the comfort-station before the rumpus started," Rex grinned. "I did as you said an' put three lollipops through the door. Whether they got him good and proper I just can't say, but I heard a sort of grunt as I turned and beat it across the landing."

'Then we left one dead for certain—poor old Anna—and four injured, of which two at least are probably dead by now. A horrible business, but quite like old times, I must confess."

"Anna's death was not our fault," remarked Marie Lou. "One of the others hit her in the dark when they were firing at Jan."

"True," the Duke nodded, "and I'm very glad that at least we have not got that nice old lady's death on our consciences. I do hope, too, that the young Pole I shot while he was putting out the lights pulls through. I didn't dare to shoot only to wound, and I got him in the head, but the bullet didn't go through his brain. It furrowed his cheek and tore his left ear; that's where all the blood came from, so with luck he will be all right."

Marie Lou's violet eyes opened wider with surprise. "I quite thought he was dead. I do hope you're right. He was the nice boy who had won something for jumping in the Horse Show at Olympia."

"Anyhow, I've no regrets over that old, stone-faced General," Rex put in, "and even less over that heel Bauer."

De Richleau smiled slightly. "No, it may mean two less enemies to fight when the real thing starts, and, even if Bauer doesn't die, he'll be out of the game for a long time to come. I put two bullets right through his chest."

They talked on in a desultory way, but their minds were only half on the conversation. All three of them were anxiously wondering how their friends had fared. Had Ignac's escape resulted in their being held up by the police long before they reached Warsaw? If they had got to the city safely, had they found Lucretia at Jan's house or had some ill chance caused her to leave it, even temporarily, which would delay their return? Perhaps Ignac had thrown his net to rope in Lucretia also, and the police would already be there when the others arrived? If they did succeed in collecting her, would they manage to evade capture on the way back? And, if they did, would Richard, who had ridden in this great lonely forest only once, manage to find his way to the hut?

Anxious as they were, they knew that there was little chance of their friends rejoining them until the following morning. To Warsaw and back non-stop was a sixteen-hour journey, so that even if Richard and Simon succeeded in reaching the Lubieszow district again that evening they would be much too done up on their arrival to undertake a long tramp through the forest, with only a vague idea where the hut lay and night coming on.

In consequence, Marie Lou and her companions did their best to still their apprehensions and while away as much of the day as possible in sleep.

Mack did his utmost to annoy them by shouting curses and indulging in long, abusive monologues, until Rex stuffed a handkerchief between his teeth and left him to sit in acute discomfort for the best part of three hours. When the gag was removed he seemed to have learnt his lesson, so they undid his bonds but kept him hobbled with a chain and padlock that the Duke had discovered among the miscellaneous gear brought from the car; and this relieved them of the necessity of either keeping him tightly bound or under constant watch.

In the evening they divided two-thirds of Rex's chocolate amongst the four of them and, as darkness fell, relinquished any lingering hopes they had had that Richard, Simon and Lucretia might reach them that night.

Having dozed a lot during the, day they slept ill and were up with the dawn. All of them hoped that the Warsaw party had spent the night in their car somewhere on the edge of the forest, and would find them in the course of the next few hours; but, as a precaution against Marie Lou being disappointed, de Richleau remarked that if their friends once lost their bearings in these almost trackless woods it might easily take half a day to pick them up again. So they breakfasted as cheerfully as they could off the remainder of Rex's chocolate and settled down to wait with the best patience they could muster.

During the morning they endeavoured to occupy their thoughts with word games, but as midday approached they became openly restless and nervy. All of them thought hungrily of lunch, but none of them mentioned it. By early afternoon they had fallen silent and were listening with strained ears for the least sound that might herald the approach of their friends.

About half past two the Duke opened one of the suitcases and produced a box of his famous Hoyo de Monterrey cigars. Offering them to Rex, he remarked laconically: "He who smokes dines."

"I've been smoking all morning," Rex answered with a wry grin, "and I feel empty as a drum, but I guess I'd forgo most meals for one of those beauties."

"Will you have one, Princess?" asked the Duke. "I've known you smoke a cigar for fun before now."

"No, thank you, Greyeyes," she smiled. "I'd almost sooner rob Fleur of her sweets than deprive you of one of your cigars."

"Almost?" he quizzed her.

"Yes, almost, but not quite," she laughed.

The episode lightened the tension for a time, and they sat there quietly while the blue aromatic smoke from the cigars filled the air and soothed the nerves of the two men; but, as the afternoon advanced, the anxiety they were all feeling began to manifest itself acutely again.

Marie Lou left the others to walk a little way in the direction from which she hoped that her beloved Richard would appear. De Richleau became irritable and moody from the oppressive thought that, if his friends were now in prison, it would be through his own carelessness; and the sanguine, happy-go-lucky Rex sought to comfort him in vain.

Afternoon merged with evening, and the shadows of the tall trees lengthened across the clearing, but still no distant snapping of twigs came to announce the approach of friends or enemies. At length dusk had fallen, and it was no longer possible to see more than a hundred yards through the scattered trees that fringed the west side of the enclosure.

"We shan't see them tonight," announced Marie Lou suddenly. "Even if they are within a mile of us, it would be too dark for them to find their way here now."

"Sure," Rex agreed, with a cheerfulness he did not feel. "But that's about the size of it. They've probably been all afternoon in the woods looking for this Ritz-Carlton of ours and failed to locate it. They'll have dossed down somewhere by now; but you can trust old Richard to find his way here somehow when they make a fresh start in the morning."

As they had no light other than their torches, it seemed that there was nothing for it but to doss down themselves. Their worry about their friends had caused them temporarily to forget their hunger, until Mack reminded them of it by a querulous enquiry about whether it was part of their precious plan to starve him to death.

He had seemed to accept his captivity with apparent resignation and spoken little during the day; but now, having overheard enough of their conversation to appreciate the cause of their anxiety, he suddenly displayed a malicious delight in aggravating their forebodings.

On being told politely but firmly for the tenth time that, as they had no food themselves, they could give him none, he gave a cynical little snigger and replied:

"Ah well, I'm not much worse off than those friends of yours. By this time they will be on a diet of bread and skilly in a Polish prison. I find your attempt to persuade yourselves that they are somewhere here in the woods looking for you rather pathetic. Once Count Ignac had told the police about you all, and a general order to watch for them was sent out, no two foreigners who could not speak Polish would have stood the faintest chance of covering more than a hundred miles in their car without being questioned."

"Can it!" snapped Rex, but their prisoner's voice continued to mock them through the semi-darkness.

"As a matter of fact, we rather pride ourselves on our police in Poland. Their organization is good, and most of them are excellent shots. Perhaps your friends are not in prison after all. They seem to have been much the same type of audacious brigands as yourselves, so they probably refused to stop when challenged. In that case, of course, it is quite likely that one or both of them is dead."

"You'll be dead yourself in another few minutes unless you stop talking!" de Richleau snarled with sudden fury.

For a moment Mack was silent, but he could not resist a final turn of the screw. "When you yourselves are arrested, as you undoubtedly will be, the police will take you to the mortuary to identify your friends' bodies."

"Oh, stop him!" wailed Marie Lou. "For God's sake, stop him!" She suddenly burst into a flood of tears.

Rex had jumped to his feet. Bursting into the inner room, he seized the squatting prisoner by the neck and banged his head violently against the wooden side of the shack until he went limp, then threw him down in his corner.

But they could not forget his words. Every one of them had been charged with such horrible plausibility that they seemed to be the actual truth, and shattered at a blow the frail illusions, built on wishful thinking, with which Marie Lou and her friends had been striving to comfort themselves through the long hours of the day.

In a few moments these brutal sentences had done what the long hours had failed to do. Marie Lou's friends knew well the courageous heart that beat in her beautiful little body; but now she was utterly undone, and she wept unrestrainedly, until, at last, with her head on the Duke's chest, she sobbed herself to sleep, while he and Rex still lay staring grimly into the darkness.

Having gone to rest early, they woke next morning with the dawn again, ill refreshed and still dejected. For an hour or so they stood about, clinging desperately to the hope that had braced them the previous day—that their friends had reached the woods, but had become lost in them, and would yet find their way to the rendezvous.

But as they paced restlessly up and down, even their anxiety was no longer enough to stave off their pangs of hunger. Their last square meal had been dinner at Lubieszow on Tuesday, the 29th of August, and it was now Friday, the 1st of September. Since, they had had nothing to eat at all, apart from a few ounces apiece of the mess of pastries which Marie Lou had brought with her and Rex's slab of chocolate. The forest was mainly larch and pine; there were no nut trees, the blackberries were still unripe, and they could find no edible roots that they might have cooked over a fire.

Mack added to their pangs by not allowing them to forget their empty stomachs for more than a few moments. A devil seemed to have entered into the man, and he now kept up an almost constant stream of shouted abuse, mingled with such tormenting questions as:

"How would you like a mushroom omelette now? Or what about some ham fried with eggs? But as we had no lunch yesterday, or dinner either, why confine ourselves to breakfast dishes? Do you prefer sole done with lobster or fresh broiled trout? Personally, I rather favour grilled salmon; it's more satisfying. Then a saddle of lamb with green peas and mint sauce, to be followed by a duck with *salade Japonaise*. Or, better still, perhaps a roast goose! Could you still manage a *soufflé Grand Meunier* after that, and a *Poire Hélène*? I think you could. But perhaps you're not hungry?"

From such patrician dishes he passed to more homely but not less tempting fare; fried bread and bacon, boiled new-laid eggs, hot toast and butter, dripping scones, lettuce and tomato sandwiches, a big juicy steak with *sauté* potatoes and fried onions.

In vain, Rex bellowed at him to hold his tongue, and even renewed banging of his head against the wooden wall silenced him for only a few moments, so, eventually, to stop his maddening flow of suggestions, they were forced to gag him again with his handkerchief.

By ten o'clock they were so ravenous that the Duke proposed that, whatever the risk, he should go in search of supplies. As far as he remembered from his rides, the nearest farm was almost two miles distant. It was a lonely place, and if the people there proved hostile, through having been warned to keep a lookout for them, he felt confident that he would be able to secure all he wanted at the point of his pistol. The probability that, even if they proved friendly, they would speak of his visit locally and thus cause the woods to be beaten for the fugitives was a danger which he felt must be accepted in such pressing circumstances.

Since the others agreed with him, he set off at once, having promised to be back by one o'clock or sooner if possible. When he had gone Rex endeavoured to distract Marie Lou's attention from her worries by a description of his holiday at Biarritz, and she gradually responded by giving him a more detailed account of all that had happened at Lubieszow before his arrival, adding as much as she knew of Jan and Lucretia's love affair. But the morning seemed interminable, and they now had the additional anxiety of whether the Duke would accomplish his mission safely or have the ill-fortune to fall in with some armed party, which might already be searching for them.

Shortly before one, however, they heard a distant rustling of leaves underfoot and speedily concealed themselves in the hut, where they waited with beating hearts to see if it were a search party, their friends from Warsaw, or the Duke.

The Duke it proved to be, with a fine heavy sack slung over his shoulder; but, even as he set it down, he distracted their attention from it by his first words.

"Hitler has annexed Danzig, and the German Armies invaded Poland at dawn this morning."

"So—so it's come then!" gasped Marie Lou. Somehow, in spite of all the bellicose pronouncements of the Nazis and the pessimism of her friends, she had never really believed that Europe's statesmen, all of whom had witnessed the world-shaking catastrophe of 1914-18, would fail to find some way to avert a second period of perhaps even more appalling suffering for the millions of helpless and innocent people for whose well-being they were responsible.

"Any details?" asked Rex.

De Richleau shook his head. "No, just the bare announcement issued over the wireless about nine o'clock this morning. The Poles are resisting, of course, and have called on their allies to assist them in their fight against unprovoked aggression, which they have pledged themselves to continue, even alone if need be, as long as one German remains on Polish soil."

"Good for them! I take it there's no doubt about Britain coming in?"

"None at all, I think. Chamberlain will almost certainly attempt to bring about a last-minute reconciliation before the real blood-letting starts. But now the German Army has the bit between its teeth I doubt if even Hitler could call it off; and nothing less than a complete withdrawal would satisfy the Poles. If the Chamberlain Government attempts to evade its obligations now it will fall. Nine tenths of the British people would have gone to war last year for the Czechs if the choice had lain with them. They know little of how ill-prepared we still are, and, even if they did, I doubt if they would stand for any more appeasement."

"How about France?"

"God knows! Every Frenchman is aware that we used them as a buffer last time and that France was compelled to bleed herself white while Britain mustered the resources of her Empire and trained her citizen armies. Any nation might hesitate before committing itself to the same appalling sacrifice of its depleted manpower a second time. Yet, what is the alternative? If she does not come in with us, Hitler will simply find an excuse to attack her whenever it suits him best, and within a few months she will be overrun."

"They have their Maginot Line," hazarded Marie Lou.

"Its invulnerability has yet to be proved, Princess, and Hitler may elect to outflank it by way of the Low Countries or Switzerland. In any case, no war was ever won by sitting behind fixed defences. How do you think the United States will react, Rex?"

The big American gave a gloomy shrug. "The best of us will be in this thing heart and soul with you from the very beginning—just as happened last time. But that doesn't go for the bulk of the people in the States. They don't see why they should be lugged into these European muddles, and, after all, Poland's as far from the Middle West as Manchukuo is from Britain. If Britain and France can stick it for a year or two, Uncle Sam will come in—just as he did before. But the folk back home have got to be educated. They'll be belligerent enough and fight like hell once they're gotten to know what it's all about; but that takes time, and I reckon the European democracies will have to stand the racket on their own for quite a bit before Uncle Sam gets out his big stick."

"Yes, that's my view, too," agreed the Duke. "Well, there is nothing we can do about it at present, and you must both be dying for a meal."

"How did you hit it off with the folk at the farm?" enquired Rex, as they emptied out the contents of the sack—bacon, eggs, butter, a loaf of rye bread, two bottles of home-made cider and a score or so of fine ripe plums.

"Excellently," de Richleau smiled. "I told them that our car had broken down after an all-night drive from Lwow, and they couldn't do enough for me. You see, these simple, honest people have taken it for granted that Britain is already in the war with them, and directly they learned that I was an Englishman they refused to let me pay for anything."

"D'you think they'll spill the beans about your visit?"

"That's a chance we'll have to take. I dared not ask them to refrain from mentioning it, as they were in such an excited state that they might easily have jumped to the conclusion that I was a foreign spy."

"Then we may not be safe here for much longer?"

"I know; but I'm afraid we must accept it now that something serious must have happened to prevent our friends getting here. I feel that the time has come for us to find out what that something is."

Marie Lou heaved a sigh of relief. "I'm so glad you think that, Greyeyes. This uncertainty and interminable waiting is simply killing me."

Rex patted her hand. "We've both been wise to that; but we'd have been crazy guys to beat it outa here while there was a fair chance they'd turn up. But now I'm with Greyeyes every time. Soon as we've fed let's get going."

Since the Duke had emptied his sack all three of them had been collecting kindling and small fallen branches to make a fire. Soon it was blazing merrily. De Richleau scraped some clay from the bank of a brook that ran through the clearing and carefully encased the eggs in it ready for baking in the hot ashes, while the other two cooked the bacon by holding it over the fire on long pointed sticks.

When they had done they brought their prisoner out to share this woodland banquet, which in their half-famished state tasted better to them than any meal they could remember; and for the first time Mack showed signs of geniality.

"I gather from your remarks," he said after his sixth plum, "that you intend to go in search of your friends. I assume that means you will take the road to Warsaw?"

"Yes," replied the Duke, "and, if the car has remained undiscovered, we shall be happy to offer Your Excellency a lift."

"Thanks," the lean statesman replied drily. "As it is my car it seems rather that it is I who will be giving you a lift. However, since war has actually broken out, I am naturally more anxious than ever to get back to the capital, so we will not quibble over technicalities. Whether I drive or am driven it will give me no small pleasure when we get there to see you all safely directed to Police Headquarters."

"Thank *you*," smiled de Richleau, "for presenting us with a valuable piece of information. Until you spoke I was not aware that it was your car that we had—er—borrowed. That it is should prove of considerable help in persuading any suspicious policeman who may pull us up that you are indeed giving us a lift, and that we have the felicity to be under your personal protection."

Mack grimaced. "I had an idea that was what you might have in mind; but you can't play that sort of game indefinitely, you know."

"Alas! No pleasure can be prolonged indefinitely," philosophized the Duke. "However, I am sure you will see the wisdom of continuing to give us your protection during our journey to the capital, as I need hardly add that your life hangs upon our reaching Warsaw in safety."

"And then?"

"Surely the fact that several million people, although apparently with long lives before them yesterday, are now being killed by one another with long-range guns, bombs, bullets and possibly poison gas, is sufficient demonstration that none of us can foresee what fate has in store for us tomorrow?"

"Oh, come on!" cut in Rex impatiently. "Let's get going."

"Patience, my friend," rejoined the Duke. "Even if the forest is now being beaten for us, it's so large that the chances are all against our being located for several hours."

"Surely you don't mean we must stay here all the afternoon?" Marie Lou cried in protest.

"No, Princess. Only for another hour or so. You see, it may well be that the place to which we are going is already in the hands of those who wish us no good, or under observation; therefore, it would be wise for us to approach it with the utmost caution. It follows that the most suitable condition would be under cover of darkness."

Mack's little niggling laugh echoed through the glade. "Thank *you*, Duke, for a piece of valuable information. You have as good as confirmed my guess that you are going to Jan's house, the Lubieszow mansion, to see if the beautiful Contesa Cordoba y Coralles can give you any news of your missing friends."

"How considerate of you, Excellency," purred the Duke, "to present us with the extent of your knowledge of our private affairs. It seems that, even at Lubieszow, you were not too heavily immersed in affairs of state to take an interest in our activities. Permit me, though, to remind you of the old tag which warns us that 'a little learning is a dangerous thing'. However, as I was saying to my friends, reasonable precaution dictates that we should not arrive in Warsaw much before midnight. It will be to Your Excellency's interest to see that we aren't held up on the journey, so we ought to do the trip in eight hours. We will allow an hour to reach the car, so if we leave here at three o'clock, barring any unfortunate accident which would prove fatal to yourself, we should do it nicely."

It was already past two, so they had no great while to wait, and they employed it selecting suitable phrases for a note they intended to leave in the hut for Richard, Simon and Lucretia, should they, after all, succeed in making a belated appearance at the rendezvous. To the uninitiated the final document would have proved extremely misleading, but its authors were fully satisfied that their friends would read between the lines and do their best either to follow them with all speed to the capital or make for the Hungarian frontier—the choice of action being left to them.

Leaving the letter on the table, they repacked their two suitcases and set out, in the same order as that in which they had arrived, for the place where they had left the car. Now that it was daylight the Duke was able to find his way more easily, and in well under an hour, to their considerable relief, they saw between the trees ahead the big pile of branches, under which they had hidden the car, still undisturbed.

Five minutes were sufficient to disembarrass it of its camouflage, and in another five it was slowly rolling through the fringe of wood towards the road.

"You quite understand?" the Duke said quickly to his prisoner. "Under my coat I have a fully loaded pistol. If we are halted you will feel its barrel as a hard lump pressing into your side. You will answer all questions—and do not forget that I understand Polish pretty thoroughly. This is your own car, and you are hurrying back to Warsaw in it; you are giving two of Poland's English allies and a friendly American a lift. If any officious policeman shows doubt and speaks of a rumour that you have been kidnapped against your will by just such a party you will laugh him to scorn. If he still hesitates to let us pass until he has consulted his superiors, you will say that your presence is required in the capital with the utmost urgency, and order my friend van Ryn to drive on. In no circumstances will you attempt to leave the car, even if requested to do so. Any divergence from these instructions will result in your immediate death."

By way of reply Mack only grunted and began to settle himself in his corner to go to sleep; but later it became fully apparent that he had taken the Duke's warning to heart; as when they were challenged for the first time at Niewierz, a small town on the Prypec about a third of the way to Brest-Litovsk, he played the rôle assigned to him, that of a Cabinet Minister in a desperate hurry, in a way that gave his companions complete satisfaction.

They were stopped again at Dwyn, Nowoziolki and Brest-Litovsk, and at several places after that; but Mack's long, grey face, so well known to the Polish people through his photographs in the press, the top priority sign on his car, and, above all, the authority vested in him, carried them safely past all posts after only the briefest delay and one slightly longer halt for petrol.

In a few cases their questioners remarked that they were stopping all cars in the hope of catching three foreign spies, but none of Mack's companions gave away their non-Polish origin by speaking and no suggestion was made that he had been, or possibly still was, the victim of kidnappers; so it seemed that his friends had decided that it would be wisest to suppress this part of their story.

With the muzzle of de Richleau's gun pressing into his ribs their hostage

impatiently waved aside all mention of these foreigners, and owing to the fact
that war had broken out that day, the police had many other urgent matters
to which to attend. In consequence, they reached the outskirts of Warsaw
without serious molestation a little before half past eleven that night.

As they had been driving through Eastern Poland, they had seen few
troops on the road, and, except for unusually large knots of people gathered
outside the still lighted cafés, there was no indication in the suburbs of
Warsaw that this day hàd prematurely sealed the fate of millions.

"Mighty quiet, isn't it?" remarked Rex, as they neared the centre of the
city. "You wouldn't think there was a war on."

As he spoke they caught a faint, distant hum. In scarcely more than
a minute it had increased to a thunderous roar. Somewhere, belatedly, an
air-raid siren screamed its banshee note. The people in the street began to
run in all directions. Blinds were hastily pulled down, lights flicked out;
a police whistle shrilled a frantic warning. A thin, wailing note followed by
an angry swish sounded above the drone of the aircraft engines. Somewhere
ahead there was the boom of an explosion. Another and another followed,
each coming nearer.

Suddenly, the road in front of them seemed to rise up. Screams of terror
were mingled with the crash of falling glass. The Nazis had begun their
ghastly work. The war was on—and on in earnest.

Chapter VIII

NIGHT IN THE STRICKEN CITY

THEY were saved only by Rex's magnificent driving. As he flung the wheel
right over it looked for a moment as though they were going straight through
the shattered windows of a drugstore, inside which something had already
begun to burn; but, as they mounted the pavement, the car swerved again,
tilted on two wheels, bumped and ran back on to the road, missing the yawn-
ing crater that the bomb had made by a matter of inches.

More bombs were falling behind them now, and a lurid flare suddenly
shot up to their right, where an oil-drum had burst on the roof of a tall building. The staccato crack of anti-aircraft guns was now added to the din, but
even by the wildest stretch of the imagination it could not be called a barrage.
Much as the Poles distrusted and loathed the Germans, they had not
plumbed the depths of the callous brutishness that would send an air armada
to murder men, women and children indiscriminately in the congested streets
of the Polish capital, without warning and on the very first night of war; so

they had sent nearly all their anti-aircraft to war stations and reserved only a few guns to protect the Warsaw Arsenal.

As Rex drove on towards the old city they could hear a second wave of bombers coming up from the west. Slowing down, he shouted: "Shall we try to make Jan's place or run for cover?"

"Keep going," the Duke shouted back. He felt that there was little to choose between the open street and the scant protection offered by the old brick and plaster buildings they were passing. Moreover, if Jan's mansion were under observation, the middle of an air raid offered the best possible opportunity of reaching it unseen, as the watchers would almost certainly have taken cover.

"It's in one of the blocks near the Zamek, didn't you say?" shouted Rex.

"Yes. When we get there His Excellency will direct us." Taking out his pistol, de Richleau pointed it at his prisoner and added: "No tricks now! For your own sake as well as ours, you will be wise to guide us to the Lubieszow mansion by the shortest route."

"All right! All right!" Mack hastily agreed. "But for God's sake don't point that thing at me. If another bomb drops near us the jolt may send it off."

He had hardly spoken when the second wave of bombers let go their eggs. All hell seemed let loose. There was a great burst of orange flame further up the street. The façade of a tall building stood out for a moment silhouetted in the glare, its empty windows lit by the red fires raging behind it. Momentarily it seemed to hover, then it bent outward with the slowness of a tired old man and suddenly collapsed, its bricks and masonry cascading into the road and sending up huge clouds of choking red-hued dust.

The car lurched from the blast, but Mack's fears were groundless, as de Richleau still had the safety-catch on his pistol. Again Rex saved them from a smash, or piling up on the great heap of rubble that now blocked the road ahead. Mounting an island and shaving the lamp standard on it, he heaved the car round by a right-angle twist into the side-street they were passing. Two minutes later he turned left and brought them out into the square of the Zamek—the Palace of the old Polish Kings—with its cypress trees and famous granite column on which the great statue of Sigismund III has stood for three hundred years.

As Mack leaned forward to give directions the legend concerning the statue flashed into the Duke's mind. Sigismund wears the cope of a bishop and a mitre-like crown. In his left hand he holds a huge cross, and in his right a curved sword which for centuries pointed upward. The Poles had a superstition that not until the sword of Sigismund pointed downward would they be free. During the 1914-18 war the terrific shocks resulting from the dynamiting of Warsaw's bridges displaced the blade, and after the war Poland regained her hard-won freedom. Sadly de Richleau wondered how long she would now be able to retain it.

From the square they passed through several short, old-fashioned streets until Mack told them to pull up and pointed to a big house on their right. They could not see its full extent, but a flare dropped by one of the German aircraft momentarily lit the narrow way, enabling them to glimpse a three-storey, stone-fronted building that had a low Roman arch with iron filigree gates leading to an interior courtyard and, further along, a tall nail-studded door reached by three narrow stone steps, flanked by ancient iron flambeau holders.

The raid was still in progress, but the bombs were now falling on a section of the city some distance away. Searchlights streaked the sky, occasionally picking up and holding one of the Nazi murder planes. They were flying quite low and made little attempt to evade the beams, knowing the hopeless inadequacy of the ground defences and treating them with contempt. An ambulance clanged past the end of the street, its bell ringing wildly : a nearby block had received a shower of incendiaries and was now blazing with a lurid glare.

Marie Lou's heart was beating wildly as she got out of the car with the others. De Richleau hustled Mack in front of him while Rex ran forward and tugged at the old-fashioned iron bell-pull that dangled beside the nail-studded door.

For a minute or two they stood clustered together at the bottom of the steps, then the door was flung back to reveal a hugely fat, bald-headed man with a small pointed beard, who held aloft a big brass oil-lamp in his free hand.

"Come in ! Come in !" he cried in Polish. "Quickly, before these accursed Germans kill us all."

As they slipped inside de Richleau asked if Jan were at home.

"No, no, my master is at the front," wheezed the Polish Falstaff as he led them hurriedly across the uneven surface of the highly polished wood that floored a wide hall. "Come down to the cellars. We shall be safe there, even if they drop a Big Bertha on us."

In the uncertain light they caught a glimpse of a great carved stairway, tapestries, bearskin rugs, old weapons on the shadowed walls and polished brasses, then they were following their guide through a low arch under the side of the great staircase and down a broad flight of stone steps.

"It's bad luck that the Germans should have put the electric power station out of action in their first raid," remarked the Duke.

"Have they ?" replied "Falstaff", wagging his bald head. "Well, that will not matter to us here. It shows only how right my master is to stick to the old ways. He has often said to me, 'What was good enough for us Poles before the partition, Borki, is good enough for us today'; and his sainted father was like that before him, so we have never defaced our fine house with the ugly contraptions of gas or electricity."

At the bottom of the stairway they entered a series of cellars, all roofed with massive Roman arches formed from huge blocks of stone. The air raid was now only a dull roar in the distance. As they entered the third cellar they saw a group of people, mainly women, sitting about with coats and dressing-gowns evidently hastily pulled over their night attire.

A slim figure whose golden hair flashed in the lamplight suddenly detached itself from the group and came running forward. Next moment de Richleau held Lucretia in his arms and was murmuring: "Thank God! Thank God you're safe."

"And you!" she cried. "And you! I've been most terribly anxious these last few days. Jan wouldn't let me telephone Lubieszow, and I feared that brute Mack had arrested you all!"

"On the contrary," laughed the Duke, "His Excellency has afforded, and is still affording, us his personal protection."

With a little gasp Lucretia recognized the Polish statesman just as she disengaged herself from the Duke's embrace to kiss Marie Lou.

"And Rex!" she exclaimed. "What in the world are you doing here? But where is Richard?"

"I only wish I knew," replied de Richleau with sudden gravity. "He and Simon left Lubieszow three nights ago to pick you up and bring you to a secret rendezvous, so that we could all make a break for the frontier together. Have you no news of them at all?"

"No, none. I did not even know that Simon and Rex were in Poland."

"And what of Jan?"

"He got back here yesterday morning, but he stayed only about twenty minutes; just long enough to tell me of the terrible treachery that had been planned at Lubieszow and that he was on the run because he had tried to kill—er—er—someone. He's gone into hiding and is now——"

"That's enough," the Duke said abruptly. "It would not interest His Excellency to know where Jan is at the moment; and that he is still safe is all that matters to us. I should have warned you," he added in Spanish, "that His Excellency is our prisoner and knows that if he makes one false move, such as appealing for help to the servants here, either Rex or I will blow out his brains."

More explanations followed, and it transpired that the Falstaffian Borki was Jan's major-domo, who had been placed in charge while his master was away. The rest of the group were all household servants, the men among them consisting of only an old butler, an even older head groom and a lame porter, all the others having left to join their reserve regiments on notification.

After Lucretia had told Borki that the new arrivals were friends of his master he accepted them with the utmost politeness; and, on learning of their long journey, himself went to the deserted kitchens in search of cold food for them, while the elderly butler was sent into the inner cellar to get a couple of bottles of hock.

By the time they had finished this most welcome repast the air raid was over. Borki ordered some of the servants to prepare beds for the newcomers and packed the rest off to their rooms; then he led the way upstairs and escorted his master's guests to a damask-hung sitting-room on the ground floor.

"What does Falstaff know about Jan's situation?" de Richleau asked, speaking Spanish again in a quick aside to Lucretia.

"I shouldn't think Jan gave him any details of the plot," Lucretia answered in her sibilant mother tongue, "but he knows that his master has quarrelled violently with some of his superior officers and, in consequence, has gone into hiding."

"Does he know where?"

"Yes, Jan is still in Warsaw. He is at his old tutor's flat, and as we didn't think it safe to use the telephone we arranged that Borki should act as messenger between us."

"He is to be trusted, then?"

"Implicitly. To him no member of the Lubieszow family can do wrong, and I am sure that he would lay down his life for any of them."

"Good." The Duke turned to Borki and spoke in Polish. "The Contessa tells me you are aware that your master is in great danger. That is the reason for His Excellency's presence here. We are holding him as a hostage for your master's safety. Can you suggest a place where he could pass the night without arousing the suspicions of the servants that we are keeping him here against his will? Comfort must be a secondary consideration to security. It may cost your master his life if we allow our prisoner to escape."

Mack stepped forward threateningly and snapped at the bulky major-domo: "If you aid these people it will cost you *your* life. I warn you. They are foreign spies—dangerous enemies of the State. Poland is now at war, and the Government will have assumed emergency powers as from this morning. To aid and abet your country's enemies is high treason and punishable by death."

"The lady whom my master left in my care, and told me to protect with my life, vouches for them, Excellency; and that is enough for me," replied Borki quietly. For a moment he stood there, fingering his little beard, then he turned to the Duke.

"One of the smaller cellars would be the safest place, but if there is another air raid the other servants will rush down and perhaps find out that he is locked up there. Wait, though—I have it. We will put him in the tower room. It is not in truth a tower—just a cupola above the level of the roof—but there is a separate stair to it, a stout door, and its windows are only slits through which I could barely pass my arm."

"Is it ever occupied?"

"No one has slept there for a long time now, but there is a bed in it which I could have made up. I could tell the housekeeper that His Excellency has asked for it particularly as the quietest room in the house, because he sleeps badly and wishes to be away from all noise. None of them will know that he has been locked in ; and for such a distinguished guest—well, perhaps it is fitting that I should take his breakfast up myself."

"Borki, you are a man after my own heart!" exclaimed the Duke. "Nothing could be better."

When the huge barrel of a major-domo had left them to see about Mack's room, Lucretia said anxiously : "I do hope Jan is all right. I've been worrying myself silly about him ever since that fiendish air raid started. If only I could telephone!"

"I don't think you need worry overmuch," de Richleau sought to reassure her. "I was in London during one of the worst raids of the last war, and, although there was a great deal of noise, it was remarkable how comparatively few people were killed."

"Oh, the last war!" Marie Lou shrugged. "Air fighting was in its infancy then, so I don't see how you can compare it with the sort of horror that's begun to happen now."

"On the contrary, Princess. For those who went through it 1914-18 will prove quite a useful yardstick. Naturally, if this conflict continues for any considerable time the devastation will be infinitely greater ; because last time aerial bombardment started from scratch, whereas this time it starts as a well-developed weapon. But it is a great mistake to imagine that air raids in the last war consisted only of machines made of canvas and bamboo from which hand-grenades and little tin canisters were dropped. The Zeppelins carried bombs as big as anything that was used twenty years later in Spain, and British scientists were developing a one-ton bomb at the time of the Armistice."

"Sure," Rex agreed. "When I was a kid and first went into flying I just grabbed every book I could get on air fighting. By 1918 air battles were no mean engagements. Some of the ace pilots bagged as many as seventy enemy planes to their own guns, and when the schemozzle ended the old Royal Flying Corps had a strength of 22,000 aircraft. I don't reckon those raids on London, Paris and Cologne can have been anything of a picnic."

De Richleau nodded. "They definitely were not. But the point I was endeavouring to make was that, however terrifying an air raid may seem and however horrifying its results in the places where the bombs actually fall, if a great city is the target the consequent casualties in any one raid can only be a very small percentage of the total population. For instance, Warsaw has a population of over a million, but the city covers an area of several square miles, and at least two-thirds of the bombs must have fallen on open spaces or commercial buildings which are unoccupied at night. From the number of bombs we heard fall I doubt very much if the casualties amounted to anything near a thousand; but if they did that is less than one tenth of one per cent of the population; so the odds in favour of Jan having escaped injury are terrific."

"You're a terribly plausible person, Greyeyes," sighed Marie Lou. "I only hope you're right, because I suppose Richard and Simon are somewhere in the city, too, locked up in a prison."

"He *is* right, darling," Lucretia supported the Duke quickly. "I've been through lots of air raids during these last few years in Spain. I never got over that sickening feeling in the lower part of my tummy; but experience soon taught us that, if we kept under cover, very few of us ever got hurt. I often used to keep my courage up by telling myself that it was much more likely that I should be knocked over by a car next day. Still, one can't help worrying about those we love in a raid, although I expect all of them are really all right."

"I'll bet they are," said Rex. "The thing is now, how do we set about finding Richard and Simon?"

"I don't think we can do anything tonight," replied the Duke. "With the war having broken out only this morning and all the new emergency measures to enforce, and the air raid on top of that, the authorities must be up to their eyes in work, and we'd get very little satisfaction out of them. In the morning, though, I think His Excellency might be able to help us."

Since Borki had left the room Mack had sat slumped in an armchair and followed the conversation without contributing a word to it. Now he stood up and said firmly:

"You are all living in a fool's Paradise if you think you can get away with this. It must have been known hours ago at police headquarters that I was seen with three of you on the way back to Warsaw. By this time the Secret Police will be combing the capital for me."

"Not necessarily," replied the Duke. "Remember, the police patrols that challenged us on the road saw you in your own car, perfectly well and in full possession of your senses, and none of them made the remotest suggestion that you had been kidnapped. Evidently your personal staff have thought it wisest to keep that to themselves for fear that if they said too much the whole of your treacherous transactions with the Germans at Lubieszow would come out. They were mixed up in that business themselves, and I don't suppose they have any more desire to be shot as traitors than you have. In fact, I should not be surprised if most of them have been hoping that you are dead."

"But my colleagues in the Cabinet . . ." Mack began.

De Richleau shrugged. "Presumably you gave yourself leave of absence when you left Warsaw for Lubieszow, and indicated that you were going off on some special mission which might result in the prevention of the outbreak of war. They probably believed up to this afternoon that you were abroad. They may think so still, as the movements of all the Cabinet Ministers are guarded with the strictest secrecy in war-time, as a matter of routine; so it is quite on the cards that the patrols who stopped us this afternoon deliberately refrained from reporting that they had seen you on the road. Even if they did no one will expect to see you back in your office till tomorrow morning."

"Then you will definitely release me tomorrow?"

"That we shall see."

While they had been talking Borki had rejoined them. He now announced that he had put the car in the garage and that their rooms were ready. Mack was escorted to his turret chamber, and after a brief examination of it de Richleau expressed himself as satisfied that their prisoner would neither be able to escape from it nor communicate with the outside world. He was then locked in.

Just as the men were saying good-night to Lucretia and Marie Lou the old butler came upstairs to announce that Jan's tutor had telephoned. He would have done so before but many of the lines were down, and the remaining ones terribly congested by thousands of people ringing up with enquiries for their friends, so the tutor had had great difficulty in getting through. Most of the windows in his apartment were broken, but he and his guest had suffered no injury. Their anxiety about Lucretia had been allayed by the old fellow's assurance that all was well at the Lubieszow mansion.

With this good news Lucretia went happily to bed, but poor little Marie Lou spent a restless and tearful night wondering what had become of Richard, and tortured by the awful thought that she might never see him again.

Immediately after breakfast next morning the Duke and Rex went up to visit their prisoner. On their appearance Mack rubbed his hands together and said cheerfully:

"Well, whatever you may have felt last night I trust you have now come to the conclusion that it would be extremely dangerous for you to hold me much longer?"

For a moment his two captors stood there regarding him seriously and almost sadly, until the smile faded from his face.

"I agree," said the Duke at last in a cold, dispassionate voice. "We *have* reached that conclusion; and it postulates an action which will be most unpleasant for us all. You are no doubt aware of the fate that usually overtakes kidnapped people once they become dangerous to their kidnappers?"

"Er—I don't understand you!" exclaimed Mack, a flicker of fear showing in his eyes. "I—I am not very well informed about the practices of the criminal class."

"Then my friend van Ryn will enlighten you as to the customary procedure in the United States."

"They get bumped off," said Rex, with unusual gravity. "Just as a precaution against their giving the lowdown later about the snatch gangs to the cops."

With a trembling hand Mack lit a cigarette. "But you cannot mean this ! You are not gangsters. You are educated men. I have done all that you asked. I have not even attempted to escape."

Rex shrugged. "Now there's a war on I guess lots of respectable characters will be acting like gangsters before they're much older, and life's going to be held pretty cheap in these parts for the next few months."

Mack's face had gone very pale, which accentuated the purple shadows beneath his eyes. "But this is not war !" he burst out. "It's murder, and you know the penalty for that. You—you can't possibly murder me in cold blood !"

De Richleau's face showed no trace of pity as he spoke again. "If we are caught your friends are almost certain to try to pin poor Anna Lubieszow's death upon me, and I can be hanged only once ; so it seems that I shall be saddling myself with hardly any additional risk by killing you. And, as we cannot possibly trust you, your elimination will at least give us a better chance of getting safely out of the country. As to its being 'murder in cold blood', those Nazi friends of yours who released their bombs last night were also, if you like, committing murder in cold blood ; but such an expression is not usually applicable to the killing of one's country's enemies or the execution of a traitor, like yourself ; and ever since I uncovered your plot to sell out to Hitler I have naturally regarded you as an enemy of my country in the first degree. So, you see, I have several excellent reasons for killing you, and no particular inducement to refrain from doing so."

"Wait !" gasped Mack hoarsely. "Wait ! You are wrong to regard me as an enemy of Britain. I am a great admirer of Mr. Chamberlain. You have referred to the bombing last night. It was just such horrors that I was striving to prevent. As for——"

"Oh, let's get through with this," Rex interrupted, pulling out his pistol and slipping off the safety-catch.

"No, no ! Please ! Wait !" Mack pleaded, now reduced to abject terror. "As I was about to say, there are the best possible reasons why you shouldn't do this frightful thing. Killing me will not help you to get out of the country. Now that war has broken out you will find that next to impossible. Every foreigner entering or leaving will be subject to a special scrutiny, and you are already being sought by the police as spies. If you will let me go I will secure special passes for you. You can have my car to take you across the frontier. I know you don't trust me, but surely—surely we could arrange matters somehow ?"

The crafty Duke, having reduced his prisoner to the required mental state, appeared to consider for a moment, then he said slowly :

"There is certainly something in what you say. However, I don't think we could possibly risk setting you free. My immediate concern is that by this morning people really will be beginning to wonder what has happened to you, and enquiries may be set on foot. If we could think of some way to allay the suspicions of your colleagues and your friends, I should be quite prepared to accept your offer to get us all safely out of the country in exchange for your life."

"I could telephone," said Mack eagerly. "Let me telephone any story you care to suggest. I could say that I was slightly injured in the raid last night and am in a nursing-home—or with friends."

De Richleau was hard put to it to suppress a smile. That Mack should do a little telephoning under strict supervision had been the very object that he had had in mind ten minutes earlier, when he and Rex had entered the prisoner's room with the grave faces suited to potential executioners.

"Yes. That might serve our purpose," he agreed none too eagerly. "I think it would make a better story, though, if you said that you had been slightly wounded in an attempt by enemy agents to assassinate you, and that you had no intention of disclosing your whereabouts for the next few days in case another attempt was made upon you. None of the people with whom you will communicate know exactly what has happened to you, and the story I suggest will help to fox those who were with you at Lubieszow, when they hear it. They will almost certainly assume that van Ryn and I were the enemy agents and believe that, having failed in our attempt, we are no longer with you, while, if it were reported to headquarters that we were together yesterday, the police may think that your English friends have persuaded you to seek temporary shelter in their Embassy."

For the first time since he had entered the room Rex's ugly, attractive face lit up with his almost irrepressible grin, as he added: "In fact, no one at all will know what the hell to think, anyhow. Come on, let's go down to that telephone."

On the way downstairs, Mack said a little dubiously: "You now intend to keep me here several days, I gather?"

"Not if I can help it," retorted the Duke. "That depends almost entirely on yourself. If all the necessary arrangements can be completed I should like to set out for the frontier tonight, or even this afternoon, if possible. By the by, you will, of course, include police headquarters among your telephone calls, to ascertain what has happened to Richard Eaton and Simon Aron, and if they have been arrested arrange for their release."

"It seems that I have no option," grumbled Mack. "But I think you have a saying in English, 'In for a penny, in for a pound.'"

De Richleau permitted himself to smile. His last, apparently casual, request had been the culminating point in the operation that he had undertaken on going upstairs that morning, and he had now got out of his prisoner all that he wanted—for the moment.

Downstairs they settled themselves round the telephone. Rex seated opposite the prisoner, covering him with his gun, and de Richleau next to him with his face close to Mack's so that he could hear not only what Mack said but also what was said at the other end of the line. He kept his finger on the instrument rest so that he could cut the conversation off instantly should any of the people at the other end begin to ask awkward questions. Upstairs they had, as usual, been talking in English or French, using whichever language came most easily to them individually, but now Mack naturally reverted to Polish, having been warned that he was to use only the simplest and most straightforward phrases; but even these sounded like gibberish to Rex, and he had to wait until the whole business was through before he could learn from the Duke how matters had gone.

Mack made four calls: the first to his office, where he spoke to his principal Personal Assistant; the second to his mistress, the third to his wife, and the fourth to the Chief of Police. All of them passed off quite satisfactorily, except for the last, concerning which the Duke reported one hitch.

After referring to another department, the harried Police Chief had ascertained that Richard and Simon had been arrested three nights earlier on the road to Warsaw, and, having been brought to the capital, were being held as suspects; but he not unnaturally refused to release them unless he received a written order to do so.

"That's no big obstacle on the face of it," Rex said at once. "Seeing we have a Polish Cabinet Minister playing along with us, he'll sign us an order, I haven't a doubt."

"I'm sure he will oblige us," agreed the Duke. "But who's to take it to the prison? That's the snag."

"I will," volunteered Rex promptly.

De Richleau shook his grey head. "No, Rex, the fact that you and I are foreigners rules us both out. At a time like this, spy mania must be running mountains high, and, remember, we have no means of securing official paper upon which to type the order. Besides, apparently we are both wanted by the police ourselves. We should almost certainly be detained for questioning, and neither of us can afford that."

"How about Jan?" Rex suggested. "He's a Pole, and an officer too."

"We have reason to suppose that he also is wanted—at all events by the military authorities. But wait a minute! I believe you've hit it. His Excellency will, I'm sure, be kind enough to sign two documents instead of one. I will go and see if Borki can find us a typewriter."

It proved that Borki not only had a typewriter but, as he handled all Jan's business affairs, was an excellent typist. Matters were explained to him, and after a short search some plain but fine quality paper was found, on which he typed two notes, the Duke giving him the gist of what was required and leaving to him the choice of the most suitable Polish expressions.

Both were headed "Commander-in-Chief's Headquarters, Polish Army, September 2nd", as it seemed plausible that Mack might either have gone there in his official capacity, or taken refuge there from his would-be assassins; and that later this might serve further to fog the issue of his disappearance.

The first was a peremptory order to the Governor of the prison to hand over the persons of Mr. Richard Eaton and Mr. Simon Aron, with their British passports and any other papers, including money, which they might have been carrying at the time of their arrest, to the bearer, who would escort them to Army Headquarters, where their presence was required with a minimum of delay.

The second, freely translated, read as follows:

"To all whom it may concern.

"This is to state that, owing to an entire misapprehension of certain circumstances, Jan Stanislas Ludovic Lubieszow, Count of the Holy Roman Empire and Captain in the Polish Air Force Reserve, made an attack on me and certain of the members of my personal entourage on the night of August 29th last.

"I hereby exonerate this officer completely from all blame, since I now know him to have believed himself to be acting in the true interests of Poland. This document cancels any order that may have been issued for Captain Lubieszow's arrest, and I am happy to take this opportunity of testifying to his patriotism, courage and loyalty."

Both the papers were signed by "General Mack" in his real name, and he was made to affix the seal of his signet ring to them. It was then arranged that Borki should take both letters to the block of flats near the University where Jan's tutor lived, and that Jan, protected by the one, should be asked to use the other and bring Richard and Simon back to his own house directly he had secured their release.

"The next thing," said the Duke to Mack, as soon as Borki had left them, "is the question of our leaving the country. All trains will undoubtedly be crammed to capacity and subject to wearisome delays owing to troop movements, so we will accept the offer of Your Excellency's car. A car, too, will enable us to change our minds on the way, if we consider it advisable, as to our point of exit. There remains the matter of special passes and exit visas."

"They should be on proper forms supplied by our Security Service," replied "Mack", "and franked by the Polish Foreign Office. But how to secure them is a problem which I leave to your fertile imagination."

"I thought as much, and I confess that I see no way at all of getting hold of such papers without jeopardizing our whole position. However, I think a personal letter signed by Your Excellency for each one of us individually should serve our purpose equally well. I suggest something on the following lines, taking van Ryn as an example :

" To the senior officers of all Military and Police Formations and the senior Civil Executives throughout Poland generally. The Bearer of this letter, Mr. Rex Mackintosh van Ryn, carrying United States Passport No. So-and-so, is personally well known to me. He is proceeding on a mission for the Polish Government and is to be allowed to cross the frontier at any point that he may select. All means of transport that he may require to facilitate his journey are to be placed at his disposal as a matter of the highest priority."

Mack shrugged and, drawing some more paper towards him, settled down to write a series of these *laisser-passer* for the Duke, Rex, Marie Lou, Lucretia, Richard and Simon, under Rex's watchful eye, while de Richleau went in search of the two girls.

He found them upstairs in a small boudoir, charmingly furnished in the style of the First Empire, where they were volubly exchanging news of all that had befallen them since they had last met in London.

When they heard the good news that Richard and Simon had been located and that arrangements had been made for their release, both girls were immensely relieved and delighted ; but when the Duke added that he hoped it would be possible for them all to leave Warsaw that afternoon Lucretia's eyes suddenly grew troubled.

The Duke noticed it but said nothing, and for a little they talked of the war. The maid who had been waiting on Lucretia for the past week spoke fairly fluent French, and ten minutes earlier she had brought the latest news up to the boudoir. The situation at the front was still vague. There had been clashes in many places, but the Polish troops were said to be fighting with their accustomed bravery and, it was reported, had thrown the Germans back across the frontier in several sectors. During the previous night the Luftwaffe had not confined its attention to Warsaw but had also bombed a number of other towns in Western Poland, and indignation at this flagrant breach of the humane conventions was widespread.

In the streets the whole population of the capital seemed to be engaged in sandbagging windows, digging trenches and erecting emergency air-raid shelters against the probability of further raids. Britain and France had not yet declared war on Germany, but the Poles had the utmost faith in their allies and expected that they would do so at any hour. In spite of the previous night's raid, the population in the capital was calm, confident and solidly behind the Government. The morale of the Army was excellent, and, as they passed through on their way to the front, the troops were boasting that within a few weeks they would have taught Hitler a lesson.

"Poor people," sighed the Duke. "I fear they are committed to a hopeless fight."

"Jan doesn't think so," said Lucretia quickly. "He says that when they are fully mobilized their Army will be nearly three million strong, and they have quite a respectable Air Force. He thinks they will easily be able to hold the Germans until the winter brings about a stalemate, and that by the spring Britain and France will be ready to launch an offensive from the west."

De Richleau shook his head. "That is simply wishful thinking, I'm afraid. One glance at the map is enough to show Poland's hopeless strategical position. East Prussia cuts right into her in the north, and her main frontier makes a huge semicircle right round to the Hungarian border in the south. There are no chains of mountains or great rivers forming natural defence lines, the country is flat and lends itself perfectly to mechanized warfare, in which the Germans will prove immensely superior to the Poles; and, vulnerable as Poland is to attack on three sides, I don't see how she can possibly hold out for more than a few weeks."

"But they are so brave," Lucretia protested; "and three million men are a lot."

"Yes, I doubt if the Germans will put more men in the field during the first few months; and no one questions the courage of the Poles. But, unfortunately, they are hopelessly old-fashioned. They live in the past and still put their faith in great masses of cavalry, just as though they were still living in the days of Jan Sobieski, who saved European civilization by his defeat of the Turks in 1683. Great masters of modern war—men of the steel age—like von Geisenheim, will, I am sure, carry out the conquest of Poland with the ease and precision with which they would undertake a peace-time military exercise."

"Oh, it's too terrible to think of!" Lucretia suddenly turned away her head, and Marie Lou and the Duke saw that there were tears in her eyes.

Marie Lou stood up. "You two have hardly seen each other since you parted at Lubieszow, so you must have lots of things to discuss," she said tactfully, "and if we are leaving again this afternoon I think I'll go and repack my bag."

When she had left them the Duke put his arm tenderly round Lucretia's shoulders. "I'm afraid you must have thought me very brutal just now, but it is best that you should know the truth. I can understand how worried you must be if you are in love with Jan. You are in love with him, aren't you?"

As she turned her face back to him it lit with a lovely smile. "Oh, of course I am, terribly."

"And he with you?"

"Yes. Last week, before he returned to Lubieszow, it was absolute heaven being with him here in Warsaw. It's the gayest place imaginable, and every one of our few nights together we danced ourselves silly. He simply smothered me in flowers and presents, and the days positively flew by before we'd said one-tenth of what we had to say to each other."

The Duke grimaced comically. "So Marie Lou was right. That's why you neglected me so shamefully. I was worried out of my wits because you failed to telephone."

"Oh, darling, do forgive me. There seems to have been a terrible mess-up; but I thought you knew that I had gone on to Warsaw to wait for you. Then Jan turned up again, and I forgot everything except that I was once more in love."

"Of course I forgive you. My anxiety was a small price to pay for the thawing out of that stony heart of yours. Is the old wound really healed for good?"

Her radiant face forestalled her answer. "Yes. Poor Cristoval's ghost is laid for ever. I can think of him now just as a dear friend of the past, and I'm sure he would be happy for me if he knew about Jan and me. We want to get married as soon as we can."

"That would be splendid," agreed the Duke, but he added after a moment —"if it were not for this wretched war."

"I know. It's a disgusting trick that Fate has played on us, isn't it? Still, I see no reason why we shouldn't get married all the same, if only Jan can get himself out of this scrape that he got himself into with that treacherous brute upstairs."

"I've already attended to that. I made Mack sign a statement this morning that Jan's attack on him was the result of a complete misunderstanding, and I don't think he'll be able to revoke it. Jan may not like the quite untrue inference that he didn't know what he was up to, but if he is wise he will make no bones about it, as the document should give him complete immunity from any trouble that may be boiling up for him and—er—enable him to rejoin his squadron."

"Yes, I suppose he will have to do that," said Lubcretia sadly. "Oh, what things I could do to that filthy Hitler! But Jan will get leave after a few weeks, won't he? And we could be married then."

"My dear," said the Duke gently, "I have been trying to break it to you that for Poland this will not be like an ordinary war. I have been through too many wars and know too much of military affairs to be deceived at my age. The Nazi campaign will be swift, ruthless and terrible. The Polish Army will go down, fighting bravely to the last perhaps, but under a series of overwhelming blows delivered simultaneously from the north, west and south. There will be no leave for anybody, and I fear few Polish fighting-men will see their homes again until some final pacification releases them from the German prisoner-of-war camps."

"It is most unlikely that Spain will enter the war, so as a neutral I could stay on here to be near Jan, even if the Germans occupy Warsaw."

"Yes, I think the Germans will refrain from molesting neutrals—at all events to start with. If, however, you *had* married Jan in the meantime, as his wife you would have assumed Polish nationality, and I prefer not to think what might happen to you in a German-occupied city. Wouldn't it really be best for you to leave Warsaw with us this afternoon, and, somehow or other, even if it means coming back here after the Polish collapse, Rex and I and the other two would get Jan out for you so that you could marry him in England?"

"Oh, darling, I know you would! But I couldn't possibly leave Warsaw without seeing Jan again. I simply couldn't do it!"

"Jan will, I hope, be bringing Richard and Simon here in the course of an hour or two. You will see him then."

Lucretia put a slim hand to her white forehead. "I love him so very much. I don't know what to do. Give me a little time to think things over."

Much perturbed, but realizing that he could do no more for the moment, de Richleau left her and went downstairs again. Soon afterwards Borki returned, bringing with him irritating tidings of an unforeseen, but probably only temporary, hitch in their plans.

It transpired that the night before, after the air raid, Jan had gone out to join a volunteer first aid squad that was dealing with the casualties in his district. Apparently he had worked all night and telephoned the professor that morning to say that he was dead-beat, so he was accepting a bed at the house of one of his fellow workers and would not be back until early evening. As his old tutor did not know from where he had rung up, or the name of his host, it was impossible to get in touch with him until he turned up again.

Borki had left the two documents with the professor, requesting him to give them to Jan the moment he came in and to ask him to act on the one concerning the two English prisoners immediately.

The delay was annoying, but it could not be helped, and when they had lunched they pressed forward with their other arrangements for departure. Mack, having been confined to his room after their morning session, was once more out of the way, so Rex was free to overhaul the car—a big Mercédès-Benz—and fill it up with oil and petrol. De Richleau visited his prisoner to extract from him a short statement that Borki had assisted his captors with reluctance and only under compulsion, for the major-domo's protection after they had gone; but, on giving it to the faithful retainer, the Duke urged him to take the extra precaution of leaving for his master's estate in the country that night. About the other servants he was not worried, as none of them had played any part in Mack's detention and were, in fact, still unaware of it. He then arranged with Borki and Marie Lou about food for the journey and assisted in packing a hamper with a plentiful supply.

It was decided that they should have an early dinner as Jan might arrive with their friends any time after eight o'clock, and the Duke wanted to get out of the city before dark, if possible, in case there was another air raid. The afternoon passed quite quickly, and they went in to dinner at seven o'clock. By eight the luggage was being carried down, and Rex was strapping it on to the grid at the back of the car.

De Richleau went up to pay a last visit to his captive and, for once, smiled quite pleasantly at him, as he said :

"We are expecting our friends at any moment now, so we shall be leaving quite shortly. I have given Borki instructions to release you at midnight. That will give us the best part of four hours' start in case you are so ill-advised as to play us any tricks. I should like to have kept you locked up for another twenty-four hours, but I want Borki to be able to say, without appearing to stretch the truth too far, that he came up to let you out as soon as he was reasonably certain that we should not return and flay him alive. In view of your transactions at Lubieszow, I trust you will see the wisdom of letting sleeping dogs lie. To explain away all the documents you have signed you would have to give a full account of your kidnapping, and once that goes on an official file all sorts of questions may arise which you would find difficult to answer satisfactorily ; and, now Poland is actually at war with Germany, things would not be made very comfortable for anyone who was even suspected of having tried to climb over to the other side of the fence."

"I'm not a fool," grated Mack, "and the sooner you get out the better. I only hope that you all break your necks."

"I could not reciprocate any wish more heartily," replied the Duke, and opening the door, locked it swiftly behind him.

On his way downstairs he met Lucretia, carrying her dressing-case. "So you've decided to come with us !" he exclaimed in delight.

"No," she said quietly. "I've only prepared to do so—so as not to delay you if I do decide to go ; but I haven't decided yet. I mean to put the matter to Jan and tell him that, if he wants me to stay here, I'm ready to marry him tomorrow morning. On the other hand, if he thinks it wiser to wait, I'll do as you wish."

De Richleau heaved an inaudible sigh of relief. He felt that Jan was not the sort of man to place the woman he loved in danger, and that, however confident he might be of a Polish victory, he would insist on Lucretia's leaving Warsaw—at least for the time being—with friends who could look after her, rather than allow her to remain on virtually alone in a city now subject to enemy bombing attacks.

As they reached the hall, Borki was just opening the front door. A smart little box-van stood outside, gaily painted pale blue and bearing in silver script the trademark of a well-known Warsaw florist. Jan was already half-way up the front-door steps, and Simon was scrambling out of the back of the van.

The Duke's heart warmed within him, and he mentally congratulated himself on the success of all his schemes. It had been a difficult and exhausting three days, but they had managed to evade many dangers, and by his skilful manipulation of Mack he had reunited the five people he loved best in the world. He felt reasonably confident that, for his own sake, Mack would not raise the issue of his kidnapping, and that the papers he had signed would carry them safely over the frontier. Given reasonable luck they might all be laughing over a good dinner at the Donapalata, in Budapest, in twenty-four hours' time.

As Lucretia flung herself into Jan's arms the Duke called out: "Hello, Simon! Thank God you're back with us! I've secured safe-conducts for us all, and we've got a car. Now you and Richard have arrived we shall be leaving for the frontier in a quarter of an hour's time."

Simon came rather slowly up the steps, and on his thin face there was only the shadow of a smile.

"Ner," he said, shaking his birdlike head as he uttered the curious negative he often used. "Sorry to disappoint you, but we can't possibly leave tonight."

"Where's Richard?" demanded the Duke abruptly. "Didn't you bring him with you? I was expecting to see him jump out of the back of that van after you."

"He's in there all right. But he won't jump out. I've taken the hell of a risk in bringing him at all. Our car crashed, and he's pretty bad. As a matter of fact, he's still unconscious."

Chapter IX

THE INDOMITABLE FOUR GO TO WAR

FOR a moment de Richleau stood there speechless. He had felt so confident that, provided Jan met with no hitch in securing the release of the two prisoners, all would be well; and now, in one brief sentence, Simon had brought his edifice of skilful planning tumbling like a pack of cards about his head. But his disappointment was almost instantly submerged in his concern for Richard.

"What happened?" he asked, advancing at once to the open door. "What sort of injuries has Richard suffered?"

"We had to pull up at an all-night garage in Brest-Litovsk for more petrol. Chap there gave it to us without any fuss, but for some reason or other it seems that the police were out to catch us. They may have learned from him later of our stop there, which would account for their knowing which road we were using. We met our first spot of bother at the outskirts of a place

called Baila Pedlas, about three o'clock in the morning. Lights were flashed
at us on the road ahead. I pulled up, thinking it was only some workmen
doing repairs. But it was the police. One of them jumped on the running-
board and told me in broken English to drive on slowly into the town.
Richard pushed him off, and I put my foot on the gas. It was dead easy, and
we got away. We tumbled to it that there'd been a slip-up somewhere, and
that the balloon had gone up much earlier than we expected. For a bit we
thought of getting on to a side road, but we decided against it. Thought we'd
probably get ourselves lost and waste too much time. At Siedlce, about
fifty miles from Warsaw, another squad of police was waiting for us. Richard
was driving then. He accelerated and drove right through them, but they
fired on us. Shot burst one of our tyres, and we were doing eighty. Poor
old Richard couldn't hold her. We piled up against a telegraph pole. By
a miracle I was flung through the roof. Didn't get a scratch except for a
nasty jolt and some bruises. But Richard's head went through the windscreen, and his hip was smashed by the steering-wheel. They patched him
up at the local hospital, then took us straight on to Warsaw. He's been in
the prison infirmary ever since."

While Simon had been giving his account of their misadventures, the
driver of the emergency ambulance and another man from inside it had been
lifting out a stretcher, and Richard's still form was carried into the house.

Rex and Marie Lou had now appeared, and, with a suddenly strained,
white face, Marie Lou bent over the stretcher for a moment before running
upstairs with Lucretia to prepare a bed.

"In spite of his critical state, we thought it best to bring him," announced
Jan. "If we'd left him in the prison infirmary there might have been some
hitch about getting him out later on. The doctor was strongly opposed to
his being moved at all, but I said that I'd get my own man to look at him the
moment I got him home; so I'll telephone at once."

"Yes," said the Duke. "Yes. We must find out the full extent of his
injuries as soon as possible, and get him the best medical attention that
Warsaw can provide."

"Let's go get the medico in the car," Rex suggested to Jan. "After last
night's bombing he's probably got his hands full, but we can run him to earth
and bring him back."

When they had gone, Richard was carried upstairs and put to bed. He
lay utterly still, scarcely breathing, and from the whiteness of such parts of
his face as could be seen between the bandages it was clear that he had lost
much blood. De Richleau spoke of his comparative youth and excellent
state of fitness as factors which would ensure his recovery, with a confidence
he was far from feeling, but in an effort to comfort poor Marie Lou. Dry-
eyed, but with ashen face, she settled herself by her husband's pillow and asked
to be left alone with him.

Simon, Lucretia and the Duke went downstairs to await the return of the others with the doctor, and they came hurrying in with him a quarter of an hour later. For another half-hour they waited in acute suspense for his verdict, then he came down to the small sitting-room and gave it to them.

Richard had cracked his skull and received a dangerous cut over his right eye. If he recovered he would be scarred for life unless he placed himself in the hands of a first-class plastic surgeon. His right ear had been practically severed, but this was only a flesh wound which would heal in time. The injury to his hip was the most severe, as it was a compound fracture, and might be causing an internal haemorrhage. X-ray photographs, which it was proposed should be taken the following morning, would give more exact data. In the meantime, although he would not commit himself, the doctor thought that, unless there were serious internal bleeding, Richard's excellent constitution would pull him through.

By the time he left it was past ten o'clock, but none of them was now even thinking of departure. Given the best possible care, it would be three or four weeks at the very least before Richard had recovered sufficiently to face a long journey, and in the meantime Marie Lou would not leave him, even if the Devil himself announced his imminent appearance in Warsaw; and none of their friends had the remotest intention of doing so either. Alone among them, Lucretia's distress at Richard's misfortune was to some extent qualified. It solved her problem and, fond as she was of Richard, the overwhelming stress of her love for Jan made her feel a guilty relief that there was now no longer any chance of her being torn away from him and hurried off to Budapest.

For an hour they sat there giving one another accounts of all that had befallen them while they had been separated, then Jan produced a pretext for carrying Lucretia off into another room, Simon said he thought he would go up and sit for a bit with Marie Lou, and de Richleau suggested to Rex that, in view of the changed circumstances, they had better have another interview with their prisoner.

In the turret room they found Mack sitting in an armchair fully dressed and apparently counting the moments until Borki came to set him free.

At the sight of his visitors he jumped to his feet and stared at them in surprise and consternation. "The devil!" he exclaimed. "You've not gone after all. What has happened to prevent your leaving?"

De Richleau told him, adding: "So you see, it is now necessary for us to reconsider the whole position."

"But you can't keep me a prisoner here for three or four weeks," Mack asserted. "That's impossible. If the Warsaw police are not looking for me already, they certainly will be in another twenty-four hours. That order of release you made me sign this morning purported to have been written at

Polish Army Headquarters. They will soon find out that I've never been there, and they're not fools. They'll trace the number from which I put through those telephone calls, and if they find me locked up here that will be the end of you."

Taking a box of matches from his pocket, the Duke lit one and put it to the big porcelain stove that occupied one corner of the room, as he replied: "Yes, I was fully conscious that we might be laying a trail back to ourselves when I made you put those calls through; but, in view of the nature of the calls, I thought it unlikely that any of your friends would endeavour to trace them until it was too late, so I decided to take that risk. However, I agree that it would be dangerous to keep Your Excellency here much longer, and I will pay your police the compliment of assuming that they would pretty soon find you if we endeavoured to conceal you anywhere else in Poland. In consequence, I have decided to let you go."

"Thank God that you are seeing sense at last! But, if you have come to release me, why bother to light the fire?"

De Richleau left the question unanswered, merely remarking: "I only trust that Your Excellency will be as sensible as you now appear to consider me."

"What do you mean?" Mack's eyes narrowed suspiciously.

"Obviously, if we had been able to place any faith in your word, we should have let you go before. Since we cannot, and we are now compelled to remain in Warsaw for some weeks at least, I propose that your departure should be preceded by the placing in our hands of certain guarantees."

Mack shrugged. "What guarantees can I give you, other than my word that I will refrain from molesting you? Of course, I could sign a statement to the effect that I have voluntarily remained in your company for these past few days; but I don't see that that would do you much good if I should choose to turn nasty afterwards and state that it was extracted from me by threats of violence."

"You almost read my thoughts," said the Duke amiably. "However, it is a statement that I want you to write and sign for us—and one which you would find it very difficult to explain away afterwards." Producing a fountain-pen and some paper, he laid them on the table, and added: "With a little prompting from me you are now going to set down a detailed account of your visit to Lubieszow and your dealings with the Nazis."

Mack's tired eyes flashed with sudden courage. "To hell with you! I'll be damned if I do!"

De Richleau picked up the poker with quiet deliberation, slid back the iron shutter at the bottom of the stove, from which a merry crackling now sounded, poked the fire gently, and left the poker in it; remarking as he did so: "It will be my uncongenial task to give you a foretaste of what we are taught to believe that damnation is like, if you don't."

"Torture!" gasped Mack. "No, no! You can't mean to torture me! Why, even the Nazis wouldn't dare do that to a Cabinet Minister."

"It has yet to be proved that the feet of an Aryan statesman are more sensitive than those of some unfortunate Jew," said the Duke. "If my reading is to be relied upon, the soles of the feet are a good place to start with; but, of course, there are more sensitive parts, and if you persist in your refusal to do as I wish we could go on to those."

"But this is frightful!" Mack's voice rose to a quavering wail. "You can't do this! You can't!"

"I can and I will." A harsher note had suddenly crept into de Richleau's voice. "The lives of my friends now depend on our giving me that statement, and I mean to have it. Yes, even if I must stoop to Nazi tricks and later answer for that in hell myself. Rex, gag the prisoner and remove his boots."

As Rex moved forward, powerful and menacing, Mack sprang away, backed into the corner of the room furthest from the stove and crouched there, gibbering:

"Don't touch me! I'll do as you wish! I'll do it! I'll do it!"

As Rex paused, the Pole drew himself a little more upright, stood panting in his corner for a moment, then spoke again.

"Listen. I'll do it if you force me to, but what use will such a statement be to you when you have it? I can always say afterwards that the whole thing was a tissue of lies concocted by yourselves and that you compelled me to write it by these appalling threats. The people who count in Poland would take my word against yours on any matter. You can be quite certain of that."

"Not on any matter," countered the Duke. "You seem to forget that Jan, Baron Lubieszow and his son Stanislas, all honourable Poles, were witnesses to the culminating scene at Lubieszow when your treachery was publicly exposed. It was clear, too, that not until then were the majority of your own staff aware of the full extent of your infamy. All their names will go into your statement and you will find it impossible to prevent any considerable proportion of them from testifying against you. Some will do so from patriotic motives, and others in the belief that, by putting the whole blame on you, they will save their own skins."

"You forget that in my position I shall be able to prevent any enquiry from taking place. The whole story will sound fantastic to any of the authorities that it might reach. It will be easy to persuade them of the absurdity of wasting time in investigating a charge of such palpable falsity while Poland is fighting for her life."

"You underrate my intelligence," de Richleau snapped. "The document will be sent under seal to the British Embassy, with a covering letter requesting our Ambassador to open and read it in certain eventualities. I shall also ask that, if he does so, he will then have copies made and, while retaining the original, send these copies to your Government with a formal demand that a full enquiry should be held, at which he and his French colleague will be represented."

"I won't do it! I refuse to ruin myself!" cried Mack.

"You can do the Nazis little good now, so you won't be ruined unless you play us false."

"You swear that?"

"I swear nothing. But you may rest assured that I place the safety of my friends and myself far higher than any desire to see you meet the just deserts of your treachery. Your absence during the crisis has probably already cost you your dominant position in the Cabinet. Both Hitler and Poland are far too heavily committed now for any machinations of yours to stop the war before the German Army has proved itself by securing a resounding victory. It is unlikely that the Government to which you belong will even exist a month from now. So, in any case, your career is virtually at an end, and I have written you off as harmless."

"You refuse to trust me; why should I trust you?"

"You have no option."

"I won't do it. I am at your mercy, and you can kill me now. But I refuse to place my life in jeopardy for an unlimited period by committing myself to paper."

"I don't propose to kill you. I am about to test the resistance of certain parts of your body to red-hot iron. This argument has gone on too long. Rex, grab him!"

Rex took two swift strides forward, seized the wretched man by the scruff of the neck and threw him face downwards on the bed. As he began to scream Rex muffled his cries by forcing his head down among the pillows. De Richleau grasped one of his ankles and, despite his kicking, began to undo his boot.

As Rex climbed astride Mack's body to pin him down more easily, the prisoner got his head free for a moment and gasped: "All right, you swine! I'll do it! For God's sake, let me go!"

"Shall we gag him and give him a taste of the iron just to show we mean business?" asked Rex.

"No, no!" came the half-stifled gasps. "I'll do it! I swear I will, by the Blessed Virgin!"

"One moment," said the Duke. "Your Excellency no doubt appreciates that my American friend has become bored by our conversation. If I ask him to let you go, there must be no more nonsense. You will write, and write what I tell you to, without protest. Otherwise, if we are put to the trouble of holding you down a second time, I shall adopt his suggestion."

"I've told you—I'll do it!" panted Mack. "I mean that! I swear I do!"

They let him get up, and, with his hair still rumpled, he sat down to write as he was bid. The language employed was French, in order that the Duke could be certain that his prisoner did not play him any tricks during its composition; but he made him add at the bottom of it in Polish: "I have written this my confession in French, having a full knowledge of that language, and because it is more widely understood than my native tongue." De Richleau's Polish was good enough for him to vet this simple statement, and Mack then affixed his proper signature and seal, whereupon his captors expressed themselves as satisfied.

As Mack began to tidy himself up, preparatory to his departure, the Duke said, not unkindly: "I'm sorry to have to disappoint you again, but we shall not be able to release you for an hour or so yet. I mean to take no chance of your raiding the house within the next half-hour with the idea of recovering your statement: I am going to write the covering letter now and take both papers round to the Embassy. As soon as I get back we will set you free."

The prisoner was not, however, destined to breathe the free air of the street until nearly three in the morning. It had been close on midnight when his confession was completed, and soon afterwards another air raid temporarily upset the Duke's plans. Marie Lou refused to leave Richard, so the Duke remained with her, but he persuaded the others to go down into the cellars by the extremely sound argument that it was absurd for them all to risk being wiped out or injured by a single bomb. His visit to the Embassy did not take place, therefore, until the night was well advanced. Even so, he found half the staff still there, at work decoding urgent telegrams; but they could give him no information, except that Britain had issued an ultimatum to Hitler, a fact which the Duke had already learnt from Jan's account of a news bulletin to which he had listened at midnight. Having left his packet in the care of the First Secretary, de Richleau returned to Jan's house and duly released his captive. In the meantime, a hospital nurse, sent by the doctor, had arrived, and, thoroughly tired out, they all went to bed.

The earlier part of the following morning was occupied by the comings and goings of doctors to see Richard. Jan's man had called in two specialists. Their preliminary reports were encouraging. Richard's heart and lungs were sound, his early treatment by the prison doctors had been efficient, and there was no indication of gangrene in his wounds. It would be a long time before he was a fit man again, but they hoped to pull him through.

Soon after breakfast the news had come in that the British Prime Minister was to broadcast at eleven o'clock, and shortly before that hour they all gathered round the wireless in Jan's study. The transmission was not good, but by listening intently they could hear enough of Mr. Neville Chamberlain's thin, distant voice to gather that Britain was now at war with Germany.

Jan told Borki to bring up some magnums of champagne, and the Duke was called on to propose the toast of "Victory".

"Let us drink," he said, "not only to a speedy victory over our enemies but to the hope that those that we love may come safely through this struggle, however long and desperate it may prove; and that Poland and Britain, with all the other nations who may share with them in the fight against tyranny, may emerge more closely wed than ever to the principles of justice, liberty and toleration, having destroyed for ever the power of the beast of Europe —as from its long history of treachery and aggression we may well term the German nation—to bring the curse of war upon innocent and peace-loving people."

"And to hell with Hitler!" added Rex laconically, upon which they all drank deep of the good wine.

Shortly afterwards, another doctor arrived with X-ray apparatus from the hospital, so Jan accompanied Marie Lou up to the sick-room to act as interpreter, and the whole party did not have any opportunity of discussing the war together until after lunch.

When coffee and liqueurs had been served in the small sitting-room Jan opened the ball by saying: "I don't think our late, reluctant guest is likely to go back on the papers he has signed, so I'm sure you'll all understand if I leave here tonight to report back to my squadron. Needless to say, the house and all that is in it are entirely at your disposal for as long as you care to stay."

Lucretia's knuckles showed white as she clenched her slender hands, but she said nothing, as Jan had already told her that morning that now he could consider himself reasonably immune from arrest he must return to his duty as soon as possible.

There was a general murmur of thanks, then the Duke asked: "Do you know where the squadron is? If it has been moved to the front we shall naturally follow the fighting in your sector with special interest."

Jan shook his round head. "No. During the past few days it may have been moved from Eastern Poland, but I shall go to the Ministry first to find out, and it's quite possible that they may send me as a casualty replacement to a squadron at the front."

Rex lifted his glass of Souverain. "Well, here's to our meeting before very long in the skies over Berlin."

"This isn't your show yet," laughed Jan.

"Shucks to that! My second name's Mackintosh, and I'm in this thing as much as any of you. A lot of the boys back home'll just be killing themselves to get into it as well, so maybe they'll give us permission to form a special squadron. If not, the moment I can get back to England I shall volunteer for the Royal Air Force—if they'll have me."

Marie Lou smiled for the first time in hours. "I'm sure they'd be glad to have an air pilot like you, Rex; and, although Richard is not in your class, I'm certain he would have volunteered also, if it hadn't been for this terrible accident."

"I want to join a first-aid squad, here in Warsaw," Lucretia said suddenly. "I saw so many terrible things in Spain that I'm no longer afraid of losing my nerve at the sight of even the most ghastly wounds; and I'm a trained nurse."

De Richleau sighed. "This is going to be a young people's war, and I fear my grey hairs will rule me out for anything except some dreary office job when I get back to London. Still, as long as we are here I can go out with Lucretia as a stretcher-bearer."

"Nonsense!" interjected Simon abruptly. "All talking through your hats. The younger people will have to fight the war, poor devils, but it's the brains of the older generations that will be needed to win it. We're cleverer than the Nazis—much cleverer. We'll think of ways to even up the odds against us. Ways to gain time. Ways to economize man-power and prevent wasteful slaughter. Ways to develop an economic stranglehold on Germany and deliver thrusts at Hitler where it's likely to hurt him most. Rex's father is one of the richest men in America, and we know he'll be behind us. Lucretia is a millionairess in her own right. My firm is not exactly the poorest in the City of London. None of us is lacking in grey matter, either. I'm willing enough to carry a stretcher with the rest of you. But that's not our real job. We've got to make our money fight, use our brains to think up some way in which it can be employed to give a real headache to Hitler."

The Duke looked at him with an affectionate smile. "You are absolutely right, my Simon. The gallantry of youth at the prow, but age and experience at the helm. That's the way to win wars."

"But we're not the Allied Governments," objected Rex, "and I reckon it's they who'll be doing most of the planning."

"Um," Simon nodded. "Of course. But the machinery of all governments is slow and cumbersome—particularly those of the democracies. While the bureaucrats at home are pigeonholing most of the best schemes put up to them for further consideration in 1941, there's no reason why we shouldn't get down to it and start a side-show on our own."

"Had you any particular thing in mind?" asked the Duke.

"Nickel," replied Simon promptly. "Means some of us going to Finland to buy up the nickel mines there, but the Germans have practically none of their own, so it's bound to be one of their worst shortages."

"Have you any idea of their present stocks?"

"Ner. But Krupps will need nickel for every fuse they make."

"True. All the same, we should be gambling with an unknown factor if we have no idea how many millions of shells they have already made and put away."

"Big guns take much longer to make than shells," said Lucretia, "so the Nazis are much more likely to be understocked with them. I think it would be sounder for us to try to corner some essential element for hardening the special steel used for gun barrels: Spanish wolfram, for instance. I own large holdings in the Rio Tinto mines, and many of the other big Spanish mine-owners are personal friends of mine; so I could help you there."

"Or chrome, for that matter," put in Rex. "My old man has quite a pull in Turkey."

De Richleau shook his head. "Much the same snag as applies to nickel also applies to these other metals, and tungsten, molybdenum and bauxite, too. Even if the Nazis have not yet had time to manufacture all the bigger weapons of war they would like to have, we can be certain they have laid in considerable stores of these raw materials. If the war is a comparatively short one, they may not even require to import another ton. I fear we should be dissipating our efforts against too elusive a target."

"The Germans are awfully clever, too," added Marie Lou. "I mean their scientists. They seem to be able to find a substitute for everything."

"The Princess is right," declared the Duke. "Even if their stocks of such metals are limited, they will manage to evolve substitutes for them. I think we should set ourselves a bigger objective. Let us at least consider the basic requirements for waging war: the things of which vast quantities are used every day, and for which no *ersatz* product can be substituted, because the basis of the substitute is too expensive or in even shorter supply than the genuine article."

"Coal, iron, corn, oil and cotton," said Simon at once. "They are the five essentials for fighting a modern war."

"Might as well add whisky and lipstick for all the hope we've got of cornering any of those," laughed Rex. "Tell you what, though, we could buy up all the asafoetida grass in South America. That would put all the belligerents out of business in a month."

Simon and the Duke smiled, as Marie Lou asked innocently: "What is asafoetida grass and why would the lack of it stop the war?"

Rex grinned. "I was only kidding, honey. It's used to make paper, and I was insinuating that if we could cut off supplies from all the thousands of people who'll soon be mushrooming the Government departments in the belligerents' capitals they'd have to quit work and go home. Old Simon is just doing a big act about his coal and iron. It's by filling up forms to eat, sleep and breathe that modern wars are really won."

"Seriously, though," said the Duke, "coal is no good because the Germans have ample supplies of their own, particularly now that they are able to process their lignite. About iron I'm not so certain. They get the bulk of their ore from Sweden. Could we do anything to check that?"

"Perhaps," muttered Simon doubtfully. "But they've got big deposits of their own in the Saar basin. If they capture Silesia, they'll have the Polish mines at Czestochowa as well. Should think they'll be able to carry on for quite a time with those, even if we were powerful enough to divert the Swedish traffic. Corn's no good either. Hungarian granary's right in their backyard; and they'll be getting supplies from the Ukraine, too, now that they've palled up with the Russians."

"Oil's about the most hopeless of the lot," commented Rex. "Even old Channock with the Chesapeake Banking and Trust Corporation to draw on couldn't make a dent in Rockefeller and the Anglo-Dutch, so that's right out of the picture."

"Is it?" De Richleau raised his "devil's" eyebrows. "It's one major essential which Germany is incapable of producing for herself."

"Ner," Simon interpolated quickly. "They've now got a synthetic process. Oil can be made from lignite as well as gas. Plant's at a place called Leuna, I believe. Anyhow, the process is reported to be quite successful."

The Duke waved the interruption aside. "I was wrong when I said 'incapable of producing for herself', and I knew about the synthetic oil factories. According to what I have heard, there are three of them. What I meant was that there is no oil-producing territory in the Reich or in any country adjacent to it."

"Hungary has oilfields which she has been developing in recent years," remarked Jan, "and we are now producing a certain amount of oil near Borislaw and Drohobzcz in South-eastern Poland."

Again de Richleau shrugged impatiently. "I know that, too, but we are talking of requirements for waging a modern war effectively. Germany will need millions of gallons if she is to make full use of her great mechanized army and her air fleets. Anything she could get from Hungary or Poland would be a mere drop in the ocean. As for her synthetic production, naturally she will develop that now as one of her highest priorities; but, as the industry is still in its infancy, it is bound to be a considerable time before she is turning out sufficient of this new product to affect her strategic oil position materially."

Simon nodded his narrow head up and down like a china mandarin, and the Duke went on: "Against the might of Spain, against Louis XIV, in Napoleonic times, and in the last Great War Britain's strongest weapon has always proved to be a blockade of her Continental enemy, so there is no doubt at all that she will use it again this time. As a matter of fact, it is rather a thrilling thought that, as we sit here on the very first night of what may prove the final struggle between Britain and Germany, the Navy must already be at its war stations, and has thus become overnight the supreme authority in all European waters except a narrow strip along the Continental coastline. Anyhow, the effect of our sea-power will be the virtual cutting off of Germany from three out of five of the world's largest oil-producing centres. For all practical purposes the United States, Mexican and Persian fields no longer exist for her. There remain Russia and Rumania."

"She won't get much out of Russia," interrupted Simon. "Transport's the bottleneck there. Different gauge railways and shortage of trucks. Now that the Russians have mechanized their agriculture, too, they need all their own oil for their thousands of farm tractors."

"Yes. And if I read Uncle Joe Stalin aright I don't think it is his intention to help the Nazis more than he has to in order to keep up this fantastic fiction that he no longer hates Hitler more than he ever did the Czar. He knows perfectly well that, if the Germans succeeded in defeating the Western Democracies, they would endeavour to grab the Ukraine and Caucasus from him without even bothering to send him an ultimatum, and he is not such a fool as to make the first round any easier for his potential enemies."

Lucretia smiled. "I know quite a lot about the Russians. The Germans may succeed in getting small quantities of high-priority goods out of them after weeks of argument, but even then all they do get will come out on a string of hay-carts. I feel sure you can rule Russia out as far as bulk supplies of oil are concerned."

"That leaves them only Rumania," murmured the Duke. "If we could find a method of preventing them from getting even half their normal supplies from Rumania we should have achieved something really worthwhile."

Rex suddenly sat forward, really intrigued at last. "The Astro-Romano Company controls the bulk of the Rumanian output. We could have a crack at that, but I doubt if they'd be willing to part with a majority holding of their shares."

"They are too big," said Lucretia. "Far too big. Even if Rex's father could find half the money and Simon's firm came into the deal as well, the Banco Coralles could not even look at such a proposition."

Simon nodded his corroboration, and for a moment there was silence, until little Marie Lou asked: "How does the Rumanian oil reach Germany?"

"By barges up the Danube, except for the few months in the winter when the river's frozen over," supplied Simon. "Some comes by rail, but only a small proportion."

"Then couldn't we find some way of cutting off the traffic?" she suggested. "If most of it comes up the Danube it must pass through that great rocky gorge near the Hungarian frontier: the place they call the Iron Gates. I may be talking nonsense, but I should have thought it would be possible to dynamite them, so that the great chunks of rock falling into the river would stop the barges coming up."

"Stop the barges!" echoed the Duke, jumping to his feet with—for him—a most unusual display of excitement. "By God! Marie Lou has hit it!"

"No, no," Jan laughed kindly. "Brave and resourceful as you are, an attempt to blow up the Iron Gates would prove beyond your powers. For that two or three score of skilled miners would be needed, and it would take weeks of drilling before a chain of charges large enough to be effective could be laid. Such extensive preparations could not possibly be concealed from the authorities, and you would all be arrested long before you were ready to bring off your coup."

"Yes, Jan, that's true enough," de Richleau replied with a smile. "But I was still thinking in terms of economic warfare rather than military sabotage. Marie Lou's 'gunpowder plot' is no wild flight of the imagination, although it is more than a handful of us could tackle. It was her suggestion of trying to stop the oil barges coming up the river that gave me another idea. This is a case where stray bits of information gathered all over the place come in useful. I happen to know that the barges are not owned by either the Rumanian State Railway or the oil combine. They are the property of an independent company controlled by a rich Rumanian named Teleuescu. The Astro-Romano Company may be outside our financial orbit, but I believe we could acquire a majority holding in the barge company for a hundredth part of what it would cost to corner Rumania's oil."

Simon's dark eyes were flickering wildly. "That's it!" he said. "That's it! How many have they got? Two hundred and fifty perhaps; wouldn't be more. But they're big things. Probably cost five thousand pounds apiece to build. It may cost us a million to get control, but we could easily raise that."

"Four million bucks would be no more than any of us would give for a shoe-shine, compared with the sums the British Government will have to shell out in this war," added Rex. "It would be worth fifty times that to them if they could get a stranglehold on Hitler's supplies of Rumanian oil."

"Make a fortune on the deal if we wanted to," shrugged Simon, "by selling out to them later. But I'm sure none of us wants a penny profit. We're simply out to make our money fight."

All of them agreed with him, and, although they considered rubber, copper, tin, sulphur, mercury, jute and numerous other commodities essential for war purposes, they could hit on no scheme liable to deal Hitler so severe a blow as the Duke's proposal of attempting to gain control of the Danube barges.

After some discussion it was decided that no time must be lost. Few private individuals possessed the resources to make such an attempt, even if they had the same idea, and if the British Government did for once cut red tape to get in first, so much the better; but similar thoughts might be simmering in some of the ugly, shaven heads poised above desks in the Wilhelmstrasse, and when they once got on to a thing the Germans could be pretty quick movers. There was no necessity for the whole party to remain with Richard and Marie Lou, so it was agreed that Simon and Rex should leave that night for Rumania in order to get in touch with Monsieur Teleuescu as soon as possible.

"It may take a week or two to fix the finance we'll need," Rex remarked.

"Um," Simon nodded. "But, in the meantime, if Teleuescu's willing to deal, we'll do our damnedest to persuade him to give us an option; so as to tie things up and stall off any enemy bidders who might come into the market later on with the same idea."

"Do try to let us know how things are going," said Marie Lou.

Rex grinned. "We certainly will if we can, but it may take us several days to get anywhere at all; and the bombing and general upset of war is bound to send the Polish mails a bit haywire, so you mustn't be surprised if you don't hear from us for a while."

"If you're going to mention this scheme on paper we must have a code-word for it," said the Duke quickly.

"Sure," nodded Rex. "What'll it be? Back home folks sometimes talk of oil as Black Gold. Could we use that any way?"

De Richleau shook his head. "The whole object of a codeword is to conceal an idea or an operation, so it should not have even the remotest inference to the thing it is designed to cover. Something like Table, Bumble-bee or Old Boot would serve admirably."

"But that's so tame," objected Marie Lou, "and if Lucretia is to put up part of the money 'Gold' is so suitable, since she was known in Spain as 'The Golden Spaniard'."

"Don't like 'Gold' alone," Simon muttered; "too near the knuckle, and if we referred to it in a letter some snooper might think we were doing an illegal deal in bullion. I've nothing against 'Golden Something-or-other', though, as the inference would be much too obscure for anyone to tumble to it that oil barges were meant by that."

"I am against any inference at all, myself," smiled the Duke, "but if you're all keen on the picturesque, as you're going on a quest to Rumania, how about 'Golden Fleece'?"

"Grand!" "Lovely!" "Oh, splendid!" came a chorus of approval; but Simon added: "What's going on a quest to Rumania to do with the Golden Fleece? Thought that was a Greek legend?"

"It is," agreed de Richleau, "but there is good reason to believe that most legends are woven about a kernel of true history. In any case, it is a fact that the Danube and other Rumanian rivers carry a light deposit of alluvial gold down from the mountains. This is still collected in small quantities by the peasants through the unusual process of pegging sheepskins fleece upper-most on to the beds of the rivers. During the course of months, thousands of gallons of water and much silt are washed through the fleece; the heavier particles of gold sinking to the bottom become entangled in the fine mesh of wool, and when the skins are dragged up again the fleece is powdered with gold dust. It may well have been such a skin that the Greek hero, Jason, went in search of and eventually brought back to Greece from some remote Rumanian village."

"That's mighty interesting," grinned Rex, "and Oil—Gold—River—

Barges all tie up pretty neatly together, but I'd eat my hat if anyone could tumble to the meaning we're proposing to hook on old Jason's travels."

And so it was agreed that this great attempt to sabotage Hitler's oil supply should be referred to between the friends as "Operation—Golden Fleece".

The only bright spot that came to lighten the tension they felt that evening was Richard's regaining consciousness. He was too weak to speak, but his eyes opened, and it was clear that he recognized Marie Lou. Apart from this, the imminence of their separation and their uncertainty as to what the future might hold weighed upon them all. Simon, going into the library to see if he could find any material on Rumania, inadvertently came upon Jan and Lucretia silently embraced and clinging to each other as if they never meant to let go. They were so absorbed that they did not hear him, and he softly tiptoed out again. Except during brief intervals of general conversation, Marie Lou's thoughts were entirely given to Richard, and the continued uncertainty as to whether he would recover. The Duke was almost equally worried about their invalid and depressed in addition by the thought that Rex, Simon and Jan were all leaving them.

They drank champagne again with their dinner, but for once it failed to enliven their spirits. Shortly afterwards Jan said his last farewell to Lucretia, then the others gathered in the hall to wish him luck wherever the war might send him, and a safe return.

At ten o'clock the Duke accompanied Simon and Rex to the Praga station, from which the trains run to Rumania. During the past few days most of the foreigners who did not intend to remain in Warsaw had succeeded in getting away, but the station was still packed with people. Many of them were reservists belatedly arrived from country districts and now passing through the capital to join their regiments. Simon had found it quite impossible to secure sleepers that afternoon, so the two travellers had to take their place in the crush and, having scrambled on to the train, were lucky to get a place in the lobby of a restaurant car, where they could sit on their suitcases. When, at last, the long train had slowly pulled out, de Richleau was unable to find a taxi to take him home; so he set out to walk, and, just as he reached the great Alexander Bridge which spans the wide Vistula in the centre of the capital, the sirens sounded.

Temporarily he took cover in a newly erected air-raid shelter and soon dropped into conversation with two Polish Artillery officers, who had also taken refuge there. Already there were rumours in Warsaw that things at the front were not going too well, and the two were so depressed that they now scarcely bothered to hide their gloomy forebodings. They knew nothing of what was happening on sectors other than their own, but they had been stationed at a frontier town in the Corridor at the outbreak of war. The German attack had come without warning towards the end of the short summer night, and had taken everybody by complete surprise. In a few minutes showers of incendiary bombs from the enemy planes had turned the barracks into a roaring hell of flame. Many of the Polish troops had been trapped before they had time even to leave their beds, and hundreds of the horses had been roasted alive, because the flames were so fierce that they could not be got out of the stables. The first treacherous blow had proved so severe that the units concerned had never recovered from it. A German tank attack had caught them still in a state of hopeless chaos, so that, after firing a few sporadic rounds from individual guns that they had managed to salvage from the burning sheds, they had been forced to beat a retreat. To add to their fury and consternation, there had proved to be many fifth columnists in the town, as its population was mainly of German origin; so that, as they hurried through it, they had been sniped at from scores of windows. Having lost most of their guns and horses, they could do nothing but continue the retreat until by a lucky chance they had come upon a train in a wayside station, and a party of them had decided to board it in the hope that, on reaching Warsaw, they could be reposted to a regiment which was still in good shape and had adequate weapons.

It was a pathetic story of gallant men sacrificed in vain by the lack of alertness in an ancient and creaking Military High Command. As the Duke had supposed, the Polish Generals had not the faintest conception of what they were up against. While even the more intelligent civilians had realized that war was imminent, these old-fashioned warriors had not so much as bothered to order adequate precautions to be taken against surprise attacks on their frontiers. He thought it certain that they still had little idea of the terrible urgency of modern war and were probably at that moment engaged in planning some vast cavalry manœuvre, with forces which were rapidly ceasing to exist under the relentless pressure of the Nazi armour. When the raid had eased he sadly made his way back to the Lubieszow mansion.

The news that trickled through during the next few days was far from re-assuring. Even by giving credence only to the least wild rumours and considering them both in relation to one another and the light of general probability, the Duke became aware that three great German armies had broken through the hopelessly vulnerable Polish frontier line to a depth that now made it irreparable. By the 5th of September the enemy had captured the two important towns of Grudziacz and Bydgoszcz, and had succeeded in severing the Polish Corridor, thus linking their main forces with those operating from East Prussia and cutting off an entire Polish army in the north. It seemed that the best hope of the Polish General Staff now lay in withdrawing their forces to Poland's only practical defence line, which ran from Grodno in the north, along the River Narew to Warsaw, and then south through Kielce and Cracow. This would mean the sacrifice of nearly a third of Poland, but it would bring about the enormous reduction in their front from

1,200 to 400 miles and give them both a secure flank in the south, based on the Carpathians, and a river line in the north on which to fight. De Richleau could only hope that sense would prevail over sentiment and that the Poles would pull out while there was still time to save the bulk of their army from annihilation.

Meanwhile, the wider situation had begun to clarify. After an agonizing wait of twenty-four hours France had followed Britain in declaring war on Germany. The Dominions had all pledged their unlimited support to Britain. All too belatedly, that grand old warrior, Winston Churchill, having warned his country of its impending peril for so long in vain, was taken into the Cabinet to fill his old post of First Lord of the Admiralty; and Mr. Anthony Eden was rehabilitated by being given the Dominions Office. Italy, Turkey, Eire, Russia, Japan, Rumania and the United States had all in turn affirmed their neutrality; so, for the moment, the conflagration was confined to the Polish and Franco-German fronts on land; but by the middle of the week the Royal Air Force had undertaken a spectacular raid against the German Fleet in its North Sea ports, and the Nazi U-boats had scored first blood in an unrestricted "sink at sight" campaign by sending the great liner *Athenia* to the bottom with many hundred souls.

Richard had passed his crisis and was now making good progress in the circumstances. Marie Lou remained almost constantly at his bedside, and Lucretia, in an endeavour to smother her anxiety about Jan, had thrown herself heart and soul into local A.R.P. work; so the Duke was perforce much alone.

To everyone's dismay the weather remained fine, and Warsaw woke each morning from its fitful sleep to skies of cloudless blue. The Polish roads were notoriously bad, and at this season the first autumn rains were due. Had they come as expected the armoured spearheads of the Nazis, which were penetrating ever deeper into the country and now appearing at most unexpected places many miles behind the theoretical front line, would have been halted, or at least materially slowed down; but all the masses said in the Polish churches for a change of weather proved unavailing, and the Nazis took full advantage of the cloudless nights to hurl down fire and ruin on the virtually undefended capital.

The inhabitants stood up to it well, continuing to dig frantically during the daytime at the earthworks which were now being thrown up round the city, and spending half their nights rescuing air-raid casualties from the rapidly increasing areas of devastation. De Richleau and Borki went out after every raid with Lucretia, and it seemed that half the population was also in the streets; even old men like Jan's butler and groom insisted on coming out to lend a hand with the casualties whenever a nearby building was hit.

On the 7th of September the Germans occupied Cracow, the ancient capital of Poland, but even this breathtaking blow left the Poles' confidence in ultimate victory unshaken and seemed to make them more determined than ever to fight on for every foot of their territory. De Richleau was horribly embarrassed by their pathetic belief that they had only to hang on long enough to receive succour from their Western Allies. Few of them knew anything about the limits from their bases at which air forces can safely operate, and they confidently expected that any night British fighters would appear to drive the Nazi murder planes from the skies. Many of them took comfort from the idea that the British Navy might force the Skagerrak and, entering the Baltic, land an Expeditionary Force on the North German coast, thus bringing speedy relief to the hard-pressed Polish armies. A rumour that the British had actually landed at Gdynia, where Polish troops were holding out, gained wide circulation.

The Duke knew only too well how groundless were all these hopes. Poland was completely isolated, and her geographical situation made it impossible for her Allies to render her the least assistance. As he had realized from the beginning, it could be only a matter of time before she was totally overwhelmed, and, knowing that, he was exceedingly anxious to get out of Warsaw while he could.

He felt that General Mack could be counted out, since, having made no move against his kidnappers up to the present, he was unlikely to do so now. But Richard's condition forbade any serious thought of travel and would continue to do so for some time to come.

On Friday the 8th a sudden alarm ran through the city. A German motorized column had reached its outskirts. De Richleau knew without telling that the next few hours might provide the last chance he would have to leave the capital; but he racked his brains in vain for a solution to his problem. Even if he could have secured a berth for Richard on a hospital train, the business of getting him to it would have undone all the progress he had made in the past week, and almost certainly cause a relapse which might easily prove fatal during a long and exhausting journey. He dared not take such a risk for another week at least, and could seek meagre comfort only in the thought that, if the Germans did capture Warsaw, it would be some considerable time before their police were able to check up on everybody in the great metropolis.

On the Saturday the news was better. The enemy penetration of the outer suburbs on the previous day proved to have been made only by a flying column, which had far outdistanced its supporting forces, and, after a sharp action, it had been forced to withdraw. But, on that afternoon, this was more than offset for the Lubieszow household by tidings which plunged all its members into the deepest gloom.

Food was now becoming short, because the farmers and vegetable growers of the surrounding countryside were no longer bringing their produce into the capital; so Borki had now relieved the cook of the job of securing adequate supplies. On returning from one of his forays, he told them sadly that he had run into an officer who had belonged to Jan's old squadron. Their aircraft had been terribly hammered on the ground by a raiding squadron of Boches. Jan's plane had escaped, so he had gone up in it at once to attack the still circling enemy and had accounted for two of their bombers; but a formation of their fighters had suddenly appeared on the scene, and he had been shot down in flames.

The blinds of the mansion were pulled down, and the gargantuan majordomo went out, weeping like a child, to the ancient church that stood on the corner of the street, to order masses for the repose of his beloved master's soul. Marie Lou had the appalling job of breaking the news to poor Lucretia, who fainted for the first time in her life on hearing it. When she regained consciousness they put her to bed, and soon afterwards she was granted the merciful relief of tears. For an hour she sobbed out her heart, then when her paroxysms eased Marie Lou gave her some veronal and had a bed made up in her room, deciding to remain with Lucretia for the night in case the effects of the drug wore off prematurely.

Thrown on his own resources, the Duke dined alone, in state. He drank some very old Madeira before dinner, a bottle of Grand Eschavaux 1923 with it, and nearly half a litre of Green and Yellow Chartreuse mixed in equal proportions afterwards. He was not drinking in any endeavour to cheer himself up, as he knew that was hopeless; but he also knew from long experience that the best way of ensuring sound sleep at a time of great distress was to get slightly tight, and that being his intention it would have seemed absurd to him to do so on anything but the best liquor available.

Solemnly staring at each glass of these magnificent potions as they succeeded one another, he thought of the merry-faced, open-hearted Polish airman who had met such an untimely end. Poor Jan, who so loved to sing, would sing no more. But, if he had shot two of those Nazi swine down, he had not died in vain; and he had met his end courageously, as all brave men would hope to do if they were fated to die while still young, in defence of his country. To be burnt alive in the flaming wreckage of an aircraft was an awful death; but the agony, searing as it must have been, would soon have been over. Lucretia would suffer more. She had to live on, haunted for months to come by gnawing memories and a hopeless yearning for what-might-have-been. This, too, was the second tragedy that had come to cast a blight upon her youth. Would she ever get over it, or would she become soured, bitter and old before her time?

As the clock chimed midnight the Duke carefully replaced the corks in the bottles and went up to bed. He was not drunk, but the potent spirit was having its effect and giving free rein to certain of his natural qualities. His hatred of the Germans, who had brought about this disaster, was stimulated to a degree which made him determine to deal with them, wherever he might encounter them in the war, with absolute ruthlessness; and it would have gone hard with any Teuton had one materialized at that moment in the passage.

While he was undressing the air-raid sirens sounded, so he slipped on the beautifully embroidered mandarin's robe which he used as a dressing-gown, and went along to Lucretia's room. She was still sleeping under the influence of the drug she had been given, but Marie Lou was awake and now, torn between two loyalties, begged the Duke to go in to Richard. Having sent the night nurse down to the cellars, he sat with Richard until the raid was over, by which time he felt quite sleepy and was glad to make his way to bed.

On the Sunday morning it was just a week since Britain had entered the war. News came through that the enemy had occupied Lodz, the largest city in the south and the Manchester of Poland, so it was clear that the favourite pincer movement of the German General Staff was now showing results.

De Richleau was one of those fortunate people who never suffer from hangovers and only feel a little sleepy in the afternoon after a night of heavy drinking; so when he went up to see Lucretia he was almost ashamed of feeling so alert and well. To his great relief he found her quite normal, apart from a natural reluctance to talk very much; but he realized that they were far from being out of the wood yet, and that she might well fall a victim to delayed shock in a few days' time. Both of them avoided the subject of Jan, and after an hour's desultory conversation de Richleau left her to go and sit with Richard for a while, as the latter was now strong enough to talk, provided he did not overdo it.

After lunch the Duke went into the still darkened library and, putting his feet up on the sofa, settled himself for a nap. He had drifted off and was faintly snoring when he was roused by Borki, who suddenly burst into the room.

The huge Falstaffian figure stood for a moment bulking in the doorway. He was trembling like a jelly and so agitated that he could not speak. His mouth was open, and his little goatee beard bobbed up and down; but the words simply would not come.

"What is it?" the Duke rapped out, wide awake in an instant, and fearing that some further terrible calamity had befallen them. "Speak, man, can't you?"

"The master!" gasped Borki. "He's safe! He's here!"

"Thank God!" de Richleau cried, jumping to his feet. "But where? Where is he?"

"It was true about his crashing in his plane. He has burns, but they are not bad ones. He has gone straight up to the Condesa."

"Hell!" exclaimed the Duke. "Don't you realize, you idiot, that this second shock so soon after the first might kill her!" And, pushing the fat man aside, he hurried from the room.

But lack of preparation for this merciful dispensation had fortunately done Lucretia no harm. The Duke found her radiant and starry-eyed, forgetful of her undressed hair and lack of make-up, as she clasped Jan's hands; while he sat perched on the side of her bed, dusty and unshaven, but vividly recounting his adventures.

Surprise attacks delivered before the Poles even knew that the war was on had wiped out so high a proportion of their first-line air force that Jan's squadron had been ordered to the front, and he had joined it there soon after its arrival. He had participated in a number of air-fights and shot down several enemy aircraft—three for certain. Then, two days ago, just before dawn, while most of them were sleeping from sheer exhaustion, the Luftwaffe had caught them. Nearly all their aircraft had been burnt out on the ground. Jan had gone up alone and got two Heinkels, but a few minutes later some of their fighters had got him. Only his long experience as a test pilot who had survived many crashes had saved him. He had escaped with some painful burns on his legs and a wrenched left ankle. But he had chased the enemy bombers some way and been shot down miles to the west of his own aerodrome. A quarter of an hour after his crash he had been captured.

He swore that his despair was such that only the thought of Lucretia had prevented him from flinging himself on to the Nazi tommy-guns as the Germans ran up. Now he vowed a thousand candles to St. Casimir, to whom he had a special devotion, for having saved him from such folly. The enemy had already taken more prisoners than they could cope with efficiently, and were, moreover, far more concerned with maintaining the speed of their advance than guarding their captives. In consequence, Jan had remained in their hands barely two hours, an easy opportunity for escape having presented itself before his captors had been able to spare an escort to take him back to a cage.

At a farm where he had sought shelter an old couple had given him their only horse without the slightest hesitation; and, despite the pain of his burns, he had ridden across country most of the previous night until he had again reached Polish-held territory. Early next morning he had fallen in with a Polish Air Headquarters that had lost touch with all its squadrons. The senior officer had decided that night that the only thing left for him and his staff to do was to fall back on Warsaw in the hope of participating in the defence of the capital. Jan had been given a lift in one of their cars and reported to the Ministry immediately on his arrival. As he was in no condition to be reposted to a fighting unit, he had been temporarily attached to the Ministry for special duty and told to bring his car there at ten o'clock that night.

"Oh!" Lucretia gave a little cry at this point in his recital. "Does that mean you are being sent off again to the front at once—but as a ground officer this time?"

"No." His smile was reassuring, but his blue eyes were sad. "In some ways I only wish it did. But it's no good concealing the truth. In fact, apart from wanting to see you, it's the main reason for my coming here this afternoon. Tonight the Polish Government is leaving Warsaw."

Chapter X

THE MAN-HUNT

"WHAT! Abandoning the capital?" exclaimed the Duke.

"Yes. Somehow, this time last week, none of us thought in our wildest dreams that anything so terrible could possibly happen. But if the Government remains here much longer the city may be surrounded; then, sooner or later, it would be captured. The idea of leaving is repugnant to us all, but at least it will ensure the continuation of the fight under proper leadership when the new headquarters have been established in the south."

"That's where you're going, then?" Lucretia said quickly.

Jan nodded. "Yes. They were hard at it burning all but their most important papers when I left the Ministry. It is to take some of the essential files that are being evacuated to a place of safety that I've been ordered to report there with my car this evening. The back of it will be as full of files as we can cram it, but there will be room in front for you, and I want to take you with me." He glanced swiftly at the others, and added: "I thought the rest of you could take Mack's car and follow us."

Marie Lou shook her head. "I only wish we could. Richard is making very good progress, but I dare not chance moving him yet."

"It's a big car. Couldn't you rig up a stretcher-bed for him in the back? There would still be ample room for you two, if I take Lucretia with me?"

"No, Jan. I daren't risk it. The jolting would be certain to affect him too seriously."

Jan fumbled nervously with a cigarette, and Lucretia gave him a light. "Look here," he said, after pulling heavily on it for a moment. "I don't want to be an alarmist, but if the capital does fall you must remember that you are not neutrals. These swinish Germans hate you English almost as much as they do us Poles. Of course, they can't arrest everyone in Warsaw, but the odds are that as foreigners here you will be singled out for special attention. They may send you to one of their ghastly concentration camps."

"Yes. But Richard's too ill to be moved, so I don't think they'll bother about him, or prevent my staying here to nurse him. For Greyeyes it's different, and I agree with you about the danger he would be in. He must leave with you tonight, and if you haven't got room for him he can go in the Mercédès."

De Richleau put his hand on her shoulder. "Thank you for the thought, my little Princess, but I'm reasonably capable of looking after myself. My grey hairs will for once prove my first line of defence. Jan will, I feel sure, give me a line of introduction to his tutor. Tomorrow I shall present it, ask him to give me a bed under an assumed name and, posing as Swiss, begin to haunt the museums. No one will interfere with a stooping old archaeologist, and they won't even bother much if he has temporarily mislaid his papers."

Marie Lou took his hand and kissed it. "Dear Greyeyes. I know it is no good starting an argument with you. I'd only get the worst of it."

"You sensible child." The Duke smiled down at her and turned to Jan, saying: "Lucretia must certainly go with you, since you are now the proper person to protect her. But can you give us any idea how long Warsaw is likely to hold out?"

Jan shrugged his broad shoulders. "No one can say for certain."

"Let us not mince mâtters. I really mean, is the departure of the Government indicative of the imminent abandonment of the capital to the enemy, or is it the intention of the army to leave a sufficient garrison here to withstand a siege?"

"I don't honestly know." Jan had suddenly become ill-at-ease and was evidently ashamed of the part his Government was playing. "I believe it is being left to the discretion of the Burgomaster, but I only heard that as a rumour. He may decide to declare Warsaw an open city in order to spare the inhabitants and save its buildings from further devastation. On the other hand, many badly mauled but still battleworthy divisions have fallen back on the capital these last few days; the High Command have not one tenth of the transport needed to deploy them elsewhere, even if they wished to, and I'm certain they will make a fight for it unless they are ordered to lay down their arms."

Realizing that Jan had given them all the information he could, de Richleau pressed him no further; but it was clear to him now that the Polish Government was finished. It had lost all control over the situation, and wherever it might establish its new headquarters, with the great industrial region of Southern Poland already in the hands of the enemy, and the capital soon to be isolated, it was most unlikely that it would be able to exercise any material influence on future events.

As Jan had been through so much and had had no proper sleep since Friday morning, he was almost dropping with fatigue, so after Lucretia had dressed his burns he hobbled off to his room to get a few hours in bed before the journey.

While Lucretia was dressing and packing de Richleau wrote a note, and when she came downstairs he gave it to her.

"This," he said, "is a letter of introduction to Sir Reginald Kent, His Majesty's Minister at Bucharest. If the Poles mean to establish their new seat of government in the south, it is a fair bet that they will choose a place near the Rumanian border. As Hitler's immediate neighbour, Hungary is more susceptible to intimidation, so should they decide to leave the country it is much less likely that they will seek asylum there. If they do go to Rumania, whatever Jan may think fit to do himself, I am sure it will be his wish as well as mine that you should accompany them to safety. Simon and Rex will almost certainly be in Bucharest by now; and, as we foresaw that they wouldn't be able to let us know their movements, owing to the chaotic state of Polish communications, I arranged with them that they should keep the Legation informed. You will find Sir Reginald a most charming man. He is a diplomat of the old school; gentle, fastidious, erudite, concealing behind these qualities a great courage and most subtle brain. He will let you know the whereabouts of our friends, and, if it isn't possible for you to join them immediately, I feel sure Lady Kent will look after you until you can."

She slipped a slim arm round his neck. "Oh, darling, I hate to leave you like this."

"I know you do," he smiled. "But, as things are, I would not have it otherwise. Besides, as you intend to help Britain by placing a part of your great fortune at our disposal, it is important that you should be in Bucharest, anyhow, before long. Rex and Simon are counting on you as the third partner in the great coup we hope to bring off, which will secure the Danube barges for the Allies."

For a moment they were silent, then the Duke went on: "I think we should let Jan sleep as long as possible, so you might see Borki and arrange for us all to dine late tonight; and be ready yourself to set off immediately afterwards."

"I shan't get a moment's sleep myself till I see you and Marie Lou and Richard all safe again," she sighed, and with tears in her grey eyes she left him.

When Jan appeared for dinner at nine o'clock he had changed his dusty, tattered uniform for a new one, and he looked once more the sturdy, debonair figure they had first known. His left ankle was still paining him, but he maintained that it was not sufficiently bad to interfere with his driving his car, and keeping it under control in an emergency. After the meal he wrote a note for his tutor, Professor Kucharski, recommending de Richleau to him, and gave it to the Duke. At a few minutes before ten the final farewells were said, and the two lovers drove away into the darkness.

For the inhabitants of Warsaw the early days of the week that followed were filled with ever-increasing anxiety and dread. As Jan had predicted, great masses of troops were now falling back on the capital, and the military authorities no longer had the means of redistributing them, so that a coherent front might be established, linking them with other Polish armies that were still resisting in Central Poland and the south. Many of the units had not even been in action, but others had been sadly cut about in desperate but futile attempts to stem the German panzers.

The Burgomaster had taken over control of the city, and in a courageous proclamation declared his intention of fighting on with every means in his power. The hugely swollen garrison had ample stocks of munitions, but the problem of feeding it was rapidly making things more difficult for the civil population, and the nightly air raids added to the general chaos. Most of the main streets were now pitted with great jagged heaps of ruins and twisted steel girders. Many roads were blocked by fallen débris or rendered unusable through unexploded bombs. Owing to the destruction of living-quarters and the great influx into the capital, such accommodation as remained was becoming daily more crowded, so the percentage of air-raid casualties was increasing with alarming rapidity. The exceptionally hot weather necessitated swift burial of the dead, and their numbers were becoming so considerable that mass graves had to be dug for them in the parks and squares. In many districts the bombing had disrupted the electric, gas and water supplies, so a great part of the population now presented a dirty and uncared-for appearance. Great numbers of people, who had been driven to take refuge in makeshift accommodation, went about, the men unshaven and the women bedraggled, still gamely sticking to their tasks, but looking haggard and depressed. Laughter and cheerful greetings were now a thing of the almost remote past in the once gay streets of Warsaw.

After the departure of Lucretia and Jan the Duke had lost no time in assuming the undercover rôle he had planned for himself. Professor Kucharski, Jan's one-time tutor, a mild-mannered little man but a great patriot, readily gave his assistance. Not wishing to leave Marie Lou and Richard during the nightly air raids, the Duke did not actually take up his residence at the Professor's flat; but by frequent visits he established himself in the eyes of the *concierge* as virtually an inmate of the block, and so prepared the ground for moving in there at any time on the excuse that he had been bombed out. Every morning he now went to the National Museum and employed himself in writing a thesis on the Teutonic influence in Polish architecture: an occupation which made the elderly *savants* who still frequented the reading-room regard him with a certain coldness, but one to which the Nazis could not possibly raise any objection if they succeeded in capturing the city.

Having once assumed this dual personality, de Richleau developed it with all the attention to detail which was so characteristic of him. At Professor Kucharski's apartment and the museum he appeared as a stooping, short-sighted old man with a slight stutter, who wore thick spectacles and a soft deerstalker hat; but every time he made his way back to Jan's mansion he slipped into the public lavatory at the Central Railway Station and emerged again ten minutes later to proceed down Jerusalem Boulevard as an upright, bareheaded figure, his hat and his spectacles in his pocket, and having shed with them ten or fifteen years of his apparent age.

The general war news continued to be scant and uncertain. The French were reported to be attacking in the area of the Saar Basin and had had some initial successes locally. It was announced that an Allied Supreme War Council had met for the first time in Paris and that a British Expeditionary Force had landed safely in France. There were rumours that the Czechs had risen and killed all the Germans in Prague. Hungary had seized the opportunity, now that the unfortunate Poles were no longer in a position to defend themselves, to reopen her claim to Polish lands in the south that she had been compelled to cede after the last World War; but in their dire emergency the Poles regarded this as only a minor misfortune and were now looking over their shoulders in apprehension towards their great eastern neighbour, as, on Thursday the 14th, Moscow had issued an ominous broadcast accusing the Poles of oppressing the Slav minorities that formed the bulk of the population in Poland's eastern provinces.

The following Sunday the blow fell. Soviet troops invaded Eastern Poland, and it was clear that, after only twenty years of freedom, Poland's new martyrdom was to be crowned by another partition.

De Richleau was no lover of the Bolsheviks, but he realized at once that this was no mere opportunist move by Russia to revenge herself on the Poles for the defeat they had inflicted on her in 1920, and even less a matter of their playing Hitler's game. On the contrary, underneath the thinnest veneer of apparent friendship Stalin and Hitler remained the most deadly enemies, and by securing Eastern Poland the cunning Georgian was simply advancing his frontier in order that he might be in a more advantageous position to meet a German attack, whenever Hitler decided that the time had come to attempt the conquest of the rich cornlands of the Ukraine.

In vain the Duke sought to comfort his Polish friends that morning by his clear-sighted arguments, and even in the hope that when the German and Russian forces met in a Central Poland there might be a bloody clash resulting in the Soviet's becoming a full partner in the anti-Nazi alliance. Most of the Poles hated the Russians, if possible, even more than the Germans. Openly and unashamedly they wept for their country, but, angry and defiant, continued to declare that they would never subscribe to a peace so long as there was a single foreigner of any nationality who arbitrarily remained on Polish soil.

During the past week de Richleau had always waited for dusk before leaving the University quarter for the northern end of the city, in order that his quick change act at the railway station might be less likely to be observed. But this being Sunday, and the museum closed, after a snack lunch with Professor Kucharski he set out for Jan's mansion.

Having discarded his hat and spectacles, he was halfway along the once splendid Marshal Boulevard when his attention was attracted by a sudden shout. A large car was nosing its way between a burnt-out bus and a recent bomb crater. An officer of high rank sat in the back, and with him was a lean man in grey. The civilian was shouting to two policemen further up the street where it formed a broad junction with Jerusalem Boulevard.

It was only after a moment that de Richleau recognized the man in grey as "General Mack", and another ten seconds elapsed before he grasped the fact that he himself was the object of Mack's excited cries.

His first indication of his danger was when a nearby pedestrian half-turned and began to run towards him. Next second he saw Mack point at him and shout: "Spy! Spy! Don't let that man get away! Seize him! Seize him!"

As the casual passerby came at him the Duke side-stepped neatly, put out a foot and sent the man sprawling full length in the gutter; then he took to his heels and began to run in the direction opposite to that in which the car was heading.

Mack's shouts and the Duke's brief encounter had now caught the attention of the two policemen and everyone else at that end of the street. The officers were blowing their whistles, several windows were thrown up over nearby shops, and the quiet of the Sunday afternoon was broken by a dozen voices joining Mack's with cries of "A Nazi! Stop him! Spy! Spy! Don't let the swine get away! Stone him! Kill him!"

It was that Sunday-afternoon quiet that gave de Richleau just a temporary sporting start. Had the incident occurred on any other day he must inevitably have been caught before he had covered fifty yards by the surging crowd that habitually frequented that busy part of the city. Yet, as it was, even with their now sadly depleted larders the women of Warsaw had done their best to provide their households with some semblance of the customary, better than average, Sabbath midday meal; and, since the war was still less than three weeks old, their families were instinctively taking a spell from their labours on this sunny Sunday afternoon. In consequence, Marshal Boulevard was as semi-deserted as Regent Street would have been on the same day at such an hour.

Having dealt with his first attacker, the Duke had a clear hundred yards in front of him. A Polish sailor and his girl were the first obstacles ahead, and the police were a good three hundred yards behind him. Mack was still leaning from the window of his car, now cursing the military chauffeur, as the man endeavoured to back and reverse amid the gaping craters and heaps of rubble, in order to give chase.

De Richleau had never been a good runner. A bullet through his lung in the second Balkan war, in which he had volunteered as a soldier of fortune, and risen to a post of importance on the Turkish General Staff, had deprived him from then on of the wind necessary to play all fast games. He could still make a good spurt for a few hundred yards, but after that he began to feel a choking sensation and had to ease his pace or risk collapse.

He knew now that he was running not to avoid capture but for his life. Those shouts of "Spy!" and "Kill him!" had in them all the menace of a blood-lusting pack. Even normally the Poles are an excitable people, and the sufferings the Germans had brought upon them were more than enough to justify the flaming hatred they now displayed. They all believed that Nazi secret agents flashed lights at night to guide the German bombers in, and the idea that one of these fiends had been identified made them see red.

In little more than a minute the almost empty street began to fill with running figures. Some emerged from side turnings, others dashed downstairs and out of the doors of the big blocks that were still standing. De Richleau knew that his legs could not save him. He must rely on his wits, and, if they failed him, he would be lynched, torn, trampled and kicked to death by the infuriated mob, long before Mack or the police could reach him.

As he came level with the sailor he sprang into the roadway, brushing aside the hands the young man had thrust out to clutch him.

A small car was passing at that moment, moving in the same direction as himself. The people in it were yelling at him, and, swerving towards the pavement, the driver tried to head him off. Instead of attempting to avoid the car, the Duke jumped on its running-board.

The driver was a fat, fair Jew, and beside him sat a pretty little hook-nosed Jewess. She screamed something at the man, on which he jerked forward his feet to declutch, jam down the brake and bring the car to a halt.

De Richleau had a firm grip on the window of the car with his left hand. With his right he pulled out the big automatic without which he now never moved abroad. Jabbing its barrel into the fat man's neck, he panted: "Drive on! Drive on, damn you, or I'll blow your head off!"

The fat man gave a gasp of fear and took his foot off the brake. The car bounded forward, nearly jerking the Duke off the running-board, and they sped past two blocks with the cries of their infuriated pursuers fading in the distance behind them.

But the advantage gained was only a temporary one. The thoroughfare ahead was half-blocked by the débris of a fallen building, and opposite it a large section of the road had given way, owing to a bomb that had torn up twenty yards of pavement.

Too late de Richleau ordered his commandeered Jehu to wheel left down a side turning. The car was already heading for the narrow gap between the heap of rubble and the crater. A careful driver could have made the passage

E

easily, even with a much larger vehicle, but the Jew, either through fright or with a deliberate courage which might easily have cost him his life—the Duke never learned which—swerved too far to the left; his front off-wheel went over the lip of the crater, the car lurched heavily and stopped with a violent jerk that hurled de Richleau from his precarious perch into the middle of the roadway.

His gun was jolted from his hand, but did not go off because the safety-catch was still on. With bruised knees and badly scraped hands, from which the blood immediately began to ooze, he picked himself up. One glance at the car showed him that it could serve him no further. Waiting only to grab up his pistol, he dashed round the edge of the crater which had proved his undoing and down the side street.

Short as it was, the lift on the car had enabled him to regain his breath; but now the fat Jew and his girl-friend were yelling "Murder!" and raising a new hue-and-cry; and, as the Duke shot round the corner, he caught a glimpse of his original pursuers, their numbers augmented by scores of people, racing up the street.

As he ran on he was now in a mood to shoot anyone who attempted to bar his path. Shortage of breath was the one and only thing calculated to make de Richleau really lose his temper. It affected him even when he had to walk upstairs. Two flights were his limit, and if it ever proved necessary for him to pant up a third he was in no mood to be argued with.

Ahead of him were two colourfully dressed and well-rouged ladies; evidently out, war or no war, to find gentlemen friends with whom to pass a quiet but lucrative Sunday afternoon. The cry of "Spy! Stop the spy!" had been taken up behind him. As the ladies caught it the clicking of their high heels ceased upon the pavement, and they turned about.

He charged straight at them, waving his gun threateningly as he came on. One of them gave a shrill scream and jumped for a nearby doorway, but the other stood her ground. As he swerved to pass her, she lifted her heavy handbag and, swinging it with all her force, caught him a terrific clout on the side of the head.

The blow took him off his balance and all but sent him flying. With one foot across the other he lurched out into the roadway, lipsticks, powder-compact, cigarettes and *zloyties* cascading down his shoulders. By a miracle he righted himself and fled on down the street.

Swerving round another corner, he momentarily shook off his pursuers. Still the three o'clock quiet of the Sunday afternoon continued to be his salvation. Every new street he entered was warm, somnolent and almost deserted, its stillness scarcely broken except for the hum of a Nazi reconnaissance aircraft that glinted silvery in the sun, high in the blue skies overhead. Yet, in each, after only a moment the drone of the plane was drowned by the angry shouts of the pursuing mob, more windows were thrown open, more people appeared from doorways, alleys and side turnings to sprinkle the vista ahead as though called up by some magical conjuration.

As he turned the corner the street seemed free of traffic, yet before he had covered twenty yards a single-decker bus rolled past him. It was almost empty and moving only at a moderate pace in order to avoid the bomb-holes and litter which here and there partially blocked the road. Transferring his pistol from his right hand to his left, the Duke put on a sudden spurt, grabbed the rear rail of the bus and swung himself on to it.

The conductor was standing on the platform. As the bus had passed the turning out of which the Duke had come he had had his back to it, so he had not seen the running crowd that was just about to debouch from its end. But the Duke's now apoplectic face and the gun that he was clutching in his hand showed clearly enough that he was on the run, and the conductor jumped to the reasonable conclusion that the police were after him. Before the fugitive had time to cover him he had seized the bell-pull and jerked it four times, for the driver to stop.

For a moment de Richleau stood on the platform, half-doubled up, gasping like a fish out of water as he strove to regain his breath; then he pointed his weapon at the man and panted hoarsely: "Pull—pull that bell again! Signal your driver to go on!"

The conductor backed away, simply putting up his hands above his head as though he had not understood. Both he and the driver had now heard the shouts of the oncoming crowd. In vain the Duke pulled the bell himself; the bus was slowing down.

The idea of forcing the driver to drive on at the point of the pistol flashed into de Richleau's mind, but he abandoned it almost as soon as it occurred to him. There was a metal partition between the passenger compartment and the driver's seat, so he could not get at the man to threaten him, except by getting off the bus. With the pack running hard behind them too much time would be lost before he could force the fellow to set his vehicle in motion again. As the bus jolted to a halt he jumped off and began to run once more.

The lift on the bus had given him a brief respite and enabled him partially to recover his breath, but he knew that he could not keep going much longer. To his dismay he saw that two hundred yards ahead the street was half-blocked again by a fallen house and that a group of four soldiers was approaching the part where it narrowed.

Suddenly a man ran at him from a nearby doorway. Swerving wildly, de Richleau thrust him off with the swift movement with which a rugby forward out for a try would have foiled a tackle by the opposing full back. The man staggered, overbalanced and sat down with a bump on the pavement, but in a minute he was up again and in hot pursuit only twenty yards behind the Duke.

Before he was halfway to the pile of débris his wind was failing him.

Every breath he drew seared his chest like a hot iron; the pain seemed intolerable. The blood was beating in his head, and his eyes were bulging. The swift running steps of the man he had pushed over were gaining on him, and ahead the four soldiers had halted with excited cries. They were spreading out at the far end of the bottleneck made by the rubble, to bar his passage.

The position seemed hopeless, but he was still determined to make a fight for it, and he knew the time had come when he must use his gun. If only he could have explained to these people, he thought with intense bitterness, that he was in real truth their devoted ally, whereas the scoundrel who had set them on to murder him had endeavoured to sell them out to their merciless enemies before the war had even started. But that was impossible, and without the faintest knowledge of the facts they were hounding one another on to do him to death. All right, then, anyone who had the temerity to join in the chase of an armed man did so at his own peril. Their blood was on their own heads.

Raising his pistol, he fired two shots at the little group of soldiers. Still running, as he was, he could not take deliberate aim at any of them, even had he wished, and they were the best part of a hundred yards away from him. Both shots went wide but had instantaneous effect. Two of the soldiers ran for cover in the nearest doorway, a third dived behind the heap of masonry; only one stood his ground at the far entrance to the bottleneck.

The man behind was now gaining rapidly on the breathless Duke. He had come up to within fifteen feet of his quarry. Half-turning, de Richleau fired again. With a curse, the man hesitated and dropped into a limping trot, the bullet having grazed his thigh.

As he had turned to fire, the Duke had glimpsed the part of the street which lay behind him. It was now half-filled with running people; two hundred at least had joined in the chase. Mack's car was in the centre of them, but could not forge ahead, or it would have run down some of the leading half-hundred. Well out in the front, a policeman and the young sailor were running neck to neck barely fifty paces behind the now wounded man.

Ahead the soldier still stood squarely in the centre of the gap, and one of his comrades, regaining his nerve, had come out of the doorway to join him. A pistol cracked somewhere in the rear, and its bullet whistled past the Duke's head. As he had started the firing himself he could not blame the marksman.

He was now in the bottleneck, but he felt nearly done and was practically certain that he no longer had the strength left to evade or fight off the two soldiers. On a sudden inspiration he swerved and began to scramble up the great heap of rubble.

An instant later he was cursing himself for his folly. The bricks and broken stone slipped and slithered beneath his feet. He felt that he would have stood a better chance if he had shot one of the soldiers at point-blank range and sought to slip past the other. But it was too late to think of that now. The pile of débris rose at an increasingly sharp angle to a height of about twenty-five feet. He was not halfway up it before the panting, shouting mob arrived at its foot.

The policeman, the sailor and half a dozen other men began to scramble after him, but one of the soldiers won him a temporary respite by shouting: "Come back there! He's armed! He'll shoot you if you corner him! Leave this to us!"

As he yelled his warning he was quickly loading his rifle, but his comrade in the doorway across the street had had the same idea and was already raising his weapon to his shoulder.

The report of the rifle echoed above the tumult of the crowd. At the second the Duke heard it the bullet pinged upon a piece of brick which an instant before had been covered by his body. But now the crowd had rounded on the soldiers with cries of "Stop shooting! He's a spy—shooting's too good for him! We want him alive! Come on, boys; up you go! Lynch him! Lynch him!"

As the leaders of the mob began to climb again de Richleau, half-blinded by sweat and dust, heaved himself up on to the top of the pile. He was now faced by the remains of an interior wall of the gutted house in which an open door hung crookedly, still supported by one of its hinges. To scale the mound he had had to thrust his pistol into his pocket. With a torn and bleeding hand he pulled it out again.

He was old enough to face most forms of death with a certain equanimity and he had always hoped that when his time came he would die cleanly and quickly from a bullet; but one type of death that he had never visualized for himself was to be torn limb from limb by a hooligan-incited crowd driven temporarily insane by the hardships and horrors of relentless bombing. It seemed now that such a fate had unquestionably been reserved for him, but the idea of mob-law, whether applied to himself or anyone else, had always filled him with intense repugnance. Even half-crazy as he had been driven by breathlessness and pain, he had instinctively recoiled from the thought of killing the soldiers who had courageously barred his path down in the street; but no such scruples weighed with him one iota where this human pack, that was surging up to overwhelm him, was concerned. Levelling his pistol, he emptied its remaining contents into the mass of struggling figures halfway up the mound.

One screamed and slumped upon the slope of broken bricks; another threw up his arms and pitched backwards, carrying several of those nearest with him. A howl of rage and execration went up from the watching throng, which now blocked the whole street for a length of a hundred yards and was still rapidly increasing. But the rest of the climbers stopped in their tracks, not knowing that the Duke had now exhausted his ammunition.

Seizing this new advantage as a last forlorn hope, de Richleau stumbled

to the gaping doorway in the ruined wall.   Beyond it the further side of the
house had also collapsed from another bomb in the same stick as that
which had brought down its front.   The ruin was open to the heavens;
the next standing wall was a good fifty yards away; all trace of the room
beyond the doorway had disappeared, except for a small square landing
from which led down a narrow flight of partially wrecked stairs.

The stairs descended in two flights to a brick-scattered tiled floor on the
ground level, which had doubtless been the hall of the building.   The banisters
had disappeared, and part of the lower flight had been blasted away, leaving
a gaping hole through which could be seen some stone steps leading to a
cellar.   At a normal time no man in his senses would have risked stepping
out on to the rickety landing without a rope round him and companions to
check his fall, if the loose boards should collapse beneath him.   But for the
Duke no hesitation was possible; death from a hundred fists and boots was
following hard on his heels.   The mob would have recovered its courage in
another few moments, and, more infuriated than ever by the casualties he had
caused, it would resume its remorseless man-hunt.   Still panting from his
exertions, he dived through the doorway, and, keeping as close to the wall
as possible, ran towards the stairs.

He was three steps down when there was a sudden grinding noise, then a
long loud creak, and the top flight gave way under his feet.   For a moment it
sank quite slowly, then in a flurry of splintered wood, dust and plaster it
crashed into the hall below.   As it fell de Richleau slid sideways from the
wall and pitched into the already broken lower flight, which bore his weight
for a second, then collapsed, sending up a great cloud of flying particles as its
fall was abruptly arrested by the stone steps of the cellar.

Instinct coupled with the still present thought of his pursuers made the
Duke scramble up at once.   Coughing, spluttering and half blinded by the
dust, he thrust aside the laths and splintered wood with which he was surrounded and crawled out on to the tiled floor.   It was only as he got to his
feet that he realized with amazement that he had suffered no serious injury.
He was scratched and bruised in a dozen new places, but the double check
in his fall had saved him from disaster.

Still coughing, and with more agonizing pains than ever racking his lungs,
he peered through the dust cloud in an endeavour to get his bearings.   The
wall through which he had come loomed dark and tall on his right, just in
front of him a part of the hole over the cellar steps still gaped open, and to
his left in the side wall of the hall he could discern a narrow archway, the
lower part of which was filled with rubble.

Again the shouts of the hunters came from above him; they had now
scaled the mound, and in another moment the foremost of them would be
peering down through the doorway that now led nowhere, to see if their
quarry had killed himself in his fall.   The dust clouds gave the hunted Duke

momentary cover as he forced himself to assess the respective merits of the half-blocked archway and the cellar steps as a means for further prolonging his precarious existence. The archway might be entirely blocked further up, whereas the cellar was much less likely to be obstructed; on the other hand, it might not have any other entrance. In either case he might be caught like a rat in a trap, so there seemed little to choose between them. His swift deliberation was decided by the thought that, if die he must, it was better to do so above ground than in some noisome hole, so, choking with the dust as though his lungs would burst, he staggered towards the archway.

Barking his shins and ankles afresh on the pile of bricks, he floundered over them into a long, dim passage, which, to his immense relief, was lit by faint daylight ahead.

At a shambling trot he ran along it, knowing that, although the fallen staircase would hold up his self-appointed executioners for a brief spell, they would soon find means to continue the pursuit by lowering themselves down the wall.

The passage ended in a half-open, nail-studded doorway. Beyond it lay a small stone-floored room with narrow, mediaeval windows set in thick stone walls. It was furnished only with a hideous pitch-pine cupboard, three wooden chairs and a deal washstand, from which most of the paint had flaked; but it showed no signs of bomb damage, except that most of the small panes in the leaded windows had been blown out. On a peg on a further door hung the black cassock and biretta of a Roman Catholic priest.

Crossing the room, the Duke cautiously pulled open the door, half-fearing that it might give on to another street, where he would find some of his enemies awaiting him; but on the further side of the door lay a burnt-out church. The walls were still standing, but the roof was gone, and its charred beams lay in blackened heaps on piles of ashes in the nave that must once have been rows of pews.

After one swift look de Richleau pulled the gown from the peg and slipped it over his torn and filthy clothes. As he snatched at the biretta and put it on his head he caught the first crunch of brick on brick, and knew that some of his pursuers were already scrambling over the heap of débris at the far end of the passage.

Slipping through the door, he tiptoed to the charred steps, taking his spectacles from his pocket as he did so. One glass had cracked across, and the other had disappeared entirely, but he put them on and, crossing himself swiftly, knelt down before the high altar in an attitude of prayer.

He was so exhausted that he knew himself to be utterly incapable of further effort. His one chance now was that, on entering the church and finding a priest immersed in his devotions, the mob would assume that their intended victim had eluded them and taken another line of escape. If they questioned him his broken glasses, his face covered with dirt and sweat, and his lacerated hands would prove an immediate give-away. He could only trust in the widespread devoutness among the Polish people and hope that it would prevent them from disturbing a priest at his prayers. Running feet sounded in the little robing-room, the door was thrown open, and the mob dashed in.

The Duke had only just got over his violent fit of coughing, brought on by the dust, and his lungs were still paining him terribly. Desperately he sought to control his heavy breathing. His head was aching as though a hammer were rhythmically pounding on the brain inside it, and his body was so bruised that it seemed to throb all over. He would have given all the treasures of his Curzon Street flat at that moment for it to be safe for him to take the weight off his battered knees and lie down unmolested on the cold stone. But his only hope of safety lay in maintaining his present attitude with absolute stillness.

The trampling ceased. The leading members of the crowd halted. There were cries and questions from those still jammed in the little room behind, and gruff calls for silence from those in front who could see the kneeling figure.

For what seemed an eternity to de Richleau he knelt before the altar, as utterly still as if he had been turned to stone. Vaguely he endeavoured to pray, but he needed every ounce of his will-power to keep himself from slumping down in a faint. In an agony of suspense he waited until the trampling of feet on the stone floor of the blitzed church sounded again. The footsteps receded, and the church became deadly still, but even then he dared not relax his pose for some moments for fear that a few of the crowd had remained behind and were still watching him. At last he turned his head very slightly and peered between his fingers; there was no one there. With a groan he slid forward on to his face.

At least five minutes elapsed before he moved again. He was only semi-conscious, but he had fought a great silent battle to prevent himself from passing out, and he had won. Exhausted and shaken by pain as he was, he still had a job to do—a job not only of the utmost urgency, but one which would require sound, skilful planning at short notice and all the clear-headed initiative that he could bring to it.

Loss of breath was the one thing which caused the Duke's capable brain to cease functioning. As long as he was gasping for air it positively refused to work, except on matters concerned with his immediate safety. During the less exacting moments of his flight a dozen questions had flashed into his mind. What was Mack doing in Warsaw? Was he still a member of the Polish Government? Had he really wished to secure his persecutor's arrest, or had he been sharp enough to appreciate that by raising the cry of "Spy!" the mob would secure him his revenge without his having to concern himself in the matter further? Was his return to Warsaw only a flying visit on some official business, or did he intend to remain there? Had he, perhaps, never left the capital? How was his presence likely to affect the plans and safety of his recent captors?

While he remained breathless and with his heart hammering as though it would burst, de Richleau had been utterly unable to assess any of these possibilities, and he was still in no state to do so. On the few previous occasions on which he had placed a similar, if lesser, strain upon himself he had found himself incapable of coherent thought for at least an hour afterwards. But he did know one thing. He had got to get back to the Lubieszow mansion and warn his friends there of Mack's presence in Warsaw with the least possible delay.

With an effort he sat up, and slowly got to his feet. Swaying slightly, he looked first round the roofless church, then down at his newly acquired habit. The priest who owned the cassock must have been a tall man, as it came well down past the Duke's ankles and partially hid his scraped and dusty shoes: a circumstance for which he was devoutly grateful. With the black biretta he was wearing on his head this clerical disguise could hardly have been improved upon; but the spectacles had served their purpose by their side-pieces showing as he had knelt with his hands covering his face in prayer, and the fact that one of the lenses was broken and the other missing would only attract unwelcome attention; so he took the spectacles off and put them in his pocket.

Crunching his way through the piles of ashes and charred wood, he went down the nave to the west end of the church, where he found one of the side doors unobstructed. With his lacerated hands thrust into the ample sleeves of the cassock, and his head bowed as though in pious meditation, he walked out into the street. Evidently the mob had not come this way and were still hunting for him in the cellars under the fallen staircase, as the Sunday-afternoon quiet here remained unbroken. In his first glance around he caught sight of a clock on a still undamaged building. Its hands stood at twenty past three. At first he thought that it had stopped, as it seemed impossible to him that barely a quarter of an hour had elapsed since Mack had shouted to the police and he had had to run for his life; but as he advanced towards the big dial he saw that the clock was going.

As he turned into the next street and with returning strength began to increase his pace, his ear caught a sound now all too familiar to him at night, but not at that hour of the day. It was the deep, heavy throb of bombers, and a second later the air-raid sirens began to wail.

Evidently, now the Germans had overcome the last vestige of Polish resistance in the air, they had decided to step up their attacks on the doomed city by daylight raids as well as nightly ones. The Duke's first reaction was to curse the Germans as he had done a hundred times in the past four weeks; but on second thoughts it entered his still dull brain that an air raid at this moment might prove to his advantage. During it Mack would certainly remain under cover, and that might give the time now so desperately needed to take precautions against him. The air raid, too, was an adequate excuse to any passersby for a priest to be seen running through the streets, and while carefully husbanding his renewed resources de Richleau broke into a gentle, loping trot.

The sirens ceased, the distant throbbing increased to a steady roar. Bombs began to crash somewhere across the river in the Praga district. De Richleau dropped back into a walk. The explosions grew nearer. An air-raid warden yelled at him to take cover, but he ignored the man's shouts and began to run again. The bombs were now falling near the Zamek, and, fearing that one might fall on Jan's mansion, the Duke reverted to his fluent cursing of the Nazis.

As he crossed the square he could see the Heinkels and Dorniers overhead. They were flying quite low, and some of them, having already unloaded their bombs, suddenly dived to machine-gun the roofs and streets.

The wicked rat-a-tat-tat was followed almost instantly by the sharp click of the bullets on stone and their whine as they ricocheted in all directions. A burst narrowly missed the Duke, sending up little puffs of dust and stony splinters all round him. His chest was hurting again, but he fought down the pain and ran on, until he reached the back entrance to the mansion's courtyard, which he had been using since he had assumed a dual personality. Panting and grey-faced, he fumbled for a key to a little side door with which Borki had provided him.

As he got the door open another stick of bombs came whistling down near by, so that the whole house seemed to rock to its foundations; but it proved the last in this attack, and the roar of the raiders' engines was already growing fainter in the distance.

Making for the back stairs, which he now always used on his nightly visits, the Duke floundered up them. They proved almost the last straw, and by the time he reached the landing he was choking for breath again.

Staggering to the door of Richard's room, he threw it open just as the "All Clear" sounded. Richard was sitting up in bed, and, as de Richleau had expected, Marie Lou was with him. Both of them stared in amazement at the dirty, haggard face and the priestly garments of the figure that had so suddenly burst in upon them; then Marie Lou jumped to her feet and cried:

"Greyeyes! For a moment I didn't know you. Why are you dressed like that? What on earth has happened?"

The Duke practically fell into a chair and lay there, panting. After three deep breaths he gasped:

"Mack is after us! Now the air raid is over he may be here at any moment! We've got to get away from here immediately!"

Chapter XI

TOUJOURS L'AUDACE

"WE can't," replied Marie Lou promptly. "You know Richard can't be moved yet."

"He's got to be !" panted the Duke, still sobbing for breath.

"But it's impossible."

"Nothing is impossible—if—if life depends on it."

"Yours may; so you must leave us again at once, darling; now you've warned us of this new danger. But his depends on his staying where he is."

De Richleau feebly shook his head. "You don't understand. The risk of moving him is nothing like as great as it was a fortnight, or even a week, ago; and if Mack gets him God alone knows if he'll ever again be a free man."

"But, dearest," Marie Lou protested, "we agreed ages ago that, even if the Germans captured the city, they were unlikely to interfere with a bed-ridden invalid and his wife who was looking after him. Your case is different, and you've already made all your arrangements for going to earth in Professor Kucharski's flat—or has that cover been blown this afternoon?"

"No, the Professor is not involved in this, thank God."

"Then what's been the point of your spending all that time in the museum and only sneaking in here at nights, during the past week, if you can't make use of your hide-out now you need it ?"

"You don't understand," the Duke repeated with almost a wail; "it's not the Germans we're up against—yet; but Mack, who has turned up in Warsaw again and is out to revenge himself."

"Well, tell us what happened, darling, then we'll be able to judge the situation better. Your poor face *is* in a mess."

"I don't wonder, after what I've been through in the past hour. Mack spotted me on Marshal Boulevard and denounced me as a spy. I had to take to my heels, and before you could count ten there was a howling mob after me, thirsting for my innocent blood. They would have torn me into small pieces and cooked me for breakfast if I hadn't managed to get away. As it is, I had to half kill myself in evading their clutches, and in the end only the heaven-sent chance of finding this priest's rig-out in the robing-room of a bombed church saved me."

"How ghastly for you !" said Richard sympathetically. "But, in spite of that, I don't see what we've got to worry about at the moment. Hasn't it occurred to you that Mack set the mob on you with the deliberate intention of getting you killed before you could be captured, so that he would never be called upon to formulate a definite and official charge against you ? It seems to me that he's the chap who has got to do the worrying now that his little scheme has failed to come off. He'll find that he has landed himself in a pretty mess when you have copies of that document he signed sent in to President Moscicki and the rest of the Polish Government."

"Will he?" The Duke's brain was at last starting to work again. "I only wish you were right, but we've slipped up over that, my friend, and slipped up badly. As you know, the Polish Government left Warsaw a week ago tonight. With it there naturally departed all the foreign missions which were accredited to it, including, of course, the British Ambassador and his staff. Most, if not all of them, are now hundreds of miles away in Southern Poland, and we have no possible means of communicating with them."

"I see. So it's now no longer possible for you to have copies of the document handed to the right people?"

"No, I should have thought of that when the Government left Warsaw, but I naturally assumed that Mack had gone too, and that we should have no further bother with him."

"Have you any idea what he is doing in Warsaw?"

"Not the faintest. Perhaps he is still prepared to act as a stooge for the Nazis and will attempt to form a puppet government under their direction when they capture the capital. He may have returned here to await their arrival. On the other hand, he may already have been sacked by his own people and come back to rescue what he can of his private property before the enemy completely encircles the city. In any case, he has little to fear from us now, and if he sets the police on to us as a gang of enemy agents, as he probably will, it will be his word against ours, and no sick-bed is going to save you. That's why, if we sit here arguing much longer, we shall all be caught and clapped into prison."

"Yes, you're absolutely right," Richard agreed, pushing back the bedclothes. "He may be on his way here now. We've got to get out, and be damn' quick about it."

"But, darling!" Marie Lou ran to him and put her hands on his shoulders to push him back. "You can't! You know the doctors said that we must not even think of moving you for at least a month."

"I know all about that, my sweet," Richard grinned up at her. "But because I didn't argue with them it doesn't mean that I was a willing subscriber to their opinion. Get me my clothes, there's a darling. I can get out of bed by myself."

"You can't, Richard! You can't! If you put your feet to the ground your fractured hip may give way again."

"That's all you know, light of my life. It's nearly three weeks since my crash now, and these Polish medicos did a pretty good job on my unfortunate carcase. But don't think that I've been gaga all this time just because I've had to stay in bed. That has given me plenty of opportunity to chew over all the less jolly bits of war news, and I made up my mind a long time ago that, when the Germans got to Warsaw, they weren't going to find me in it. Ever since that little night nurse left us I've been testing out my rickety limbs and exercising the muscles a bit. These past four nights, while you two innocents have been sound asleep, I've made the tour of this nice large bedroom unaided."

"Richard! You haven't!" cried Marie Lou, aghast.

"I certainly have, my poppet. Of course, I have to cling on to the furniture for support, but that makes it all the more exciting. It's rather like a game we used to play as children, where you have to get all round the room without touching the floor; but in my case it was just a matter of getting from piece to piece."

"But you must have been crazy. If you'd fallen . . ."

"I'm only crazy about you; and, in any case, I didn't, darling. If we fall into Mack's clutches we won't stand much chance of getting out of Warsaw before the Nazis arrive; and then the moment I'm fit enough they'll pop me into a concentration camp. That's what I've been trying to take precautions against. In spite of the climate, I have a definite preference for wintering in England, now there's a war on. When you've helped me on with my bags it will be interesting to see if I can get downstairs under my own steam."

"Oh, you're crazy, but I love you!" Marie Lou threw her arms round his neck and kissed him. The Duke, meanwhile, had hoisted himself out of his chair and was saying:

"Well done, Richard! Well done! To hear you talk like that has been as good as a magnum to me, and, God knows, a few moments ago I needed one badly enough. What a relief, too, to have you back in the game, sane and determined as ever, even if you do have to lie up most of the time."

"It's my reward for being a good boy and taking my nasty tonic," laughed Richard.

"It's Jan's good red Burgundy that I've ordered for you every day. That's the stuff to make new blood. It's that and your own good British guts that have made a live man of you again so quickly."

When they had helped Richard on with most of his clothes the Duke sponged his own face and hands in the fixed basin and, leaving Marie Lou to finish dressing her husband, hurried from the room, feeling much more his own man, to arrange about transport.

Downstairs he unearthed Borki, told him what had happened, and went into swift consultation with him.

"To leave in our ex-prisoner's car would surely add to the risk of capture," said the fat major-domo.

"Yes. That's one of the points that worries me," agreed the Duke. "But we've a long journey to make, and the military have already commandeered all the cars that were for sale in Warsaw."

"Why should you not take my master's shooting-brake? He would wish it, I know. Normally, we keep it in the country, but it was brought up for a thorough overhaul a few weeks before war broke out. It's in tiptop condition now and is a good, stout vehicle. Besides, we could remove some of the seats and put in a bed for Mr. Eaton. He would travel much more comfortably that way."

"Excellent! Nothing could suit us better." De Richleau clapped his rotund companion on the shoulder. "How soon can you get it ready?"

"In ten minutes—a quarter of an hour, perhaps, if we must take out some of the seats to get mattresses inside."

The Duke glanced anxiously at his watch. He had been in the house a quarter of an hour already. It was most unlikely that Mack would come to search it unaccompanied. He would go first to Police Headquarters and would have to make some sort of statement before they would give him a squad of men to raid the place. It would have taken him ten minutes or so to reach the headquarters after the "All Clear" had sounded and another fifteen at least to find somebody in authority, tell his story and collect a squad of police. If they succeeded in getting away at all it looked as though they would only do so by the skin of their teeth.

"All right!" he said. "But hurry. Every moment counts."

As Borki called to his elderly henchman and hurried out into the courtyard, de Richleau made for the kitchen. Picking up two baskets, he strode past the astonished cook and entered the larder, merely remarking over his shoulder: "I'm sorry to have to raid you when supplies are so short, but we are leaving tonight and need some emergency rations."

A swift glance round showed him that Borki had proved an excellent *chef de commissariat* in spite of the recent difficulties of procuring food. A half-cut ham, a joint of pork, the remains of a goose, some tins of sardines, three lettuces, a dozen tomatoes, as many apples and four loaves of bread all left their marble shelves to find places in the Duke's baskets.

When he took them out to the courtyard he found the shooting-brake already facing the gate, and Borki puffing heavily as he helped the old groom to dismantle some of its seats.

Hurrying back to the house, the Duke slipped upstairs and thrust all his things pell-mell into his suitcase. By the time he got it out to the brake two good but narrow mattresses from the servants' quarters were being thrust into the vehicle. The next thing was to get Richard down.

He found that two maids had just finished doing the Eatons' packing for them, and while the girls carried the bags down, de Richleau and Marie Lou got Richard into a basket chair. Despite his protests they would not let him try to walk, and, thrusting two broomsticks through the basketwork of the chair to make a sedan of it, they carried him out to the yard.

The old butler had now appeared on the scene with a basket full of bottles.

The Duke had thought of visiting the cellar himself, but, much as he loved good liquor, had decided against it on account of the shortage of time.

"I sent him to get these," wheezed Borki. "I wouldn't have you leave my master's house and go thirsty on your journey."

"Borki, you're a man in a million!" cried the Duke, giving him another friendly pat on his huge back. "Jump in now, and we'll be off."

"But, *Excellence*, I am not coming with you."

"You must. The rest of the staff have nothing to fear if they answer the questions of the police truthfully, but our recent visitor will not have forgotten the part you played in helping us to prolong his stay here. You *must* come."

The others had already assisted Richard on to the makeshift bed. Marie Lou was seated beside him; the baskets of provisions and drink and the suitcases had also been stowed away, but Borki obstinately shook his head.

"No, my master left me in charge of the house; whatever happens, I cannot leave Warsaw."

"That's your affair," replied the Duke hastily. "But you must leave the house, anyhow for a few days. You would only deprive your master of your future service by remaining here now to be arrested. Quick! Get in."

"There's sense in that," Borki agreed with an unhappy glance round, and he clambered into the seat next to the driver's. As the Duke took the wheel there was a chorus of good-byes from the little group of servants, and shouts of thanks in return from the departing visitors. A minute later the brake was running smoothly out of the back entrance of the courtyard.

Having turned the car north towards the Jewish quarter, as the direction in which they were least likely to run into Mack if he were already on his way from Police Headquarters, the Duke said to Borki: "Do you intend to remain in Warsaw, even if the Germans occupy the city?"

"Yes, *Excellence*. It is only by staying on that I can hope to protect my master's property."

"Then I suggest that you should remain under cover for the next few days with relatives or friends. It is myself and Mr. and Mrs. Eaton that our late prisoner will be most anxious to catch. When he finds that you have gone I don't think he will make any great effort to find you, and the police are desperately overworked these days. It should not be difficult for you to contact some of the servants, and they will let you know when they think it safe for you to go back to the house. Have you anyone in mind with whom you could pass the next few nights?"

Borki pulled thoughtfully at his little pointed beard. "I think I will go to my sister's. She has a house of her own out by the Gol Station, on the other side of the river. My size makes me a conspicuous figure, but I can sit in the garden all day there, and there will be no gossiping *concierges* or apartment servants to talk of my presence."

"Good. Then I will take you there. Has your sister's house, by any chance, a garage?"

"Yes. My brother-in-law is a timber merchant and a prosperous man. His business adjoins the house, and he has a garage for three lorries as well as his own car."

"Would it be possible for us to leave the brake there for a few hours? I have some business still to attend to, so I do not mean to leave Warsaw until to-night."

"But yes, *Excellence.* There will be ample room, and you will be welcome, I am sure."

"Thank you, Borki. That's a big help."

Having run through a few streets, they now turned right towards the river, and, on reaching the embankment, turned right again until they came to the great Alexander Bridge, by which they crossed the Vistula. On its far side they headed north again. When they were opposite the Gol Station, now a battered wreck from the German bombing, Borki began to give directions, and a few minutes later they pulled up in a quiet street at the entrance to a timber yard. Next to it there was a two-storeyed house, with shattered windows, but otherwise undamaged, that stood a little way back from the road in its own trim garden.

Borki hoisted himself out, and, on going up to the front door, learned from a plump maid that his sister, Madame Wojciechowski, was from home and not expected back until the evening; but, recognizing him as her mistress' brother, the girl said that he and his friends must make themselves at home until Madame's return. An elderly foreman was found who opened the yard gates for the brake, and it was run into the garage, Richard remaining in it while the others went into the house.

The maid insisted on serving them with coffee and biscuits, although these were already becoming luxuries in the half-devastated city. They partook of them on a verandah at the back of the house, and when they had finished the Duke asked Borki if he could arrange for him to have a very badly needed bath, on which the major-domo left them to see about it. Quite apart from the fact that he really wanted a bath, de Richleau had deliberately raised the matter because he also wanted as soon as possible to have a word alone with Marie Lou.

Having led her out into the small but pleasant garden, directly they were out of earshot of the house, he asked:

"What jewels have you got with you, Princess?"

"Not very many. My pearls are not real ones, they're copies I had made some years ago to take on our trips abroad. I have the sapphire clasps Richard gave me, a diamond brooch, two bracelets and three rings. Most of the Schulimoff jewels are in the bank at home."

"Which would it distress you to part with least?"

"Why, are you in need of a big sum of money?"

"I need two or three hundred pounds, at least. It is, of course, to help us get safely out of the country. Communications have now broken down so badly that I don't think Mack will find any means of cancelling the *laisser-passers* that I forced him to sign; so once we are clear of Warsaw we ought to be all right, as long as we are in territory still held by the Poles. Bu' the Russian invasion of Eastern Poland may complicate things for us further south as the Russians may have occupied the territory adjacent to the Rumanian frontier by the time we get there."

"Then you have been thinking up some way to get us through the Russian lines?"

De Richleau smiled ruefully. "I haven't had much time to think about it so far. The Russian invasion only started this morning, and I've been pretty fully occupied this afternoon. Still, before Mack set the mob on to me I had been considering it in a mild sort of way. Of course, it did not seem a matter of any urgency then, so I didn't get very far. Anyhow, the only line that occurred to me requires a fair sum of money, or its equivalent, so, much as I hate to do it, I'm afraid I'll have to ask you to part with some of your jewels."

"That's quite all right, dearest," Marie Lou smiled up at him. "I'm far better off for trinkets than most women. You can have the lot if it will help to get us home; but I'd like to keep the clasps that Richard gave me, unless you need them very badly."

"Of course. One of your bracelets should be quite sufficient, but I had better take the diamond brooch as well to be on the safe side."

Marie Lou believed in always carrying her jewels on her person when she travelled, and, lifting her tweed skirt, she slid her hand into a specially constructed pocket beneath it. After a little fumbling, she produced the two articles and handed them over. They then went back to the house.

Borki appeared, to say that the Duke's bath was ready. Upstairs, on undressing, he found that he was scraped and bruised in a dozen different places. But his hurts were only superficial, and the hot water did much to lessen the ache in them. As soon as he was dressed he went with Marie Lou round to the garage to see Richard and, after telling them that he hoped to be back in three to four hours, set out towards central Warsaw.

He had some distance to cover, but his thoughts were now moving rapidly again, and his steps kept pace with them. As he was still wearing the priest's cassock and biretta he had little fear of being recognized, unless he was unfortunate enough to come face to face with Mack; so he took the shortest route and contented himself with giving the occupants of the few cars that approached him a keen scrutiny while they were still some way away.

On reaching the Zamek he walked down a street on the opposite side to the direction in which Jan's mansion lay, and soon afterwards entered the region where most of the Foreign Embassies and Legations were situated.

The majority of those that had not suffered severely from bomb damage now had their shutters closed, and he knew that all their principal personnel would have departed from Warsaw with the Government a week before, or very soon afterwards. However, he felt reasonably confident that in some of them junior officials would have been left behind to clear up.

He had decided that his first bet should be the Turks. They had long had close relations with the Poles, even continuing to recognize Polish sovereignty long after the partitions had expunged from the map an autonomous Polish State, and their Embassy was one of the largest in Warsaw. Moreover, they were one of the few peoples who could be said to have reasonably good relations with the Russians.

But at the Turkish Embassy he drew blank. A wooden-faced porter who had been left in charge informed him that the Ambassador had departed with all his staff on the previous Monday.

His next bet was the Bulgarians, as they were also on good terms with Moscow, but when he reached their Legation he found that it had been reduced to an empty shell. It then occurred to him to try one of the small Baltic States that bordered on Russia, and the first of their Legations that he came to being that of the Esthonians he rang the front-door bell.

As no one came to the door he rang again and, after waiting for a few minutes, had just decided that the house must be empty when it was opened by a fair, square-faced man of about forty, with masses of tiny wrinkles round his bright blue eyes.

"Well? What can I do for you, Father?" he asked in Polish, naturally assuming from the Duke's garb that he was a priest.

"May I know whom I have the pleasure of addressing?" enquired the Duke blandly.

"My name is Fincks, and I am the Second Secretary here."

"Then, Monsieur Fincks, I should like to discuss a very urgent matter with you ; so I trust that you are not too busy to grant me a few moments of your time?"

The wrinkles round the blue eyes gathered in a quick smile. "I am not in the least busy, Father. I only wish I were ; but the moment my Chief and the rest of his staff drove away to join the Government our routine here came to a dead stop, and, of course, all sensible Esthonians left Warsaw days ago. I remained here myself only because my wife is in hospital and cannot be moved. Come in, and I will help you in any way I can."

The Esthonian led de Richleau upstairs to a pleasant, book-lined room on the first floor, and when they were seated he said : "Well, Father ? Tell me about this urgent affair of yours."

"I have come," said the Duke calmly, "to buy your car."

"Really !" Monsieur Fincks' eyebrows shot up as he replied somewhat coldly : "I'm afraid my car is not for sale."

"Ah!" said the Duke. "But I only require a very small piece of it, and, having taken that, I propose to return the car itself to you as a free gift."

The Secretary sat back and crossed his legs. De Richleau could almost read the thoughts flickering through his mind. "This poor priest is not all there. Bomb-shock perhaps? Anyhow, he seems quite a harmless sort of madman, and it would be best to humour him." After a moment he said:

"How did you know that I had a car?"

"I didn't," the Duke admitted with perfect frankness, "but I am delighted to hear that my hopes are justified. How much will you take for it?"

"Do you mean to say that you are prepared to buy it without even knowing what make it is? Perhaps the part that you want is not even fitted, or in the make I own quite unsuited to your requirements."

"Please don't concern yourself on that score. It is there, and its removal will in no way interfere with the running of your car. I should have given you that assurance to start with."

"Really, Father. You intrigue me enormously. What is this mysterious part that you are so anxious to acquire?"

"I want," said the Duke, "your *Corps Diplomatique* plates."

"Ho, ho!" exclaimed Monsieur Fincks, suddenly realizing that he was not dealing with a madman after all, and jumping at once to another conclusion—that the Duke was not a priest at all, but a secret agent.

"May I ask, *Father*," he emphasized the last word, "if you obtained your cassock and biretta by the same means as you propose to acquire my number-plates?"

"No," smiled the Duke. "I didn't pay anything for them at all; but you are quite right in your assumption that they are not mine and that I am not a priest."

Monsieur Fincks' freckled hand stretched out instinctively towards the telephone. "I think," he said with sudden sharpness, "that I ought to hand you over to the police."

"I greatly doubt if that telephone is working," remarked the Duke pleasantly.

"True. I'd forgotten. The line was severed days ago. However, I've still got a voice, and if you're not out of the house inside two minutes I propose to use it."

"That," said the Duke in his mildest tone, "would be a very great pity; because if you did you would never use it again." As he spoke, he produced his gun from under his cassock and went on quietly: "I came in peace, and I trust that you will allow me to go in peace. In either case the *Corps Diplomatique* plates of your car are going with me. I have made up my mind about that, and here is the price I propose to pay you for them."

As he finished speaking he withdrew his left hand from his pocket and threw Marie Lou's diamond bracelet on the desk-table behind which the astonished Esthonian was sitting.

For a moment Fincks stared at the little pile of scintillating gems as they flashed and sparkled in the afternoon sunlight, then he picked up the bracelet to examine it more closely.

"It is a lovely thing," he said at last, "and it must be worth a lot of money. It is real, of course ?"

De Richleau nodded. "Please accept my word for that. The lady to whom it belongs bought it from Van Cleff and Appels at Deauville, if my memory serves me. May I take it that I shan't need my pistol and can put it away ?"

"Your offer is certainly a tempting one," smiled the Esthonian. "But first I should like you to answer a few questions."

"Certainly."

"Your nationality ?"

"British."

"Are you in the pay of your Government ?"

"No, I'm not in anybody's pay."

"Why are you dressed as a priest ?"

"Because I want to get home to England. The first stage of my long journey lies through Polish territory, and the Polish Army is now disintegrating. In such a state all armies become more or less lawless. The Poles are a particularly devout people, and dressed as a priest I am far less likely to be held up and robbed or otherwise molested."

"Are you prepared to give me your word that if I let you have my number-plates you will not use them for any purpose which might harm my country ?"

"Yes, willingly."

"All the same, I think I must ask you why you are so anxious to obtain these plates."

The Duke drew the *laisser-passer* which he had forced Mack to sign for him from his pocket and handed it across, as he replied : "This, as you will see, is a *carte-blanche* to pass all posts and cross the frontier, signed by a member of the Polish Cabinet. That would have fulfilled all my reasonable requirements yesterday ; but it does not do so today. I propose to cross the frontier into Rumania, but by the time I get there the Russians may be in control of it. Therefore, I need something other than this Polish document to serve as a special credential with the Russians. It occurred to me that if I posed as a neutral diplomat on his way to rejoin his chief the Russians would allow me to proceed without argument."

The Esthonian nodded. "Yes. That is sound and plausible. If you were not in such a hurry you could easily have had *Corps Diplomatique* plates made for you at any garage and fitted them on yourself ; so I see no reason why I shouldn't sell you mine."

"Thank you. I am most grateful to you."

"It seems rather that I should thank you," said the Esthonian with a smile, pocketing the bracelet as he stood up. "Let's go down to the garage."

"There is just one other matter," the Duke remarked casually, also coming politely to his feet. "And it would be as well if we got it settled before we go downstairs."

"Oh! What is it?" Fincks' blue eyes narrowed a shade suspiciously.

"You mentioned that your poor wife was in hospital and gave that as a reason why you have not been able to leave Warsaw."

"Yes, that is so."

"Well, I have recently been in a somewhat similar difficulty, but in my case the invalid is a man friend to whom I am greatly attached. Incidentally, his wife has also stayed with him, and she is the lady who owned the bracelet which I now hope will soon be gracing your wife's arm."

"Thank you, yes. But what is it you want?"

"Simply that my friend has sufficiently recovered for us to attempt the journey in an emergency ambulance. But he is still a very sick man. Naturally, I want to avoid any delay as far as possible, and spare my friend the exhausting business of being questioned by minor officials. If by chance you doubt my story and have an hour to spare, I would willingly take you to see my friend."

"I don't doubt your story in the least, since you offer to take me to him. But what is all this leading up to?"

"If you were about to make the journey with your wife you would be able to spare her these annoyances I have mentioned, would you not?"

"Yes, I should certainly hope to."

"I think you would succeed, because, in addition to the *Corps Diplomatique* plates, you would have proper papers."

"Of course, and I take it you have your British passports?"

"Certainly. But the Russians are not showing any particular fondness for the British just now. In fact, their attack on Poland has virtually made them Hitler's ally, at all events for the time being. That was why I had in mind that it would be much more preferable for myself and my friends to travel as Esthonians. In fact the *Corps Diplomatique* plates will be almost worthless unless we have proper papers to support them. Would it be troubling you too much to ask you to provide three Esthonian passports for us?"

For a moment Monsieur Fincks stared at him, before he exclaimed: "Well, I'll be damned! Of all the impertinence!" Then he burst out laughing.

Having at last come to the real reason for his visit, de Richleau watched the Esthonian like a lynx, to see what his next reaction would be.

"*Toujours l'audace*," murmured the diplomat, when he had stopped laughing. "So that's what you really came for, eh? All this business about the plates was merely to get me interested."

"How can you think that of me?" smiled the Duke. "I have bought and paid for the number-plates already. This little matter of the passports is only a request which I trust you will grant to make a sick man's journey easier."

"If I did and were found out I would lose my job."

"There is not the least reason to suppose that you would be found out," de Richleau said, now speaking with the utmost seriousness. "I promise to destroy the passports immediately we are over the Rumanian frontier. Even if they fell into someone else's hands before that it is most unlikely that they would be traced back to you, as the issuing officer. If they were you could always say that I had forced you to give them to me at the point of my pistol. Much stranger and more terrible things are happening in Warsaw now, every day. Both of us may lose not only our jobs but our lives in the next raid. I would not ask it of you in normal times; but will you not please help me to get an injured man and a beautiful young woman out of this hell to which poor Poland has been reduced?"

"Yes," replied the Esthonian, without further hesitation, "I will. I don't know who the devil you are, but you're a better diplomat than any I've ever met. And you've convinced me absolutely. Esthonia is a little country, and I dread for it the fate that has overtaken Poland. All we ask is the right to live in peace and friendship with all other peoples, but now that the Great Powers have decided to fight it out I doubt whether we shall keep our freedom for more than a few months longer. Anyhow, while Esthonian passports still have the power to save decent human beings from the horror that Hitler has brought upon the world, they should be issued to anyone who wants them."

De Richleau did a very unusual thing for him. He silently extended his hand, and Monsieur Fincks clasped it firmly.

Half an hour later the Duke had in his pocket three old passports selected from a pile sent in for cancellation as being the most suitable on account of their descriptions. He also had an invitation to a reception at the Esthonian Legation held the previous month, on which Monsieur Fincks had written the name on the passport which he had chosen, and a number of letters that he was supposed to be taking on to one of Fincks' colleagues who had actually been killed by a bomb; while, under his arm, he carried a flat brown-paper parcel containing the *Corps Diplomatique* plates.

As they were about to part the Esthonian produced the bracelet, saying: "I don't think I ought to take this. It is worth several hundred pounds, and in any case at such a time decent people should help one another without thought of payment."

After a second's hesitation the Duke took it back. "If it were my own property I should insist on your keeping it, but as things are I can hardly refuse your generous gesture. However," he added, producing the brooch, "this is of considerably less value. Please accept it for your wife with our best wishes for her recovery. I am sure the lady to whom the jewels belong would wish you to retain some souvenir of us.''

"If you put it like that I should be very pleased to have it. Perhaps all too soon our safety may also depend on the few things of value which we could trade in an emergency."

"You really fear then that Esthonia may soon become involved?"

"Yes. Now that Stalin has invaded Poland the Germans and the Russians may be fighting for her carcase within a week. In a Russo-German war the three Baltic States make such a perfect jumping-off ground for a direct Nazi attack on the Soviet that Hitler is almost certain to seize all our ports, unless Stalin forestalls him. In either case, poor Esthonia will lose her freedom."

De Richleau nodded. "I fear you may be right. But if the worst happens the name in the Polish document I showed you is my real one, and I am not without friends in England. Should you seek refuge there do not hesitate to enquire for me, and we will do everything in our power to make your exile as pleasant as possible."

They shook hands once more, and the Duke set out on his long walk back to the northern outskirts of the city.

He reached his destination just before seven, to find that Madame Wojciechowski had returned and was now busy preparing supper for her unexpected guests. She was almost as thin as her brother Borki was fat and proved to be a silent, uncommunicative woman, who appeared interested in little except the running of her own house. Her husband, a grey-haired, thick-set man, joined them soon afterwards, and they all sat down to a good meal which Marie Lou had insisted on supplementing from the baskets that the visitors had brought with them. Richard had had a sleep during the afternoon, but his meal was carried out to him, as it was thought wiser not to move him from his makeshift bed in the brake unless it became absolutely essential to do so.

At half past eight they all went out to the garage, and, having said their farewells to the excellent Borki, who had proved such a stalwart friend to them, and to his relations, they started on their long and hazardous drive to the Rumanian frontier.

The Germans had now brought up heavy guns and were beginning their evening "hate" on the doomed city. Although they had not yet completely invested it, large formations of the enemy had established themselves at many points on its circumference, and some of their armoured spearheads were now reported to be as much as a hundred miles to the east. The whole situation was so confused that no one had anything but the vaguest idea of the enemy dispositions, and, although the Duke said nothing about it, he regarded capture by the Germans as a far more potent danger than the possibility of their coming to grief through any endeavours Mack might be making to catch them.

To minimize the chance of running into detachments of the enemy he drove them out of the capital through its north-eastern suburbs, then followed the bank of the Czarna river south-east to the little town of Okunew. During the short run of twenty miles they were challenged no less than eleven times. Any attempt to ignore these challenges in territory where German armoured cars and motor-cycle machine-gunners were known to be operating would have been the height of madness, and, as it was, on three occasions warning shots were fired over their heads.

Each time they were pulled up they waited in agonized suspense for their papers to be examined; but the production of their British passports and the *laisser-passers* that Mack had signed to go with each acted like a magic charm; so it was clear that in the widespread confusion it had proved quite impossible for him to circulate a general order for their arrest.

From Okunew they ran south through the night to Kotbiel, Garwolin and Deblin, all in the centre of Poland, but even then they were rarely out of earshot of artillery fire, and twice during this lap great flights of enemy bombers roared overhead on their way to devastate some unfortunate open town. Several times they saw the glow of burning villages on the horizon, where the Nazis had strafed Polish troops only a few hours earlier, and all the towns they passed through had had a share of the bombing.

There was not much traffic on the roads, yet throughout the night they were never free of people. Occasionally they met long files of Polish cavalry on the march or a battery of artillery, but the wayfarers were mostly pedestrians, or little groups of country people trudging beside one or two farm wagons. They did not seem to be moving in any particular direction but were just the terrible flotsam of war; city-dwellers who had been bombed out and were trying to reach friends in the country, or poor peasants whose farms had been ravaged, making for the towns in the desperate hope of finding safety there.

Soon after dawn a flight of Nazi marauders came over and machine-gunned the road from two hundred feet. De Richleau drove the brake in under some trees, and the heroes of the Luftwaffe had roared out of sight in less than a minute, but they left an old cripple, two peasant women, one of whom was carrying a baby at the breast, and a man in a bowler hat, lying mutilated and bleeding in the road.

Having done what he could for them, the Duke pressed on, and just before eight o'clock they entered the city of Lublin. It had taken them over nine hours to cover less than a hundred miles, but as de Richleau drew the brake up in front of a still undamaged café in the partially ruined main square he was well satisfied. It was more than probable that during the night they had passed within a mile or so of several enemy detachments from which only the darkness had saved them, and by this time he felt confident that they were well out of Mack's clutches.

The café was crowded with officers, but after a short wait they managed to get some hot coffee and sausage, which they eked out with their own provisions.

The eight hours that followed proved less exacting. They were passing through rich farmlands which the Germans were not yet attempting to occupy, and, to keep clear of their forces that were operating against the Polish industrial centres of the south-west, the Duke veered south-east, through Krasnystaw and Hrubieszow towards Brody. On crossing a bridge over the Styr, some ten miles to the north-west of Brody, the tollgate-keeper told them that he had heard from two people that the Russians were already in the city, so the Duke made a wide détour to the west by way of Krasroc with the intention of trying to reach Tarnopol for an early dinner.

But the distance proved too much for him. He had not yet fully recovered physically from the grievous strain he had been under the previous afternoon. It was now nearly forty hours since he had had any proper sleep, and, although Marie Lou had relieved him at the wheel for several long spells during the day, he was now all in. They pulled up on the grass at the side of a small lake a few miles outside Zloczow, and there, three hours later, just as dark was falling, the Russians found them.

The encounter proved far from a happy one, as the sergeant in charge of the Soviet tank, which had pulled up at the lake to renew its water supply, was both surly and illiterate. The *Corps Diplomatique* plates meant nothing to him, and he and his men were living on the land, so they promptly confiscated all the remaining provisions.

The Duke, who spoke Russian much better than he spoke Polish, argued and pleaded for some of the supplies to be left for his sick friend, in vain. Fortunately, however, another tank with an officer in it soon appeared on the scene. He was a small, bright-eyed man and looked as tough as they make them, but he was good-humoured and intelligent.

Having examined the Esthonian passports, he ordered the food to be given back, but his grin had a shade of cynicism in it as he returned the passports to the Duke, saying: "You won't need these soon. You'll have Soviet ones, and so will most of the other people in Europe."

Having been roused from their sleep, they had an early supper as soon as the Russians had left them, then pushed on again. They were pulled up twice more on the road to Tarnopol, but in the city itself they were not interfered with, although they found it in full Russian occupation. It was still only a little after nine when they passed through the town, so, refreshed by his sleep, the Duke determined to do the remaining seventy odd miles to the frontier and endeavour to get across it that night. They were only halted once more and, as on the two previous occasions, directly the Russians had examined their papers they proved not unfriendly and extremely punctilious.

As they neared the little frontier town of Zaleszezyki on the Dniester the road became more congested, and it was clear that a great number of people from all parts of Poland were also attempting to seek safety in Rumania. The dusty and dishevelled state of many of them showed that they had been on the road for several days, but these refugees were not sufficiently numerous to impede the progress of the car seriously, and they reached the town with half an hour still to go to midnight.

In spite of the late hour the narrow streets and small square were crowded with both pedestrians and vehicles, so the Duke began to take a pessimistic view of their prospects of getting over the frontier until the following day. But his *Corps Diplomatique* plates now proved of unexpected value to them. A stalwart Russian military police girl in a smart uniform, who was controlling the traffic in the square, spotted the plates immediately, held up the other traffic and smilingly directed him to the frontier post. For the girl the war had been on for less than thirty-six hours, and she was thoroughly enjoying this picnic campaign.

At the frontier post they met with equal politeness. Despite the number of people trying to get through and the fact that the Russian officials had only taken over that morning, they were handling the situation with efficiency and despatch.

Although de Richleau did not know it, many foreign diplomats accredited to the Polish Government had gone through during the past few hours, and, at present, the Russians had no quarrel with the smaller powers. He was directed to a special enclosure; only a cursory examination was made of the contents of the brake, and a smiling Russian waved them on without their having had to wait in the mile-long queue.

The Rumanian frontier guards were equally accommodating, as they, too, had passed many foreign diplomats through that day. To his amazement, soon after one in the morning de Richleau found himself twenty miles inside Rumania and just entering Cernauti, the capital of the Bukovina. Never did he remember having crossed a frontier so easily and so quickly.

But that they were now safe was their sole, if considerable, cause for congratulation. Czernowitz, as it used to be called, was crammed to capacity, and neither for love nor money could either food or a bed be found there. After half an hour of fruitless questing they decided that they had better make the best of things and both sup and sleep in the brake.

They were tired again from accumulated fatigue, but they still had ample provisions, and they opened the best bottle of the wine that Borki had given them from Jan's cellar. With it they celebrated their arrival in a still free country, which was so largely due to the Duke's planning, and drank to the success of "Operation—Golden Fleece". Then, thoroughly tired out, in spite of their makeshift accommodation, they fell sound asleep.

The following morning they woke at a little after seven. They had parked the brake in a crescent of middle-class houses, but from their exploration late the night before they knew that every spare foot of floor space in them was occupied by Polish refugees. The possibility of securing a bath or breakfast in any of these houses was zero, so they decided to eat their last sardines and remaining bread, then take the road for Bucharest.

They had accomplished their four-hundred-mile journey from Warsaw to Cernauti in just under twenty-nine hours, thus averaging fifteen and a half miles an hour exclusive of their three-hour halt. Considering the many hold-ups they had met with in the first part of their journey and the notoriously bad state of the Polish roads further south, it was by no means a bad performance; but in Rumania the trunk roads were far better, and they had every reason to believe that they would now be able to proceed unmolested, so they expected to achieve a much higher average. If all went well they had every hope of covering the three hundred miles to Bucharest before nightfall.

As they drove out of the city the congestion on the road soon lessened. Rumanian aircraft were patrolling the frontier, but their drone soon faded, and the brake sped smoothly through the peaceful farmlands of the Bukovina, still mercifully free of any signs of war. Their only worry now was the comparatively minor one that great clouds of dust made driving uncomfortable and delayed their progress when they had to pass other vehicles.

After covering forty miles they entered the valley of the Sereth, and the road rose steeply to wind its way through the mountains of Moldavia, which constitute the southern end of the great Carpathian range. All the lower levels were covered with vast forests, above which great rocky peaks reared their summits to the blue skies. It was a sparsely populated country of smiling peasant folk who waved to them in the pleasant villages through which they passed. Here and there in some charming but lonely bend of the valley stood an ancient monastery, but they did not house the cloistered communities such as usually inhabit them in more western lands. From time immemorial they had served as both centres of peasant industry and wayside inns for travellers passing through this lovely land, as yet almost unknown to globe-trotting tourists.

At midday they pulled up at one of these and after a meal rested for a while in its great sunny courtyard. Richard had so far sustained the journey well, as he had not been compelled to move from his mattress, but the Duke and Marie Lou were very tired. Nevertheless, anxiety to know what had happened to their friends, and particularly whether Lucretia had reached Bucharest or was still with Jan somewhere in Poland, drove them on.

At Focsani the country to their left began to open out and fall away towards the great marshy area of the Dobruja, in which lies the Danube delta, but the road steadily curved south-westward, hugging the foothills of the mountainous country on their right until they had passed through Rimnik and reached Ruzan. Here they left the mountains behind and entered the great Wallachian plain, driving across it to Ursitzem, which they entered at seven o'clock.

They had hoped to reach Bucharest in time for dinner, but the dust and hairpin bends skirting terrifying and unprotected precipices in the mountainous region through which they had passed had kept down their speed, and the fact that they had not slept in beds for the past two nights was now telling on them heavily; so they decided to feed in the town and do the last lap of forty odd miles after dinner.

The only inn they could find was a quiet, unpretentious place, but the landlord served them himself and produced a plain but excellent meal which they helped down with the strong resinous wine of the locality.

At nine o'clock the Duke and Marie Lou forced themselves wearily out of their comfortable chairs and went out to the brake to find that after his meal Richard had fallen asleep. He did not even turn over when the engine was started up, and he was still sleeping soundly when an hour later they entered the suburbs of Bucharest.

The Rumanian capital is one of the most delightful in the world, and it owes this largely to the fact that the great majority of its houses stand in their own gardens. In consequence, the city covers a great area; but in shape it is long and narrow. It is, in fact, mainly built about one immensely long street, the inner section of which, called the Calea Victoriei, is lined by nearly all the big blocks of office buildings, hotels and shops, and the Chaussée Kisseleff, a great boulevard on which stand most of the finest private residences, leading into it.

Some way down the Chaussée Kisseleff the Duke pulled up to ask a policeman the way to the British Legation.

De Richleau did not speak Rumanian, but nearly all well-educated people in the Balkans are able to talk a second language, which is usually German or French. The policeman called over a passerby, and between them they managed to supply the required directions.

At the Legation, which proved to be just off the Chaussée in the Strada Jules Michelet, the porter spoke enough English to tell them that Sir Reginald and Lady Kent were dining out, but he showed the Duke into a waiting-room and shortly brought one of the junior secretaries to him.

It transpired that during the past three weeks, owing to the war, they had had an exceptional number of callers, so at first the young man could not remember having seen Rex and Simon, but on the Duke's giving a closer description of them he exclaimed:

"Of course! I know the two you mean. They have been to see Sir Reginald several times and are, I feel sure, staying at the Athenée Palace."

"Has another friend of mine yet turned up here by any chance?" asked the Duke. "A young lady, the Condesa Cordoba y Coralles."

"Why, yes, poor girl."

"What do you mean by that?" De Richleau strove to hide his sudden alarm.

"Well, she is such a lovely person, and it's so sad that she should have been overtaken by such a terrible tragedy. She arrived here two days ago with her fiancé—a Polish airman. They hadn't been in Bucharest for more than two hours when he was knocked down and killed by a passing car."

Chapter XII

DEATH IN THE AFTERNOON

"Are you certain?" asked the Duke, aghast.

"I didn't actually see it myself," replied the young secretary, "although it happened right outside the Legation. The two of them were leaving just after having made their number with Sir Reginald; and, naturally, all of us here heard about it. His name was Lubitski, or something like that."

"Lubieszow," prompted the Duke.

"That's it. He wasn't killed instantly, but he was pretty badly knocked about the head, and he died soon after they got him to the hospital. The poor girl fainted, and some of our people brought her inside. Lady Kent took charge of her and kept her here for the night. Then Sir Reginald got into touch with her friends, and they came to collect her the following morning."

"She is at the Athenée Palace, too, then?"

"Yes. I suppose so."

"Thank you. Thanks very much," murmured de Richleau, still half-stunned by this terrible news. "I'll go there at once. When Sir Reginald comes in you might be good enough to tell him that the Duc de Richleau called, and say that I should consider it a great kindness if he would spare me half an hour tomorrow morning. Any message about time can be telephoned to me at the Athenée Palace."

His tiredness forgotten, but with slow steps, he rejoined the others in the brake and broke the sad tidings to them. Ten minutes later, Richard, now fully awake, was being moved from his bed to an invalid chair by the porters at the hotel. At the desk de Richleau learned that Lucretia was up in her room, but the others had gone out, and it was not known at what time they would be back.

It was now close on eleven o'clock, and, owing to the late hours that the upper classes in Rumania habitually kept, the gay crowd in the foyer was still drifting in to dinner, but the Duke hoped that Lucretia might be asleep. In any case, both he and Marie Lou felt far too done up to face her in her grief that night, or to wait up for Simon and Rex, who might quite possibly not return until two or three in the morning. Having left a message for their friends, they escorted Richard upstairs, and after making him comfortable went to their own rooms, where they wearily pulled off their clothes and flopped into bed.

De Richleau was wakened about nine o'clock by a house-call from Rex, who greeted him with restrained cheerfulness and asked him to come along to breakfast in the suite that he was sharing with Simon and Lucretia. Normally the Duke required very little sleep and, having just had the best part of ten hours, he felt quite recovered from the fatigue which he had been feeling all through the previous day. Slipping on his dressing-gown, he crossed the sitting-room that separated him from the Eatons and gently opened their door to peep in.

The heavy curtains were still drawn, but bright streaks of sunlight coming through their chinks faintly lit the room. Richard was awake and, raising himself on his elbow, whispered: "Hush! She's still asleep, and the last two days have taken *it* out of her pretty badly. I want her to sleep as long as possible."

"That's right," de Richleau whispered back. "I'm going along to Rex and Simon."

After a wash and shave he joined the others in their private suite. Lucretia was not present, but the two men were overjoyed to see him safe and well, as he was to see them; and it was not until they had given rein to their pleasure in their own reunion that Simon said:

"Not so long ago I'd have taken big odds against all six of us getting safely out of Poland. 'Fraid, though, that you don't find us in quite the mood for a celebration. As a matter of fact, we've got some pretty bad news for you."

"You mean about Jan? I know; they told me at the Legation last night. Is it really true?"

"Yes. 'Fraid so. Rex and I didn't know about it till the following morning. We went round to the hospital, but he had died within an hour of being brought in. A French-speaking doctor told us all about it. Van went right over his body, and he was so badly crushed that he had no chance."

"Poor Lucretia's real bad," Rex supplemented. "She was still all in when we went to collect her from the Legation, and they wanted to keep her there, but we figured that she'd be better with us. We wouldn't let her attend the funeral, so Simon and I were the only mourners. We bought a burial plot and tidied everything up as well as we could, though it wasn't all that easy, as neither of us could speak Rumanian, and the French around these parts is pretty queer."

"You'll find German useful with the middle classes," remarked the

Duke, as they sat down in a decidedly chastened mood to breakfast. "But, tell me, what was poor Jan doing in Bucharest? I should have thought he would have remained in Poland as long as the Polish Army was putting up a fight."

"We're keeping Lucretia as quiet as possible," said Simon. "Haven't liked to question her much. Seems, though, that all that was left of the Polish Air Force was brought down to the Rumanian border to protect the Government's new H.Q. Then, when the Ruskies decided to walk in, the Poles saw that the game was up and ordered their airmen to fly their planes over into Rumania. Preferred the idea of their being interned, I suppose, to their falling into the hands of the Nazis or the Bolshies."

"Yeah," Rex cut in. "That was the line they took, and, although Jan wasn't one hundred per cent, after his crash, he still felt up to flying a plane. Having gotten hold of one, and knowing that Lucretia wanted to join us as soon as possible in Bucharest, he took a chance with the Rumanian flyers that were shepherding the Poles down, foxed their patrols and flew her straight through."

"Didn't fancy the idea of Lucretia's being shut up in an emergency internment camp for several weeks, I expect," added Simon.

"Pretty risky, though," muttered the Duke through a mouthful of mushroom omelette. "They might easily have been shot down."

Rex shook his big, curly head. "No, slipping through these Rumanian boys would have been dead easy to an ace like Jan. They've got a few good pilots, but most of them are only enthusiastic amateurs, and their machines are just old crates. Besides, there would have been plenty more Poles in the sky to keep them busy, and they'd know that Jan would have to come down further on in the interior and be interned just the same. They probably thought he was some dumb cluck who didn't understand their signals. Still, the poor old chap is a gonner now, and it's Lucretia we've to worry about."

"Yes," said the Duke. "It seems doubly frightful that, having mourned him as dead ten days ago, she should have had him restored to her again, only to lose him now. We must get her back to England as soon as possible. Richard has made a marvellous recovery, thank God, but he will still be out of the game for some time to come, so I want Marie Lou to take him home. If Lucretia goes with them the two girls are experienced enough travellers to manage, and helping Marie Lou to look after Richard will give Lucretia something to occupy her mind, poor darling."

"I'll say it was a mighty fine feat your getting him out of Poland," said Rex, "and we're dying to hear how you did it."

"It's a long story, so do you mind if we leave that till later, and you tell me first what luck you've had with the Golden Fleece?"

"Good and bad." Simon jerked the narrow shoulders under his silk dressing-gown. "Sir Reginald has been very helpful—quite unofficially, of course. We've met Teleuescu, chap who owns them, several times. He's—er—well, a pretty tough customer, but he doesn't like the Nazis. Got a Jewish wife. Nice woman. Had tea with her the other day, and she's pushing the boats along in our direction for all she's worth. It's boodle that's the trouble."

"He's sticking out for a very big price, eh?"

"Pretty big. About four times what they're really worth. But that was to be expected. The good news is that he's prepared to deal at all."

"What is the hitch, then?"

"Trouble is, when we got here, we found that immediately after Britain's declaration of war, she froze all her assets, and most other countries followed suit. Consequence is none of us can now lay our hands on any ready cash or get the sort of credit that's needed to carry through a deal like this."

"How about an option? One should be able to secure that for a tenth of the capital sum, and once we have it there shouldn't be any great difficulty in persuading the British Government of the wisdom of taking it over from us."

"Um. We thought of that. In fact, those are the lines we're working on at the moment. But even the purchase of a thirty-day option needs a pretty tidy sum—about fifty times what the whole lot of us could raise by pledging our personal credit here in Bucharest."

"That's the devil, isn't it?" said the Duke meditatively.

"It certainly is," Rex agreed. "Simon can't get a nickel out of England, and I guess Lucretia will find it just the same with Spain. That leaves me as the White Hope at the moment. I've cabled my old man, and the wording of that cable was just as strong as they come. But it's a big wad of dollars to ask for, when I dared not put it in clear over the international wires what I was up to. We can only hope that he comes across, but it's trying him pretty high."

"When do you expect to hear from him?"

"Today, with luck. We've got another conference with old man Teleuescu this evening, and he's promised to have the option all drawn up for us to sign. We didn't dare to put him wise to it that we might not have the money, and he certainly won't play ball unless we can produce the cheque. So that's how we're situated right now."

"How about your own Legation? If Channock lets us down, would they be prepared to help you at all?"

"Nope. I was not acquainted with the American Minister here, but I got him to see me all the same. Simon and I agreed that no harm could come of my spilling the beans to him, because if he passes the idea on it will only be to the United States Government. If they decided to cash in on it, that would be all to the good. Some of us may not like Franklin D. Roosevelt's domestic politics, but he's no friend of the Nazis. Putting the half-Nelson on this barge traffic is just the sort of thing that might appeal to him. It's such a whale of a chance to give a hand to the British without having to enter into a public argument with all those isolationist diehards in the Senate, who are out gunning for him all the time. Anyhow, the Minister could suggest no line by which we might raise the cash to carry through the deal; and when I asked him to lend me a million bucks on my own personal say-so, he just burst his sides for laughing.''

"One can hardly be surprised,'' smiled the Duke.

"No, I've only just stopped laughing myself at the idea of asking him; but you never know your luck.''

De Richleau nodded. "I am hoping to see Sir Reginald this morning, but, of course, he is in exactly the same position as your man, and, however sympathetic he may be to our intentions, I don't see how he can help us financially. Anyhow, I'd better go and dress now, in case a call comes through from the Legation.''

While the Duke was bathing a call did come through, to the effect that Sir Reginald would be pleased to see him at twelve o'clock.

Marie Lou was now getting up, and when they were dressed she and de Richleau went along to see Lucretia, while Simon and Rex came in to talk to Richard.

Lucretia was up but lying on a sofa in her room. She looked very pale, and there were great circles under her grey eyes. She smiled faintly at her visitors and tried to put them at their ease by saying at once:

"You'll have heard all there is to hear from Rex and Simon, so don't let's talk about it. I know you'd both do anything you could for me, but there's nothing you can do.''

In an attempt to take her mind off her grief, the Duke and Marie Lou launched into a description of their own adventures; but after a little they realized that for the time being she no longer had the power to concentrate on anything but her own bereavement and was hardly listening to what they said. When de Richleau suggested that she should return to England with Richard and Marie Lou she roused a little and agreed without protest; so they left it at that, and the Duke went to get ready for his visit to the Legation.

Bucharest is subject to great extremes of climate—more so than any other capital in Europe; in summer it is as hot as Madrid, and in winter nearly as cold as Moscow. During September it is still beautifully warm, and as it was a lovely morning when he left the hotel, de Richleau took one of the open *droshkys*, which are such a feature of the city. They are much more numerous than taxis, and both their drivers and horses come of a special breed; the former, who always wear long black velvet caftans, being Russian *Skoptzi*—a religious sect that emigrated to Rumania many generations ago—and the latter black *Orloffs* of splended proportions.

F

Arriving at the Legation punctually at midday, the Duke was shown straight up to Sir Reginald's room, which overlooked a charming little garden. After they had exchanged greetings and the Minister had enquired kindly about Lucretia, the two old friends settled down to an informal chat about the international situation.

Pacing slowly up and down, his hands thrust deep into his trouser pockets and his grey head slightly forward, Sir Reginald discoursed quietly and amusingly on the position of Rumania.

The present régime, he said, was well disposed towards the Allies, and the bulk of the Rumanian people were most strongly opposed to any form of dictatorship. Few countries had a greater variety of foreign minorities included in its population, and these had always been treated with the greatest toleration. The Hungarians in Transylvania would, of course, seize on any excuse to make trouble, but this was due to their comparatively recent absorption. The Russians in Bessarabia showed little desire to place themselves under Soviet rule, and in other parts of the country communities of Turks, Germans, Greeks, Armenians, Tartars and Jews followed their own ways of life without the least interference. Commercially, Rumania was much more dependent on Germany than on Britain and France, but this was mainly the result of her geographical situation, and, Sir Reginald felt, the Rumanians would do anything to retain their independence.

The danger, of course, lay in the possibility of Hitler going into Hungary and then arriving on the Rumanian border. If the Hungarians decided, or were forced, to throw in their lot with the Germans, they would undoubtedly point out to Hitler the wisdom of securing their genuine goodwill by getting back for them their lost province of Transylvania. The poor Rumanians would then be in a pretty fix, since they could certainly not resist the might of Germany for long, and the Allies were in no position to assist them.

The permanent retention of Transylvania was the thing nearest every Rumanian heart, but there were two schools of thought as to how this could best be achieved. The great majority, remembering that, although the Germans had overrun their country in the last great war, the Allies had triumphed in the end, and enormously increased Rumania's territories after their victory, were for fighting their old enemies, if need be, and putting their trust in God and the Allies once again. But a small though powerful political minority were for cutting the ground from under the Hungarians' feet by going in with Hitler as the price of his allowing them to retain Transylvania.

This minority was the Rumanian Iron Guard, an association which had risen as the result of the totalitarian doctrine gaining a certain number of converts in the army and the cities. It was mainly composed of discontented young blackguards who admired the Nazis and was rapidly becoming a menace. To achieve their ends these gangsters resorted to intimidation.

blackmail and even murder; and it seemed beyond the power of the Government to stop their violent activities; although their original leader, Codreanu, had been arrested more than a year before and shot dead with twelve of his leading adherents during an attempt to escape which they had made while being transferred from one prison to another. In the event of Hitler's occupying Hungary, the Iron Guard might even attempt a *coup d'état*, and, if it succeeded, as the Minister put it mildly, his own position might become one not altogether lacking in difficulties.

The Duke then gave him the latest news out of Poland, and his host congratulated him on the timing of his exit, remarking that he had had news that morning that the Russian and German Armies had met the previous day at Brest Litovsk. He added that the Rumanians were behaving extremely well to the defeated Poles and had already given many of their leading personalities sanctuary.

After listening patiently to all that the Duke had to say about his project of buying up the Danube oil barges, Sir Reginald remarked that he was already endeavouring to interest the British Government in the matter, but it might well be some time before they could reach agreement on the formula to be adopted and secure the necessary funds from the Treasury. There was also the factor that, if the barge traffic were cut off, Rumania would lose a great part of her oil revenues, and her Government might decide to intervene. But Sir Reginald thought it would be time enough to consider that when further progress had been made.

He warned his visitor that, if the German agents, who were already swarming in the city, or their friends of the Iron Guard got wind of his intentions he and his associates in the deal would find themselves in grave personal danger, and that he feared the police might not be able to afford them adequate protection. He then went on to say that, although he could be of no assistance in the matter of funds, should the Duke succeed in securing the option he would willingly have it sent by fast bag to London with a personal recommendation as to the advisability of the Government's considering its purchase as a matter of the utmost urgency; but he added a further warning that the option should on no account be sent by post, but be brought to him personally, as he had reason to suppose that the local mail was at times subject to scrutiny and that the postal authorities were not altogether free from Iron Guard influence.

While enjoying a glass of fine Amontillado they talked for a little of the war, after which de Richleau thanked the Minister for his valuable if unofficial co-operation, and took his leave.

Back at the hotel he found a radiant-faced Rex waiting for him in the lounge. The cable from America had arrived, and old Channock van Ryn had come across with the big sum they needed. Rex had already been round to the bank at which the credit had been opened, and had in his pocket a banker's draft for the option money. It seemed that all was now set for the completion of the deal with Teleuescu that evening, and, having collected Simon, they went out to lunch at a *grădină*, as the garden restaurants, for which Bucharest is famous, are called.

Much of Rumania's wealth lies in her great herds of livestock, and, as her cultivated lands range from temperate to semi-tropical and she has abundant fish from both her many rivers and the Black Sea coast, food is incredibly cheap and of the greatest possible variety. As a result of this, her cuisine is perhaps the best in Europe and rivals that which obtained in the Russia of the Czars.

The *grădină* to which Rex and Simon took the Duke was one of the best among the innumerable selection to be found in the tree-lined streets of the outer city, and, as he sat eating his caviare, his *ciorbă*—a chicken soup made with sour cream—and his *sărmala* of rice and meatballs wrapped in vine leaves, he thought more than once of the terrible contrast between the gay and happy scene about him and the empty, shattered cafés that he had so recently left in Warsaw.

Marie Lou had elected to remain with Richard, and Lucretia had made it plain that, for the time being, she preferred to be left alone with her grief ; so that afternoon they all subscribed to the Rumanian custom of the siesta, which Simon and Rex had already adopted. In Bucharest the wealthier population keeps hours which would be thought extraordinary in England. They rarely dine before ten o'clock or go to bed before three or four in the morning, and, although the appointment with Teleuescu was not until nine that night, the friends were under no illusion that he had asked them to dinner.

At half past eight the three of them set out for the Rumanian magnate's great mansion on the Chaussée Kisseleff, and on their way the Duke said in a low voice : "Tell me a little more about this man we are going to see. Do you feel reasonably confident that he can be trusted ?"

"Don't think he'll back down on us once the thing is signed," replied Simon. "Put through an enquiry to my office in London about him. They say he drives a hard bargain but sticks to his word once he's given it."

"I take it he is not mixed up with the Iron Guard in any way ? It's scarcely likely that he would be if he's prepared to do business with us."

"He's the sort of wise guy who doesn't believe in getting himself mixed up in politics," said Rex. "Money is what he's after, first, last and all the time. He's out to become the wealthiest man in Rumania, and he doesn't give a damn who rules the country, provided they let him alone."

"I thought you said he'd taken a bias against the Nazis ?"

"Sure. His wife's a Jewess, but I don't reckon he'd let that interfere with his business deals."

"Then it's just on the cards that he may be double-crossing us and has put our idea up to the Germans with the hope that they might pay a higher price."

"Ner. Don't think so." Simon shook his head. "He named his price the first time we went to see him. It was an outrageous one, of course, but he wouldn't reduce it by a *lei*. Naturally, we tried to get him down. That didn't cost us any time, as we hadn't the boodle to close until this morning, anyway. But he wouldn't budge an inch. He jumped to it that we were acting for the British Government first go off, and probably named the top sum he thought they'd pay, right away. If we swore on the Bible, the Koran and the Torah that this was a private deal, he still wouldn't believe us. But now we're prepared to come across I'm sure he'll be satisfied. Just pat himself on the back for having opened his mouth so wide in the first place, and take the cash."

Their taxi drew up before a tree-screened mansion through the shrubberies of which there penetrated a long glass-roofed porch. The door was opened to them by a liveried manservant, and, after a short wait in a huge colonnaded vestibule, they were ushered into an ornate room on the ground floor, where the Rumanian millionaire transacted his business.

Rising from a tall, stiff-backed, brocaded chair of the Louis XIV period, which stood behind a big satinwood table inlaid with ormolu, Teleuescu came to meet them. He was a very tall man with a red face and a small paunch that stood out curiously in view of his otherwise lean figure.

"My friends!" he exclaimed. "Come in, come in. But I see there is now a third in your party. Be so kind as to introduce me."

The introduction was effected, and the Duke looked about him, attempting to assess from the room something of the character of its owner. Its furnishings were mainly French and of the eighteenth century, but some fine Persian rugs were scattered about the parquet floor, and among them two beautiful Oltenians of native Rumanian craftsmanship. Most of the pictures on the walls were not by recognizable old masters, but, nevertheless, very fine portraits of Boyars, as the great Rumanian landowners of the eighteenth century and earlier were called; their richly embroidered, fur-trimmed robes, jewelled ornaments and high papenkas—or great turban-like hats—gave the paintings a sombre magnificence which did much to lend character to this otherwise ornate apartment.

De Richleau decided that their owner was no mere money-spinner who had bought French antique furniture because it was showy and expensive; the Oltenian rugs and the bearded figures of semi-barbaric splendour on the walls showed that Monsieur Teleuescu had very marked tastes of his own and had surrounded himself with gilt, bronze and ormolu because he liked it.

Although he transacted all his business in this room, not a single paper was to be seen; but as soon as they were seated the millionaire pulled open a drawer and laid a closely typed document of several pages upon the desk.

"Gentlemen," he said, "you will be aware that a deal such as that upon which we are engaged has many complications. Nevertheless, I have made my lawyers work overtime upon it, and they have drawn up this deed in consultation with the firm that you appointed to act for you. Both parties have now expressed themselves as satisfied with its contents, and I have here covering letters from them both."

Rex nodded. "Sure. I heard from our people that they'd okayed it after lunch today."

"Good. I ordered it to be drawn up in French, as that is a language common to us all, and the one in which we have found it most suitable to converse. Perhaps you would now like to read it through?"

"Er, thanks." Simon, who was nearest, took the paper, and the other two drew up their chairs so that they could see over his shoulders. It took them ten minutes to run through the clauses and much of the legal jargon was almost incomprehensible to them, but they had ample faith in the international lawyers who had vetted it for them, as the same firm acted for both the British and American Legations; and the main fact in the preamble was perfectly clear. In exchange for a cash payment of one tenth of the full sum involved, Teleuescu was giving them an option to acquire on payment of the balance within thirty days the whole of his majority holdings in the Danube barge companies; but, if the balance were not paid within thirty days, the option became null and void, and the holders of it forfeited their deposit.

When they had finished reading it they nodded to one another, and Simon handed it back with the remark: "That seems quite all right to us; but—er—I see you have not filled in the name of the purchasing party."

Teleuescu shrugged. "I will, if you wish, but I must confess that I had formed the impression that you were acting for the British Government, so I thought that, if I left it blank, the name of anyone they might select as their nominee could be inserted."

"Ner," Simon shook his head, "this is a private deal."

"Then," smiled Teleuescu, "I am happy to congratulate you and your friends on your great wealth, Mr. Aron. Please fill in your own names at your leisure. You have, of course, brought the money with you?"

Rex produced the banker's draft and passed it across. "I had that drawn this morning. It is okayed by your State Bank, and on presentation the cash will be placed to your credit."

The Rumanian gave the flimsy paper a swift though apparently casual scrutiny, and flicked it back. "Thank you, that is perfectly satisfactory."

"Heh!" exclaimed Rex. "What's the idea? We exchange papers now. You keep that and give us the option."

"Not yet." Teleuescu put the document back into the drawer of his desk and shut it firmly, but his smile was most friendly. "There is still a small formality to be observed. To make it fully operative the option must first be countersigned by the Rumanian Prime Minister."

"But surely," remarked the Duke, carefully concealing his sudden alarm, "to secure his signature may take days—or even weeks. It is strictly necessary?"

"Yes. It is absolutely essential. A large part of Rumania's wealth, you know, lies in her export of oil, and Germany is now her principal customer. In the event of my barges becoming inoperative for any reason, the quantity which could be sent to Germany would be reduced to a trickle—or at least the comparatively small amount that is always going through by rail. It is not for me to suggest a reason why you should be willing to pay—yes, I will be frank with you—nearly five times the real worth of my barges to gain control of them. But it would not surprise me, in view of your nationalities, if, immediately you have gained the control, you decide to lay the barges up, or find some other use for them.

"Oil is the life-blood of modern war, and by such a move you could deal Hitler a blow the results of which are quite incalculable. By next summer you would probably have reduced the effectiveness of the Luftwaffe by sixty per cent and have rendered most of Hitler's armoured divisions inoperable. But how would Rumania come out of all this? Last time she lined up with the Allies, she suffered grievously by so doing, but in the long run she was amply rewarded by Austro-Hungary being forced to cede Transylvania, which has always rightly belonged to her. The retention of Transylvania dominates all Rumania's foreign relations.

"If Hitler can be speedily defeated, there is no doubt at all that we shall be left in full enjoyment of all our present territories. To cut off the bulk of his oil supplies would enormously accelerate an Allied victory, but in the meantime Rumania would be compelled to forgo a great part of her revenues. Directly it becomes known that this is happening, the Government will be faced with a great public outcry; not only from the shortsighted masses, who will resent the new taxes that will have to be imposed, but also from more powerful interests, who are of the opinion that we can have our cake and eat it too."

Teleuescu paused for a moment, then went on thoughtfully: "I am not altogether certain either that these people are not right. Even if Hitler continues to receive his full supplies of Rumanian oil, that is no guarantee that in the long run he will emerge from the conflict as the victor; and an Allied victory at any time, however distant, would result in Transylvania either remaining Rumanian or becoming Rumanian again.

"Then there are those who argue that a German victory would serve us equally well, provided we are prepared to adopt some form of National Socialism. I am a business man, and in Germany big business has not suffered under the Nazi régime; on the contrary, it has prospered exceedingly.

So, you see, although I have a slight personal bias in favour of the Allies, I am virtually a neutral so far as this business is concerned."

"Yes, I get that," Rex agreed, with a puzzled frown. "But I still don't see where your Prime Minister comes in."

"It is because, if I sell you my barges, I wish you to get what you pay for," Teleuescu smiled, tapping his table. "If I were to give you the document as it stands, the control of the barges would become yours on your paying up the balance of the purchase price. So far so good. But, if you then decided to lay them up, as I have told you, a public outcry would result. Such pressure might then be brought upon the Government that it would decide to frame a special Act of Parliament nationalizing the barges—or commandeering them, if you prefer—in order that the oil traffic with Germany could be resumed."

"I see," breathed the Duke. "And your idea is to commit your Government to a definite policy beforehand?"

"Exactly! If the Rumanian Prime Minister countersigns the document, it will show that the deal was carried through with the Government's full knowledge and consent. In such a case, even should the Government be changed in the meantime, I do not believe for one moment that it would go back on a previous Rumanian Prime Minister's signature."

For a moment they were silent, then de Richleau said: "I think we all owe a great debt of gratitude to Monsieur Teleuescu for his forethought in seeking to protect our interests in this way."

The Rumanian spread out his hands. "Gentlemen, it has been my good fortune to make a great deal of money, and I have found that honesty always pays. Whether you are prepared to admit it or not, I am of the opinion that you are acting for the Allied Governments. At the moment I am interesting myself in shipping, and with a war on they should prove my best customers. I want them to know that they can buy from me with confidence, because I shall do everything humanly possible to ensure the delivery of the goods."

"This—er—signature?" Simon hazarded. "Are you quite certain that you can get it?"

"Yes. I have discussed the whole affair at great length on three occasions with the Prime Minister. Armand Calinesco is a great little man, you know. It takes courage to commit oneself to a policy like this; as, if the Germans go into Hungary, it might even plunge Rumania into war. But he has complete faith in an eventual Allied victory and is prepared to face the music from his own people in order to bring it about, and peace to the world again, more speedily."

"Will you be able to get it within the next few days?" asked the Duke.

"I shall get it tomorrow morning. I already have an appointment with him for that purpose. I only asked you to come here tonight to make certain that everything was in order and—I will be honest—to see, as they say in

English, the colour of your money, before asking him to countersign the deed."

"Well, both the deed and the money are all right," laughed Rex.

Teleuescu nodded. "Yes. I am very glad you managed to secure the banker's draft. I will confess now that I had some doubts about your ability to do so. That is no reflection on your stability, of course; but I was just a little worried that you might find some difficulty in getting so large a credit transferred to Rumania now that the Allies have frozen all their assets. You see, rich as I am, I need that money very badly at the moment. War, terrible as it is, presents us financiers with unrivalled opportunities for increasing our wealth, and I practically took a gamble on your option money being in my bank the day after tomorrow, in order to meet a new liability to which I have committed myself in connection with the shipping that I mentioned just now. Still, all is well that ends well. If you will be here at midday tomorrow, the document will be ready for you. Now, may I offer you gentlemen a drink?"

On their accepting he pressed a concealed bell, and a servant, dressed in a long, royal blue caftan edged with gold, brought in a decanter and glasses on a silver salver. The contents of the decanter proved to be *Tuica*, a national spirit of Rumania, somewhat resembling the Hungarian *Baratsk*, which can be drunk at any hour, although it is usually taken as an apéritif, and varies in quality from the newly distilled fiery spirit on sale in every little tavern to a beautifully smooth, heart-warming liquor found in the better restaurants and private houses of the well-to-do. The present example had been matured for many years, and the visitors drank it with due appreciation.

As they set down their glasses Teleuescu rose again to see them out, remarking pleasantly as he did so: "I'm afraid my next interview will not be such a pleasant one. Owing to your having produced the option money as agreed, I shall have to disappoint the gentlemen who are coming to see me quite shortly."

De Richleau stopped dead in his tracks. "Do you mean that a third party is interested in this matter of the barges?"

"Please don't be alarmed," smiled the Rumanian. "After this evening's talk the option is as good as in your pocket. But I felt it only sensible to ensure against the freezing of credits preventing you from finding the necessary money. I will confess that it was Mr. Aron and Mr. van Ryn who first put the idea of parting with my holdings into my head. But, having once decided to do so—well, as the English say, 'I am not a man who allows the grass to grow under his feet.' I naturally began to consider how I could utilize the money that is coming to me to the best advantage. Having decided to go into shipping, I at once began negotiations for the purchase of Rumania's biggest line. If you had failed me I should have had to part with assets which I do not yet wish so dispose of, in order to finance the

F*

purchase of the line. I felt confident that another buyer could be found who would willingly pay as much as you are prepared to do, in order to keep the barges out of your hands."

"The Germans!" exclaimed the Duke.

"Of course. A few days ago I saw to it that the German Legation here got to know that I was thinking of disposing of my holdings, and they got in touch with me immediately. But you have not the least need to worry. As far as I am concerned, the sale has now taken place, and I can give you my honest assurance that I would much rather have sold to you than to the Germans."

"Hope to God you haven't let them know who was negotiating with you!" Simon jerked out.

Teleuescu frowned. "Mr. Aron, I am surprised that you should even suggest such a thing. I have naturally regarded your approaches to me as a matter of the strictest confidence."

"Sorry," Simon apologized, "but we can't be too careful, you know. Bucharest is full of German agents. If they knew we had this option, to prevent our getting it back to England they wouldn't think twice about bumping us off, even though we are in a neutral country."

The Rumanian smiled again and patted his little paunch. "I quite understand your alarm, but you haven't the least cause to be afraid, because they would never guess that any private buyer would have sufficient resources to make such a purchase, and will naturally have assumed that I am dealing direct with Sir Reginald Kent at your Legation." With a glance at the clock, he added as an afterthought: "However, perhaps it would be as well if you left here now. It is unlikely that the Germans would even connect you with the deal as you are not on the staff of the British Legation. All the same, it would be wiser if you did not run into them on my doorstep, and I am expecting them at half past ten."

It was only twenty past, so there seemed no need for undue hurry, but nevertheless the visitors did not linger over their farewells. Having thanked the Rumanian millionaire, they collected their hats from the footman in the hall, and a minute later were walking down the paved way under the glass portico to the street.

The car that they had hired was waiting for them, and just as they were about to get into it another car drew up with its front buffers only a few yards from their rear light.

"Hurry!" whispered the Duke, who was a little behind the other two. "This may be the Germans, arriving early."

As Simon jumped in and de Richleau waited for Rex to follow, he gave a quick glance at the other car. A slim man a little above medium height had just got out and was looking in his direction. There was something vaguely familiar in a gesture the man made as he flicked a cigar which he was smoking, but the brim of a soft hat threw a strong shadow on his face, and the Duke could not place him. Swiftly turning his own face away, de Richleau dived after Rex, and a moment later their car was spinning down the Chaussée Kisseleff, bearing them back to their hotel.

Richard and Marie Lou were waiting impatiently to hear the outcome of the interview with Teleuescu, and had ordered dinner to be served upstairs in the sitting-room of their suite, so that the invalid could be made comfortable on a sofa and enjoy it with them. Lucretia had excused herself from joining them, so, having given her a sleeping draught at ten o'clock, Marie Lou had left her ; and when the others arrived with their good news the rest of the party were able to give free rein to their elation.

It was no small triumph to have virtually achieved, in the short space of eighteen days, the tremendous task they had set themselves on Britain's entry into the war—no less than dealing what should in time prove a mortal blow at Hitler's war economy. Teleuescu had been much too definite in his promise to secure the Rumanian Prime Minister's signature on the following day for them to have any serious doubts of his ability to do so. That he had opened the matter with the Germans at all was regrettable, but there was no reason whatever to suppose that the enemy had any idea that anyone outside the official staff of the British Legation was concerned in it ; and by now they were probably scratching their bristly pates as to how best to break the bad news to Berlin.

All they could do was to report their failure and take such measures as they could to step up the oil traffic by rail during the coming months. By the time it leaked out that the deal had been engineered by private enterprise, the new controllers of the Danube barges would be out of the country and well on their way to England. If ever there were grounds for a celebration they certainly existed in the completion of this great *coup*, and, temporarily putting poor Jan and Lucretia out of their minds, Marie Lou and her guests did ample justice to the excellent dinner and fine wines that the hotel provided.

It was nearly two o'clock in the morning before they separated—early for Bucharest, but they were not yet used to such late hours. As de Richleau undressed, he thought again of the man in the soft hat who had stepped from the car outside Teleuescu's mansion just as they had been leaving. He had seen that little gesture with the cigar somewhere before, but where he could not think. However, his own face must also have been in shadow except for a few seconds, so it was unlikely that he had been recognized ; and, even if he had, there was nothing by which the German could connect him with Operation—Golden Fleece.

Getting into bed, he read for a little, and for the twentieth time, a few passages of that wonderful book of Joan Grant's, *Winged Pharaoh*, a copy of which always travelled with him. Then he put out the light.

Except on very rare occasions the Duke always slept soundly but lightly, and tonight was no exception. The usual noises of the street or of people passing in the hotel corridor outside his room did not disturb his rest, but a small noise close at hand was quite enough to rouse him. The window some ten feet from his bed creaked slightly as though it were being opened wider. Instantly the Duke was wide awake, and, slipping his hand beneath his pillow, closed his fingers round the butt of his automatic.

The window creaked again, and there came the muffled sound of the curtains which hid it billowing out slightly as they were caught by a sudden draught. De Richleau drew his gun from under the pillow and, while remaining almost motionless, levelled it at the place from which the sounds came. As he did so, something clicked in his brain. It may be that while he slept his consciousness had been on a higher plane and brought back to his waking memory the answer to the question that had been puzzling him when he went to bed. He knew now the identity of the man in the soft hat who had jerked the ash from his cigar. It was Herr General Count von Geisenheim.

Chapter XIII

MIDNIGHT VISITORS

THE Duke lay very still and waited. Someone was climbing in at the window now. He caught the faint scrape of a boot as it was drawn across the sill, and wondered who his stealthy visitor by night would prove to be. That it was a hotel thief or burglar was the most probable explanation, and before his memory had been revived by sleep de Richleau would have accepted that.

But now the thought of von Geisenheim had become like a nagging pain of which he could not rid himself. Had the German General recognized him from some trick of gesture such as that by which he had betrayed himself? Would he associate the three men he had seen getting into the car outside Teleuescu's house with the barge deal? Not in the ordinary way, perhaps, because Teleuescu might have been transacting any one of a score of different business projects with them, or they might have been making a social call, perhaps not even on the Rumanian magnate himself but on some member of his family. Yet, if von Geisenheim had recognized the man who had held him up at Lubieszow, that quick brain of his was capable of forming some very swift conclusions.

There was a faint whispering at the window now, as a second uninvited visitor climbed inside. De Richleau raised his gun a little, and the thoughts racing through his mind about von Geisenheim sped on. The Germans knew that Teleuescu was thinking of disposing of his majority holdings in the barge combine to someone, and who could that someone be if not the British? And, if the British did not wish their Legation to appear openly in the matter, what better agent could they select to act for them than that widely travelled and most knowledgeable man, Monseigneur le Duc de Richleau, whose personal prestige all over Europe was such that even kings would speak with him on the same terms as they would to a properly accredited plenipotentiary extraordinaire?

Yes, that was it, de Richleau decided. Von Geisenheim had spotted him and lost no time in acting on his shrewd assessment of the situation. That one of the men now stealthily fumbling with the curtain was the General himself the Duke did not think likely for a moment. Von Geisenheim would never undertake such a mission in person. But these were his agents whom von Geisenheim, no doubt believing that the Duke already had the signed option in his possession, had sent to procure the deed. "Well, they will be disappointed," thought de Richleau. "What is more, they will look extremely foolish in a few minutes' time when I hand them over to the hotel detective at the point of my gun."

One—or both—of them was through the curtains now and advancing cautiously towards the Duke's bed. He had been waiting for that in order to be able to cover them before they could get away, and, in any case, make certain of seeing their faces.

Suddenly sitting up in bed, he stretched out his left hand and switched on the bedside light.

The two intruders were caught right in the open, with the Duke's gun aimed at them. They made no attempt to run for it, but neither did they put their hands up in token of surrender. One was slightly in advance of the other.

The leader was a dapper little man with smooth black hair brushed straight back above a good forehead; his face was bronzed and his chin determined; he looked as though he might be a cavalry captain, and the likeness was accentuated because he was wearing a blue shirt without any coat over it, a pair of well-cut breeches and brown riding-boots. His companion was dressed in the same manner. He was younger, taller, and a fair, good-looking young stripling.

From their costume the Duke knew that they were two members of the Rumanian Iron Guard. "So I was wrong about my visitors being von Geisenheim's people," he was thinking. "But what the devil do these fellows want with me? Perhaps, though, von Geisenheim has sent them to pull his chestnuts out of the fire for him? Anyhow, we shall soon see."

The dark man took another step forward.

"Stay where you are!" snapped de Richleau, raising his gun a little.

The man advanced no further, but he waved the pistol aside with a faintly contemptuous gesture, as he broke into rapid French. "You can put that thing away. We have not come here to harm you or to rob you."

"If he is speaking the truth they are not after the option, then," thought the Duke. Aloud he said with a shade of sarcasm: "I am glad to hear it. In that case, perhaps you will tell me why you have broken into my room like a couple of thieves while you supposed me to be asleep"?

"We wanted to talk to you undisturbed and to offer you a little advice, which for your own sake we hope you will take. But I wish you would stop pointing that gun at me; you might let it off by mistake."

"That is unlikely," replied the Duke coldly, "as I have had long experience in the handling of firearms. I see no reason, either, why I should lay it down, seeing that the two of you have automatics strapped to your waists. However, if you will both put your hands well home in your breeches pockets I will lower my gun-barrel so that it rests on the bed."

They both complied with de Richleau's suggestion, and he went on: "Now, perhaps you would like to give the advice which you have put yourselves in some peril to offer me?"

"It is," said the dark man, "to leave Rumania."

"And what if that doesn't happen to suit me at the moment?"

"It has got to suit you, because to certain important people you and your friends are now *persona non grata* here."

"And who may these important people be?"

"It is unnecessary for me to name them. You must know from our uniforms that we are members of the Iron Guard. Our leaders have decreed that you should leave the country."

"Your leaders have no official status, and I and my friends can place ourselves under the protection of our respective Legations."

The dark man shrugged. "If you think that will do you any good you must be very ill-informed about the present state of affairs in Bucharest. Our organization may still be an unofficial one, but our powers enable us to dictate the actions of most private individuals at will. The Legations you mention are always picketed, and from now on the members of your party will be prevented from entering them. You will not be able to communicate with them by telephone or messenger either, as the operators on the exchange here have been told that they are not to put any more outside calls through for you, and the staff will 'lose' any letters or notes that you may send."

"I congratulate you," said the Duke, "upon the perfection of your organization. What happens if we still refuse to go?"

"You would soon find cause to regret your decision. I have come here with an invitation and a warning. The invitation is for you to call at Cook's Travel Bureau at ten o'clock this morning. You have only to state your name, and reservations will be handed to you on the express that leaves Bucharest at midday for Turkey. You will hand in your passport and those of the three men and two ladies who are accompanying you. They will all be visa'ed for Turkey and returned to you on the train. An ambulance will be outside the hotel at eleven-thirty to take your invalid friend to the station, and you will accompany him in it. You have no need to bother about money, as your tickets, etc., will all be paid out of the funds of the Iron Guard."

"Most handsome," murmured de Richleau. "And now let me hear the warning."

"From the moment you leave this room until the train steams out of the station you will be under constant surveillance. If you attempt to reach your Legation, or, in fact, if you diverge at all from the direct route to Cook's Bureau and back, you will meet with an accident. What sort of accident I cannot for the moment say, but it may possibly be a fatal one. If any of your friends leave the hotel at all, until it is time to go to the station, they, too, will meet with accidents. Finally, if you fail to accept this invitation to leave Bucharest on the midday train, there will be trouble here tonight. Again, I cannot yet say precisely what kind of trouble, but a fire might break out in your suite, or a criminal wanted by the police might try to take refuge here. In any case, during the excitement you and several of your friends would get very seriously hurt. Have I made myself plain?"

"Absolutely so. Either we all leave on the midday train without attempting to communicate with our friends, or you will put a gang of young hooligans on to beat us up tonight."

"We are not young hooligans but patriots who have the true interests of Rumania at heart. Apart from that, you are quite correct in your assessment of the situation."

"May I know why your leaders are so anxious to have us out of the country?"

"That is not my affair. I am simply acting under orders; but you must have been up to something, and, if you search your own mind, I have no doubt that you will be able to find some perfectly good reason."

As the Duke had not mixed himself up in politics during his short stay in the Rumanian capital, he felt convinced that there could be only one reason. Von Geisenheim had recognized him, and the German Legation had asked the Iron Guard to get his party out of the way as quickly and quietly as possible. A hint from the Germans that the Duke and his friends were trying to stop the oil traffic going up the Danube would have been quite enough to ensure the Iron Guards' immediate co-operation.

"Very well," he said, "I will discuss the matter with my friends over breakfast. And now, if you have nothing further to say, I will go to sleep again."

"You agree to depart?"

"I did not say so. I will talk over the matter with my friends."

"You will all be very ill-advised if you ignore the warning I have given you, as you will get no second one."

"We shall see about that," de Richleau shrugged. "By the by, you might as well leave by the door. In fact, since you can intimidate the hotel staff into becoming your accomplices, I don't see why you bothered to come in by the window."

A darting smile illumined the dark man's face. "We assumed that your door would be locked, and we thought you might be armed. If we had had to break in, you would have been ready for us with your gun, and we had no wish to be shot before we could explain the object of our visit. The fire-escape below your window presented a better chance of getting into your room while you were still asleep. I'm sorry to have disturbed you, but we were acting under instructions."

"Don't mention it," replied the Duke politely, as the other turned towards the door and, accompanied by his silent companion, let himself out.

Seeing that it was only a quarter past five, de Richleau read a few more passages from *Winged Pharaoh*, then put out the light and went to sleep again.

He woke at eight and spoke to Simon on the house telephone, asking him and Rex to breakfast. When they had joined him and Marie Lou, and Richard had hobbled from his bedroom to the sofa, the Duke gave them all a cynically humorous account of the visit he had received from the two Iron Guards.

"Don't see anything to laugh at," commented Simon when the recital was completed.

"Neither do I, really," rejoined the Duke mildly. "It's the memory of their faces when I switched on the light that makes me regard the affair with undue lightness. They were actually extremely businesslike young men, and there's no doubt that their organization is an exceedingly powerful one."

"What filthy luck," said Marie Lou, "that they should have insisted on our going on the midday train, at the very hour you were going to collect the Golden Fleece from Teleuescu !"

"They're not the only guys who can come and go by a fire-escape," Rex grunted. "Soon as we've finished breakfast I'll slip out that way and get to Teleuescu somehow. I'll find out at what hour the Prime Minister is signing, and, if it's too late for him to get the thing to us by hand, ask him to send it direct to Sir Reginald at the Legation."

"Better ask him to do that in any case," supplemented Simon. "Even if he could get it to us, it doesn't look as though we'd stand much chance of getting it to the Legation now."

"No," said the Duke firmly. "This is not just a question of eluding a handful of the enemy for a matter of half an hour. The Iron Guard has hundreds of members and is extremely well organized. You may be quite sure that they will picket the back of the hotel as well as the front. Our suites make very comfortable cells, but for all practical purposes we are now

under arrest in them.   These people are not the least afraid of the police and
have already got away with murder in open daylight on a number of
occasions. If any of us attempted to leave by the fire-escape, we should be
shot before we had covered a hundred yards. I fear that, in this case, discretion is quite definitely the better part of valour. I see nothing for it but to
put as pleasant a face as possible on it and knuckle under."

"What, leave without the option !" exclaimed Richard.   "We've never
yet walked out of a game with our tails between our legs."

"He who fights and runs away . . ." quoted the Duke.   "Honestly,
Richard, these young blackguards will think up some devilry for us tonight
that will cost us pretty dear if we don't accept their so-called invitation ; and
we dare not risk a shooting affray with you still crocked up and the two girls
to think of."

"Um. Always have hated these shooting parties," Simon agreed. "Still,
must be something we can do.   How about sending the banker's draft to Sir
Reginald via Cook's ?   Ask him to collect the Golden Fleece from Teleuescu
for us ?"

"Yes. I thought of that."   De Richleau sprinkled a lavish helping of
sugar from the castor on to the slice of cantaloup which he had just fetched
from the sideboard.   "We'll get out something pretty non-committal but
clear enough for him to understand, in a minute."

When they had finished eating they composed the note and enclosed the
banker's draft in it ; after which the men went off to bath and dress, while
Marie Lou went along the corridor to warn Lucretia that they were leaving
and help her to pack.

At a quarter to ten de Richleau left the hotel and was soon walking down
the sunny Calea Victoriei in its most congested part, where it twists and bends
and becomes as narrow as Bond Street.   He had already identified his escort :
one middle-aged man, who was walking just ahead of him but kept glancing
round, apparently at nothing, and two youths looking like students, who were
walking abreast, a few paces in his rear.

When he reached Cook's office the middle-aged man stopped at the door,
as though undecided whether to go in, waited until the Duke came up,
politely made way for him to pass and followed him inside.

On reaching the Foreign Travel counter, behind which there was only one
clerk disengaged, de Richleau found the man beside him, so he said amiably
in French : "I think you were really first, so do go ahead."

"No, no," the man protested.   "I am in no hurry, but the enquiries I
have to make will take some time. I would not dream of holding you up
while I make them."

Out of the corner of his eye the Duke saw that the two youngsters who
looked like students had now come in and were standing by a rack in the
middle of the floor, from which they had taken some travel brochures which

they were pretending to study with interest. He knew then that the possibility of his trying to send a message to anyone through Cook's had been foreseen and guarded against. Even if he could have got rid of the man beside him, the others were watching him also and would intervene at once if they saw their comrade leave him.

But de Richleau had also foreseen such a possibility, and he had placed the note for Sir Richard between the passports and written on the top left-hand corner of the envelope : "It is requested that this letter be despatched by hand to the British Legation as a matter of the utmost urgency."

He produced the pack of passports from his pocket and was just about to pass them across the counter.

Suddenly the man beside him snatched them from his hand and, turning, stared into his face with a bright, false smile.

"Permit me to help you. It always is a pleasure to assist a foreigner in the intricacies of travel."

Before the Duke had time even to protest, the man had shuffled quickly through the little pack, found the letter and removed it.

With a beaming display of teeth he handed it back, exclaiming brightly : "Ah! This has got among them by mistake, I expect. Put it safely in your pocket. Tell me where you wish to go, and I will arrange everything. It is such a pleasure to help a visitor to Bucharest. Do you not think it a lovely city ?"

"Turkey," grunted the discomfited Duke, who could cheerfully have pushed the man's teeth down his throat, but there seemed little choice but to stand by while this officious stranger did his business for him.

When the transaction was completed de Richleau made a show of thanking the man in front of the travel agent, gave him one look that had it been the thrust of a dagger would have killed, and walked stiffly back to the hotel.

His friends saw at once that he was in one of his rare tempers, and Marie Lou asked him tactfully if anything had upset him.

For a moment he could hardly speak, then he burst out : "I've been made a complete fool of by a little twerp of an Iron Guard agent. On the pretence of helping me get those tickets he simply took the passports out of my hand, found our letter and handed it back to me, while I stood there like a ninny !"

"Oh, Greyeyes, darling! How horrid for you!" exclaimed Marie Lou, her big eyes opened wide in sympathy. But the mental picture of the Duke's discomfiture proved too much for her, and, her sense of humour overcoming her pose, she suddenly gave way to peals of laughter.

The others joined in, and after a moment even de Richleau's fury with himself was dispelled to the extent of his muttering with a smile : "Yes, I suppose there is a funny side to it, but I've a very good memory for faces, and if I ever come up against that impertinent little brute again I'll choke the life out of him."

In spite of their amusement, they were quick to appreciate the serious side of the matter, and very soon their laughter had given way to anxious consultation.

They had counted more than they realized on getting this letter to Sir Reginald, the sands of their time in Bucharest were rapidly running out, and, rack their brains as they would, they could think of no other way of communicating with either the Minister or Teleuescu ; and, if they could not get the banker's draft to the latter that day, they might never have another chance to secure the all-important option.

Silent and anxious, they dispersed to finish their packing, and while doing it rack their brains afresh, but when they met again in the Duke's suite a few minutes before half past eleven none of them had any suggestions to offer.

Downstairs in the hall two white-coated ambulance men were waiting for them, and, taking the carrying-chair, in which Richard had been brought down in the lift, from the porters, they bore him out to the street.

As the Duke followed with the others, he saw that a long, low, open car was drawn up just behind the ambulance. In it were his two visitors of the night before and two other stalwart young men; so it seemed that the deportees were not to be given any chance of jumping out of the back of the ambulance on the way to the station. They all crowded into it, and the doors were not only slammed but locked behind them.

De Richleau was crushed up next to Lucretia, and it was the first chance he had had to have a proper look at her that morning. He thought she was looking a trifle better, but decided that might be due to the soft glow from the shaded electric light. In any case, she was still listless and silent and refrained from speaking unless a direct question was put to her.

The ambulance pulled up smoothly, its doors were unlocked, and they descended into the station yard. The car with the four Iron Guards in it had pulled up just behind them, and the short, dark man got out, followed by his companions.

Having saluted the Duke's party politely, while his fair friend was securing porters for them, the leader handed them their passports and escorted them through the barrier and on to the platform. The long train was already in the station, and their reservations were all in order. Richard was carried through on the stretcher by the ambulance men, but he was now sufficiently recovered to get into the train unaided and lie down on the day berth that had been considerately ordered for him. The others sorted themselves out and made themselves comfortable, while the dark man kept a watchful eye on them.

Just before the train was due to leave, the two Iron Guards who had remained out in the yard to supervise the stretcher party reappeared with a pile of luncheon baskets, an armful of periodicals in several languages, two large bunches of flowers and two big boxes of chocolates.

As they were handed in, the leader said to de Richleau : "We would not have you leave Rumania thinking us inhospitable. Please accept these trifles with our best wishes for a good journey."

"Thank you," the Duke smiled. "That is most considerate of you. Please believe that, whatever you may imagine about us now, we have the true interests of Rumania at heart, and in happier times we shall all hope to make a longer visit to your beautiful country."

The door was closed, the whistles blew, and the train steamed slowly out of the station.

"Aw, hell!" muttered Rex, as it gathered speed, and they passed the extreme end of the platform. "Did you ever hear of such lousy luck?"

"Yes. Beaten on the post," sighed Richard.

"Um, we'll never get the Golden Fleece now," added Simon gloomily, as he turned in the doorway to go to his place in the next compartment.

De Richleau was standing in the corridor with him, and Marie Lou suddenly noticed that he was smiling.

"What is it, Greyeyes?" she asked quickly. "You've got an idea. You always have when you smile like that."

"Haven't you noticed anything?" he replied with tantalizing slowness. "Something they forgot when they gave us that splendid send-off?"

"Noticed anything? Why, no. What more could they do than give us lunch, papers, chocolates and these flowers, which are quite heavenly?"

"Yes, they were a charming thought. Those young devils could hardly keep their eyes off you and Lucretia. But let me put it then that someone is missing in our party."

"There can't be. Lucretia is tucked up in a corner of the compartment next door, and the rest of us are all——"

"Good God!" cut in Richard. "I see what you're driving at now. They haven't saddled us with an escort."

"Exactly," laughed the Duke. "I took it for granted that some of them would see us safely across the frontier, but apparently that didn't occur to them. So we've a sporting chance yet."

"Where's our first stop?" Simon jerked out.

"On an express like this I shouldn't think we'll pull up until we reach Giurgevo. That's the frontier town before we enter Bulgaria."

"Oh, darling," sighed Marie Lou. "I expect that's hours away and much too far for any of you to get back to Bucharest before tomorrow. You shouldn't have raised our hopes like this."

"On the contrary," smiled de Richleau, "Giurgevo is less than fifty miles from the capital. Mind you, there's many a slip . . . They may have telephoned some of their friends to meet the train and see us over the border. But, if not, any of us who has a mind to it should easily be able to get back to Bucharest by the evening."

Richard groaned. "May the devil take those Polish policemen who made me wreck that car. I've the mind to go back all right, but crocked as I am it wouldn't be fair to ask you to let me come with you."

"No, Richard, I'm afraid we must leave you out of this." The Duke's tone was sad but firm. "You know how we shall miss you, but you couldn't run ten yards, and anyone who comes on this party must be able to take care of himself."

"You can count me in with knobs on," cried Rex enthusiastically. "I'm just pining to have a second crack at old von G."

"He wouldn't have turned up in Bucharest if I'd been on that landing at Lubieszow," Simon remarked with unusual sharpness. "Don't like fire-arms, but you leave him to me if we run up against him tonight."

"O.K., Simon," Rex grinned good-naturedly. "He's your meat next time; but I only hope there's not a darn' great door between you to interfere with your shooting."

"That's settled then," remarked the Duke. "You two will come back with me, unless we are prevented from getting off the train. Richard, Marie Lou and Lucretia had better go straight through to Istanbul, since the Iron Guard have been considerate enough to pay their fares that far. Once they are there it shouldn't be difficult to secure passages to England."

"No fear!" exclaimed Richard. "We're not going back to England until we know you're safely through with this. We'll sit tight in Istanbul at the Pera Palace Hotel until you three can join us there. Now, what about some lunch?"

They opened the baskets and found them to contain excellent fare. De Richleau took his into the next compartment to keep Lucretia company; but she ate automatically and roused from her lethargy only when he told her that Rex, Simon and himself were returning secretly to Bucharest that evening.

"Oh, be careful, darling!" she pleaded. "Be careful, please. I have so little to cling to now, and you are my biggest sheet anchor. I can't think what I should do if I lost you."

"I will," he assured her. "I've never taken a risk yet that was not justified by the circumstances. It's you who must take care of yourself and, hard as it may be for you now, try to realize that time heals all sorrows."

Over an hour had sped by while they were lunching, and soon afterwards the three who were to attempt to leave the train began to make their pre-parations. They repacked their suitcases, filling one bag with their most immediate requirements, then the good-byes were said, and the Duke, Simon and Rex made their way to the extreme end of the train.

They did so in the hope that, the train being very long, the rear coaches might be left standing outside the platform, and their hope proved to be justified. With Rex carrying the suitcase, they slipped off from the last exit before the guard's van.

The guard shouted something after them, but they ignored his cries, and within a minute had disappeared behind an array of coaltrucks in the outer sidings of the station.

Having reached the street by one of the entrances to the goods yard, they gave the train ample time to pull out. Then, silent from anxiety as to whether they would find a posse of angry Iron Guards searching for them, they made their way round to the station's front entrance.

No Iron Guards were present in the booking-hall, and they learned that there was a train leaving for Bucharest in twenty minutes.

They took their tickets and went on to the platform. Still no Iron Guard uniforms were to be seen, except for two worn by obviously casual travellers, both of whom had bags beside them at their feet.

The anxious moments ticked away. The train drew in, they boarded it without anyone paying special attention to them. There was another agonizing wait, then it rolled out, and all three of them sighed with relief.

There were three stops before Bucharest, but only a ticket collector came in to disturb them for a moment. On reaching the capital, they felt increasingly nervous. If for some reason or other their absence on the train had been reported from the frontier, the little dark man would be there to meet them, and every exit to the station would be guarded. But it seemed that their luck was in. They passed through the barrier among the crowd of passengers, and the collector who took their tickets did not even look at them.

Outside in the station yard the Duke caught sight of a clock. It stood at ten past four, so they still had several hours of the day before them, and he thought it most unlikely that Teleuescu would give up hoping to see them before midnight.

"We've as good as done it," laughed Simon.

"Yes," the Duke agreed. "Thank God the Prime Minister was to sign the thing this morning, and not tonight. We've only got to get out to Teleuescu's house and collect it now."

It was at that moment that he saw an unusual stir among the crowd outside the station, and noticed that there were many more people to be seen about the adjacent buildings than was usual at that hour, before the siesta was fully over.

Newsboys were shouting excitedly, and the people were grabbing their papers from them. The Duke knew little Rumanian, but that language has a marked resemblance to Italian, and he spoke Italian fluently.

For a moment the repeated cries rang meaninglessly in his ears, then he stopped dead as he grasped their terrible import. The newsvendors were shouting :

"Prime Minister assassinated! Calinesco murdered by Iron Guard this morning!"

Chapter XIV

THE AMBUSCADE

"WHAT's it all about?" asked Rex, as the Duke stopped, turned and stared with an expression of shocked distress at the crowd. "What are all those palookas so het-up over?"

"The Prime Minister!" gasped the Duke. "He's been assassinated by the Iron Guard. It happened this morning."

"Now we *are* in a muddle!" Simon's head jerked in a nervous spasm. "What time did it happen? We must try to find out."

They turned in their tracks and hurried back to the station entrance. The Duke bought a paper, and the other two peered over his shoulders at the black banner headlines and the apparently incomprehensible script underneath.

The Rumanians are now a mixture of many races, but their purest stock comes from the Roman Legions that were left stranded in the ancient Province of Dacia after the fall of Rome. When the nations of the west were still semi-barbarous tribes Rumania was already a civilized country with Latin as her most commonly used form of speech; and through all the centuries the Roman influence has never been entirely submerged.

In consequence, although de Richleau could speak only a few phrases of Rumanian, his knowledge of Latin and Italian enabled him to get the rough sense of the front-page news. Few details were, however, as yet given. The Prime Minister had been attacked in the street on his way to his office that morning. His car had been held up by a lorry driven across the road, and a score of men both in it and on the nearby pavements had drawn pistols and fired upon him.

He had been riddled with bullets before the police could come to his aid, but some of his assailants had been caught and they had all proved to be members of the Iron Guard.

"Wonder whether the poor chap signed before they got him?" muttered Simon, when the Duke had finished translating the few paragraphs.

"We're sunk if he didn't," said Rex.

"I'm afraid so," agreed the Duke. "If the Iron Guard felt themselves strong enough to perpetrate a national outrage like this it can only be because they feel confident that whoever replaces Calinesco will be much more favourable to them; and any man who is well disposed towards the Iron Guard would certainly refuse to countersign our option."

"That's so," Rex nodded. "But better the Golden Fleece with no Prime Minister's signature on it than no Golden Fleece at all. Let's get along out to old man Teleuescu's place and learn where we stand."

"Not yet," said the Duke. "We have plenty of time before us, and I think we would be wise to secure some sort of base before we go out to the Chaussée Kisseleff. The Prime Minister's assassination may be the opening act of a *coup d'état* by the Iron Guard. By tonight the police may be openly under their control and all the stations be guarded to prevent their political enemies escaping from the capital. If it becomes known to them that we have returned we shall be among the hunted; so, if only as a reasonable precaution, we ought to find a place where we can go to ground should the need for it arise."

"Sure. Let's find a place where we can dump this, anyway." Rex looked down at the heavy suitcase he was carrying. "And beds where we can doss down for the night."

"Pity we haven't got that shooting-brake you brought Richard in from frontier if we have any difficulty in getting on a train."
Poland," Simon remarked. "Would be jolly useful now to get us to the

"It is still in the hotel garage," said the Duke. "But I don't think we dare risk going there to get it. You're right about our needing a car, though. I think we'll try to buy one."

He thought for a moment, then went on: "As for accommodation, I think we will make our headquarters some little hotel in the Dambovita; that is, at the far end of the city among the wharves down by the river. It is very unlikely that we shall run into anyone who knows us there."

They hailed a passing *droshky* and half an hour later had installed themselves at a clean, unpretentious-looking hotel called the Peppercorn.

While they were upstairs unpacking their solitary bag, Simon remarked: "How are we off for boodle to buy a car?"

They all produced their wallets, and a check-up showed that, while a luxury car was out of the question, they had ample to buy a moderately priced model in good secondhand condition.

Leaving the hotel they went in search of a car-dealer and found a big garage in an adjacent street that had cars for sale. As Rumania was not yet involved in the war, secondhand cars were still plentiful and their prices at pre-war level. Having selected a Chrysler that the proprietor said he had bought only that morning from two Frenchmen, Rex drove with him in it round half a dozen blocks and then spent a quarter of an hour inspecting its engine. After a little bargaining they closed the deal, had their purchase filled up to capacity with petrol and drove away in it.

"Clothes are the next thing," said the Duke. "So many people are mixed up in this Iron Guard business, and unfortunately there are scores of them that we don't know but who might recognize us. Most of the servants at the Athenée Palace must have tumbled to it that we were run out of town by the Iron Guard this morning, and if any one of them happened to catch sight of us he might put them on our trail; so we ought to alter our appearance as far as we can."

Rex pulled up at a large secondhand clothes shop a few blocks further on and they went inside. Simon's beaky face lent itself so naturally to his posing as a Jew from the Bukovina that he at once selected one of the tall hats trimmed with red fox fur that they had worn as a distinguishing mark of their caste for centuries, and a rather threadbare black coat to go with it. Rex bought a long caftan and shiny peaked cap in which he could easily pass as the driver of a hired car, and de Richleau contented himself with a cheap gaberdine suit in which he would look as much like an underpaid clerk as was possible for him.

Having carried their purchases out to the car they drove up a deserted dockside *cul de sac* between two warehouses and changed, packing their own clothes into the boot. It was now half past six and, not knowing when they might have another chance to get a meal, they decided to feed before going out to Teleuescu's.

After driving round for a little they selected a fish restaurant in which the unadorned marble-topped tables looked suitable to the clothes they were now wearing. The choice proved a good one as they dined off deliciously fresh écrevisses, those miniature lobsters found in the Danube which are almost all claws, and Black Sea sturgeon stewed in a paprika sauce, and finished up with big plates of wild strawberries; so that even the epicurean Duke declared that they could not have fared better had they dined at Prunier's in Paris.

According to Rumanian habits their meal had been a high tea rather than dinner, and as most of the restaurant staff were off duty the service had been slow. By the time they had settled their bill it was getting on for eight o'clock, and dusk having fallen they decided to delay their visit to Teleuescu no longer.

On their arrival at his mansion the servant who opened the door at first displayed some reluctance to let them in; but recognizing them after a moment, despite their shoddy clothes, as visitors to his master of the night before, he took their hats and left them in the colonnaded vestibule while he went to ask if Teleuescu would receive them.

A few anxious minutes elapsed, then he returned and ushered them into the millionaire's private sanctum.

Teleuescu was seated behind his table, but he made only a show of rising to greet them. He looked much older than he had on the previous night, and tired and depressed. As he took in their shabby raiment his eyebrows lifted, and he exclaimed:

"My poor friends! I see from your clothes that you are on the run. I was informed that you would receive a visit from the Iron Guard. Oh, what a day it has been! You find me plunged in grief. I have lost a dear friend, and I fear too that my country may now fall into the clutches of this gang of murderers."

For a few moments they condoled with him and Rex described how, after the Iron Guard had attempted to deport them, they had managed to get back to Bucharest.

The Rumanian nodded gloomily. "You have shown much courage as well as resource in returning here, because you will receive short shrift now if the Iron Guard catch you. I will not conceal from you that your visit tonight has placed me also in danger. Some of them came to see me first thing this morning. They told me that they meant to deport you and warned me that, should you succeed in evading them and come here, if I received you I should pay for it with my life. I only hope that the men who have been on watch in the street outside most of the day have gone now."

"May have been someone on the other side of the road," Simon volunteered, "but there was no one loitering near enough to recognize us— especially dressed as we are."

"Let us hope you are right," Teleuescu sighed. "Yesterday I would have laughed at such a threat, as the play-acting of a lot of blustering young fools. But not today—no, not today. If they are bold enough to kill the Prime Minister they are capable of killing anyone."

"We all regret most sincerely that we may unwittingly be the cause of bringing you into danger," said the Duke. "But it was imperative that we should return to pay you your money and collect the option." He added the question the answer to which they were all on tenterhooks to hear. "Did the Prime Minister countersign it this morning before he met his tragic end?"

Teleuescu nodded. "Oh, yes, he signed it. He had just left me and was on his way to his office when that gang of brigands set upon him."

Not a muscle of de Richleau's face moved, but his grey eyes lit up. Rex's huge shoulders straightened slightly as though a load had been taken off them, and Simon's nails, which he had been gently digging into his clenched palms, relaxed their pressure. Terrible as was the event which had so soon followed the countersigning of the option, it was no personal concern of theirs. The task they had set themselves was to deal a mighty blow at Hitler by securing the Danube barges for Britain, and it seemed that through fantastic luck—by a bare half-hour and the thoughtlessness of the Iron Guard in not sending an escort to see them over the frontier—they had succeeded.

Carefully as their reactions were concealed, Teleuescu's sharp eyes caught them, and he spoke again with a sad shake of his head.

"I am sorry, my friends, to disappoint you ; but the fact that poor Calinesco signed before he died will not now do you any good."

"But hang it all, the deal's still on !" exclaimed Rex.

"No, it is not. It ceased to be on at midday today."

"What the hell d'you mean ?" snapped Simon in a most unusual display of anger.

The Rumanian ignored the remark and continued to address himself to Rex. "Much has happened on this most unfortunate of days. Let us start at the beginning. While I am still having my breakfast two of the Iron Guard arrive and demand to see me. I come downstairs in my dressing-gown, and they tell me that their leaders have given orders for you to be deported, and that, should you elude your escorts and come here, I must refuse to see you or face the consequences. I tell them that this is my house and that I shall receive whom I like in it and that they can go to the devil. Naturally, I am very worried on your account, and, Iron Guard or no Iron Guard, I hope that you will somehow manage to keep our appointment. An hour or so later I am rung up by the German Legation. A certain General who has come from Berlin specially to negotiate with me about the barges on behalf of the German General Staff."

"Von Geisenheim," broke in de Richleau quietly.

"All right then, since you know him, the General Count von Geisenheim asks me if I am prepared to reconsider my decision of last night. Well, I will be frank, I hedged. In view of the visit of the Iron Guard, there was now at least a strong probability that you would be prevented from completing your purchase of the option. I have to find a large sum of money by to-morrow. This is no fairy story concocted on the spur of the moment because I wish to excuse myself from wriggling out of my bargain with you. . . ."

"Ner," Simon grunted. "You told us so yesterday."

"Did I? So I did. I am glad of that. Well, I tell the General Count that in certain eventualities I might yet be prepared to accept an offer from him. He wishes to come round to see me at once to discuss the matter. But no! I refuse even to see him until this afternoon. In due course the Prime Minister arrives. He countersigns the option, and as he does so he says: 'I do this for Rumania. It is right that we who have always loved freedom and won our own freedom from the Turks should bear our share in freeing the world from an even greater tyranny. When this transaction becomes public it may cause the premature fall of my Government, but that is of small consequence if at the same time it shortens this war by a year. The eventual good of the country must always be placed before party politics, and, even if this act of mine results in our having to fight, I shall not regret it, because I am convinced that only by an Allied victory can Rumania hope to retain her independence and full sovereignty over her present territories.' "

As Teleuescu paused there were tears in his dark eyes, and the three friends were deeply moved. Overcoming his emotion, the Rumanian went on: "We agreed that the affair should be kept secret as long as possible. It was for that reason that he came here to sign rather than have me take the document to his office. My presence there might have aroused unwelcome speculation, and all our talks upon the matter have been held in private either at his house or mine. Well, poor Armand left me. You know what happened then. Ten minutes, or a quarter of an hour perhaps, after he had gone my servant rushed in to me with the terrible news. I am thunderstruck! I am heartbroken! What to do now I do not know. The man who is most likely to be the new Prime Minister is no friend of mine. If the Iron Guard decides to go after me he will give me no protection. I say to myself, why should I sell the damn' barges at all? After poor Calinesco's last words to me how can I sell them to the Germans, anyway, even if you do not turn up? And, if you do turn up, why should I risk my life to sell them to you? Somehow I must find the money I need another way; but that will not be easy."

Teleuescu wiped his drawn face quickly with a silk handkerchief, then spoke again. "I am, as the English say, between the devil and the deep sea. But the principles of a lifetime come to my aid. I say to myself, never yet have you broken your word. If Mr. van Ryn or either of his friends arrives in this room by twelve o'clock they must have their option and be damned to the consequences. But all the same I hope very much that you will not manage to get here. Twelve o'clock strikes, and I heave a great sigh of relief. All the same I force myself to give you another half-hour. It is for me a very long half-hour, but at last the clock strikes again. I get up and go to my club for lunch to hear from my friends the details of the great tragedy that has occurred. From that point, as far as I am concerned, the deal between us is off—finished—as though it had never even been discussed."

"I fully understand your attitude," said the Duke slowly. "And, of course, it was entirely our responsibility to be here at the time arranged. In view of the way in which you were threatened, we all appreciate your courage in determining to go through with the business if we had turned up; and even extending to us half an hour's grace. Nevertheless, the very words of the late Prime Minister surely stress the immense importance of this deal being carried through, not only for the Allies but also, in the long run, for Rumania. Can we not . . ."

"No. I refuse to reopen the matter. In any case it is now too late."

"D'you mean you've already sold out to the Germans?" asked Rex.

"Not yet."

"Then for the sake of your dead friend," de Richleau pleaded, "for the sake of the great patriot that Rumania has lost today—if for no other reason—let us at least . . ."

"No, no!" Teleuescu violently shook his head. "I tell you I can discuss the matter no further with you. I am now committed elsewhere."

"Thought you said you'd made up your mind that you wouldn't sell to the Germans in any case?" Simon interjected.

"What does it matter if I sell to Germans now or not? Since I cannot .

sell to you the barge traffic will go on just the same whether the Germans gain control of the combine or I retain it."

"But if you haven't closed with them you're still free to deal," Rex protested. "After all, we were first in the field. I know the fact that we are several hours late for our appointment lets you out. But . . ."

"Wait. You do not understand," Teleuescu cut in. "I have not yet told you all. When I got back from my lunch the Germans were here. I could not refuse to see them, but thinking still of poor Armand's words, I had made up my mind not to sell. I told them that I had decided to retain my interest in the barge combine. But they were not satisfied. They say that, although you are out of the game, that may not be the end of the matter. Even the Iron Guard is not yet powerful enough to expel the British Legation from Bucharest. They know that you have been in touch with Sir Reginald Kent. They think that, although they have succeeded in expelling you from the country, as soon as you reach Turkey you will get in touch with him through your Ambassador at the Porte and ask him to complete the transaction on your behalf. Or even, perhaps, that you have only been acting as his agents all along and that he will quickly replace you with others. They say that their Fuehrer has given a personal instruction that the barges are to be brought under German control. No chances whatever are to be taken of the Allies interfering with the traffic either now or in the future. Therefore, the sooner I make up my mind to sell, the better. Hitler is not a man who can be kept waiting, and he is expecting a report that the matter has been settled, by tonight. I say that Hitler is not my master—yet, and that for once he will be disappointed. The barges are not for sale."

"Well done," murmured the Duke. "Well done."

Teleuescu shrugged wearily. "Yes, I did my best; but that is not all. The Germans departed, very stiff, very correct, but much annoyed. I rest on my bed for a little and try to sleep; but sleep does not come. At six o'clock I have more visitors; the Iron Guards are back again. They say, 'Our leaders have good information that France is rotten. They do not believe that the masses in the United States can be made sufficiently aware of what is at stake to allow their Government to intervene before it is too late; and Britain is no longer powerful enough to resist the might of Hitler alone. Therefore, his victory is assured. Once he has defeated the Western Democracies his word will be law in South-eastern Europe, and our only hope of permanently retaining Transylvania lies in our securing his goodwill now, while our friendship is still of some value to him. He regards it as imperative that he should safeguard his oil supplies from Rumania, and, in consequence, it has been decided that you must sell your barges to him. If you refuse . . . Well, we killed Calinesco this morning and we are quite prepared to come here and kill you tonight.'" Teleuescu spread out his hands. "Now you have the whole situation. What could I do but agree?"

"Yes. I don't blame you in the least," said de Richleau quietly. "You still have the document, though?"

The Rumanian gave a faint smile and shook his head. "Yes, I still have the document, and I know what you are thinking, but it is no good. You three are saying to yourselves: 'There is a war on. Plenty of people are dying these days. Poor Teleuescu is in a mess and we are sorry for him, but we cannot let his life stand in the way of this thing which would do so much to assure an Allied victory. If the Germans come here later on to-night and, finding the document gone, call in the Iron Guard, they may kill him, which would be very sad. But we are three to one, and we have our duty to do as we see it. Why should we not take the option from him by force and leave him to get out of his trouble as best he can?'"

Those were in fact the very thoughts that had been simmering in the minds of his visitors, and they all looked slightly guilty as he went on:

"But it is no good, my friends; I like my life and I yet have much to do. I do not mean to die, if I can help it, for a long time to come. The option is no longer in the drawer of my table here. When my servant announced that you were here I foresaw that in your disappointment you might be tempted to resort to desperate measures; so I transferred the option to a wall-safe of which I alone have the combination. I have a concealed bell which I should press the moment any of you made a move to attack me, and, even if you succeeded in stunning me before I could raise an alarm, you would be found and arrested hours before you could get the safe open."

"I give you full marks," grinned Rex. "But, say, what time are you expecting the Germans here?"

Teleuescu's smile deepened. "Ah, that is a different matter. The place where the name of the person to whom the option is granted should appear still remains blank. What happens to it after I have handed it to the General Count is no affair of mine. They have made an appointment for the same time as last night. A quarter of an hour or twenty minutes should see the business through. I expect they will leave the house about ten minutes to eleven."

"Thank you," said the Duke. "Have you any idea how many of them there will be?"

"On their previous visit there have been just two of them: the General Count and the Commercial Attaché from their Legation. I see no reason why there should be more than those two tonight."

De Richleau stood up, and his friends rose with him as he said: "Then we will not detain you further. I am only sorry that we have not been able to secure the option by orthodox means."

The Rumanian had risen too. "The transaction I am about to enter into with the Germans is not an orthodox one, either. Had it been I should certainly not have given you the information that I have just supplied. I am forced to make the sale against my will, so I do not feel in any way responsible for doing my best to see that Hitler gets what he is paying for. But whatever may happen later on tonight I trust that none of you will attempt to seek refuge here or come to the house again. I should not like to have to give you up to the police or to the Iron Guard, and my life would almost certainly be forfeit if I failed to do so.''

"You needn't fret yourself on that score," Rex smiled. "We're pretty capable of taking care of ourselves."

"Then let us say *au revoir*." Teleuescu extended his hand. "I wish you all good luck, and I hope that we shall meet again in happier times."

They all echoed his wish and shook hands with him, then he led them to the door, and his footman showed them out into the street.

"How long have we to go?" asked Rex, as soon as they were outside.

De Richleau glanced at his watch. "Well over an hour and a half before von Geisenheim will be leaving here. We had better drive round for a bit."

"No," said Simon. "May need all the petrol we've got later. Let's find a café and kill time by having a drink."

They got into the car, and Rex drove slowly down the long tree-lined avenue until they came to a small, inexpensive-looking *grădină*. Alighting, they walked through to a table that was only faintly lit by the coloured fairy lights swinging gently in the trees and ordered some *tuică*. A small gypsy band was playing in another corner of the garden, and the few people in it were not yet thinking of dinner, but enjoying an early apéritif. It was very peaceful there, and Hitler's "positively last demands", the now slowly smouldering Western Front and murdered Poland seemed a very long way away.

Since the previous morning they had heard little war news, but they discussed the scraps they had picked up in a desultory way. It was said that the Russians had occupied Vilna in the north and had reached the Hungarian border in the south. They had now come face to face with the Germans in many places in Central Poland, but they had not started to fight one another, as many people had hoped they would, and it was even reported that on some sectors the Germans were voluntarily retreating before the advance of the Soviet forces.

They felt that Hitler must be chewing up a lot of carpets in his rage at having to give away captured territory to Stalin. But what else could he do unless he were prepared to take on Russia as well as France and Britain—and the odds were that the German General Staff knew their own business too well to let him do that. He had another headache coming to him, too, if the rumours current that morning were to be believed. The formation of a Czech Legion to fight the Nazis had been announced over a week before, and now, it was said, the principal cities of Bohemia, Moravia and Slovakia were all in open revolt against their German overlords.

After a little Rex said : "How're we going to play this thing ?"

"Going to be pretty tricky," murmured Simon. "Don't want any shooting, if we can help it, in the open street."

De Richleau was just lighting one of his long Hoyos. "It is," he said, releasing the first cloud of fragrant blue smoke, "always a good thing to get quite clearly in one's mind the object of any operation before one starts to plan it."

"That's easy," laughed Rex. "The object here is to beat up those blasted Germans and snatch the option off them."

"Ner. Beating up's not part of the object. Might achieve the same end by a trick. The object is to get hold of the option."

"Simon is nearer the mark, but you're both wrong," smiled de Richleau. "The object is to get the option into the hands of Sir Reginald Kent."

The other two thought for a minute, then nodded acquiescence, as the Duke went on : "You see, that makes all the difference. We have not only to get hold of the thing but to do so in such a way that there will be no hue-and-cry immediately afterwards which might prevent our getting it to the British Legation."

"Suits me," said Simon. "Means no shooting. But oughtn't we to use the codeword when we're talking about the option in semi-public places, like this ?"

"Sure," Rex grinned. "I guess you might add a bit to your object, though. Shouldn't it be 'to get the Golden Fleece into the hands of Sir Reginald Kent *at the earliest possible moment*?' "

"That's a good amendment," agreed de Richleau. "Sir Reginald told me that the Iron Guard keep illegal pickets on all the Allied Legations to prevent known Rumanian democrats getting in to give the Allies information about pro-Nazi activities. We can hardly hope that our assault on von Geisenheim and Co. will remain unreported for more than half an hour ; and, once it is known at the German Legation, they will warn the Iron Guard and ask them to increase the picket on the British Legation, so that we shan't be able to get into it."

"We'll have to work mighty fast then."

"Unless," suggested Simon, "we could think of some way of kidnapping von G. and his friends—so that they won't be able to report us. People at their Legation won't get anxious about their not turning up for an hour or two. That would give us more time."

"That certainly is an idea, Simon," de Richleau said after a moment. "The devil of it is, though, that there are only three of us, and with their chauffeur there will not be less than three of them. It would be no easy matter for us to overcome three men in a public highway without their raising an outcry."

"We could tackle the chauffeur first—while the others are in the house."

"True, and one of us could take his place at the wheel of their car."

"Holy mackerel!" Rex exclaimed. "You've got something there. Then whoever's driving takes the other two for a ride out into the open country and slugs them quietly, some place where there won't be any rubbernecks to see the fun."

"Aren't you being a bit optimistic?" objected Simon. "Can't quite see old von G. and his friend quietly allowing themselves to be driven out of Bucharest, then lamely throwing their hand in to a solitary fake chauffeur."

"I'll drive," volunteered Rex, "and you two could keep on our tail in the Chrysler. When I pull up we'd be three to two, and even if we have to mix it we three ought to be able to give 'em the works."

"No," said de Richleau. "That's no good, Rex. They are sure to be armed. The moment you turned their car out of the Chaussée Kisseleff they would know something was wrong. The next thing you'd know was that you had a gun-barrel pressed against the back of your neck, and Simon and I, driving along behind, wouldn't be able to lift a finger to help you."

Simon nodded his beaky head up and down. "Greyeyes is right. We've got to get them before they get into their car. Look. How's this? We tackle the chauffeur first and put him in the back of the Chrysler. We then go into Teleuescu's garden. Nice and quiet there behind that high wall. Must be a good thirty yards of that glass-covered passage too, between the front door and the gate. We wait till the front door is closed, then jump the other two just before they reach the gate. When it's all clear outside we carry them out and put them in their car. Rex drives it out into the country while we follow in the Chrysler. Soon as we've dumped the bodies and got the Golden Fleece we drive to the British Legation with it, and the trick's done."

"That's much the best scheme that's been put up yet," said the Duke. "The idea of tackling von G. and Co. in the garden is a real brain-wave. I don't see why both cars should be driven out to the country, though. Surely, once we've laid the chauffeur out it would be better to put him into the back of his own car, and the other two on top of him. Two of us are enough to dump them in a quiet spot, and while we are doing that whoever is left to drive the Chrysler can take the option—I mean the Golden Fleece—direct to the Legation."

"How'll the two of us who dump these birds get back?" asked Rex.

"Why, in the Germans' car, of course."

"Nope. That'll be too hot. Much safer to leave them in it."

"Perhaps you're right. We'll have to walk then, or pick up anything we can."

"Who'll drive the Chrysler?"

"Simon had better do that. You and I, Rex, will do the laying on of hands in the garden, while Simon stands by. I am thinking now of your very sound amendment to our object. One of them will probably be carrying a brief-case. The moment we have felled them it will be Simon's job to secure the case and make certain that the option is in it. If not, we'll search them. Directly he has got it he will leave us to clear up the mess, dash straight to the Chrysler and drive hell-for-leather to the Legation. Even if you and I are caught after that, it doesn't matter; we shall have pulled off our coup. But, if all goes well, the three of us will rendezvous as soon as we can get there at the Peppercorn. Is that all clear?"

"How about if there's a slip-up?" asked the cautious Simon.

"If anything goes wrong we must act according to the dictates of the moment. If there is no other way we'll have to shoot it out. If we do have to shoot we must shoot to kill, because the gaining of a few seconds before the police come on the scene may mean the difference between success and failure. Rex and I will do the shooting and you, Simon, must not get yourself mixed up in any rough-and-tumble that may occur. Your part is to keep your eye glued to that brief-case and get hold of it somehow. Never mind what is happening to Rex and myself. You've got to get the Golden Fleece to the Legation if it's the last thing you ever do."

They all realized that there were perforce many imponderables in such an attempt, but it seemed the best plan that they could make with the data they had at the moment and they were satisfied that it had a reasonable chance of success.

Having whiled away an hour they settled their score and drove back along the Chaussée Kisseleff. The part of it in which Teleuescu's mansion stood was as quiet as Kensington Palace Gardens, and, at this hour, little sign of life was to be seen on either side of it except for occasional lights glimmering through the branches that above high walls screened the big private houses. Yet the broad thoroughfare itself, being the main entry to the city, was never empty down a quarter of a mile of its length for more than a few minutes at a time. In the daytime both sides of it were occupied by a constant stream of buses, cars, lorries, vans, *droshkys* and farm-carts, and even up to a late hour each night there was no part of it in which one could not hear the clop-clop of horses' hooves and the swish of motor tyres. The best protection that it offered to anyone of criminal intent was the shadow cast by the big trees that lined it on either side, the broadness of its sidewalks and the width of the road, which enabled motor traffic to pass at such a speed that the chances were against its occupants noticing anything that was happening outside the circles of light cast by the arc lamps.

They pulled up the Chrysler halfway between two tall lamp standards and outside the next house but one to Teleuescu's. It was twenty past ten, so they had ten minutes to go before the Germans were due to arrive. The wait seemed interminable, but at last a passing car slowed down and drew in to the 'kerb thirty yards in front of them. Rex had switched his headlights off, so from that distance the Chrysler looked as if it were empty and had been parked there. Two men got out of the car in front and walked purposefully towards the glass portico before which it had halted. As they crossed a belt of light which shone down between two trees from a nearby lamp standard, de Richleau muttered :

"There they are all right. Better give them a few minutes to get inside."

Again they waited, for what seemed an eternity, until at last Rex said : 'Come on, let's go."

Slipping in his clutch, he drove quietly up behind the other car. As he brought the Chrysler to a halt a man and a girl came into view ; they were strolling slowly along arm in arm in the deep shadow cast by the wall.

"Hell !" murmured Rex. "We'll have to give them time to cover a couple of hundred yards before we start anything."

To the fury and chagrin of the three watchers the couple elected to come to a halt just beside Teleuescu's portico. The girl leant against the wall and the man embraced her.

De Richleau groaned. "Those two may be there an hour ! And why in God's name choose a place opposite two cars to make love in when there are hundreds of yards of dark wall facing the empty street . . . ?"

"Can't stay here, now," said Simon jerkily. "Chap in front must have heard us drive up. If we just sit he'll start to wonder wh_ we pulled in here."

"Get out, Rex," urged the Duke. "Start to tinker with the engine. Pretend something is wrong. Then go and ask those two the way to the nearest garage in French and German. Anything to break the party up."

Rex climbed out, lifted the bonnet and played for a moment with the engine. While he was doing so a solitary soldier walked by and, pausing, came up to him to ask for a light. Another two minutes elapsed before the soldier was out of sight. Rex then walked over to the courting couple. Neither of them understood him, but the ruse took effect. The man muttered something to the girl, they both gave a surly look at Rex and, turning, strolled off down the street.

Instead of returning to the Chrysler, Rex walked towards the big limousine in which the Germans had arrived, but at that moment its chauffeur, apparently not noticing his approach, started it up and began to turn it round so that it would be facing towards the city when his passengers came out of the house.

Guessing that Rex had decided to tackle the limousine driver, de Richleau and Simon had just been getting out to go to his assistance ; but they managed to scramble back in time, before the big car swung round towards them. Rex, left halfway across the sidewalk, turned a little and, coming back to the Chrysler, resumed his tinkering inside its bonnet.

The Germans' car had drawn up behind them and faced the other way.

It was now dead under the arc lamp, and from a quarter of a mile away anyone in the street looking in that direction could see its driver.

"We can't slug him under that light," Rex muttered to the others.

"We've got to," replied the Duke tersely. "Time's getting on. They've been in the house ten minutes already."

"Daren't start a rumpus while we're getting the chauffeur," objected Simon. "We'll never get the others if there's a row going on in the street when they come out."

"We must get the fellow here then," de Richleau whispered. "Quick, Rex. Say you need his help. Say your torch has given out and you want him to shine a light on your engine for a moment. He's sure to speak German."

"Okay," drawled Rex, but just as he was about to leave them a maid-servant came out of a nearby house with a little dog. For five precious minutes she stood about while it sniffed round the nearby trees, and four more pedestrians passed.

At last she went in, and Rex quickly crossed the twenty odd feet that separated the two cars. But, instead of returning after a moment with the other man, as they had expected, he remained there for some minutes talking to him.

The Duke looked at his watch and groaned again. "Oh, God, I wish Rex would hurry up! It's a quarter to, and they may be out any minute now."

At length they heard approaching footsteps. Making themselves as inconspicuous as they could, they sat well back in the darkened interior of the car. Rex and the Germans' driver passed within a foot of them, but neither looked inside.

Pausing at the bonnet, they both bent over it, and the chauffeur shone his torch inside. Rex had not dared to disconnect any of the leads in case they had to get off in a hurry, and there was nothing wrong with the engine. The two inside the Chrysler saw the heavy face of the chauffeur as he leaned over to look down into the bonnet, and they saw Rex suddenly draw back to strike him down from behind. But at that instant they both caught sight of something else as well.

"Rex!" cried the Duke suddenly and loudly.

The shout came only just in time. As Rex checked the raising of his arm a policeman emerged out of the shadows.

He walked slowly towards them, and they both turned at his approach. Then he and the chauffeur began to talk together in Rumanian while Rex stood helplessly by.

To justify his shout de Richleau had now put his head out of the window of the car and began to upbraid Rex in French as though he were intensely irritated at his not being able to get the car going.

The minutes were ticking away. Simon, who hated shooting, sat there miserably thinking: "Oh, hell, we're in a muddle! We'll have to shoot it out after all."

All three of the men on the kerb had been peering into the bonnet, but at last the policeman shrugged his shoulders and turned away. The chauffeur made to do so too. He could see nothing wrong with the carburettor, with which they had been fiddling, and he was now mildly abusing Rex for wasting his time.

On the inspiration of the moment Rex called him back and, producing a packet of cigarettes, offered him one. The man took it, and they lit up. The policeman had not covered more than twenty yards, but they knew that it was now or never. As the fellow turned away de Richleau was just about to call to him again when Rex produced a heavy spanner that he had been holding ready in his pocket and, lifting it, brought it crashing down on the back of the man's head. He stumbled once, lurched sideways against the car and sprawled in a heap in the gutter.

In less than thirty seconds they had hauled him into the Chrysler. The policeman had seen nothing and was still walking away with his back turned; but he had only just passed the other car, so it was impossible to adhere to their original plan and put the chauffeur into that.

As quickly as they could they secured the man's ankles and his hands behind his back with some straps that Simon had been holding ready for the purpose. Then they stuffed a gag into his mouth, pushed him down into the bottom of the car and got out.

"Well, that's that," sighed Rex with relief. "I thought that squarehead would never stop asking questions before I could induce him to come along and take a look at the perfectly good innards of this old bus."

"Quick!" whispered the Duke, who was already leading the way towards Teleuescu's gate. "Into the garden! We haven't a moment to lose!"

But it was already too late. As he reached the grilled iron gateway he saw through it the lighted front door of the house standing half-open and the two Germans coming down the steps towards the path.

Chapter XV

STREET BATTLE

THERE was no time now to get into the garden unseen. The passing of odd pedestrians, the courting couple, the servant with the dog, the reluctance of the chauffeur to leave his own car and the inquisitive policeman had all conspired to delay the execution of the first part of their plan.

The policeman was still no great distance away, and his attention would be caught by the slightest cry. Even if he glanced back over his shoulder he could scarcely fail to see any scuffle that might be going on outside Teleuscu's mansion. Yet there seemed no alternative now but to attack the Germans in the open.

"It's the first plan we thought of or a shooting match," de Richleau whispered angrily, as he took a quick catlike step back into the shadows. "Rex, you take the wheel of the car; Simon and I will tackle them as they get in."

The car was not dead opposite the iron gate, so Rex was able to run to it and scramble into the driver's seat unseen. De Richleau had picked him for the part because in the indifferent light his peaked cap made him look not unlike the chauffeur. As he huddled himself down into his seat to disguise his height the Duke and Simon ran round to the far side of the car and stooped down behind its body so as to be out of sight of the approaching Germans.

When they emerged from the gate Rex saw with relief, out of the corner of his eye, that there were only two of them. The many unforeseen delays in carrying out the first part of the plan had put it badly out of gear, but things would have been infinitely worse if there had been a third member of the enemy party.

They were walking almost abreast, with von Geisenheim slightly in the lead. He was carrying a black leather brief-case, and the short fat man beside him, no doubt the Commercial Attaché, was speaking to him in an unctuous, deferential voice that oozed satisfaction.

De Richleau had the far door of the car very slightly open, ready to pull it back and spring on the first of them to step inside. He waited there, hardly breathing, like some huge, grey cat. Simon was crouching behind him. The palms of his hands suddenly became unpleasantly moist, and he felt terribly jittery, as he did on all such occasions when violence was about to be employed. He just caught the Duke's whisper:

"Slip round the back, Simon. Force them into the car at the point of your gun. As soon as you can grab the option, run for it."

As the Germans reached the car von Geisenheim stepped in front of his companion and spoke sharply to Rex. Evidently he was accustomed to having the doors of cars opened for him.

"*Schlaffun sie da!*" he exclaimed angrily, but Rex, taking the cue, just mumbled something and shook himself as though he had been asleep.

The General impatiently pulled the door open for himself and, with a curt order to Rex to drive to his Legation, stepped inside.

De Richleau gave him just time to sit down, then wrenched the opposite door open, jumped in, thrust his pistol into the astonished General's face, and cried :

"If you open your mouth I'll kill you !"

The fat Attaché was half in and half out of the car. As he made to draw back, Simon came running up behind him ; but he tripped on the kerb, lost his balance and staggered against the car with such force that his gun was knocked out of his hand.

Seeing what had happened, Rex leaned right out and caught the German a glancing backhander on the side of the head. The blow was just in time to stop the shout that was already rising in his throat. On drawing back he had half turned, but the heavy smack on the ear knocked his head back inside the car again.

Recovering his balance, Simon suddenly dived forward, seized the man by both ankles and, exerting all his strength, pitched him head foremost through the doorway. As the German rolled over and opened his mouth again to shout, the Duke lifted his foot and jabbed it down hard on his face.

To do so he had had to take his eyes off von Geisenheim for a second. The General saw his chance, grabbed the Duke's gun-wrist and forced it up, but he could not draw his own pistol because with his other hand he was still clutching the brief-case.

The Attaché swallowed two teeth and let out a muffled, choking cry. With the edge of his left palm de Richleau hit von Geisenheim a sharp crack on the wrist. The General winced and relaxed his grip. Simon had snatched up his pistol by the barrel from the pavement. The Attaché's stumpy legs were still flailing wildly in the open doorway of the car. With an effort he jerked them in and strove to sit up, while the Duke was still struggling with von Geisenheim ; but Simon was too quick for him. Jumping on to the running-board, he lifted his gun and brought its butt smashing down right in the centre of the German's square forehead.

De Richleau had now got his pistol-hand free and was pointing his weapon at the General's head again. As Simon's gun-butt smacked on to the Attaché's skull Rex's voice reached them, a hoarse, urgent whisper through the windscreen :

"Got that brief-case, Simon ? Come on, man ! For Mike's sake make it snappy !"

Simon was still sprawling on top of the now unconscious Attaché. Reversing his pistol, he thrust it in his pocket and stumbled to a kneeling position on his victim's chest.

"There it is ! There !" cried the Duke, pointing to the brief-case, which von Geisenheim was endeavouring to push behind him. Leaning across the General's knees, Simon grasped the case and hauled upon it. The case came towards him, slowly, reluctantly, as the General's arm straightened from the pull upon it.

Rex's voice came again. "Come on, can't you! Shoot if you've got to, but get that case!"

Von Geisenheim's arm was now almost fully extended. De Richleau lifted his hand again and brought the side of it smacking down on the General's other wrist. With a gasp of pain he let go the case and Simon, still clutching it, almost fell out of the car backwards.

"Hell!" exclaimed the Duke, as he saw what it was that had brought Simon up with a jerk. The brief-case was fastened to the General's wrist by a chain such as bank messengers wear when carrying wallets containing money or negotiable securities.

At that instant the car suddenly slid forward. Simon rolled over into the empty seat, and de Richleau, who had been crouching with his back to Rex, was flung forward on to the General.

Von Geisenheim gave a shout, but it was half stifled by the Duke's shoulder, which had fallen across his face.

As they picked themselves up the car gathered speed. Simon still had the brief-case and was tugging upon it, but he let go with one hand to slam to the door. De Richleau, his face pressed close to his enemy's ear, snarled: "If you try to shout again I'll blow your head off!" Then he heaved himself up, pushed down the small seat opposite the General and lowered himself into it.

The car raced round a corner, and they heard Rex shout: "Look out of the back window. See if we're being tailed?"

Simon squirmed round and peered through the square pane above the back seat.

"No!" he shouted back, after a moment. "Don't think so. Can't see anything."

"Why in thunder did you drive off like that?" the Duke flung over his shoulder.

"Had to!" The boom of Rex's voice came in reply above the humming of the engine. "That darned cop had turned round and was patrolling towards us. I tipped you off as soon as I spotted him, and he was within ten yards of us before I slid in the clutch. Hope to glory he didn't catch sight of what was going on inside there."

For the first time von Geisenheim spoke, his cold eyes on the Duke. "It is always a tragedy when a gentleman turns thug. I am sorry to see an old acquaintance, such as yourself, in the guise of a gangster."

De Richleau raised his "devil's" eyebrows. "It surprises me, *Herr General Graff*, to find that you still retain memories of those now distant happier days when we were both guests at Schloss Werzenstein, for the shooting. I should have thought that all niceties of conduct had long since been eradicated from your mind by the gangster you have made your master."

Von Geisenheim shrugged. "Adolf Hitler may not be one of us, but he has served the end for which he was placed in power. Germany is no longer weak and a beggar among the nations. The Great General Staff, which has now come into its own at last, at least owes that to Hitler."

"And you will throw him aside like a worn-out boot when he is no longer of any use to you," commented the Duke. "I've always suspected that you *Junkers* were the real power behind that neurotic, blustering puppet."

"Perhaps," von Geisenheim shrugged again. "But he is a man to be reckoned with all the same."

"So the horse is becoming master of the rider, eh? And you are afraid there will be times when this little Austrian corporal may try to interfere with your strategy?"

"You need not worry, Duke, the *Stabscorps* is perfectly capable of taking care of itself."

"I wonder? It is a dangerous business to call up the Devil and try to make him your servant."

"As long as the German Army continues to be victorious there will be no clash of opinion, and it will continue to triumph to the end. After that—well, we shall see."

"You would not be there to see yourself if that little bounder could hear you. He has fifty times more gunmen than Al Capone ever had and, it seems, seeks far less excuse to use them."

"Yes. Most of these Nazis are unspeakable brutes straight out of the gutter, and it certainly is not wise to air one's opinions anywhere they are likely to get wind of them. However, this fool," the General gave a contemptuous kick at the body of the unconscious Attaché, "is as near dead as makes no matter, so during this little ride we can talk quite openly as friends and equals."

"Equals perhaps, but hardly friends," corrected de Richleau. "It is surely unnecessary to remind you that our countries are at war."

"Oh, the war! It may result in the killing of a few hundred thousand of our respective nationals, but what difference does that make? I was thinking of much broader issues, and in those you and I inevitably find ourselves on the same side. The future holds only one question of real significance. Is our caste to continue its task of maintaining civilized order among the masses, or is the world to be given over to the dictates of a blood-soaked Bolshevik rabble?"

"Are you suggesting that in recent years Germany has set an example of maintaining civilized order?"

"That is only a phase. Hitler's thugs and their filthy concentration camps are a necessary evil to purge the State of its irresponsible elements."

De Richleau shook his head. "I think there are very few British people, whatever their caste, who would not prefer to take their chance with the blood-stained mob for masters rather than stand by passively while such horrors are perpetrated as has been the case in Nazi Germany.''

"Then they are bigger fools than I thought. Obviously they cannot appreciate the sort of fate that would be in store for them. Yet the writing on the wall is plain enough for you all to see. Look how the brutal Russian giant has licked the wounds we inflicted on him last time and is getting to his feet in an attempt to crush us all. Does not the fact that Stalin has felt himself strong enough to send an army into Poland mean anything to you ?''

"It means that he is barring his front door against the possibility of future German aggression. And, after all, he did not seriously embarrass your campaign in Poland."

"Oh, that !" Von Geisenheim laughed a little bitterly. "That was hardly more than an exercise, and Stalin would be getting a bloody nose by now if he had attempted to go in before he did. That reminds me. I have a score to settle with that big American rough-house man of yours. I should have been commanding one of the armies that were sent into Poland if it had not been for him. He put one of his accursed bullets through my shoulder. That's why, instead of doing my proper job, I have been side-tracked and sent on this mission to Bucharest."

"It is regrettable," said the Duke sarcastically, "that we should have been the cause of interfering with such a distinguished career. Perhaps, though, your absence from the front resulted in quite a few less of those unfortunate Poles being murdered."

"My career does not matter," von Geisenheim replied quietly. "But the success of the German Armies does. It is the only thing which stands today between the world and Bolshevism. As for the Poles, they are a stupid, pigheaded lot, and since they would not co-operate with us, what does it matter if a few thousands more or less of them got killed ?"

"Really !" exclaimed de Richleau. "I do wish we had a professional psychologist with us. It would interest me greatly to hear his report upon a brain which shows such callous indifference to suffering as yours. How can you be quite so inhuman when you have every reason to fear that we are taking you to your own death ?"

The General shrugged. "It is just that which makes me speak so frankly. If you don't kill me the loss of the paper that you mean to take from me will probably result in my having to face a firing squad when I get back to Berlin. As I now regard my days as numbered I am taking the opportunity of trying to make you face the wider issues that lie behind the present conflict. You have influence with your people. If you succeed in getting home, for God's sake tell them to ignore this mountebank Hitler for another year or two, and line up with us Germans to save all that we value in this world from being trodden underfoot by the Bolshevik scum."

The car had been speeding along at a good pace, first through streets of houses, then through a less built-up area. It was now on the edge of the open country, and, slowing down, Rex turned it into a narrow lane between two orchards. Having run along the lane for a hundred yards, he brought the car to a stop.

"*Herr General*," said de Richleau seriously, as the car halted, "I am afraid that tonight you have failed in both your missions. May I have the key to that brief-case which is still attached to your wrist?"

"So be it." Von Geisenheim thrust his free hand into his breast pocket. "It is quite pointless for me to make a fight; and, after all, the *Stabscorps* still has some power where the protection of its own Generals is concerned. This may mean no more than retirement for a few months. If so, I may yet be able to play a hand against you pig-headed British in the war."

"You seem to have gained a sudden confidence in the belief that we do not mean to kill you. Perhaps it would be better if we did."

"No. You would shoot me if I put up a fight, but you would not murder me unarmed as I am. I congratulate you, Duke, on your triumph. Here is the key to—*Sieg Heil!*"

At the end of the sentence the German raised his voice to a sudden shout. On his cry of "*Sieg Heil!*" he whipped from his pocket, not the key of the brief-case, but a small flat, snub-nosed automatic. In the one swift movement he had it levelled straight at the Duke's heart.

During the first few minutes of their drive de Richleau had kept his pistol pointed at von Geisenheim's head, but in a moving car it is not easy to keep an upraised arm steady, so for the latter part of the journey he had let the pistol rest on his knees. He was still holding it there. Only a flick of his wrist was needed to jerk the barrel round and send a bullet into the General, but before he even had time to flick his wrist the General might now send a bullet into him.

For once the Duke had made the fatal error of underrating his opponent, and it looked as if his carelessness was going to cost him his life. During the split second that he stared down the small deadly muzzle of von Geisenheim's little pistol he was bitterly conscious of how easily he had let himself be tricked.

They never knew if it had been the German's intention to kill the Duke first and take his chance with the other two afterwards or if he meant to attempt to barter de Richleau's life for his own freedom.

The pistol flashed, making, small as it was, an ear-splitting crash in the confined space of the car. But whether he deliberately squeezed the trigger, or the gun went off because his hand was jolted, remained uncertain.

Throughout the German's conversation with the Duke, Simon had sat quietly in his corner, a cynical and watchful listener. All his native suspicion had been instantly aroused on seeing von Geisenheim's hand go to his pocket. The General and the Duke were so engrossed with each other that neither of them saw him lift his own pistol; but as the German's hand left his coat Simon's weapon swung in a swift, vicious back-hander, crashing sideways against their enemy's face.

As the spurt of flame issued from the pistol-barrel de Richleau flung himself sideways. The bullet streaked over his shoulder and crashed through the glass screen of the car just where Rex's head had been a moment earlier.

Before von Geisenheim could fire again Simon had flung himself upon him and brought his gun smashing down, once, twice, thrice, on the German's head.

A muffled cry came from outside, but it was drowned in the thudding of the blows, and none of those inside the car heard it.

"Phew !" whistled the Duke, as he picked himself up from off the unconscious Attaché. "That was a near one. Thanks, Simon, you can let him be now. What a lesson not to talk politics with old *friends*."

"Let me finish him off," Simon panted, lifting his arm again.

"No !" De Richleau caught the raised arm swiftly. "You have had your cut at him now. So has Rex. If he recovers from those head wounds, and Hitler spares him, we may come across him again. And he is my meat next time."

Von Geisenheim was now slumped in his corner. He had dropped his little automatic ; blood was streaming from his nose and trickling through the grey hair in two places on his scalp. It looked as if it would be a long time before he was capable of making further trouble for anyone.

As Simon picked up the brief-case again and the Duke leaned forward to search von Geisenheim for its key the car door was pulled open, and Rex said angrily :

"What in thunder's been going on in here ? Couldn't the two of you take care of one old hoodlum ? That bullet landed up in my arm."

"My fault," said the Duke contritely, as he stopped his searching and got out. "I'm sorry, Rex. I slipped up badly and I'm lucky not to have been killed myself."

Rex peered at the neat bullet-hole through the glass screen. "So am I, from the look of that. I was wriggling out from behind the wheel and it got me through the flesh just above the elbow."

Blood was running from a jagged tear in his caftan. They got it off, slit his shirt-sleeve and examined the wound by the light of the car lamps. Fortunately the bone was not broken and the small slug had gone clean through the flesh, but on straightening his arm Rex gave a quick yelp of pain. There was no clean water readily available to bathe the wound, so they cut off the shirt-sleeve at the shoulder and bandaged it up with that ; then they used a silk muffler that the Attaché had been wearing, to make a sling.

Having attended to Rex, the other two resumed their search for the key of the brief-case and soon found it in von Geisenheim's waistcoat pocket. On undoing the case the Golden Fleece proved to be the only paper in it.

A quick examination showed that the four sheets of stiff typescript were just as they had last seen them, except that Armand Calinesco's signature had been added below Teleuescu's. The place for the name of the party to whom the option was assigned still remained to be filled in.

Folding the sheets into a small square wad, de Richleau thrust them into his breast pocket and said:

"The delay caused by that couple and the policeman has blown our original plan sky-high. What is the best thing for us to do now?"

Simon knew that he must still be pretty shaken from his recent narrow escape even to ask, so he stepped into the breach.

"Got to get the 'Fleece' to the Legation before half Bucharest is after us. Better dump the two Boches here and drive straight back in the car."

"This car's too hot," Rex disagreed. "That cop may have seen you all kicking around inside it as I drove off. If so, the night squads will be out looking for it already."

"Let's drive back part of the way then, and try to pick up the Chrysler. We'll need that to get over the frontier in."

"Sure, if it's still there. It'll be okay if the cop didn't see anything, but if he did he'll have looked inside it and found the Germans' chauffeur."

"It's not far from Teleuescu's to the Legation. Well worth going there just to see if it's still possible to get hold of the Chrysler."

"Let's get going then. Haul out those two stiffs."

Between them Simon and the Duke dragged the two unconscious Germans out of the car and propped them up with their backs against a nearby fence. It was certain that von Geisenheim would be out for a long time, but they were not so sure about the fat Attaché. He was jerking slightly and breathing stertorously, so it looked as if he might come round fairly soon. It was still possible that no alarm had yet been raised, and they did not want him to start a hue-and-cry earlier than could be avoided, so they tied his hands and feet with some wire that they found in the boot of the car and stuffed his handkerchief in his mouth.

Simon took the wheel of the car and, when the other two had got inside, backed it out of the lane. Turning it there, he drove at a moderate pace back towards the part of the Chaussée Kisseleff in which its biggest private houses were situated; but when he was within half a mile of the Boulevard he turned the car into a dark *cul de sac*, and they all got out.

Ten minutes' swift walking brought them to the wide tree-lined thoroughfare and another five to a long blank wall, above which branches rustled lightly in the wind, opposite Teleuescu's mansion. The Chrysler was no longer outside it.

"Keep walking," whispered the Duke. "It's a hundred to one that there are police in the shadows over there waiting to see if we come back."

When they had covered another hundred yards he said: "Leaving their chauffeur behind was fatal. He will have described us to the police and to his own people half an hour ago. By this time the Germans will have got the Iron Guard to warn their picket on the British Legation and increase its strength. They will probably have reinforced the picket on the American Legation too, in order to prevent Rex getting the 'Fleece' to Sir Reginald by way of his own Minister; and by now I expect our description is being circulated. We had better separate. Rex is the most conspicuous of us. His height and breadth are such a give-away. Besides, that wound must be washed as soon as possible. I think you had better get back to the Peppercorn, Rex, while Simon and I see if there is any chance at all of getting into the British Legation."

"That's sound," Rex agreed without argument. "I wouldn't be much good to you now in a mix-up, anyway, with one arm in a sling."

For a moment they paused to wish one another luck, and it was agreed that the Duke and Simon should join Rex at the hotel as soon as possible. He then crossed the road and left the others to proceed on their reconnaissance.

Soon afterwards a night-hawk *droshky* came clopping by, so de Richleau hailed the driver and, as they got in, told to him to drive through the Strada Jules Michelet.

Five minutes later they were drawing level with the Legation. A sickle moon had now risen above the trees, so they could see the sidewalks more clearly, even where the big trees cast patches of deep shadow. Two men were walking slowly along on the inner side of the pavement, a little group of four more stood silent and watchful almost in the gateway of the Legation.

"It's no good," muttered the Duke. "Of course they *may* not be waiting there specially for us, but in view of that chauffeur having been picked up it's a hundred to one that they are. Still, we'll have a look at the back on the chance that it may not be so well guarded."

He let the *droshky* drive on until it was out of sight of the watchers, then pulled him up and paid him off.

When the cab had clattered away they walked down a side turning, turned again and after a few moments reached the back wall of the Legation garden. Two more men were standing on its corner and another two were patrolling up the street.

"Whole place is surrounded," muttered Simon, stepping back into an open gateway. "If Rex were fit and we had him with us he's tall enough to push me over that wall while you held those chaps off. But we wouldn't stand a dog's chance alone."

"No," the Duke agreed, as they began to retrace their steps. "We would only get ourselves killed if we attempted to force our way in now. We must think up some ruse by which one of us can get inside tomorrow."

"We'll need to alter our appearance to pull that off."

"That is just what I was thinking. You are slight of build, Simon, and could easily pass for a woman. Directly the shops open you must buy some kit. In the meantime, I will get hold of a taxi somehow, and a driver's cap and tunic; and I will drive you straight up to the front door in the morning."

Simon wriggled his shoulders nervously. "Don't like it. If a man tries to disguise himself as a woman his feet are always such a give-away."

"You must hide them then. A nun's robe would do the trick, and there are plenty of nuns to be seen in Bucharest."

"Don't they always hunt in couples?"

"Not always. The ones here belong to the Orthodox Greek Church, and some of its Orders have considerable freedom. A nun's get-up would do away with the necessity for a wig too. I'm sure it's the best thing we could hit on."

"All right," Simon agreed, a shade reluctantly. "How are you going to get hold of a taxi?"

"Heaven alone knows!" De Richleau paused under a street lamp to look at his watch. "It is twenty-five past twelve now, so I still have the best part of the night to get one somehow and to do another little job that I've had in mind. The shops won't be open till about nine, so you had better go back to the Peppercorn and get some sleep. Say it takes you two hours to get the nun's outfit in the morning and to change into it; you should be able to meet me by eleven-thirty. I'll pick you up outside the west door of the Cathedral."

"Why not come back with me and get some sleep yourself? There'll be time for you to see about a taxi in the morning."

"No. I may have to steal one, and that will be easier during the night. I don't feel like sleep, anyhow."

"Then let me come with you. I can keep cave while you pinch the chariot."

"I'd rather you got some rest, Simon. You need much more sleep than I do. I shall manage quite well on my own."

"Well, just as you like. It's been a pretty tiring day, and I'll be glad to get a shut-eye. You sure, though, that there's no other way of getting this thing to Sir Reginald? Couldn't we post it, or send it by special messenger?"

"No. Sir Reginald warned me himself that the postal clearing centres are full of Iron Guard people whose job it is to tap all letters to the Foreign Legations that look as though they might be interesting. As for a special messenger, this thing is so darned important that I wouldn't care to trust its delivery to anyone except one of ourselves."

"Couldn't we telephone Sir Reginald? Ask him to come out and meet us somewhere?"

"If the mail is tapped you can be pretty certain that his telephone is too.

We don't want to draw him into some hornets' nest where he may get shot as we hand the Golden Fleece over to him."

"Then let's send him a message by hand, asking him to meet us."

De Richleau shook his head stubbornly. "We daren't, Simon. It's not as though we had only a few German agents to be wary about. We are up against an organization thousands strong, this time, and we now have the police on our track into the bargain. Some of them may recognize and pick us up any time after daylight tomorrow. Apart from that, if Sir Reginald goes out they will almost certainly tail him in the hope that he will lead them to us. In either case, a lot of people that we have never even seen may start shooting at us without a moment's warning. We must not risk bringing Sir Reginald into such great danger. Many of these Iron Guards are real pro-Nazi hot-heads. They are quite capable of jumping at the chance to shoot him and pretending that it was a mistake afterwards."

"Looks as if there's nothing else for it, then." Simon shrugged. "Well, I'll get along. See you at the west door of the Cathedral at eleven-thirty. For goodness' sake take care of yourself. We'd be lost without you."

"It was I who was very nearly lost with you, tonight," laughed the Duke. "I really am beginning to lose my grip. By Jove, though! That was a true word spoken in jest, if ever there was one. I haven't given a thought yet to our line of retreat, and there will be no time to discuss that tomorrow morning."

"Should have thought of it myself," murmured Simon. "We could drive the taxi out into the country, abandon it as soon as its description as a stolen car is likely to be given out, then go native for a bit in some small town."

The Duke considered for a moment, then he said: "We don't want to be stuck in Rumania for longer than we can help; and wherever we abandon the taxi the local search will get pretty hot for us. I think we would do better to try to get over the frontier into Bulgaria right away."

"Well, there's only road and rail; and it's certain that they'll watch the stations for us."

"Wait! I think your saying there's 'only road and rail' has given me an inspiration. There is also the river."

"Then they'll watch the Port, too."

"I doubt it. Small steamers ply down the Arieshu to the Danube, but no foreigner would ordinarily travel by such a route; and as the boats call at all the little river villages no criminal would normally choose such a slow method of getting away from the capital. While you are buying your nun's outfit tomorrow morning Rex can make enquiries. Ask him to find out the times of the sailings and to take three tickets for us on the first boat that leaves after one o'clock tomorrow. If we succeed in our job at the Legation we will go straight back to the Peppercorn and pick him up there."

Having settled these details, they wished each other luck again and, on reaching the next corner, separated.

After walking for five minutes, Simon picked up another *droshky* and drove in it down to the Dambovita. When he entered the hotel, its proprietor was still up, having only just put out the lights of the little bar that opened into the small square hallway. He was a fat, dyspeptic-looking man with a crop of close, dark, greasy curls.

With an unfriendly, suspicious look he pointed at the cuff of Simon's shirt, and said something in Rumanian.

Glancing down, Simon saw that his cuff was heavily stained with von Geisenheim's blood.

Without waiting for a reply, the landlord tapped his own left arm, held it up as though it were in a sling, then pointed at the ceiling. Obviously he was referring to Rex, whom he must have seen come into the hotel half an hour or so earlier.

Simon did some quick thinking, then raised his elbow and his right hand, half-open, as though he had a glass in it, thus making a pantomime of drinking. Next, he started to sway about, then struck out with his fists at the empty air.

The landlord relaxed a little, taking it, as he was intended to do, that they had been mixed up in a drunken brawl. Such episodes were common enough down in the dock area, but he was still not altogether satisfied, as he now pointed at Simon's hat.

Simon had forgotten for the moment that he was wearing the black hat trimmed with red fox fur traditional among the Jews of the Bukovina. All his outer clothes, and Rex's, were different and of a considerably lower social level from those they had been wearing when they had arrived at the hotel the previous evening.

He tried to think of a suitable excuse for this change, which had clearly raised the landlord's suspicions; but with no common language between them it would have been difficult to put over a plausible story, even if he could have thought of one. His imagination failing him, he resorted to that universal language which has so often averted unwelcome suspicions. Taking out his pocket-book, he laid a Rumanian bank-note high enough in value to pay for a week's keep on the ink-stained desk, put his finger to his lips, his hand on his heart and smiled confidingly.

The Rumanian pocketed the note without the least hesitation, but he did not smile in reply. Merely shrugging his broad shoulders, he jerked his thumb towards the stairs and turned away, apparently placated.

They had managed to get two rooms adjoining, a single one for the Duke and a double which the other two were sharing. Rex had washed his wound and roughly rebandaged it before going to bed; he was still awake.

While Simon adjusted the bandage properly he told him of his brush with the surly landlord and outlined the Duke's plans for the next day. Then he undressed, got into bed and put out the light. Within a few minutes they were both asleep.

Next morning they went out soon after nine on their respective assignments and met again in their bedroom at the Peppercorn an hour later.

Rex had ascertained that the little river steamers left their jetty twice daily, at nine o'clock in the morning and three in the afternoon. Tickets were not necessary, as they were not unduly crowded, and fares were collected on board. Simon had emptied their suitcase to take with him, and it now contained the robe and coif of a nun of one of the Greek Church Orders.

Had it been any male form of disguise he would have changed into it in a public lavatory, but he could not possibly go into one for men and come out of it dressed as a nun, so he could think of no alternative but to bring it back to the hotel and change there.

"Hope to goodness that nosy landlord doesn't see me going out," he said nervously, as he struggled into the unaccustomed garments.

"I'll beetle down before you," Rex volunteered. "You wait on the bend of the stairs, and when I cough you'll know it's all okey-doke. Sit tight till I do, then beat it across that hall for all you're worth."

A few minutes later he wished Simon luck and walked heavily downstairs. The landlord was not about, so, having had a good look round, Rex coughed loudly.

Simon came down the stairs at a run, forgot to hold up his skirt, tripped on it and took a header into the hallway.

At the noise of his fall the door leading to the kitchen was pulled sharply open, and the landlord stood there gasping with amazement, while Simon scrambled awkwardly to his feet.

Looking at Rex and pointing at Simon, the landlord burst into a torrent of Rumanian which, from its tone, was clearly protest mingled with abuse.

Simon did not stay to listen but, red in the face with rage and mortification, picked up his skirts and ran out into the street.

Rex could only pretend that he thought the whole matter a terrific joke. Roaring with laughter, he clapped the landlord on the shoulder, and pointing after Simon gave way to positive shouts of faked hilarity.

The landlord did not appear to see the joke. First he scowled darkly, then he shot a series of staccato questions at Rex, but as Rex could not understand a word he said he threw up his hands in disgust and made to turn away. But Rex caught him by the shoulder and pronounced the only Rumanian word he knew "*Tuica*—two, *deux*, *zwei grosser*."

This the fat man understood, and going to the bar he fetched out the bottle and two glasses. It was fiery stuff, but Rex drank it down without batting an eyelid. The landlord drank his with the unconcern of a professional but he became no more genial and after a few minutes reached for the telephone.

Rex refilled the glasses, and they drank again, then he paid for the drinks with a useful note and waved aside the change. But his sop to soothe the landlord's ruffled feelings came too late. He could not know it, but the man had already telephoned for the police.

Simon, meanwhile, had got himself a *droshky*, and was driving in it to the Cathedral. When he arrived there, he found that there was still twenty minutes to go before the time of his appointment. The only thing to do seemed to be to enter the building, although he was extremely troubled about doing so as he had no idea at all what sort of procedure an Orthodox nun would follow in it.

Walking as sedately as he could, he took a chair behind one of the pillars and knelt down there. The trappings of the building were magnificent in the extreme and far outdid the average Roman Catholic Cathedral in their splendour. He wished that he could walk round and examine some of the old Byzantine paintings at his leisure, but he did not dare to do so from fear of coming face to face with some of the priests.

Kneeling there he had ample opportunity to consider the fact that in less than an hour's time he might well be dead. It was pretty certain that by this time somebody would have come across von Geisenheim and the Attaché. The German Legation would give the Rumanian authorities no peace until they received satisfaction for this brutal assault on one of their leading Generals, so all the best brains in the Bucharest police would now be exerting themselves to trace and catch his attackers. But, far worse, the whole Iron Guard organization would have received urgent orders to hunt for them. And if they were caught it would be no mere matter of being deported this time. The men who had shot Calinesco yesterday would not hesitate to shoot them today. And it was probably that very bunch of assassins who had been posted outside the British Legation, as the most likely place at which von Geisenheim's assailants might appear. And he, Simon, was just about to go there. If he were recognized, or even if they questioned him— and they were probably questioning everybody who attempted to get into the place—that would be the end. Simon's mouth was so dry that he found he could not swallow, and he choked loudly into his outspread hands.

The wait seemed interminable, but at last he felt that sufficient time must have elapsed for the Duke now to be at his post ; so he got to his feet, tripped over his robe again, just managed to smother a curse of fright, dipped awkwardly before the altar, said a swift, agonized prayer, and made his way as calmly as he could to the west door.

Outside there was a solitary, yellow-painted taxi. Its driver, a peaked cap pulled well down over his eyes, lounged at the wheel. His heart pounding under his ribs, Simon approached. The driver did not even appear to see him until he was within two paces of the cab; then, raising himself a little, he swung open the door and murmured quietly:

"Good morning, Simon. In you get."

The sound of de Richleau's well-loved voice restored Simon's nerve a little. "Thank God you're here," he breathed, as he got in. "Did you get this without any trouble?"

The Duke swung the door to without looking behind him, as casually as if he were a taximan born and bred, then started up the engine, and his voice came back through the half-open glass partition:

"Yes. I had no trouble at all. I bought the clothes first, then simply went to a rank and drove this taxi off while its owner was in a little eating-place having his breakfast.

"Look on the seat beside you," he went on, after a moment. "There's a small fat packet there. That's the Golden Fleece. For goodness' sake don't drop it. Better put it in your pocket."

Simon had already seen the packet. Picking it up with a trembling hand, he secreted it safely under his robe. Then he leant forward as though to give directions to his driver.

"Rex's wound doesn't seem too bad, but he's going to see a doctor and have it properly dressed while we're doing our stuff. I'm a bit worried about the landlord at the hotel, though. Surly sort of chap. He saw that I had blood on my clothes last night, and I'm afraid he spotted that it was me going out dressed up as a nun this morning."

"Plenty of time to think of 'crossing the Vistula . . .'," quoted the Duke cheerfully. He seemed in a high good humour this morning and Simon felt with no little envy that he had never had greater reason to admire his courage.

"Got your gun handy?" sang out de Richleau a few minutes later. "We're coming up to the Rhine. Just walk forward looking at the pavement. Don't take any notice if anyone speaks to you. Remember you are a nun. Just side-step politely and walk on. If they question me and I am recognized, that may start the shooting. Just look round once as though you were scared, then run like hell for the Legation gate, as if you were dashing for cover. If the worst happens and they tackle you, try to throw the packet into the Legation garden. If you have to use your gun shoot to kill, but don't fire unless it is at somebody barring your way to the Legation gate. If you have to run for it before you can get near enough to throw the packet over the wall your job is to try to get away with it. Don't try to help me, whatever sort of mess I may be in. Pull up your skirts and run as though all the devils in Hell were after you. Here we go. *Bonne chance*, Simon!"

De Richleau had purposely refrained from giving his final instructions till the last few moments in order to take Simon's mind off the dangers that lay ahead. When the taxi slowed down Simon saw that four men were still posted outside the Legation gate, but suddenly he had lost all sense of fear and found himself completely calm and collected.

As the taxi drew up two of the men walked purposefully towards it, but when they saw Simon get out they halted, gave him only a casual glance and strolled back to their companions.

With his eyes cast piously on the pavement, Simon, now playing his part to perfection, went forward with short, firm steps. The sidewalk was a wide one, and to his surprise he realized that he had already covered three-quarters of its width without any of the men making a move to stop him. Another few measured steps and the men parted to let him through while two of them murmured a "*God be with you*".

He bowed slightly in acknowledgment. His heart was steady now and high with elation. He was so near the gate that whatever happened they could not possibly stop him throwing the Golden Fleece over it. He had got it out while still in the taxi and had it clutched firmly in his left hand, which was thrust into the wide sleeve of his robe. In his right hand he grasped his pistol, similarly hidden.

Suddenly there was a shout behind him. Automatically he faltered and looked round. A man dressed as a taxi-driver was running diagonally across the street and yelling wildly as he pointed at the number-plate of the taxi at the wheel of which the Duke was sitting.

In an instant Simon grasped what had happened. By an almost inconceivably ill chance the taxi-driver whose cab the Duke had taken earlier that morning had been walking down the street, and had recognized his stolen taxi.

The gibberish the man was shouting meant nothing to Simon, but it did to the passersby, and to the men posted on the Legation gate.

The second they realized the cause of the man's excitement two of them dashed forward towards the taxi. The other two closed up in front of Simon.

He stepped aside and tried to pass, his eyes still desperately fixed on the ground. One of them grasped his arm. It was that of the hand that held the packet. He wrenched his arm free, but in doing so his hand was pulled from his sleeve. The other man saw that he was trying to conceal something and with a cry of triumph grabbed at it.

Simon snatched his hand away. A shot rang out somewhere behind his back—another and another. Both the men now flung themselves at him.

Suddenly he heard a loud smack. The forehead of the man who had grabbed his arm seemed to cave in, and blood gushed out over his left eye. With splendid marksmanship the Duke, ignoring his own attackers, had put a bullet through the man's head.

As Simon jumped aside the man fell against his companion, who staggered back, then recovered; but only to lurch again with a second bullet from the Duke's gun in his body.

The dead man now lay sprawled upon the pavement, the other was reeling back against the wall. De Richleau's shooting had freed Simon for the moment. Spinning round, he thrust the precious packet into the pocket of his robe, grabbed it up and ran towards the car. Then he remembered that he must not go to it and, swerving, dashed off in another direction.

But he had glimpsed it as he started forward. Four other men, all with pistols in their hands, had suddenly sprung up from somewhere. All six of them were blazing away at de Richleau, who, crouching over his wheel, was blazing back at them.

Even as he glimpsed the Duke he saw him jerk as a bullet hit him. Another had sent his chauffeur's cap flying, and there was blood streaming down his face.

As Simon ran an awful thought came to him. He was still grasping the accursed Golden Fleece. In the excitement of the moment he had forgotten to throw it over the Legation gate. But it was too late now; he was twenty paces past the end of the Legation garden.

He turned to throw one desperate glance over his shoulder as he ran. The police had now come on the scene and were firing at the Iron Guards. The crash of firearms and the whizz of bullets seemed to come from every side. Three men were now writhing on the pavement, but some of the Iron Guard were still firing at the taxi, and de Richleau now lolled out of its side, his gun dropped from his hand, limp and deathly still.

Chapter XVI

AND THEY WEPT BITTERLY

SIMON's every instinct was to dash back to the Duke; to pull his gun, which he had not yet even used, and shoot down some of the assassins who were still blazing at the limp body in the taxi, before he himself was killed or captured. But even as his footsteps faltered he knew that to do so would be to betray his friend's last trust.

In an agony of self-reproach he cursed himself for having bungled his part in the affair. After the Duke had disposed of his two assailants for him he had had a clear thirty seconds in which he could have thrown the packet into the Legation garden. It was addressed to Sir Reginald and marked "Most Urgent". As de Richleau must have foreseen, the sound of firing outside would immediately attract the attention of the people in the Legation; and that had proved the case. The first shots had scarcely echoed down the street when the porter on duty had opened the door; Simon had even glimpsed him as he came out on to the top step. If the packet had been thrown in he would have picked it up, and even the Iron Guard would have hesitated before actually attacking a servant of the Legation on his own ground.

Yet, once the real taxi-driver had raised the alarm and the shooting had started, everything else had followed with such frightful swiftness. As the Iron Guards had grabbed at Simon every thought had gone out of his head, except to keep the packet from them. When he should have thrown it to the porter he had made the mistake of turning round, and lost precious seconds stumbling towards the taxi. The sight of the Duke, crouching over the wheel, hatless, wounded, fighting for his life, had recalled to him the order to run for it if there were trouble. Now he had his wits about him again and knew that his one paramount duty lay in retrieving his blunder by saving the option from capture.

Half blinded by tears, which had welled up into his eyes at the sight of the limp, bullet-riddled body of the Duke, he raced on. As he swerved round the first corner that he came to he cast one glance back. The police and the Iron Guards were still shooting it out. Most of the passersby had run for cover in gateways and behind trees; and their horrified attention was riveted on the street battle that had begun so suddenly. It seemed as though those who had noticed him had taken him for a frightened old woman running, as many of them were themselves, to get out of danger. No one was now looking in his direction, except the survivor of the two Iron Guards who had stopped him getting into the Legation.

The Duke's second shot had only winged him, and he was staggering along behind Simon, supporting himself with one hand against the wall. In the other he grasped his pistol. As Simon turned the corner the man raised his weapon and fired, but the bullet whistled harmlessly over Simon's shoulder.

He was thinking fast now. He had a good hundred yards' start, but, encumbered with skirts as he was, he knew that he would never be able to keep it. The wounded man knew that he had been trying to smuggle a paper into the Legation. Although he could only stagger along himself, he would soon succeed in attracting the attention of some of his comrades and send them careering after the pseudo nun. In the use of his wits and not his legs lay Simon's only hope of escaping capture.

Fifty yards down the street he had entered he saw a small box-van. Its driver was just going into a house to deliver some vegetables. He must have heard the firing but could see nothing of it and probably thought that it was none of his business. The half-door at the back of the van was open. Everyone else at that end of the street had run to the corner and was cautiously peering round it at the fracas outside the Legation. As Simon passed them he had dropped into a quick walk, as though, now that he was out of danger of a stray bullet, there was no longer any need for him to hurry. On reaching the van he gave a quick glance behind him. No one was looking in his direction. The delivery man was now hidden by the shrubs which bordered the tradesmen's entrance.

Quick as thought Simon slipped in through the open half of the van door and, making himself as small as he could, curled up behind the still closed half. With his heart pounding in his chest he crouched there, waiting.

A minute later he caught the sound of running feet. They stopped on the pavement just beside the van. Several voices were all talking excitedly in Rumanian. Simon guessed that it was the Iron Guards and part of the little group of onlookers that he had passed on the corner. It was probable that the delivery man had just come out of the tradesmen's entrance and they were asking him if he had seen a nun. A nervous shudder shook Simon. He knew that his life hung on his not being discovered in the next few moments.

For what seemed an age, but was actually only the time it would have taken him to light a cigarette, he sat doubled up, straining his ears for sounds that meant life or death to him.

The patter of running feet came again. Suddenly, without warning, an empty crate crashed on the boards beside him as the greengrocer's roundsman threw it into the back of the van. The door was slammed to. The bright daylight gave place to sudden semi-darkness. There was a moment's silence, then the engine of the van was started, and with a jerk it drove off.

Simon let out a long sigh of pent-up emotion. But he knew that he was still very far from being out of the wood. If the roundsman had another call to make in the same street he would open his van to get out the goods and almost inevitably discover his stowaway passenger. Then the hue-and-cry would start up all over again.

The van ran on smoothly and turned a corner. His nerves strained to breaking-point, Simon strove to calculate the distance they were covering as it sped along. It turned another corner, and he began to breathe more freely. Then it stopped.

Simon's nature revolted at every form of violence. He positively loathed the desperate encounters in which his friends always seemed to be getting themselves involved. De Richleau was a born fighter who never sought to disguise the fact that he got as much joy out of shooting an enemy as in outwitting him by some skilful plan. Rex always enjoyed an opportunity to use his great physical strength. Even the mild, good-natured Richard seemed to derive a quiet satisfaction from delivering a well-aimed blow; but to poor Simon the very sound of crunching bone or sight of bleeding flesh was purgatory.

If he had been able to speak Rumanian he would have attempted to fool the roundsman by some plausible story concocted as he went along, or, if necessary, protest that he was an innocent party and plead with him for continued sanctuary from the pursuing killers. But he was not capable of doing that, and the man, even if, like most Rumanians of the working classes, he feared and hated the Iron Guards, was probably under the impression that a criminal dressed as a nun was wanted by the police; so he would raise an outcry the second he set eyes on his passenger.

Simon knew there was only one thing for it. Taking out his gun, he reversed it and clutched it tightly by the barrel.

The door opened, and the man thrust his head and arms inside, reaching in the semi-darkness for his next delivery of fruit and vegetables. His forward movement ceased abruptly as his downcast eyes lit on the skirts of Simon's robe. At that second Simon let him have it with the gun-butt, hard on the back of the head.

With a little moan the man pitched forward half in and half out of the van, his head bumping with a loud knock on the empty crate that he had thrown in after his last call.

Suddenly Simon felt himself shaking all over with silent semi-hysterical laughter. The phrase to "stick out one's neck" had just flashed into his mind, and there could rarely have been a better example of the dire consequence likely to follow such an act than that which had just occurred.

Fighting down his absurd, unnatural giggles, Simon pocketed his gun, grabbed the unconscious roundsman by the coat collar and, exerting all his strength, hauled him inside.

Having covered the man's feet with two potato sacks that lay handy, Simon waited for a moment, then cautiously peered out through the still open half-door. The van was in a side street. There was a coalcart standing stationary outside an open gateway about a hundred paces behind the van, and on the opposite side of the road two small boys, somewhat nearer but with their backs turned, were walking away from it. No one else seemed to be about, so, gathering his courage, Simon slipped out and swung the door to behind him.

He spent a moment adjusting his robe, then peeped round the corner of the van on the pavement side. A fat, stupid-looking woman carrying a heavy shopping bag was just level with the bonnet. She gave him a startled glance, but he stepped out, piously lowered his glance, and, controlling his gait to a slow, measured pace, walked past her down the street.

After passing two cross-roads he came to a broader thoroughfare in which buses were running. Taking the first that was going towards the centre of the city, he sank down on one of its seats more dead than alive from heartrending distress about the Duke and nervous exhaustion from the appalling half-hour he himself had just experienced.

While he was in the bus he knew that he should be thinking of the future and trying to formulate some new plan for getting the option safely into

Sir Reginald Kent's hands, but his mind refused to function on those lines. The one fact which hammered in it repeatedly, to the exclusion of all else, was that their Great Planner was now out of the game for good.

Simon could not yet bring himself to accept it that never again would he look upon that charming debonair face and that the master mind that lay behind it would fashion no more subtle schemes for the discomfiture of their enemies; although the evidence of his eyes told him that de Richleau was dead It had all come about with such appalling suddenness. It was still too close to be fully realized; yet one thing was quite certain—the Duke could not aid them now. Richard was crippled and out of it altogether. Little Marie Lou and Lucretia, both of whom had so often helped in the past with good ideas, were out of it too. Poor Jan, who might have proved a useful standby, if he had still been with them, was dead. The whole battle, both its direction and its waging, lay now with him and Rex, and even Rex was wounded.

He had simply produced a small coin and taken the ticket that was handed to him. The conductor roused him from his nightmare thoughts on his reaching the limit to which his fare took him. He got out to find himself in the centre of the city, opposite the National Theatre. Hailing a *droshky*, he had himself driven back to the Peppercorn, still with tear-dimmed eyes that took in nothing of the scene about him.

Upstairs in their bedroom he found Rex waiting. How to break the news was another problem. Simon had not even thought of that. He sat down on the bed to gain a moment's respite.

"Well! D'you get it in?" Rex asked eagerly.

"No," Simon muttered. "I've got it here," and he produced the flat, square packet from his robe.

"Where's the Great White Chief?" suddenly enquired Rex, sensing from Simon's manner that something had gone seriously wrong.

"There was shooting, Rex. I was almost inside the Legation gate. He covered me and shot two of them who got in my way. But there were six of them at least. He told me that whatever happened to him I was to run for it. When I looked back . . . Oh God!" Simon sank his face into his hands and burst into a flood of tears.

For a moment Rex stood there, stunned.

"You don't mean . . ." he stammered. "Oh, for Christ's sake!" He seemed to wilt as though someone had hit him, and as his great shoulders sagged he lost height.

Then, recovering a little, he burst out: "It can't be! I refuse to believe it!"

Walking over to Simon, he sat down on the bed beside him and put his good arm round his friend's shaking shoulders. "Let's hear the whole of it, Simon," he urged. "Come on, old boy. You've had a packet, a blind mute could see that. But try to tell me just what happened?"

It was some time before Simon became sufficiently coherent to give a detailed account of the scene outside the British Legation. Rex listened without comment and was forced to admit to himself that there could be little hope for the Duke.

When it was done they sat plunged in silent despair, until at length Simon said : "What shall we do now ? We've got to get the Golden Fleece to the Legation somehow."

"Oh, to hell with the Golden Fleece !" Rex groaned. "What's it matter now ?"

"It matters no more, but every bit as much, as it did before," replied Simon logically.

"I know, I know ! But it was for that accursed bit of paper that he got himself rubbed out. We'll win the war sooner or later whether the barge traffic is stopped or not. Why should you and I deliberately follow Greyeyes into a death trap ? And it's certainly shrouds for us if we try making that Legation."

"But we *must* !" cried Simon, spurred for the first time since his return into a positive reaction. "We must, Rex. We've got to get this packet to Sir Reginald somehow. Of course we'll win the war sooner or later ; but every single day it goes on hundreds of people are being killed and maimed. The chance to shorten it is in our hands. If Hitler's oil is cut off he *must* collapse far sooner than he would otherwise do ; or else occupy Hungary and Rumania in order to get his supplies going again. And even if we compel him only to do that it means a great dispersion of German effort, which again will enable the Allies to win considerably earlier than there is any hope of their doing at present."

"You're crazy, but I'll say you're right about it all the same," Rex admitted. "Well, how'll we set about it ?"

"Goodness knows ! I don't." Simon shivered. "Don't think I could face walking into that hornets' nest again, even if I had ten men all standing round armed and ready to protect me."

"No. I reckon to try that way again means curtains for both of us for sure. But there must be some other line ? Does it have to go to Sir Reginald ? Why ? Only because he's the British Diplomatic representative here and could get it by fast bag to London for us. We've got thirty days to go before the option runs out. We ought to be able to reach London in that time. Why not let's fade right out of here and take it to London ourselves ?"

Simon looked up, and his tear-dimmed eyes showed a little flicker of light. "Um," he nodded. "I believe you've hit it, Rex. As long as it reaches the British Government in time for them to cable the money here so that Sir Reginald can complete the deal by midnight on the 20th of October we'll have pulled off our coup."

"How long d'you figure it'll take for us to get back to London, under war conditions?"

"No need to worry about that. If we can get safely out of Rumania, into any of its adjacent countries, the job's as good as done. British Minister in Sofia or Istanbul will despatch the Golden Fleece to London by fast bag for us just as readily as Sir Reginald would have done."

"Sure," said Rex. "Sure, you're dead right about that. And the little river steamer'll take us down the Arieshu to the Danube where Bulgaria forms the southern bank. Come on, Simon, we'll have more time than we want later being lonely for the smile of the Great White Chief. I don't like the face of our dyspeptic-looking landlord one little bit, so the sooner we're out of this joint the better. Get those 'Hail-Mary' clothes off while I pack the bag. We've still got all the time we want to catch the three o'clock boat."

Simon pulled the coif off his head. He was just about to struggle out of the robe when there came a sharp rattle of the doorknob, and the door was unceremoniously thrown open.

"Well! Talk of the devil . . .!" Rex exclaimed on seeing the landlord bulking in the doorway. Then his eyebrows drew together in a frown as he saw that behind the fat man was a little fellow wearing a trilby hat and that they were accompanied by two uniformed policemen.

The landlord had already stepped into the room. Pointing at Simon accusingly, he broke into a spate of Rumanian; then, picking up the discarded coif from the bed, he waved it excitedly in front of the others, before throwing it down with a gesture of angry disgust.

The little fellow came forward, giving a quick flick to his hat that pushed it on the back of his head as though he were a detective in a Hollywood gangster film; they guessed at once that he was a plain-clothes officer.

"I spek Engleesh," he announced with a sibilant accent. "You not conduck yourselves nice 'ere, no. Ze managaire, 'e telephone complaint zis morning. I say you 'phone me gen when zey comes in. 'E 'phone; I come. What you make in zose woman's clothes, eh?"

Simon strove to raise a smile, as he replied: "Well, I'll tell you. This is a kind of fancy dress. I've been trying it out for a party."

"You wore et in ze street. In Bucharest zat ess an offence. We no allow men to walk aroun' in ze clothes of women. Get me pleese your passports."

Simon produced his and the detective turned to Rex, who produced his also. The little man looked carefully through them, then put them both in his pocket.

"Hi!" exclaimed Rex. "Give me that back. I'm not going to have you walking off with my passport."

The man shrugged and displayed a police badge which he was wearing under the lapel of his coat. "I take et for check-up. Ef et ess O.K. you get it back later. You call tomorrow, twelve o'clock, at ze Dambovita Distreck Office. I gif you." Then turning to Simon, he added: "You comes with us."

"I was only wearing it for fun," Simon protested.

"You make zat story for magistrate tomorrow ten o'clock. Perhaps 'e sink you tell truth." The detective shrugged again. "Now, no argues. You comes to police office. We lock you up for night."

With the two stalwart, dark-visaged policemen standing in the doorway there seemed little choice but to obey. It was a bitter pill to Simon that after what had happened barely an hour before he should now be lugged off to a lock-up, instead of being left in peace to nurse his grief; but at least he could thank his stars that his visitors were not Iron Guards and that he was only being arrested for a misdemeanour.

Rex was silently cursing the interfering landlord who had brought this infuriating and possibly dangerous complication on them. It was de Richleau who had done all the shooting outside the Legation, so Simon could not be called to account for that. But if the Iron Guard learned of his arrest they would endeavour to fix the assault on von Geisenheim, the Attaché and their chauffeur, and the theft of their car on to him. That was where the danger lay. Fortunately he was being taken only to a local police station on a minor charge, so there was at least a possibility that the higher authorities and their Iron Guard friends would not receive information that he had fallen into the hands of the police.

Simon had been thinking on much the same lines, and was just about to ask if he might change into more suitable clothes before they took him away, when he checked himself in time. His proper clothes had been in the back of the Chrysler, so he had none to change into except the Bukovina Jew outfit which was hanging up in the wardrobe. He had been wearing that the night before, and, even if von Geisenheim were half dead from his injuries, the chauffeur, and probably the Attaché as well by this time, would have described their attackers. If he put on his black clothes and fur-trimmed hat the local police might identify him from any description that had been circulated as the man wanted by Headquarters on an entirely different and much graver charge. Once that happened his number would be up; but, if he could keep his two identities separate, there seemed a fair chance that within twenty-four hours he might wriggle out of this minor mess and the people he really had reason to dread would never know that he had slipped through their fingers.

"All right, then," he said to the perky little detective. "I'll come along if you wish." Then, with his heart in his mouth, he produced the envelope containing the Golden Fleece and, tossing it to Rex, said as casually as he could:

"You might post this, will you? If I'm held by the police for a day or two on some formality I'd like to know that it's on its way."

The onlookers made not the slightest attempt to interfere, and Rex pushed the packet into an ugly, wide-mouthed vase on the mantelpiece, remarking lightly: "I've a letter of my own in that thing so I'm less likely to forget it than if I put it in my pocket. Sorry about all this. It's too damn' silly, and I shall get high on my own at the party tonight. If I don't fall in the river on the way home I'll be seeing you in the morning."

As the two policemen were about to march Simon away the landlord said something in Rumanian and tapped Rex's suitcase with his finger.

The detective translated. " 'E say you pack an' go. Zis 'otel family place. Verrie quiet, verrie respectable. 'E not want you 'ere. Peoples like you bad for 'is business. 'E say you get out."

"Tell him I wouldn't stay in his lousy joint if he paid me," Rex said angrily. "So long, Simon."

The door closed behind the little group, there followed a trampling of feet on the thinly carpeted stairs, and Rex was alone with his unhappy thoughts.

For a little he thought miserably about the Duke, then he forced his mind back to the present and what he had better do. The ball was now with him. He was last man in, and his side had fared pretty badly. He hated the thought that he might have to abandon Simon, and debated whether he dared go along to the court the following morning to find out if Simon got into a real jam through additional charges being preferred against him, or if he would get off with a fine and a caution; but he decided that he must not risk it.

If the police did identify Simon as one of the men who had attacked von Geisenheim they would jump to it that he, Rex, was another of the gang; and immediately he appeared at the police court he would find himself popped in the cooler, too. Then their last hope of getting away with the Golden Fleece would be gone.

"Come to that," he said to himself, "if the police have a lucky break, or attempt any serious check-up on this phoney nun stuff, they'll tumble to it that I was one of the bunch that got after old von G. long before tomorrow. They'll be coming round here to pull me in any time after the next hour or so. Perhaps it's just as well that sanctimonious heel of a landlord has handed me my check. I'll have to beat it outa here anyhow, and his having given me the bum's rush provides an explanation for my quitting."

When he had said to Simon, "If I don't fall in the river on the way home I'll be seeing you in the morning," he had purposely left himself free to choose whether he left Bucharest at once or decided to stay on. He knew that if Simon did not see him in the morning he would at once realize that the alternative had been adopted, and that by "falling in the river on the way home" Rex had meant taking the river steamer down the Arieshu as the first stage of his journey back to England.

But now Rex suddenly saw that it was no use his taking the river steamer. When he had made enquiries at the jetty that morning the man in the office had told him that it was not necessary to take tickets in advance but that he should bring his passport with him, because the steamer touched on Bulgarian waters when it reached the Danube and no one was allowed further than the mouth of the Arieshu unless they had proper credentials. And now he no longer had a passport, because that "so-and-so" of a detective had taken it from him.

To call for it at the police office at twelve o'clock the following day entailed exactly the same risk as going to the court to find out what happened to Simon. And that was quite definitely off. There did not seem to be any point in going on the river steamer if he was to be turned back even before it reached the Bulgarian frontier, so he tried to consider the whole position afresh and get a new angle on it.

For some ten minutes he sat on one of the cheap iron bedsteads with his head in his hands, trying to think of a safe, speedy way of getting through to Bulgaria ; but whatever route he took the loss of his passport now presented a major obstacle, and he dared not apply for another at the American Legation because that was one of the places where it seemed certain that the Iron Guard would be on the look-out for him.

He wondered how the Duke had meant to proceed when they got down to the Danube. Probably he had intended evading the Rumanian frontier guards, by hiring or stealing a small boat in which to row across at night, or even that they should slip off the river steamer at some place where it passed close to the Bulgarian shore and swim for it. Some bold stroke of that kind would have got them past the Rumanians, and by hitch-hiking to the border Rex felt fairly confident that he would find a way of evading the frontier police ; but now, without a passport, it would be necessary to outwit the Bulgarian frontier patrols as well, and he did not feel that the odds were very good on his managing to cross such a wide river as the Danube without being spotted by the trained watchers on the far bank. If he were caught trying to enter Bulgaria without a passport the authorities would not simply turn him back ; they would hand him over to the Rumanians, and falling into their hands was the one thing above all others that he must avoid.

"How would the Great White Chief have played it ?" he asked himself. "Now the river steamer's a washout and the police are even more on their toes about us than they were when he planned that line for our get-away. Maybe he'd go to earth right here in Bucharest for a while ; adopt a masterly policy of inactivity, as he used to say himself. It would certainly be up his street to remain right in the thick of things when the enemy were wasting their shoe-leather looking for us all along the Bulgarian frontier ; and that sure is where they'll have turned on the heat, seeing that it's the quickest way out."

The thought gave him another idea. As the Bulgarian frontier was by far the nearest to Bucharest, de Richleau would probably have chosen another route for their attempt to get out of the country. Yugoslavia, Hungary, Poland and Russia also had frontiers bordering on Rumania, but all of them were at a much greater distance from Bucharest than Bulgaria, and, even when reached, were in the opposite direction to that in which Rex wanted to go.

Russia and Russo-German-occupied Poland he ruled out at once, as, if he arrived in either without a passport, he might have great difficulty in getting any further and would probably be clapped into prison right away. Hungary and Yugoslavia offered better prospects, and there was no great river to cross into either, so the odds were against his being caught trying to enter and turned back at once. If only he could get twenty miles or so into one of them he might still be arrested, but it was hardly likely that the authorities would then return him to Rumania before he had had a chance to get in touch with his Legation, and once he had done that he could count on the protection of the American Minister.

But how to reach either still remained a problem; and there was, too, the unpleasant prospect that, lacking a passport, he might be held while enquiries were being made about him for days or even weeks in the gaol of some little mountain town. And time mattered.

If only he could have got hold of an aeroplane the whole thing would have been so simple. Aircraft were to Rex what horseflesh had been to the hunting squires of Georgian England. When he was at home in the United States hardly a day passed without his going up in a plane. He had flown everything from a Tiger-Moth to a Pan-American Air Liner and possessed four planes of his own. If, by hook or by crook, he could obtain one now, the crossing of the desolate mountain chains to the west would hold no terrors for him. He could fly straight out to Belgrade, or even Rome if the aircraft had sufficient range and fuel. Once he reached one of these capitals, being arrested on his arrival would not matter. Within twenty-four hours American diplomatic representatives on the spot would have vouched for him, and he would then only have to get the Golden Fleece despatched by fast bag.

The more he thought about it the more convinced he became that an aircraft was the answer to his problem. But how was he to get hold of one?

The civil airport would certainly have its own police, and, if his description had been circulated, they would already be on the look-out for him there. Yet where else could he get an aircraft? On the outskirts of the more Western capitals there were numbers of private flying clubs, but Rumania was a backward country, as far as aviation was concerned, and from his wide knowledge of such matters Rex felt certain that he was most unlikely to find an aircraft of the range he needed on any Bucharest airfield, apart from the Military Aerodrome and the Civil Air Port.

For a bit he racked his brains for any other place where aircraft of a fair size might be found, and suddenly an idea came to him. All that remained of the Polish Air Force was being flown out for internment in Rumania. Up in the north, just this side of the Polish border, there must be scores of aircraft lying idle, in any one of which he could make the trip out to Budapest or Belgrade. And the odds were that once the Poles had turned their machines in they were not heavily guarded.

The only thing against the project was that it meant going right up to Cernauti in the Bukovina. That was almost the most distant part of Rumania from Bucharest, but on that count it had the advantage that it was the least likely place in which the police would look for him. He wondered if they, or the Iron Guard, would be watching the trains going to the north for Simon and himself, and thought it quite probable that they would not bother to do so. To be on the safe side, though, he decided to hitch-hike out to a station some miles to the north of the capital and take a slow train from there.

Having made his plan, he stood up and finished the packing of the suitcase, putting Simon's incriminating garments into it as well as his own bits and pieces. While he did so he was considering how best to let Simon know of his intentions.

As the British and American Legations were ruled out, the only place where Simon, if he succeeded in getting out of the mess he was in, could hope to pick up Rex's trail was here, at the Peppercorn ; but Rex knew that any letter he might leave would go, via their officious landlord, straight into the hands of the police.

It was with this in mind that he had tossed the option into the ugly wide-mouthed vase on the mantelpiece, and made his casual remark that he would not forget it because he had already put in it another letter of his own. Simon knew that he had written no other letter, so, if he were discharged with a fine the following morning, he would come straight back to the hotel and somehow gain access to their old room, probably on the excuse that he had left something there, in order to look into the vase to see if Rex had left in it a letter for himself.

The snag was that in the interval the chambermaid might find the letter while doing the room and either throw it away as of no importance or give it to the landlord.

Realizing the necessity of disguising the meaning of any note that he left behind, Rex gave the matter quite a little thought and eventually wrote two notes, the first of which, scrawled on a plain piece of paper, simply read, "Base over Apex", and the second, written as small as he could on a strip of sticky-backed stamp paper, ran, "Plenty of Jan's Toys where your hat came from."

H

By Jan's "toys" Simon would know that he meant "aeroplanes", and Simon's fur-trimmed hat had come from the Cernauti district, so he would jump to it at once that Rex had gone there in the hope of getting out of the country by his favourite means of travel.

Having taken the Golden Fleece out of the vase, Rex stuck the second message to its bottom and put the first one in it. If the chambermaid threw away the piece of paper with "Base over Apex" on it, that would be no great loss, as, should Simon succeed in getting back to the room for the deliberate purpose of looking in the vase, he would pretty certainly look under it as well ; but if the paper remained, then it would serve as a quick way of letting him know where to look should the landlord accompany him on his visit.

Going downstairs, Rex settled the bill for his party and went out into the street. In order to disguise his height as much as possible, he adopted a slouching walk, and, as he knew that the taxi garages in most capitals were happy hunting-grounds for the police when they were trying to get on the track of foreigners, he took a bus as far as the Royal Palace, then changed into another which served the northern suburbs. He did not remain on it to the end of its run, again to avoid being remarked by the conductor and information later reaching the police about his movements, but got off when the vehicle reached the outskirts of the city and was still about a quarter full of passengers.

He then walked for about three miles until a motorist on the now semi-deserted road, seeing him trudging along with his bag, slowed down and offered him a lift. As this good Samaritan did not speak anything but Rumanian, Rex was spared any embarrassing questions as to where he was going. The car took him on his way for another five miles, then pulled up in the square of a village, and the driver indicated that he was not going any further.

On finding that the village had no railway station Rex set out north again. It was late afternoon now, and the country looked very lovely, although, owing to the great heats of summer, the ground was parched and the leaves of the trees already yellow. As he walked along, little traffic passed him, and he thought how strikingly different it was from any place within a similar radius of New York, London or Berlin. From all the great metropoli, modernity, with its hideous jerry-building, frequent petrol stations and advertisement hoardings, had stuck out its ugly tentacles twenty to thirty miles deep on every side. But here, although Bucharest itself was a fine city with many great modern buildings, less than twelve miles from its centre he was in the depths of utterly unspoiled country, where great fields of corn stretched unbroken by comfortless little houses, and the scattered farmsteads were great, picturesque, rambling places that appeared to have remained unaltered for many generations.

There were now very few motors on the road, but occasional farm carts trundled by, and when he was tired of walking he got a lift in one for a couple of miles. Just as he left it and was thanking the farm-hand with a pantomime of smiles, a petrol wagon pulled up outside the gate of the farm they had arrived at, and its driver came into the yard to ask for a fill-up of water. After some difficulty Rex learnt that the man was taking his wagon back to Ploesti, the centre of the Rumanian oil industry, and as that was directly on his way he asked to be taken there, to which the driver agreed readily enough.

Soon after they left the farm the landscape began to change; the rich cornlands and orchards gave way to a more desolate part of the Wallachian plain. There were no trees, and coarse grass covered the great open sweeps of land that ran unbroken to the horizon, until they came in view of the first oil wells. When they had covered another mile or so the square, tapering wooden shafts above the wells rose up out of the black earth to either side of them like clusters of lighthouses, but lacking their grandeur, strength and beauty. Here and there among them were ugly wooden sheds, and the atmosphere was polluted with the unpleasant stench of petroleum. It was a dreary and depressing scene, and Rex was heartily glad when about six o'clock the driver reached his journey's end in the equally dreary and depressing little town that provides such a big proportion of the revenues of Rumania.

He was now the best part of thirty-five miles from the centre of Bucharest and felt that he should be safe in continuing his journey by train. Ten minutes after he had been dropped he was making enquiries at the station and, with the aid of a German-speaking commercial traveller, learned that the night train from Bucharest to Cernauti stopped to pick up passengers at Ploesti at twelve-forty-five.

Going out again, he made himself as comfortable as he could in the bleak-looking lounge of the station hotel, where he drank four *tuicas* at reasonable intervals to while away the time. At ten o'clock, the earliest he could get it, he went in to dinner and found the food of surprising excellence for such a place. But he ate only because he thought he ought to and to get through another hour of his wait, being still too burdened with sorrow about de Richleau to take the least interest in his food or the bottle of Odobesti wine that he was drinking.

At twelve-thirty he went back to the station and bought a second-class ticket for Cernauti, feeling that if he travelled first he was much more likely to be drawn into conversation with people who spoke a language he could understand, and have to give an account of himself; and, in any case, that second class was much more suitable to the clothes he was wearing.

When the train came in the first-class compartments were comparatively empty, so that Rex could have got a sleeper had he wished, whereas the seconds were fairly full and not even a corner seat was available; so he had to sit up practically straight all night, but he tried to console himself with the thought that as a second-class traveller he was much less likely to arouse anyone's interest and be remembered afterwards.

When he and his fellow passengers roused themselves from their uneasy dozing the grey light of morning showed that the train was running through a country of rugged mountains, great forests and picturesque waterfalls. But they had some hours to go yet in one another's company, as the run from Bucharest to Cernauti takes the best part of twelve hours and they were not due in until shortly before mid-day.

Just before they pulled in to Cernauti, Rex took down his bag and went along to the rear end of the train with the intention of slipping off the last coach and getting out of the station by one of the entrances to its goods yard, just as he had done with the Duke and Simon two days previously at Giurgevo; but this time he was unlucky. He ran into a friendly, but in this case most unwelcome, train conductor, who, finding him to be a foreigner, insisted on taking his bag from him.

In consequence, during the next ten minutes Rex suffered acute apprehension. He tried to restrain himself from looking about too anxiously, but he knew that if a check-up had been made the previous evening on Simon, linking him with the assault on von Geisenheim and the theft of the option for which the Germans had paid so much good hard cash, his own description, in full detail and much more accurate than any the Germans' chauffeur could have supplied, would have been obtained from the little detective who had carried Simon off, and circulated during the night to all railway police.

But no one challenged him, and outside the station he found a German-speaking *droshky* driver who took him, on his request, to a small, inexpensive hotel, called the Roebuck.

The hotel was run by a family of Jews named Levinsky who had relatives in the United States and spoke a little English, as they were learning it in the hope of migrating to that Mecca of golden promise to all their race. They were hard-working, kindly people, and, although their hotel was packed with Polish refugees, they could not do enough for Rex. They provided him at once with a hot bath, although it was the middle of the day and most of their usual guests bathed only on Friday nights, the eve of the Jewish Sabbath, and while he was having it they specially prepared for him a good hot meal.

Feeling much restored after this, he made a determined effort to throw off his crushing sorrow about the Duke and his anxiety about Simon as he sallied forth into the town to learn what he could about the evacuation of the Polish Air Force.

He found Cernauti as unlike Bucharest as any town could be. The capital of the Bukovina had none of the spaciousness and splendour of the capital of the State. It was a congested, shabby place that yet had bright garish spots in its cinemas, theatres and dance halls. To his surprise he heard little Rumanian spoken in the streets, but quite a lot of German, and considerably more of a language he guessed to be Yiddish from the appearance of its speakers.

It was the 23rd of September, a Saturday, and the Jewish Sabbath was obviously being observed by a high proportion of Cernauti's inhabitants. The main street and principal square might in some respects have been a section of the Jewish quarter of New York or of Whitechapel. The more prosperous of the population, all of whom seemed to be Jews, were wearing the bright, flashy clothes that pass for smartness with the middle classes of their race wherever it is to be found. Nine-tenths of the shops, all bearing Jewish names, were shut, and these children of Israel were taking their leisure, the older people strolling along here and there, greeting their friends with grave courtesy, the younger ones chi-iking each other and shouting rowdy witticisms as the groups intermingled in the roadway.

In strange contrast to this modern scene, many poorer members of the same community thronged the sidewalks clad in threadbare blue gaberdines and the high black hats trimmed with red fox fur that had been the costume of their people for centuries. Many of them still wore their hair long, and it dangled in red, greasy curls down on to their shoulders. They were representatives of that great portion of the Jewish race rarely seen in England and America, who lack quick wits, a flair for moneymaking and no small ability in the world of music, literature and art. Their only culture lies in a parrot-like ability to repeat long passages from the Torah by heart; in all other ways they are abysmally ignorant, and stupid, dirty and poverty-stricken almost beyond belief.

Rex had often discussed the Jewish problem, thinking in terms of the flashy Americanized Jews who throng the second-class cinemas and restaurants of the great cities of the Western world, and by their overbearing brazenness give a false impression of their numbers. He knew, too, that there existed a small sprinkling of really cultured Jews—men of quiet demeanour and unshakable integrity, such as his own friend Simon Aron—and he had often argued that, in spite of their reputation for sharp practice, the average Jew was honest and industrious and made a useful contribution to any country in which he settled. Here, for the first time in his life, Rex was brought face to face with the real Jewish problem, and he wondered unhappily how any country could make useful citizens out of these dirty, stupid-looking off-scourings of humanity.

How these myriads of Jews had come to settle there he had no idea, but as he thought about it he remembered that Cernauti lay in the very heart of Middle Europe. It was almost equidistant from the Baltic and the Black Sea and occupied a position where four frontiers, those of Russia, Poland,

Hungary and Rumania, very nearly met, and with that of a fifth, Czecho-slovakia, only a little distance to the west. Perhaps the Jews had chosen it so that, whenever the Governments of any of those countries were affected by a wave of anti-Semitism, there were still others into which their surplus population could overflow without meeting such rigorous persecution. That they were still breeding like rabbits was clear from the swarms of ill-clad children in the streets, and Rex no longer wondered why the world's statesmen found the Jewish problem such a headache.

The only Christians to be seen were a sprinkling of peasants, attending the Saturday cattle market in the square, and the Polish refugees, who, in the main, were easily distinguishable by their appearance. Somewhat to Rex's surprise, however, nearly all the Poles were civilians, and he saw very few men in Polish uniforms.

Those that he did see were hurrying through the crowd, evidently intent on their own business; so, finding no groups of Polish officers idling and at a loose end, with some of whom he had hoped to get into conversation, he returned to the hotel and, sitting down in its small lounge, began to talk to some of the refugees who were its principal occupants.

All of them had tales to tell, varying in their excitement and hairbreadth escapes from death or capture, but all ended in the same pathetic refrain—gnawing anxiety about the fate of loved ones left behind, destruction of homes and things held dear; the loss of businesses and the savings of a lifetime, the terrible uncertainties of the future.

Rex listened in sympathy to those who could tell him of their tragic flight in English, French or German, and gradually obtained the information he wanted, without appearing to enquire for it. The Rumanians had shown great humanity to their suffering neighbours, but naturally they had to abide by established international procedure. Under the laws of war any defeated force might seek sanctuary in a neutral country, instead of sur-rendering to the enemy, but a neutral was under an obligation to intern any such force for the duration of hostilities.

The Polish officers that Rex had seen in the streets were representatives of the Commondature of the interned Polish Forces, who had been released on parole for the purpose of making arrangements about quarters and supplies for their companions. A state of emergency still existed on the frontier, owing to the continued influx of Poles, and the Rumanian author-ities were occupied in making encampments for them. These had not yet been completed, but the main body of Polish servicemen who had escaped over the frontier were already behind barbed wire some miles to the north of Cernauti near a little town called Grodek.

It was now well on in the afternoon, and, seeing that only three out of the thirty days for which the option was good had so far elapsed, Rex decided not to go out to Grodek until the next morning. His wound, the terrible shock he had sustained the previous day and his uneasy night in the train had all combined to take it out of him, so he got the Jewish owners of the hotel to fix him up a high tea at six o'clock and went upstairs immediately afterwards.

As he hung his jacket on the back of a chair he took the packet from his pocket for the first time since Simon had passed it on to him, and wondered where it would be best to put it for the night. After a moment he decided that until he could get it out of the country it would be safest in the money-belt that he always wore round his middle when travelling abroad. Opening the envelope, he refolded the sheets lengthwise and slid them into the longest pocket of the belt. To do so he removed the banker's draft that he had been carrying there since Teleuescu had refused to accept it two nights before, and, as its purpose had now been fulfilled by other means, burnt it. Within five minutes of his getting into bed he was sound asleep.

Next morning, although his wound was doing well and the clean punctures in his healthy flesh already beginning to heal, he thought he ought to have it dressed again, so he consulted Mr. Levinsky, who sent him to a Jewish doctor.

On his way there he saw that the town had now taken on a completely different appearance. Quite a number of true Bukovinians were strolling up and down resplendent in the peasant finery that they wore only on Sundays ; but practically every shop in the place was open and the streets were packed with thousands of Jews shrilly driving their Monday morning bargains.

The Jewish doctor impressed Rex as cleverer than the man he had seen in Bucharest, and warned him when he was leaving that, although neither of the punctures was any longer discharging, he ought to keep his arm in the sling for another ten days at least. As Rex hoped to be flying an aeroplane long before that he did not expect to follow this advice, but he had every intention of taking as much care of his arm as he could.

Anticipating that as Grodek was right on the frontier it would be even more crowded than Cernauti, he decided to leave his bag with Levinsky— at all events until he had made a preliminary investigation of the frontier town. The next problem was to get out there.

It was the best part of twenty-five miles away, and normally he would either have gone by train or hired a car ; but, with the uneasy idea never far from his thoughts that the police might be on the look-out for him, he decided not to risk arriving right on the frontier by such conspicuous means, and set out to hitch-hike again.

On leaving the city the road crossed a low range of hills and wound down again to the River Pruth, all the land beyond which had been Russian territory up to 1918. Just after Rex had crossed the river a lorry picked him up, and from his slightly higher elevation beside its driver he saw that the country both in front and to the right of him was one vast level plain. The lorry was going into Grodek, but he saw the huge internment camp that was still in process of being erected to house the Poles long before they came to it, and slipped off at one of its barbed-wire entrances, hoping that the lorry-driver would think that he was a Pole who was visiting the camp to look for a friend.

Indeed, that was the rôle he would have adopted had he been able to speak any Polish, but, as it was, he had to content himself for the time being by just looking up and down the road as though he did not know which way to go, then setting off at a fast walk parallel with the wire as if he had made up his mind that the entrance he wanted was further along.

It took him over an hour to circle the great camp, but by the time he had done so he had a pretty good idea of its lay-out. The Poles had not just been dumped down in the centre of the open plain, and, in view of the desolate country thereabouts, the site of the camp had been well chosen. Its main feature was a group of buildings about three-quarters of a mile from the road, which appeared to consist of an old manor house surrounded on three sides by stabling and farm buildings. At its back there was a wide stretch of almost treeless parkland, and it was here that the machines of the Polish Air Force had been parked. In front of the group of buildings there was an avenue of elm trees, and on each side of it a number of wooden hutments formed the nucleus of the camp, while many more were in process of erection.

Apparently the Poles had been given the task of guarding themselves, as only sentries in Polish uniforms were to be seen at the gates and loitering outside the wooden guard-house that stood near each of them. But on the side of the camp nearest to Grodek Rex saw that there was a Rumanian military airfield with permanent buildings and under canvas near by what he estimated to be a battalion of Rumanian Infantry.

He wondered if all the Polish planes had been rendered inoperative by the removal of some of their essential parts, but considered it unlikely, as, even while he watched, Rumanian aircraft in the sky above were shepherding new Polish arrivals down into the park that had been made a temporary aerodrome for them. He thought it probable that the Rumanians were quite content to have their Polish visitors behind the wire, as, once there, they were under the discipline of their own senior officers, and it was most unlikely that any of them would attempt to fly out again.

On a rough count he estimated the Polish aircraft to number at least two hundred, and practically any of them would serve his purpose provided it had enough petrol in its tanks. That and getting into the camp were, he foresaw, going to be his main difficulties. After their tragic defeat the Poles themselves would undoubtedly be depressed and slack. There was no reason why they should even set a guard upon their aircraft now that they were no longer in a position to use them. Probably the most they bothered to do was to post a small picket as a formality, and that would be quite inadequate to prevent a trained big-game stalker, such as Rex, getting away with one of their machines at night.

He noted where the latest arrivals were being parked, as it was less likely that they would have had their petrol drained out of them by nightfall. If he could once get to the machines there was a good stretch of level ground facing the front row, so he did not think he would have any difficulty in taking off.

The question was, how to get into the camp? He noticed that all the men arriving at the gateways, whether on foot or by car, had to show passes before they were allowed inside. But quite a lot of them were civilians, as a considerable number of workmen was supervising and assisting in the erection of the new hutments.

Clearly his line was to try to get in as one of these workmen, perhaps the following morning, then hide somewhere in the camp when they left at night. It seemed, though, that he would have to show some sort of pass. Perhaps that evening in the town he would be able to contact some of the workmen and either buy to steal the pass he needed.

Having gathered all the information he could from outside the cage, Rex walked into Grodek. The sight of the place positively horrified him. It consisted of a single row of board shanties patched up with hammered-out petrol tins. Its poverty and filth beggared description. Beyond it lay the broad sluggish sweep of the Dniester and on the far bank a continuance of the seemingly endless windswept plain. During the snows and gales of winter it must have been sheer purgatory to live there, but at least the snow would have mercifully hidden some of its filth and decrepitude.

Its population consisted entirely of the poorer-class Jews that Rex had seen in Cernauti on the preceding day, yet these, if possible, looked still more dirty and destitute. The shacks that passed for houses and shops were even more tumbledown than those inhabited by the very poorest class of negro in the Southern States.

Outside the hovels, which displayed pathetic little assortments of shoddy goods for sale, swung painted signs showing that the population of the place was so backward that a good part of it could not even read, and he doubted if any slum in Europe or the United States could show evidence of such dire and universal poverty. The people of the place, red-haired Jews without exception, apart from a handful of uniformed officials, crept rather than walked about, their greasy caftans hanging in tattered rags, their faces pinched, their dark eyes furtive, and stinking to high heaven.

In spite of its poverty this nightmare township boasted several rather larger hovels that did duty for inns. Rex visited them all in turn, and selecting the least repulsive, ordered himself a meal. Somewhat to his surprise, there did not appear to be any Polish refugees in Grodek, so he could only assume

H*

that after crossing the frontier they all gave the place one horrified look, shuddered, and hurried on to Cernauti. There was, however, one Polish officer, whom Rex assumed to be on pass from the camp. He was a thin but muscular-looking fellow as tall as Rex himself, with china-blue eyes and fair smooth hair.

Rex got into conversation with him in the hope of picking up some information about the regulations governing permits to enter the camp. He found that the Pole spoke French and a little English, and said that he came from Radom.

While the shadows lengthened they ate the indifferent fare the place provided together, and, after a while, Rex learned to his annoyance that none of the men in the Rumanian working parties were local people. They had been imported from further south and both worked and slept in the camp.

Rex saw that he would have to bide his time until he could get in touch with some of them in their off-duty hours when they took a stroll outside the cage, or think of some other way of entering it. After his meal, with great reluctance he booked a bed at the inn, but it was still early yet and dusk had not long fallen ; so he thought it would be a good idea to stroll up to the camp again to see if it were as well guarded at night as it was in the daytime.

Having paid for the tall Polish airman's dinner as well as his own Rex wished him good-night and went out into the street. Turning south, he set off between the two lines of dismal buildings towards the camp. The place boasted no pavement of any kind, and there were no street lamps. The only light came from guttering candles set in bottles which could be seen glimmering through some of the grimy windows that he passed.

After he had covered a couple of hundred yards he suddenly got the impression that he was being followed. There were very few people about, so once on the *qui vive* he was soon able to identify his shadow by the simple process of alternately quickening and slowing his pace. It was the Polish officer with whom he had been feeding, and there was no doubt that the fellow was following him, as each time Rex paused to light a cigarette or peer into one of the ill-lighted windows the tall airman stopped too.

Rex had always been so confident in his own strength that, forgetting about his injured arm, he was not the least perturbed, and when he reached the end of the town walked briskly on into the darkness of the open country. He had covered another quarter of a mile when he caught the soft footfalls of his shadow, who was now evidently hurrying as quickly but as quietly as he could to catch up with him.

Even then Rex only wondered vaguely what he wanted, and surmised that perhaps the poor fellow was going to ask him for a small loan, having been ashamed to do so in the public room at the inn.

When the footsteps were only a few yards behind him Rex turned and said : "Hello ! *Que voulez-vous ?*"

To his amazement, instead of replying, the man crossed the remaining space between them in two swift bounds, whipped out a black-jack and slashed with it at his head.

Taken by surprise, he jumped aside only just in time. But his assailant struck again, and the second blow caught him on the side of the head above the ear.

It was only as he reeled back half blinded by pain that he remembered his injured arm, and strove in vain to jerk it out of its sling.

His foot caught in something, and he lost his balance. With silent ferocity the man leapt upon him and bore him to the ground.

Next moment, with not the faintest conception as to why he had been attacked, Rex found himself fighting for his life.

Chapter XVII

UNEQUAL COMBAT

As Rex went over he fell backwards on to the grassy verge at the roadside. The Polish airman came down on top of him, driving the breath out of his body ; he had thrust out his left hand to get a grip on Rex's throat, and his right, in which he still grasped the black-jack, was raised for another blow.

Gathering his great strength, Rex suddenly hunched up his knees and lifted his shoulders, throwing his antagonist off. But the man came at him again like lightning and forced him back on to the grass before he could even struggle to his knees.

Rex knew that normally there were few men, apart from professional boxers and wrestlers, who could have bested him in a physical combat, but his injured arm robbed him of a great part of his powers, and the Pole was not only as tall as himself but extremely muscular and fit. He could not for the life of him imagine why the fellow had attacked him, yet he cursed himself for having been caught unawares. He had known for a good ten minutes that the man was following him, and on a lonely road at night in an area given over to a defeated army he should have realized that there might be desperate characters about, and at least have had the sense to pull out his gun as the man came up with him.

He thought now as he lay on his back writhing under his assailant that if he could only get at his gun he might yet put a swift end to the combat in his own favour. But he had only one free hand, and he needed that to protect his head.

As the Pole swung the black-jack up again Rex caught his wrist and gave it a savage twist. With a grunt of pain the Pole let the weapon go, but it fell only to dangle from his arm by a leather thong. Next second he had smashed his left fist down into Rex's face.

Rex flinched under the blow, but hung on to his opponent's wrist. Jerking it towards him, he gave it another violent wrench, at the same time heaving himself over sideways. To save his arm from being broken the Pole let his body follow through and was flung right over Rex's head. As his shoulders and back descended heavily on Rex's wounded arm, Rex let out a yell, but for the moment he had freed himself.

With an effort he jerked himself up into a sitting position and reached for his gun, but the Pole was up too, on his knees, and hit him a stunning blow with his clenched fist on the side of the head.

Rex heeled over under the impact. He was being attacked now on his crippled side and was thus almost defenceless. The Pole slogged at him again, and before he could grasp the butt of his gun he was forced to snatch his hand from his pocket to protect his head.

The Pole, seeing his advantage, struck with both fists alternately, raining a hail of blows at him. As the only way of avoiding them Rex flung himself backwards again on to the grass, and once more thrust his hand down to his pocket in an attempt to pull out his pistol.

Suddenly the Pole jumped to his feet and delivered a terrific kick at Rex's body. It got him under the ribs. The pain was excruciating, and the breath was driven out of his lungs. Gasping for air, he rolled over in the hope of getting away; but his attacker ran at him and kicked him with all his force again. This time the man's heavy boot landed on Rex's head.

Stars, circles and flashes flickered and gyrated in the intense blackness that abruptly veiled his eyes. His head was singing like a kettle, he was still fighting for breath, an agonizing pain was tearing at his ribs, his skull seemed to be opening and shutting, there was the salt taste of his own blood in his mouth. New pains stabbed at him as he lay, now inert and helpless, and he knew subconsciously that the Pole was ruthlessly kicking him into unconsciousness. Then the pain eased and he passed right out.

When he came to he lay quite still for a time, staring at the starlit sky above his head and wondering what had happened to him. Then memory trickled back. The Duke riddled with bullets, Simon arrested, himself left as the sole hope of getting the Golden Fleece safely through to London, his journey to Cernauti, the tall, blue-eyed Polish airman and the bitter, uneven struggle.

There was a dull ache in his side, and his head hurt intolerably. Suddenly he shivered and realized that he was very cold. Next moment the reason seeped into his still bemused and pain-dulled mind. He was lying there on the grass in his pants and vest. While he was unconscious he had been stripped of all his outer clothes.

As he struggled into a sitting position pain stabbed at him in a dozen places; his chin dropped heavily on his chest, and he moaned. Then the thought of the Golden Fleece came into his mind again. If that had been taken with his clothes it was the end, as he had not the faintest idea who his attacker was or any means of tracing him.

With bruised and aching hands he fumbled at his waist. His wounded arm had been pulled from its sling when the Pole undressed him. As he moved it he felt a sharp twinge of pain above the elbow, but it seemed now the least of his hurts.

Suddenly he let out a sigh of relief, and relaxed. The money-belt was still there, and he could feel the fat flat wad of the option in it. Fooled, beaten up and robbed as he had been, the worst had not happened. He had the bulk of his money in the belt, too, so once his pains eased a little he could buy other clothes and be able to carry on the big game, which was the only thing that really mattered.

He did not think that he had been unconscious for very long, as the moon was only just rising above the flat horizon. Lifting himself painfully to his feet, he shivered again. Then as he looked round his eye lit on a tumbled heap of stuff a few yards away from him. Something on the top of the heap shimmered dully in the faint moonlight. Walking over, he saw that it was a button, and that the heap consisted of the Polish officer's clothes.

Turning them over, he found that the whole outfit was there; uniform greatcoat, cap, tunic and breeches, belt, shirt, collar, tie and even the black boots. The man had been his own height, so the clothes should fit him. Shivering again, he began to put them on.

As he did so he formed an idea of the probable reason why he had been attacked. Many of the Poles were, he knew, splendidly stout fellows and had already expressed their determination to fight on, although their country had been overrun. Perhaps this chap had intensely resented the idea of being cooped up in an internment camp and made up his mind to get to France or Britain in order to join in the fight against the Nazis again as speedily as possible. He had spoken a little of both French and English, so the difficulties of the journey should not prove insurmountable if he could once get away from the area where his compatriots were interned. To do that his most urgent need would be a suit of civilian clothes. Meeting Rex, who was the same height as himself, and very vulnerable to attack through having one arm in a sling, must have proved too much of a temptation for him, and he had decided to knock him out and strip him as the most certain way of getting what he wanted.

The uniform proved a little tight across the shoulders, but to Rex's relief the boots were big enough; the cap, however, was a hopeless misfit, being at least three sizes too small.

As he pushed it on to the back of his head it suddenly came to him that his recent ill luck might in reality prove a blessing in disguise. Here he had been all the afternoon and evening battling his wits for a way to get into the camp, and a Polish officer's uniform had now been thrust upon him.

Regretfully now he thought how stupid it had been for the Pole and himself to fight it out when, had one of them only disclosed his desires to the other, they might have simply swapped clothes and parted the best of friends.

The idea made him laugh, but directly he did so his mirth was checked by a dozen pains stabbing at him. This caused him to make a careful examination of his hurts. His head was very sore, and the blood had congealed on top of two nasty cuts, but his thick, curly hair had saved his skull from being cracked. His side now throbbed dully, but he did not think any of his ribs were broken as the pain was well below them. The wound in his arm had opened and bled a little, but he knew that it would soon heal again if he refrained from using it. All things considered, he had come off far better than might have been expected. He knew that for some hours to come he would continue to feel sick and giddy, but he had sustained no serious damage that time and rest would not put right.

He next debated whether to make his attempt to get into the camp that night, but quickly decided against it. For such an undertaking he needed all his wits about him, and, even if he pretended to be tight, so that it might be assumed that he had been mixed up in a drunken brawl, to arrive at one of the gates with blood all over his face was a sure way to invite questions from the guard, and, as he could not speak Polish, that was the one thing he must avoid. Still badly shaken and half-bemused as he was, it would have been madness to risk ruining the whole business through some stupid slip that he would not normally make when rested and more or less recovered from his beating up. Besides, there was no great urgency about getting hold of a plane, as only four days were gone out of the thirty for which the option was valid.

In consequence, he began to wonder how he could best get himself cleaned up and where to pass the night. He could walk back to the town and claim his bed at the inn; but the odds were that by this time it would be shut and to get into it he would have to knock up the evil-smelling travesty of Shylock who ran the place. Even if it were still open, its single room giving on to the street, which served as hall, lounge, dining-room and bar, was much too small for there to be any chance of his slipping through it and up the rickety staircase at its far end unnoticed. Shylock's visitors were not so many or his eyes so slow that he would fail to remark that Rex, having gone out dressed like a fairly prosperous mechanic, had returned clad in the uniform of a Polish officer, and his instinct for keeping on the right side of the authorities would probably send him creeping hurriedly round to the police station to lay an information about the strange metamorphosis of his visitor.

Rex could have gone to one of the other inns but he thought it a hundred to one that wherever he showed himself his state would attract attention, so he dismissed the idea and decided to spend the night in the open. He remembered that, about halfway between the town and the camp, the road ran over a low stone bridge that spanned a sluggish stream. There, at least, there would be water to wash in and, with luck, under the arch he might find shelter from the possibility of rain and wind.

The moonlight was now brighter, and before leaving the place of his fierce encounter he looked carefully round to see if either he or the Pole had dropped anything during their struggle. But he could find nothing. All his clothes had disappeared, and with them his gun, his torch and the wallet in which he had kept all his notes of low denomination.

The bridge was only ten minutes' walk away, and on reaching it he found that it would serve his purpose admirably. Under it, on the north side, there was a bank between it and the stream amply wide enough for him to stretch himself out without any risk of his rolling into the water. Stooping his head, he got down below the ancient blocks of stone and spread out the Pole's greatcoat on the ground. The night was moderately warm here out of the wind, and, having stretched himself at full length, while he was still worrying about his throbbing hurts, he fell asleep.

In the morning he woke to find that his head and side were still sore, but he felt considerably better. Partially undressing, he knelt down by the stream and bathed his hurts in the cool water. As he was about to pull on the tunic again he felt something crinkle in the left breast pocket. On looking inside, he found a square piece of flimsy paper. It had some words in ink neatly written on it in a language he took to be Polish; below them was an indecipherable signature scrawled in pencil, and imposed upon it a circular rubber stamp in the centre of which the figures 24.9.39 stood out clearly.

The date was that of the day before, so it seemed highly probable that this was the pass on which his Polish assailant had left the camp the previous afternoon. The camp authorities would have had no time yet to get proper forms printed, and the circular stamp was probably part of the office impedimenta that had been flown out with one of the Headquarters.

Rex grinned. It really looked as if his luck were in, and that he was receiving very valuable compensation for his bruises. Having no further use for it, the Pole had probably forgotten to remove it from his pocket when he collected his other things. In any case, whether it was a pass to the camp or not, it would serve admirably to flash under the nose of the sentry in the semi-darkness.

He now felt hungry, so, having peeped cautiously from his hiding-place to make certain there was nobody about, he emerged from it and walked into the town. After visits to several of the miserable shops he secured a loaf of dark rye-bread, some liver sausage, chocolate, half-a-dozen apples, a flask of some sort of spirit, a new torch with a spare battery, a bottle of disinfectant, some cotton wool and rolls of bandage.

Carrying his purchases back to his hide-out under the bridge, he first had a meal, then set about washing and dressing his wounds more thoroughly. When he had done, his face as well as his head was half-swathed in bandages, which he had so adjusted on purpose as they partially concealed his features and made it less likely that any of the guards who were acquainted with the Pole whose pass he now believed himself to carry would recognize him as an impostor. Many of the Poles were, he had noticed, bandaged for wounds they had received before escaping from the battle, so his would not make him particularly conspicuous. In addition, as he had tied a big wad of the cotton wool under his jaw he had only to point to it as a good excuse for not answering if he was questioned.

He then lay down to sleep again and spent most of the day dozing. About five o'clock he ate some more of the bread, sausage and chocolate and, not feeling inclined for any more sleep, began to contemplate the tricky business that he meant to undertake that night.

He was full of confidence that he could get away with an aircraft provided that it was in a condition to take the air. Even if the wind were not in a favourable direction, and he had to taxi her round to get off, he knew so many tricks that the feat of taking her up before he could be stopped presented no more difficulty to him than a cowpuncher would have had in mounting a bucking bronco. The only real snags were getting into the camp and finding a plane with an adequate supply of petrol. The question of petrol had to be left on the knees of the Gods for the moment, but it seemed that his prospects of passing the guards were now pretty good. It was not as though they were posted to protect some vital headquarters or even an operative air station, so they would probably be slack and lazy. It was a comfort, too, to think that the Rumanians would almost certainly have deprived the interned Poles of everything except their rifles and side-arms, so the odds were against their having machine-guns with which to try to bring him down once the noise of his engine raised the alarm and he was in the air.

The evening dragged by very slowly, and about seven o'clock he suddenly began to wonder what would happen to him if he were caught. Rex was such an optimist by nature that it had not even occurred to him to think seriously of such a possibility before; but now that he had thought of it he was quick to realize that he ought to have some excuse ready to offer for trying to get into the camp, or getting into it, under false pretences.

After cogitating for a little he decided that the best line would be to use the assault that had been made upon him the night before. He could say that he had been laid up by his injuries all day and now presented himself full of righteous indignation to claim compensation for the assault made on him and the theft of his clothes by a Polish internee.

They would soon find out that he was not one of the local inhabitants, so he had better come clean about being an American. If they wanted to know what he was doing in that neighbourhood he could say with a certain amount of truth that, like hundreds of other people of all nationalities, he had fled from the Nazi-Soviet invasion of Poland and landed up here as a piece of the flotsam of the war.

The story was based on such a nice substratum of truth that it seemed pretty good to him. With luck they might only put him under open arrest while making enquiries, in which case he would stand a good chance of getting away with a plane the following night.

There was only one rather disquieting factor about it. If the guards did not know about his assailant's desertion, before checking up on it they might disbelieve the story and insist on searching him. If that happened it was hardly likely that the money-belt round his waist would escape them, and they would come across the option. Should that fall into the hands of an interpreter he would realize at once that no man carrying such a document was just a casual refugee.

For a moment he thought of going straight to the camp, demanding to see the Commandant, telling him the whole business from start to finish with complete frankness, and asking to be given one of the Polish aircraft for the purpose of flying the Golden Fleece out to Yugoslavia. But he discarded the idea as having too many imponderables.

The defeated Poles had been honourably received by the Rumanians and would have now given their word not to allow any of their aircraft off the ground. Any Polish officer would hesitate to go back on his pledged word and, in addition, risk serious trouble with people upon whom they were relying for food and shelter. Again, if the Commandant proved to be some old Cavalry General who knew a lot about horseflesh but nothing at all about Economic Warfare, he might even fail to see the immense importance of the document and think that Rex was just some get-rich-quick Yankee out to feather his own nest. He might even be one of Mack's people and hold the secret belief that the best outcome for Poland would be a short war, after which his own country would be allowed semi-independence while enjoying the protection of a greatly strengthened Germany against the Soviet.

If he were caught, Rex decided, he would play that as a last card, but not before. Far better rely on his own wits and courage, and with a little luck he would be in Belgrade by this time tomorrow. But, in the meantime, he must certainly hide the option from any preliminary search as skilfully as he could.

Had he had a needle and thread he would have sewn it up in the lining of his jacket, but he lacked those useful requisites, and the packet was too thick for him to get it into his boot, as his foot would not go in with it there. After a little thought it occurred to him to put it in his cap, and removing the oilskin lining, which disguised its colour to the casual glance when put back, he secreted it there.

Another two hours dragged by, then about ten o'clock he crawled out of his hiding-place. On his way to the camp he saw only two Poles, and, in view of the hundreds of them that were interned in the camp, he judged that they were allowed out only on passes granted for special reasons. That made him a little more anxious about the validity of the one he was carrying, seeing that it was dated for the day before, but he went forward with a firm step.

When he reached the first wire he slowed down his pace and gave it a careful scrutiny again. The day before he had come to the conclusion that the strands were too close for a man of his size to get through without having most of his clothes and a good bit of his flesh torn from his back and legs by the barbs ; and, although he could not be certain, he thought that some unbarbed wires which ran through the lower part of the fence were probably connected with burglar alarms in the guardhouses. If so, he would be caught long before he could painfully wriggle through such a tangle. His second examination confirmed his first impression, so he felt that he would stand a much better chance of getting in uncaught by slouching past some bored sentry at one of the gates.

At the first gate he came to three men were talking under an arc lamp, so he maintained his unhurried pace and went on to the next. Here, too, there was an arc lamp, but the solitary sentry, evidently taking advantage of relaxed discipline, was leaning against one of the posts smoking a cigarette. Producing with his free hand the piece of paper that he hoped was his late antagonist's pass, Rex marched boldly towards the gate and stepped inside it.

The sentry came to attention and muttered something. Rex acknow-ledged the salute and proceeded a few paces. The man repeated the words he had said in a much louder voice. Halting for a moment, Rex waved the paper so that the sentry could see it, then made to move on. Again the man spoke ; his tone still held the normal difference usual in a private address-ing an officer, but underlying it there was a definite note of firmness.

Rex had hoped to get through without having actually to present the paper for inspection, but he saw now that he would have to do so. If he ignored the sentry the man would call his sergeant, and, if the paper were not after all a pass, the fat would then be in the fire ; but there was still a chance that a sight of the rubber stamp would be enough to satisfy the sentry.

Turning back a little, Rex walked over to the soldier. He tried to remain calm and to appear completely indifferent; but his heart was in his mouth as he held out the paper.

Chapter XVIII

UNDER SUSPICION

THE sentry took the paper and read it carefully. He was so long in doing so that Rex wondered if he were semi-illiterate. He was a big, blue-eyed, fresh-complexioned man who looked as if in normal times he might be a labourer from some Polish farm.

His blue eyes left the paper to search Rex's face, then went back to the paper again. Rex was worried now. He felt instinctively that there was something wrong. Next second he had proof of it.

Suddenly the sentry thrust the paper into his pocket, took two swift paces backwards, presented his carbine at Rex's chest and shouted something that Rex instantly guessed to be the Polish equivalent of:

"Guard! Turn out!"

There was a clatter and shuffling in the nearby hut. Out of it came tumbling a squad of soldiers, still hastily adjusting their accoutrements. A small, wizened man with a sergeant's stripes on his arm hurried over to the sentry. While the others lined up the sentry produced the piece of paper and gabbled something to the sergeant, who stared at Rex and asked him a question in Polish.

Rex was seriously alarmed. The sudden belligerence of the sentry and the turning out of the guard seemed excessive measures to take against an officer simply because his pass was out of date, or because he had produced some other document in lieu of it, and, as might reasonably be assumed, by mistake.

As he did not understand a word of what was being said and could not answer he pointed to his heavily bandaged jaw and shook his head.

The sergeant turned and spoke to one of his men, who promptly turned and ran off towards some hutments further inside the camp. There was then a pause while nobody said anything, but the whole of the little group of Poles stood about eyeing Rex curiously and, he felt, with a definite hostility.

After a few minutes the soldier returned with a young Lieutenant. Having examined the paper and spoken about it briefly with the sergeant, he addressed Rex.

As before, Rex pointed to his bandaged jaw and shook his head.

Again the Lieutenant spoke, but this time in halting German.

"You are Captain Kilec, are you not? Or I should say the man who is passing for him."

Rex hardly knew what to make of this. Kilec, presumably, was the man who had attacked him, and he certainly had endeavoured to pass as the Captain for the purpose of getting into the camp. But how did these people know that anyone was impersonating Kilec? That unscrupulous individual would hardly have attacked a stranger, robbed him of his clothes, left his own uniform behind and then returned to the camp with a story that someone had stolen his uniform and was now masquerading as himself. It did not make sense.

While Rex was still wondering what sort of a mess he had got himself into a car coming from the centre of the camp drew up just inside the gate. It was empty except for its driver, a fat little Major with a dark moustache, who leaned out to present his pass.

The Lieutenant went over to him, saluted smartly and showed him the paper with which Rex had endeavoured to enter the camp. They exchanged a few rapid sentences, then the Major got out and came over to Rex.

"So we've caught you, eh?" he said in fluent German. "Saints alive, what a nerve you've got attempting to get back into the camp on your own pass! What do you take us for, a pack of fools?"

The Major's sneering outburst gave Rex the first clue to the situation in which using his attacker's uniform and pass had landed him. Evidently Kilec had not been a patriotic Pole made desperate by the thought of a long internment and prepared to take any measures which would enable him to get out of Rumania to a place where he could resume the fight against the Nazis. It seemed that he must have committed some misdemeanour against his own people. Perhaps he had even already been under arrest and awaiting court-martial. In any case, it was clear now that he had assaulted Rex and stolen his clothes for the purpose of escaping from Polish military jurisdiction.

Rex saw at once that his only line now was to tell the story of how Kilec had attacked him, and say that he had come to the camp to claim compensation.

Shifting his bandage a little, he said in German:

"You've got this thing all wrong. I'm not Captain Kilec."

"We know you're not—now," the Major cut in. "We succeeded in tracing up the real Kilec this afternoon. He was killed a fortnight ago in the fighting outside Lodz."

"Well, I'm not the fellow who impersonated him, then. I'm an American citizen recently escaped out of Poland. I was . . ."

"You can tell that story to the Rumanians," the Major interrupted again, with a grunt of disbelief. "You're an optimist if you think it will prevent them from having you put up against a brick wall and shot."

"Hey! What's all this?" exclaimed Rex, suddenly galvanized into extreme perturbation.

"You know well enough—you filthy Nazi spy!"

"Nazi spy!"

"That's what I said."

"Now, wait a minute. For Mike's sake, listen. This is all one hell of a mix-up. My name's Rex Mackintosh, and I'd never even heard of this fellow who's been passing as Kilec until you mentioned him just now."

"There has been only one mix-up," broke in the Major swiftly. "And that was caused by you treacherous German swine invading Poland without warning. We had no chance to put up a decent fight, and in the ensuing retreat thousands of officers got separated from their units or killed without their deaths being reported. That made it child's play for scores of Nazi agents like yourself to pose as Polish officers and mingle with us. It will take us weeks to sort ourselves out and check up on everyone. In the meantime, we naturally made use of the most fluent French speakers we could find for liaison duties with the Rumanians, and you managed to get yourself picked for such a job while posing as the unfortunate Kilec. That's where the mix-up's come in."

"So I'm supposed to be one of your liaison officers with the Rumanians, am I?"

"Yes. Do you deny it? And do you deny that when you were in their camp yesterday morning, and were left alone for a few minutes in the Adjutant's room, you stole a document from his safe giving the situation of all the Rumanian airfields on their Polish and Hungarian frontiers?"

"I do deny it. I tell you I'm not Kilec, or the man who impersonated him."

"You are a fool. Lying like this will do you no good. How can you pretend that you are not the man for whom we have been hunting for the past twenty-four hours while you stand there in a Polish Captain's uniform, which is far too big to fit any ordinary man, and you present at the gate here the pass that was issued to the man who posed as Kilec yesterday morning? And, what is more, you speak excellent German!"

"I may speak fair German but I can't understand a word of Polish, so if I am the man you believe me to be, how the hell do you think I could have passed myself off as a Polish liaison officer?"

"You say *now* that you cannot understand Polish because it suits you to do so, but what proof have we of that?"

"For Mike's sake, keep your dirty cracks for the man you're after and give me a chance to speak. I'm an American. Get that. I recently came out of Poland in the general mix-up, but before going further south I stooged around here a bit in the hope of getting news of a friend of mine, a Captain in the Polish Air Force Reserve named Jan Lubieszow."

"Never heard of him," grunted the Major. "And it wouldn't do you any good if I had. Since you have been mixing with us as a spy you've probably got to know scores of Polish airmen without their suspecting you to be the scum you are."

"All right, all right. Anyhow, I was coming up to the camp yesterday evening to enquire for news of Jan when this fellow who's been kidding you that he's Kilec set on me. He's a big chap like me, just as you say; but all the same I would have pasted him plenty if it hadn't been that one of my arms is out of action. A stray bullet from a Hun aircraft zipped through it a few days back before I crossed the border with a bunch of refugees, so the set-to didn't go my way. Your friend laid me out and kicked me on the head until I was unconscious. When I came to I was in my pants and he'd beaten it with all my clothes, leaving his uniform behind. My baggage is somewhere in Poland, so I only had the things I stood up in. I couldn't walk around in my pants so I put on the uniform, and I came up here tonight to tell you all about it. Believe me, I'm as anxious to get that guy as you are."

"Very nice," said the plump Major sarcastically. "And what sort of story have you made up to account for the past twenty-four hours?"

"I haven't any story at all. I felt mighty sick by the time that so-and-so had done with me; and ever since I've been taking things quietly to get over the ill effects."

"Anyhow, you stick to your story that you are an American. In that case you will have a United States passport. May I see it?"

Rex managed a wry grin. "I certainly had one, but I haven't any longer. That Nazi we're both so anxious to meet took it off me with the rest of my things last night."

He felt that the lie could do no harm, and it saved him from having to tell some other which might be less readily believed.

"How very convenient!" sneered the Major, and went on after a moment: "Well, I don't believe one word of the account you give of yourself, and the best thing we can do is to hand you straight over to the Rumanians."

"Hey, wait a minute!" exclaimed Rex. "I'd rather you didn't do that. Can't you sort this thing out yourselves?"

"Why shouldn't we hand you over? Our relations with the Rumanians were delicate enough as it was, but there's been hell to pay since yesterday morning. Naturally they think it was a Polish officer who stole their damned defence plan. It wasn't till this afternoon that we were able to check up on Kilec and found out how we had been tricked. Of course, they don't believe us. They think we're lying to save our own good name, but you're the living proof that it was not a Polish officer who abused their hospitality, and it will be a real satisfaction to turn you over to them. I've a long drive ahead of me, but, by Saint Stanislas, I'll hand you over myself before I take the road south. It will be well worth half an hour's delay to see their faces. Get in that car while I telephone Headquarters to let them know we've got you and that I'm taking you across."

"Listen!" said Rex urgently. "For God's sake, listen! You'll regret it if you don't. I'm a Secret Service man—or, at least, I'm on that sort of work."

The Major had been about to turn away, but he stopped in his tracks. "You're a quick thinker, aren't you? I suppose you're going to tell me now that you're working for the Allies?"

"Yes. That's just what I am doing, and I'm on to a big thing. I demand that you take me to the senior Polish officer in this camp."

"Thanks, but we are not interested in secret documents stolen from the Rumanians, who, by and large, have behaved very decently to us."

"I'm not talking about this wretched defence plan. Who cares where they've stationed their antiquated kites, anyhow? I'm on to something of real importance to the Allies, and it's imperative that I should not fall into Rumanian hands."

"You don't like the idea of facing a firing party, eh!" The Major grinned. "You know that's what you'll get from them, and you think that if you can cook up some story to interest us we will save your skin by keeping you here."

"I don't have to cook up a story. I'm acting with some British friends, and, by hook or by crook, I've got to get out of Rumania."

"By heavens, you're a cool one!" cried the Major, and suddenly burst out laughing.

Rex promptly lost his temper. "You damned fool!" he roared. "Can't you get it into your thick head that I'm not the man you want, and that I'm not a German? I'm on your side—on the side of the Allies. It matters every bit as much to Poland as it does to Britain or France that I should get the information I've got to London. I demand to see your Commandant, and he's got to help me."

The Major's laughter stopped, and he suddenly stiffened, as he said frigidly: "There is only one thing we have *got* to do. That is to protect the honour of Poland, which has been brought into question by this theft. Nothing else is of the least importance compared with that, and it is a matter upon which no Polish officer would subscribe to the least delay. Your build, uniform, the pass you presented and your excellent knowledge of German all identify you with the man who stole the airfield layout plan from the Rumanians yesterday. Personally I am convinced that you are that man, and even if you are not we shall prove our good faith to the Rumanians by handing you over to them. Get in that car!"

"Please!" pleaded Rex. "You don't know what you're doing. You're wrecking the biggest coup that the Allies could pull off in this war. All I ask is to be allowed to see your Commandant."

"It is you who do not know what you are saying. 'The biggest coup the Allies could pull off in this war'!" The Major sniffed contemptuously. "That is overplaying your hand with a vengeance. Do you take us for fools that we should believe such twaddle? Evidently you think that the Commandant may prove more credulous than I am, and you hope to prolong your miserable existence by making a long tissue of such wild statements to him. But I will not permit it. I will not allow the good name of Poland to remain in question even five minutes longer than need be. Get into that car at once."

Rex started to plead again, but, after issuing an abrupt order to the Lieutenant, the Major stalked pompously away to the guard hut to report what had happened over the telephone to Headquarters.

The wizened little sergeant felt Rex over to see if he was carrying a weapon and, finding none, pushed him towards the car. Under the threat of the Lieutenant's revolver Rex climbed into the back seat, and one of the soldiers got in beside him. After a wait of two minutes the Major returned and took his place in the driver's seat. As he did so he said to Rex:

"I have spoken to Headquarters, and they entirely agree with me. Where the honour of Poland is concerned there can be no delay, so you had better think up some other story for the Rumanians. The Commandant is delighted. He is patting himself on the back now because, instead of keeping the affair secret, he had it broadcast through the whole camp last night so that every sentry should be on the lookout for 'Captain Kilec'. None of us thought that you would dare to return here, but it is great good luck for us that you were fool enough to do so. It was lucky, too, that I happened to arrive at the gate so soon after your attempted entry, because I am the Assistant Military Attaché. I shall be able to explain the whole affair to them, and, of course, bringing you to them like this will put up my personal stock."

The Major was now in a high good humour, but Rex hardly took in what the fat, pompous little man was saying. His last-ditch plan of coming clean with the Commandant of the Polish Internment Camp and begging his assistance had been frustrated through his most unfortunate encounter with this Assistant Military Attaché, who, either through stupidity or a desire for his own glorification, placed the urgency of satisfying the Rumanians before the possible chance of serving the Allied cause. All the Major's talk of "the honour of Poland" made Rex sick with fury, because had he only been allowed a chance to establish the point that he was not the man who had impersonated Captain Kilec, this very fact, with a description of the impostor's attack upon him and the clothes he had been wearing at the time, would have given the Poles themselves a better chance to help the

Rumanians catch the culprit, and, perhaps, retrieve their stolen document more speedily.

The very thought of the document made Rex shiver. Directly the Rumanians got him, whatever he might say, he would be searched, and searched with extreme thoroughness. They would not find their air defence plan, but they would find the option on the purchase of the Danube oil barges.

That would be the end of everything. It must be prevented at all costs. But, in God's name, how?

Poor Rex, jolting from side to side in the ill-kept car as he stared over the Major's shoulders into the darkness, would have given his wounded arm for an answer. The Rumanian Air Force Station was barely half a mile away. Within a matter of minutes they would be entering its gates. Once they were inside he would certainly never get out again without the Rumanians having gained possession of the Golden Fleece.

If only he had been fit and with both arms at his disposal he would have risked a car smash. With one good blow he could have put the soldier beside him past caring what happened for several moments. Then he would have grabbed the idiot Major by the back of his neck, hauled him bodily over the seat and used his body as a screen from the flying glass when the car ran into the ditch and turned over. But with only one hand he knew that any such desperate venture was beyond his powers. The soldier was sitting on his right, so he could not get a free swing at him or the power into a blow sufficient to knock him out; and if he failed in that the fellow would be on him before he had a chance to get at the Major.

The lights of the Rumanian Air Force Station loomed up ahead. Deciding on one last desperate attempt to make the Major see reason, Rex leaned forward and said loudly:

"Look! Don't drive in. For God's sake, listen to me! If only you'll help me to get out of this God-damned country I can stop Rumania's oil getting to the Germans. Honestly I can. I'm prepared to prove it."

The only response he received was a curt laugh and the Major's acid comment: "You're the most audacious liar I've ever met. I must tell the Rumanians that. It will ensure you a good reception."

Rex jerked back into his seat as though he had been hit. He had gone too far; said too much. If this self-centred little moron did repeat what he had said the fat would be in the fire with a vengeance. The fact that he was carrying the option was damning enough, but, if they learned the purpose for which it had been secured, the Iron Guards who were certain to be among them would see to it that he was shot before he had even had another breakfast.

Never had Rex been in such a frightful predicament. Beads of sweat had started out on his forehead, and his hands were clammy. He tried to imagine what the Duke would have done in such circumstances, but there was no time left even to wonder about that. The car was already turning into the gates of the Air Force Station, and its interior was flooded by the arc lamps outside the guardhouse. It was too late now even to attempt the desperate hazard of attacking the Major in the hope that the car would overturn. It had slowed up and the Rumanian sentry was calling his sergeant out of the guardroom.

Rex received one minute's grace while the car was at a standstill and the sergeant, having spoken with the Major, saluted and signed to him to proceed. As the car moved on again at a slower pace towards the Headquarters Offices of the camp Rex knew that he no longer had minutes but only seconds in which to think. Once he was in the hands of the Rumanians he would be stripped, and all his clothes would be gone through with a tooth-comb. It was a thousand to one against experienced searchers failing to examine his cap.

Between the gate of the camp and the big block of permanent buildings that housed its offices lay a quarter of a mile of tarmac road lit only by faint blue guiding lights. The moon was not yet up, and the interior of the car was once more in darkness.

With a sudden desperate resolve Rex took off his cap, fanned his perspiring face twice with it and laid it on his knees. The soldier beside him, knowing that he was not armed, was sitting quietly back, not even looking at him but staring straight ahead.

Gripping the peak of the cap with his knees, Rex thrust his one free hand inside it. Quickly but quietly, and making as little movement as possible, he crumpled back the oiled-silk lining and pulled out the packet from beneath it.

The car was already slowing down as it approached the main entrance of the office buildings. There was not a second to lose. In one swift movement he covered all of the packet but its corners with his great leg-of-mutton hand and taking it from the cap thrust it down out of sight beside his hip. His fingers came in contact with the tight-pressed fissure where the cushion of the back seat of the car met the upholstery of its side. As the car drew up before the entrance he thrust again with all his force, pushing the flat packet down until it was right under the heavy leather seat.

The soldier sat forward suddenly, but he had noticed nothing; he was simply stretching out his hand to open the door of the car. Rex lay back for a moment with an inaudible sigh of relief. Next minute the Major was shouting to him to get out, and he silently accompanied his guards into the Air Force Headquarters.

In the doorway he turned to give a quick look at the car. It was a dark blue Ford V.8. that had evidently seen much service. The dirt upon it was not only superficial, showing that it was not often cleaned really thoroughly, so he felt there was a good chance that the option would remain where he had hidden it at least for some days. As he followed the others he kept on silently repeating its number, UCZ827, to himself.

They were shown into a room on the right of a bare but spacious hallway. In it the Duty Officer, a dark young man of medium height, was seated at a desk. The Major excitedly explained his business, now speaking in French. The Rumanian gave them seats and, picking up a telephone, rang through to his Commanding Officer.

There was a short wait, and during it Rex thought agitatedly of the drastic step he had just taken. Now he had parted with the Golden Fleece, would he ever be able to get hold of it again?

Having freed himself of it, he did not think that he was in any great personal danger. He had nothing on him now which could lead the Rumanians to associate him with von Geisenheim's attackers, and he thanked his stars that he had had the sense to speak of himself as Rex Mackintosh to the Poles instead of giving his full name. Sooner or later they would have to produce somebody to identify their captive as the German who had posed as Captain Kilec, and then it would emerge that he was not the man they wanted. Once that was clear he did not see on what either the Rumanians or the Poles could hold him. There seemed no reason at all why they should not accept his story that he was simply an American refugee from Poland who had been attacked and had his clothes and papers stolen the previous night. If things went well they might even let him go right away or, at the worst, after a full enquiry had been held the following day.

As these thoughts sped swiftly through his mind he began to cheer up a little, but he soon became a prey to fresh anxiety as he wondered how on earth he was to set about retrieving the option. The Major had said something about having a long drive before him but that the pleasure of handing Rex over to the Rumanians would be well worth the delay in starting on his journey south. He had also said that he was the Assistant Attaché, so he was not an internee like the other Poles but free of the whole country to go and come where he pleased. The probability was that he had come north for a few days only to assist in making the arrangements for the interning of his fellow countrymen and was now about to return to his Legation in Bucharest.

If so, Rex saw that unless he were freed immediately after the coming interview with the Rumanian Station Commander, and could somehow get the option back that night, he would have to follow the Major to Bucharest; and the Duke, Simon and himself had already made Bucharest too hot to hold them. Rex did not like the idea of returning to the Rumanian capital one little bit, but it looked as if that was what he would have to do, and with the least possible delay; as otherwise the packet might be discovered before he could retrieve it.

How he was going to get free access to the Major's car he had not the faintest idea, but that must wait on circumstances and it would be time enough to worry about it when he had secured his own freedom.

He had got so far in his anxious speculations when a tall, thin officer entered the room. Speaking in French, which seemed to be the *lingua franca* in use between the Rumanians and Poles, he introduced himself to the Major as the Senior Intelligence Officer on the Station. He then went on to say that the Station Commander was waiting for a trunk call from Bucharest, but as soon as it had come through he would join them. In the meantime, he had given orders that the prisoner was to be searched.

Rex protested to the Rumanian that he was not the man they thought him to be, but his protest was ignored, so he shrugged resignedly.

While they helped him off with his clothes the station doctor was sent for to remove his bandages. This worthy, a fat, jolly-looking fellow, arrived a few moments later, bringing with him a dressing-gown to cover Rex's nakedness after his clothes had been taken from him.

The doctor, apparently, did not speak French, as he gabbled away in Rumanian with a joking manner after he had unwound the bandages from Rex's head, pointing at his chin and evidently drawing attention to the fact that, although his jaw had been heavily padded with cotton wool, it had not even a scratch upon it. However, the dried blood in Rex's wavy hair and the rainbow-hued bruises on his body clearly bore out his story that he had been badly knocked about.

While the doctor was making his examination the tall Intelligence Officer was going over his garments with the utmost care, ripping open the linings of his outer clothes here and there and even examining the buttons to see if they were genuine or could be unscrewed to hold small pieces of folded paper. But neither search revealed anything at all, and the pockets of Rex's money-belt were found to contain only a considerable sum in Rumanian banknotes.

The telephone shrilled, and after answering it the young Duty Officer said to the others: "That was the C.O. He has finished his telephoning now, and I told him of our disappointment, but he wishes to see the prisoner."

Rex's clothes were handed back to him and he dressed as quickly as he could; then he was escorted by the whole party across the hall to a much larger office. A square-jawed, determined-looking man with grizzled hair, evidently the Station Commander, was sitting there behind a large desk and near him was standing a beaky-nosed, dapper little fellow, who proved to be the Station Adjutant.

The moment Rex entered the room the beaky-nosed man muttered something in Rumanian, and the Station Commander shook his head. He then spoke sharply to the Polish Military Attaché in French:

"This is not Captain Kilec; and except for height this fellow bears little resemblance to him."

The Pole looked distinctly crestfallen, but he bridled at the implication that they still regarded a Polish officer as the culprit. "As we had the honour to inform *Monsieur le Commandant* this afternoon, the real Captain Kilec died for his country some ten days ago," he said huffily. "*Monsieur le Commandant* means that he does not think that the prisoner resembles the man who impersonated Kilec."

"I have no grounds yet for accepting your ingenious theory that a German had succeeded in foisting himself on you as your Captain Kilec," replied the Station Commander coldly. "If it were so, it shows an extraordinary lack of elementary security precautions in the Polish Command."

As Rex listened to this chilly outburst he gained a much clearer understanding of why the Poles had been so anxious to hand him over to this fire-eating Rumanian with the least possible delay. Evidently he had been creating hell's delight about his missing document, and the Poles, being virtually his prisoners, had the best possible reasons for endeavouring to pacify him and so regain his goodwill.

"I saw the man known as Kilec only once," the Station Commander went on, "but I am sure that he was of slighter build, and I think his hair was fair."

"But can you be certain of that?" the Major almost pleaded. "After all, if you saw him only once you may be mistaken, and men of such a height are uncommon in any army."

"It is not the man," cut in the dapper Adjutant decisively. "I saw Kilec . . ."

"The man who was impersonating Kilec," insisted the Major.

"As you will. I saw the man you sent to us as Captain Kilec on several occasions; half a dozen times at least. It was from the safe in my office that he stole the document when I left it for a few moments because the Station Commander had sent for me. He was as tall as this man but not quite as broad. There the resemblance ends. The other had fair hair, as the Station Commander says, and bright blue eyes; also he had slightly protruding teeth."

"Thanks," said Rex, entering the discussion for the first time. "Now, may I give you my end of the story?"

The Station Commander nodded. "Yes. As the Poles don't seem to know their own officers from Nazi agents and you are dressed as a Polish officer, let us hear who you are and how you came to be mixed up in all this."

Rex had now been over the story he meant to tell so often in his own mind that he was able to tell it clearly and convincingly. When he had finished it was obvious that the Rumanians believed him; but the Polish Major, angry and disgruntled at being made to look an impetuous fool, through having dragged Rex over to the Rumanian camp without first finding somebody in his own camp who had worked with the false Kilec and could identify him, continued to display a pigheaded antagonism.

"If he is not the impersonator of Kilec, who is he then?" he demanded. "He says he is an American, but he had no papers to prove it . . ."

"Oh, nuts!" Rex cut in. "I've told you half a dozen times. They were stolen with my clothes."

But the Major would not be stopped, and hurried on: "He says that he tried to get into our camp to secure redress against the man who attacked him. If that is so, why did he try to slip past the sentry by just waving a pass that did not belong to him? Why did he not come in the daytime when it was light? Why did he not take the pass straight to the guardroom and ask to be taken up to the Camp Offices? Why did he swathe his jaw in bandages when his only injuries were on the top of his head?"

"I've perfectly good explanations for all those silly little points," Rex replied briskly. "You're simply wasting time with all this nit-pecking, and I expect these gentlemen want to get back to their evening's work or amusements, even if you don't."

"I, too, have a perfectly good explanation for these not so silly little points," declared the Major, now determined to justify himself in the eyes of the Rumanians. "You did these things because you are another impostor. Yes, I have it! You are not the German agent that stole the defence plan, but you are another Nazi spy. The man who passed as Kilec would have known that after stealing the document our camp would be no safe place for him; but, for reasons best known to themselves, the Nazis still wanted a man inside it. You met him last night by arrangement. You gave him your clothes to help him get away from this part of the country unsuspected, and he gave you his uniform and pass so that you could slip into our camp. Once safely inside, you would have taken the name of another of our missing airmen and got to work at your filthy espionage."

"You're crazy!" cried Rex angrily. "How about the cuts on my head and all those bruises on my body that you saw just now? If the fellow had been a friend of mine is it likely that he'd have handed me out things like that?"

"Why not?" snapped the Major. "None of your hurts are at all serious. A big man like yourself would think little of such punishment if his life might hang upon receiving it. Those cuts and bruises were deliberately accepted by you in order that, should you be caught entering the camp, they would support the lies you have just been telling us about being attacked and having your clothes taken from you. There is another thing. You did everything in your power to persuade me not to hand you over to our Rumanian friends here. Why was that? It was because you know that the Polish camp is still in great confusion, owing to the constant arrival of new officers who have only just escaped over the frontier, and that we had to leave all our own dossiers about enemy agents behind in Poland. But not so the Rumanians. Their routine for dealing with suspects like yourself has not yet been interfered with. You were afraid that if you fell into their hands their Intelligence Department would soon be able to check up on you."

Rex was now acutely worried again. He was in constant fear that the Major would make mention of his rash assertion that he was acting for the British and, given help to get out of the country, could prevent further supplies of Rumanian oil reaching the Nazis.

The manner of the Rumanians had noticeably hardened towards Rex while the Major was speaking, and he felt that to prolong the argument would only serve to increase his own danger. The one thing now was to stop the Pole talking before he excited really dangerous suspicions in the Rumanians' minds by some mention of the oil traffic. So, with great reluctance but from a feeling of essential caution, Rex made no effort to answer in detail the charge made against him. He simply shrugged his shoulders and said : "This is all absolute nonsense."

"I am by no means satisfied that it is," announced the Station Commander. "I think Major Serzeski has made a reasonably strong case against you, and you do not seem to be in a position to refute it. In any case, I shall certainly hold you here until our Intelligence people have gone into the matter and checked your description against their files of suspects."

With an awful sinking feeling in the pit of his stomach Rex thought of the Golden Fleece, which in a few minutes now looked like being whisked away, God alone knew where, under the seat of the Major's car. True, he had the car's number and now the name of its owner, which had just been mentioned by the Station Commander, but it might be the most frightful job to trace it once Major Serzeski had left the Bukovina.

In a last effort to retrieve the situation he tried an angry bluff and boomed : "You can't do this to me. I'm an American citizen. You've got no right to detain me just because I've had the bad luck to be attacked by some Polish crook or dirty German."

"In the circumstances I have every right," snapped the Station Commander. "Unless, of course, you can prove your *bona fides*. If you are really an American perhaps you have friends in the United States Legation in Bucharest. If there is anyone there who would vouch for you I will have a trunk call put through."

"No," said Rex a little lamely. "No, I don't know anyone at our Legation in Bucharest."

"Very well then. I shall keep you confined in our lock-up here until we are fully satisfied as to your identity."

"Holy Mike !" Rex gasped. "How—how long's that likely to be ?"

The Station Commander shrugged. "I've no idea. It largely depends on the information you are prepared to give us about yourself. A week perhaps, but in the present state of things it might easily be a month if the friends to whom you refer us outside Rumania are dilatory in answering our enquiries."

As he finished speaking he made a sign to the young Duty Officer, who slipped out into the hall and returned a moment later with two armed guards.

While the Rumanians were saying good-night to Major Serzeski the guards placed themselves one on either side of Rex, and, with the Duty Officer in attendance, marched him from the room.

He was taken down a long passage, then through several others at the back of the building until they came to a row of cells. One of the cells was unlocked, and the soldiers pushed Rex into it, locking the door behind him.

One look round was enough to show him that he was in a proper military "glasshouse", from which there was little hope of escape. The walls were solid brick, the door had a glass peep-hole in it, and the windows were barred. The place was furnished only with a truckle bed, a wooden chair and a tin pail.

Wearily he sank down on the bed and drew his hand across his eyes. He felt utterly done and absolutely overwhelmed by an agony of depression. His beloved and trusted friend, dear old Greyeyes, was out of the game for good. Simon had by this time almost certainly been identified and was probably facing a charge of violent assault, if not murder, for the attack on von Geisenheim and the German Commercial Attaché. Poor old Richard had been half-killed in the car-smash and, still a cripple, was now hundreds of miles away in distant Turkey. While he, the last of that splendid company, had messed up the final hand that they still had left to play and had landed himself in a military prison—perhaps for a week, perhaps for a month.

"A month!" And the option was only good for thirty days from the 21st of September. It still had twenty-five days to go; but how long would he remain cooped up in prison? There was no one to whom he could appeal to go surety for him in Rumania without giving away to the Rumanians that his real name was van Ryn, and if any of the Iron Guards got to know of his whereabouts they would pounce on him for being mixed up in the von Geisenheim affair.

In a fresh wave of distress he realized that this would also apply if he endeavoured to get himself vouched for by his father or other friends outside the country. To reveal his full name in any circumstances was as good as asking to be allowed to join poor Simon for a term of years in the Rumanian equivalent of Sing Sing.

But even if he could find some means of persuading the Station Commander to set him free, he no longer had the Golden Fleece. His friends had relied on him to get it through, and he had let them down. That was the last straw. They had given everything they had to give, and in the end they had trusted him with a thing they valued more than their lives. Yet he had lost it and now had no hope at all of retrieving it.

Exhausted, still aching in every part of his body from his cuts and bruises, utterly overwrought, Rex felt like letting his head fall into his hands and sobbing like a child. But he did not do so. The stubbornness with which his American forbears had fought the prairie and the Indians and the drought came to his assistance now, and all the best of the courage and chivalry that had been the light of Europe for many generations lit a beacon in his mind as he thought of the Duke.

De Richleau would not give way to a sentimental flood of tears inspired by his own inadequacy. Shrewd as he was, there had been times when he, too, had made mistakes, and many a time the luck had turned against him. But never had he thrown his hand in and blubbered like an ill-used school-boy. He had been like a blade of pure, fine-tempered steel that could take it and take it and yet come up again finally to run an antagonist through the heart.

There must be a way out if he, Rex, could only think of it, and there *was* a way out. There was one card in the pack that had not yet been played. It was a card that needed very skilful playing and a dangerous card that, when played, might easily cost him his life ; on the other hand, it might prove the Ace of Trumps. Rex knew that he must wait to play it, but a few days would not make all that difference. He must hold his hand when they questioned him tomorrow, and perhaps the next day and the next.

That was an appalling risk to take, because at any time Major Serzeski might have his Ford V.8. properly cleaned out, which would result in the discovery of the Golden Fleece. But that was a risk which must be taken. Rex knew that he could play his card effectively only if he pretended that he had no cards at all and then produced it casually, so that he would be allowed to exploit it instead of its being brushed peremptorily aside.

He lay down on the bed and within a few minutes, instead of sobbing like an impotent child, he was sleeping as peacefully as a great Commander who, faced with enormously superior odds, is at least content in the knowledge that he has made the best plan possible before the day of battle.

Chapter XIX

PRISON BARS

On the following morning Rex was wakened by the sound of bugles blowing the *Réveillé*. He had been so done up the night before that, faced with the difficulty of undressing with the use of only one hand, he had flung himself down on the bed and slept in his clothes. He had not been able to shave since he left Cernauti, so his chin was now covered with a bristly stubble, and he felt generally ghastly.

However, he was allowed little time to commiserate with himself on his parlous state, his torn and muddy garments, or the fact that he had lost the Golden Fleece and was now in prison. The bugles had hardly ceased sounding when there came the jingle of keys and the noise of doors being thrown open. His own cell was unlocked, and he was beckoned out to join a line of men, who were then marched off to a wash-house. One of the guards, noticing that Rex had his arm in a sling, very decently helped him get his upper garments off, and two out of his five fellow prisoners lent him soap, a towel and shaving equipment. None of them seemed to speak any language he understood, but they were a decent crowd of simple, cheerful airmen, and they extended a ready sympathy to their new comrade in misfortune.

Feeling considerably refreshed by his clean-up, Rex was marched back to his cell, where his breakfast, consisting of a bowl of porridge, two door-steps well spread with butter and a mug of coffee, was passed in to him. A quarter of an hour later, from a variety of sounds out in the passage, he guessed that the other prisoners were being led off to work, but he was left undisturbed until half past nine, when he was taken from his cell and escorted to an office two doors away from the one in which he had been brought before the Station Commander the previous night.

The tall, gawky Intelligence Officer and the dapper, beaky-nosed Adjutant were both there. The former told him to sit down and began to interrogate him. In the interval since breakfast Rex had had an opportunity to collect his thoughts and work out the details of the account he meant to give of himself.

His story was that his business was selling cars in a big way, and he was the European representative of a new United States make called the Stuyvesant. The outbreak of the war had caught him in Poland. When Britain and France had come in he had thought it just on the cards that the United States might follow suit. If that had happened and he had been caught by the Nazis, he would have found himself interned for the duration. As he didn't care to risk that, he had made his way to the Rumanian border and crossed it with a number of other refugees. Having reached Cernauti, he heard that all that was left of the Polish Air Force was being flown out to Grodek and decided to go there to see if he could learn what had happened to his friend Captain Jan Lubieszow of the Polish Air Force Reserve. He had been on his way up to the Polish camp two evenings before when the man whom they knew as Kilec had come up behind him on the road and suddenly attacked him, without giving the least indication why he did so.

There followed a long interrogation about his age and circumstances, his movements in Poland and during the four days which were all that he admitted to having spent in Rumania; about how he had received the bullet wound in his arm and about how he had been dressed when he was attacked. Finally, they asked if he had no business connections in Rumania who could speak for him.

"No." He shook his head. "I'm sorry, but in Rumania I just don't know a soul. You see, my firm's a new one, and as motor manufacturers go we're not starting up in a very big way. My first trip was to include only Scandinavia, Poland and the Baltic States, but I'd figured to do a run round South-eastern Europe next spring, but naturally there was no point in making contacts in these parts until I was due to undertake the journey."

"What about Britain, France and Germany?" enquired the Intelligence Officer. "I should have thought you would have gone for those big markets before bothering about Poland or the Baltic States."

Rex gave a knowing grin. "I had a hunch that if I could place our automobiles in some of the smaller countries the bigger boys would be more prepared to listen to me when I tackled them. I figured they'd feel they were slipping a bit and getting behind the times if they weren't stocking Stuyvesants when I could show them orders from Warsaw, Riga, Bucharest and Belgrade. Anyhow, that's how I intended to play it."

The Adjutant asked him to describe the new car, and Rex promptly launched into a spate of technologies. He had an extremely wide knowledge of both car and aeroplane engines, so it was easy for him to create in his imagination a sporting guttsey bus, somewhat on the lines of an M.G. and calculated to have a wide appeal to young men of moderate means, whatever their nationality.

This invitation to talk on a subject that he knew was the very thing for which Rex had been angling. It enabled him to speak so convincingly that his listeners now tended to gloss over in their minds a few hesitations in the replies to their previous questions.

When he had done the Adjutant asked him in an almost friendly way whether he objected to being photographed, and Rex replied at once:

"Of course not. Just lead me to the camera. You can take my finger-prints, too, if you like. I'm just a plain American business man, and I haven't a thing to hide."

After the photographs had been taken, full physical particulars of Rex were noted down, then he was led along to the First Aid Room, where the jovial doctor re-dressed all his hurts. It was now midday, and back in his cell he was given a plain but quite eatable dinner.

During the afternoon and evening no one disturbed him, and when he turned in that night he felt that he had not had an altogether profitless day. By and large, the interrogation, which he had been rather dreading first thing that morning, had gone extremely well, and he felt that his captors were now inclined to believe him. The report, together with his photographs and measurements, would by now be on its way to Bucharest. These could not possibly be identified with any Nazi agent or German living in Rumania and listed as a suspect, that the Rumanian Secret Service might have on their books. In consequence, within another two days a clean bill on that score should come in. His captors had said that they meant to hold him until he could produce proof of his identity, but, once they had satisfied themselves that no dossier concerning him existed, it was reasonable to suppose that they would regard him as more probably unfortunate than dangerous and allow him a reasonable degree of liberty until his affair could be cleared up.

When that point was reached he meant to ask the Station Commander to give him the freedom of the camp, and, if necessary, he was even prepared to offer his parole in order to secure it. He would then put into operation the plan that he had thought of the night before. He would mingle with the officers, talk flying to them without disclosing his own prowess as an airman and, quite suddenly, on the first occasion that he saw one of them do a stunt, make a big bet that he could beat it. Once in the air he hoped to elude any pursuit, land in some lonely valley, hide the plane, go after Major Serzeski, retrieve the Golden Fleece, return to the hidden aircraft and fly out of the country.

It would be much more dangerous than his scheme to steal a Polish aircraft, as he was now on a military airport equipped with Ack-Ack, and fighter aircraft that would certainly go up after him, or even go up with him, as in this case he had the additional handicap of being a prisoner; but he put considerable faith in his great skill as a pilot to keep out of trouble if only he could get into the air.

The thought that he might have to break his parole had caused him a good deal of worry; but he had argued the matter out with himself and come to the decision that no individual should allow his own honour to weigh in the scales against the possibility of bringing victory for his country nearer by many months, if not years; and, as far as the war was concerned, Rex thought of Britain as his country.

It was now the evening of Tuesday, the 26th of September, and he reckoned that a clean bill on his case should arrive from the Secret Service Headquarters in Bucharest by the 28th. It might take him two or three days to become friendly with some of the Rumanian pilots, and the chances of any of them doing stunt flying would largely depend on the weather; but he thought that with luck he might be able to get away about the 2nd of October. The option would still have eighteen days to run; so, if only he could regain possession of it, there would still be plenty of time left to get it to London.

On the Wednesday morning he was sent for again at about ten o'clock, but this time it was only to see the doctor, who re-dressed his wounds. After the business was finished, as the doctor could speak no French or German, Rex wrote out a message, which he handed to him, asking to be taken to see the Adjutant.

About a quarter of an hour later he was marched to the Adjutant's office, and the dapper little man received him with a non-committal courtesy.

Rex asked at once if he could have some books to read, preferably in French.

"Certainly," was the prompt reply. "It must be very boring for you sitting in that cell all day simply waiting to hear if we find you to be a perfectly innocent American or a case for incarceration in a fortress. What kind of books would you like?"

"I'd be very grateful if you could lend me some on flying."

The Adjutant looked up with sudden interest. "Are you a flying man, then?"

"Well," Rex answered modestly, "I wouldn't exactly say that. I've flown a bit, of course. Just amateur stuff off Club Airfields back home. But motor engines are my job and I know quite a lot about their innards, so naturally I've always been keen to witness their performance either on the road or in the air. I'm no great pilot myself, but just love being in the air, and I've done hundreds of hours as a passenger in all sorts of aircraft."

"Really!" The Rumanian's dark eyes lit with enthusiasm, and Rex felt the most awful cad as he saw that 'Brotherhood of the Air' which knows no bars of language or nationality function so spontaneously, and heard the little man go on: "In that case, if the people in Bucharest don't identify you as a suspect and you have to hang around for a while until you can produce proof from abroad about your *bona fides*, I'll take you up with me some time."

"Thanks, I'd like that a lot," Rex grinned.

Twenty minutes later, back in his cell, while he was still congratulating himself on the success of his first move, an orderly arrived with a stack of a dozen volumes on aeronautics.

He had read several of them in the original English, but a selection of the others served to while away the time for him quite pleasantly during the rest of the day.

It was about eight o'clock when his cell door was opened and he was taken along to the Adjutant's office again.

The black-eyed little fellow did not look so cheerful as he had done that morning, and he seemed to be preoccupied with some other business when Rex was brought in. Having excused himself, he continued to shuffle through the papers on his desk for some moments. Then he said abruptly:

"Our 'I' Headquarters in Bucharest have just been through on the telephone. They don't seem to know anything about you, but they are making further enquiries. In the meantime, they have given orders that you're to be transferred to the proper military prison in Cernauti. Sorry I shan't be able to take you for a flip, but there it is. I think that Polish Major was an idiot, myself, and barking up the wrong tree. Still, that's none of my business. I hope you manage to convince our people in Cernauti that you're all right. Good-night.''

Rex realized at once that it was utterly futile to protest. As far as the Adjutant was concerned, an order was an order, and in this case there was not even the remotest reason for questioning it. He had already turned back to the papers over which he was worrying and merely nodded as Rex muttered a good-night before he was marched from the room.

It seemed that instructions had already been given regarding his transfer, as he was taken straight out of the building and put into an Air Force box-van with an armed escort of a sergeant and two airmen. Almost before he had time to realize the full import of the blow he was sitting on the narrow bench between his guards, and the van was in motion.

With a wave of sick despair he forced himself to accept the fact that the plan he had been cherishing and elaborating for the past forty-eight hours now lay in ruins. He had been so pleased with the groundwork for its development that he had laid that morning, and now, without a moment's warning, the whole basis of his plot to escape had been swept from beneath his feet.

It was quite certain that there would be no easygoing fraternity of airmen, or aircraft, at the military prison in Cernauti, and both were absolutely essential to the getaway on which he had been counting almost as much as if its success were beyond question.

To attempt to escape from the box-van while it was in motion and he had an escort of three armed men with him was quite hopeless, and the journey passed without incident. Three quarters of an hour after leaving the Air Force Station the van pulled up, and when Rex got out he found himself in a high-walled prison courtyard.

His escort marched him into a grim old-fashioned building of grimy nineteenth-century brick and duly handed him over. A truculent-looking warder took him up to a cell on the second floor and locked him in.

The cell was considerably roomier than the one he had occupied at the Air Force Station and better furnished, having a small marble-topped washstand, a deal table, a chest of drawers, two chairs and a brass bedstead. It did not look like convict accommodation, and he formed the impression that it had probably been used to house several generations of political prisoners in the days when Cernauti was Czernowitz and the easternmost city of the old Austrian Empire.

The prison certainly seemed to date from the days when the authorities relied more upon the strength of stone and iron than carefully worked-out technique to prevent prisoners from escaping. As Rex thought of the open cages in modern American prisons he was grateful for the privacy and comparative comfort of the room into which he had been put, but as he noted the wrist-thick iron bars across the window and the double lock on the heavy door he knew that, without friends outside to aid him, escape from such a place would be virtually impossible.

His transfer had, apparently, cost him his supper, as, although he sat about for an hour, no one brought him any, and he did not think it good policy to start his sojourn there by kicking up a row and banging on the door. So he undressed and got into bed.

Next morning another tough-looking warder brought him his breakfast and a jug of water to wash with, so it seemed that he was to be given no opportunity to communicate with any of the other prisoners; a point that depressed him as it lessened still further any prospect of escape.

Just after ten o'clock his cell door was unlocked, and two men came in. The first was a pale-faced officer of slim build, with thin sandy hair and pince-nez, who did not look like a Rumanian; the other, who carried a writing-board and paper, was obviously a clerk.

The officer introduced himself as Captain Ferari and mentioned at once that his mother had been an American of Swedish extraction, and that it was owing to his knowledge of English that he had been given Rex's case. He added that he was not actually on the prison staff but attached to the Headquarters of an Infantry Division stationed at Cernauti.

The clerk sat down at the table, Captain Ferari took the other chair, while Rex made himself comfortable on the bed and submitted with the best grace he could muster to another long and searching interrogation.

Ferari spoke English with great fluency and only a slight accent, but as his words tumbled out he sometimes misplaced them and frequently muddled his tenses. His manner was mild and pleasant, but Rex soon saw that he was much too sharp to be easily fooled and so told his story with considerable circumspection.

When the examination was over Ferari asked the same old question as to whether Rex could not possibly think of anyone in Rumania who would come forward and identify him, or at least substantiate the fact that a Mr. Mackintosh was the European agent for Stuyvesant cars.

On Rex replying in the negative the Rumanian said: "Well, I will be most frank with you. Your photographs and descriptions bear no likenesses to any agent or suspected agent in the Bucharest files. But you were taken in circumstances most suspicious. Nothing convinced me that you did not bandage your face for purposes of hiding. You say you tried to make access to the Polish camp for purposes of redress. Why then should you slink in? To make this approach normally you would have ask at the guardhouse, 'Please take me to the office, I wish to make complaint to the Commandant.' The theft of our defence plan by the man called Kilec is a matter most serious—especially at this time when there is war. If the Germans go into Hungary they will be then our neighbours. That they should now have the location of our airfields in the north is bad. The Poles are convinced that you are associate with Kilec. Of Nazi agents there are great numbers, and comparatively few of them are known to us. How can we tell if the Poles are right or not? Why should we take a risk? If there were not war things would be different; but Rumania may become involved. For our own protections we must keep you locked up until you can provide the proofs that you are who you say."

"Sure," Rex agreed. "I see your point of view all right; but I'm mighty anxious to get out of here. Have you any ideas on how we could set about securing these proofs you want?"

"We could send photographs of you to the Police Chief in your home town in America and if he okayed them that would be proof sufficient enough."

Rex had foreseen that, if they really meant to hold him until they were a hundred per cent satisfied that he was not a Nazi spy, this was the sort of line they might suggest; and it was for that reason he had purposely made the information he had given about himself very broad. Plenty of people to whom photographs of him might be sent could identify them as of Rex van Ryn, but very few would be prepared to say that they were of Mr. Rex Mackintosh. He was therefore now able to reply:

"As I said in my statement, my home town's little old New York; and that burg's a bit too big for the Police Chief to be on christian-name terms with everyone in it."

"I meant the town you came from before you live in New York," said Captain Ferari.

"Sorry," Rex grinned. "But I can't claim to be one of those village kids that made good. I was born right in the heart of Manhattan and I've been kicking around there most of my life. No. I'm afraid the police angle's no good. I guess I never thought the day would come when I'd be sorry I've no criminal record, but I haven't; so we can't ask for any checkup on that either."

"Where was your passport issued?"

"New York."

"We could send your photograph to the Passport Office and ask them to make a check of it."

"Sure!" Rex replied casually, hiding his sudden concern. "But unfortunately I've forgotten its number, and without that they'll take the whale of a time to trace it up. You know what Government Departments are, and I don't want to be stuck here till Christmas."

"Naturally not, if it can be avoided. Your Bank then?"

"They'd certainly give us what we want quicker."

Rex was prepared to use his Bank in an extremity, as he could see to it that the enquiry was made direct to his father, and he felt confident that old Channock would read between the lines and play up; but that meant the letter would be addressed to Mr. van Ryn, and he did not wish to bring his own name into the matter if it could possibly be avoided; so he added: "Wouldn't my firm do as well, though?"

"I think your firm would do," Ferari nodded. "If they replied that the photograph we send is of Mr. Mackintosh, their European representative, that makes sufficient enough for us."

"Okay. Better address your enquiry to F. V. Stuyvesant, Stuyvesant Motors Inc., 1062, Park Avenue, then."

Actually F. V. stood for Florence Venetia, and the lady of that name who occupied a charming penthouse on the top of 1062, Park Avenue was Rex's aunt. It was for that reason he had chosen the name Stuyvesant for his imaginary make of car. The old lady would be a bit puzzled when she received a letter addressed to her as a man and inferring that she was the head of a motor manufacturing firm, but Rex knew that on seeing his photograph she would have the sense to take it to his father before answering the enquiry, and Channock would handle the reply. In his mind's eye Rex saw the old man's slightly twisted grin as he ordered some suitable note heading to be specially run off for the job.

Rex's scheme for manœuvring the enquiry in a direction where it could do him no harm and should ultimately secure his release had now come off; but such mild satisfaction as he felt was more than offset by the knowledge that it was only a long-term policy and most unlikely to bear fruit in time to be of any value to him so far as the Golden Fleece was concerned.

Before he had gone to sleep the night before, and again from his waking onwards, he had thought of nothing except how he might secure a speedy release; yet all his mind-searching had been of no avail, and his brain was now stale with that apparently insoluble problem. More for something to say than anything else, he asked in a genuinely depressed voice:

"How long d'you think it will take to get a reply from my firm?"

Ferari shrugged. "We can send the photo by air mail to Gibraltar. That will take three days; but no air line crosses the Atlantic yet, so from there it will have to go by sea. If it catch one of the fast Italian ship like *Conte di Savoia*, count six days for the crossing, but it must probably wait the ship or go on a slower boat, so ten days is a better allowance, and a day for deliver in New York. If your peoples make prompt reply you can expect to hear in just one month, but there is more likely that it take five weeks."

I*

"Hell!" muttered Rex. "Isn't there some quicker way you can get yourselves happy about me than writing to the States!"

"I fear, no." The sandy-haired Rumanian blinked through his *pince-nez*. "I can only repeat that someone themselves above suspicion must vouch for you to us. If you had the connection in Sofia, Belgrade, Athens, Rome, that would be all right. But you say you have never travel in South-eastern Europe."

Suddenly, at the mention of South-eastern Europe, a light flickered and then blazed up in Rex's mind.

"How about Turkey?" he asked, striving to keep his voice from betraying his excitement.

"Yes. Turkey is not under German influence, so a person of responsibility to speak for you there would serve good; and we could get a reply from Istanbul in a matter of few days."

"The friend I'm thinking of is in Istanbul and he's British, so that should suit your book all right."

"Ah. He is not then an official of the Turkish Government," said Ferari warily. "That is not so good."

"In Mike's name, why?" exclaimed Rex, now frantically concerned to put over his new idea. "My friend is a Mr. Richard Eaton, and he's British born and bred. No Britisher would be mutt enough to go surety for a German agent, and your only worry is that that's what I might be. I've known him for years, and if you put your enquiry through to him I'll bet my last dime you'll get a satisfactory reply by return of post."

The Rumanian shook his head. "I am regretting, but I do not like it. No, I do not like it at all. Turkey is as full of German agents as any other Balkan country. This Mr. Eaton has an English name, yes; but what proof should we have that he is not by reality some Nazi friend of yours?"

Rex suddenly roared with laughter.

"Well?" said Ferari patiently. "If I have made a joke let me please hear of it."

"I'm sorry," Rex apologized. "It was your suggesting that Richard Eaton might be a Nazi agent. He's just about the most English thing that ever came out of that great little island. You'd get the joke all right, if only you could see him."

"Ah, if I could see him," Ferari took the suggestion up seriously, "that would be different. If he presented himself here with a British passport, and I could talk with him so as to make assurance with myself, then his word for you would be sufficient enough. Is he so close a friend perhaps that he would make the journey to Cernauti for securing your freedom?"

"Yes, I'm sure he would," replied Rex without hesitation. "But the snag is that when last I had news of him he'd just been mixed up in a bad car smash. Maybe he's not fit to travel yet."

As he spoke Rex wondered just how far Richard had progressed in his recovery. When he had left Bucharest he had been able to hobble from room to room on crutches and was his old cheerful self to talk to; but his smashed hip was still a matter for considerable concern and there was small reason to believe that he would be fit enough to undertake a long and tiring journey on his own for some time to come. With Marie Lou to help him while bathing and dressing, and in and out of trains and cars, he would be all right; but Rex knew that as long as the Iron Guard were after them Richard would never agree to Marie Lou re-entering Rumania.

The slim Rumanian was now looking down his rather long nose. The mention of the car smash had strengthened his suspicions that this Mr. Eaton might be anything but the pure-blooded Briton that his friend made out. After all, the journey from Istanbul to Cernauti could be made in from three to four days, and if they were such old friends, for one to suggest that the other should make such a trip in order to get him out of prison was not asking a great deal; so it looked like a hurriedly thought-up excuse to avoid a request which would either be ignored or result in some extremely dubious character turning up in Cernauti and making the prisoner's case far worse than it was at the moment.

"You don't believe me, do you?" said Rex, who had guessed the workings of Ferari's mind. "But I'd like you to put an enquiry through to Mr. Eaton, all the same, and ask him if he's yet up to making the trip."

"As you wish. You understand, though, that only when I have assure myself by personal interviews that he is really English can I recommend to let you go. Do you wish also that I should write to your firm in the States?"

"Sure, and the sooner the better. Why not cable both of them?"

"That will not help. We cannot send your photograph by telegram. The firm of Stuyvesant may reply that they are representative in Europe by a Mr. Mackintosh, but that would not be proof that you are him."

"No. Still, you could wire Mr. Eaton."

"All right. I will do that. What is his address?"

"Send it to the Pera Palace Hotel. He was there when I last heard, and as he's been laid up it's hardly likely that he would have moved on yet. I'll follow it up with a letter, if you've no objection."

Ferari shook his head. "No, I cannot allow that. Remember you are suspect of being a Nazi agent, and for all we knows he may be another. I cannot risk your communicating to him."

This refusal was a sad blow to Rex, but he had no option other than to accept it, and, their business being concluded, he asked Ferari if he could get him some more suitable clothes than the Polish uniform he was still wearing, shaving tackle, washing things and some books and magazines, out of the money that had been taken from him when he had been arrested.

The Rumanian agreed to do so, and Rex's two visitors left him.

When they had gone he pondered the prospects of Richard's being able to come to Cernauti. That now seemed his only hope of getting out of prison before the option expired. Rex knew that, if Richard realized how much was at stake, he would charter a private aircraft and come to the rescue, even if he were at death's door. He would bring Marie Lou, too, if need be. But the trouble was that they could not possibly know what had happened since they left Rumania. They did not even know if their friends had succeeded in getting the Golden Fleece from Teleuescu, let alone the difficulty and urgency of getting it out of the country. And, unless Richard had made the most remarkable progress in the past week, or Marie Lou believed that the life of one of their friends hung upon his making the trip, Rex greatly doubted if she would allow him to leave Istanbul.

If only Rex had been allowed to write he could have indicated that his regaining his freedom was a mattter of vital importance; but all the Eatons would get was an enquiry as to whether they knew an American motor salesman named Mr. Rex Mackintosh, with the information that he was now in prison at Cernauti and would be released if Richard cared to come and identify him. There would be no suggestion that he was in any danger or that the duration of the war might be enormously shortened by his swift release.

Rex could only hope for the best and endeavour to console himself with the thought that he now at least had one lifeline out that might possibly prove effective.

In the afternoon Ferari returned with a selection of outsize ready-made clothes for Rex to choose from and a number of other items he had bought for him in the town. Rex selected a dark blue lounge suit and two of the quietest from a rather gaudy selection of ties. Then with considerable relish he shed his dirty Polish uniform and dressed himself in his new things.

At midday the following day Ferari appeared again and greeted his prisoner with considerably more affability than he had shown the day before. He had received a reply to his telegram to Richard, and it ran :

"REX MACKINTOSH CITIZEN OF UNITED STATES IS AIRCRAFT EXPERT HAVE KNOWN HIM INTIMATELY MANY YEARS STOP OWING TO INJURIES REGRET DOCTORS FORBID TRAVEL TO CERNAUTI FOR AT LEAST A FORTNIGHT BUT FOR PURPOSES OF IDENTIFICATION MACKINTOSH SIX FOOT FOUR IN HEIGHT BROAD IN PROPORTION BROWN WAVY HAIR BROWN EYES STRAIGHT NOSE CLEFT CHIN GOOD TEETH READY SMILE VERY LARGE HANDS STOP IF FUNDS REQUIRED BY HIM DRAW ON ME OTTOMAN BANK ISTANBUL UP TO FIVE HUNDRED POUNDS STOP PREPARED TO VOUCH FOR MACKINTOSH'S INTEGRITY ABSOLUTELY AND CONVINCED HIS ARREST MUST BE THROUGH MISTAKE IN IDENTITY STOP TELL HIM ALL OF US SEND FONDEST LOVE."

"Hell!" thought Rex. "A fortnight!" But the blow was softened for him by his having half expected something of the kind.

Meanwhile Ferari was saying with a smile: "This Mr. Eaton must certainly be a good friend to you to make offer of five hundred pounds. But why does he say, in reply to my question, 'What business does Mr. Mackintosh make for a livings?', that you are an aircraft expert?"

It was Richard's only slip, and even in that he had made a pretty good guess, which enabled Rex to answer casually:

"Well, I was in aircraft before I went into motors. The Stuyvesant is a new venture, and it's many months since I've seen Eaton so he wouldn't know about that."

The Rumanian nodded. "In all other ways the telegram is good for you. It make no mention of his car smash but he implies it by his mention of injuries. Also his description of you is very good."

"You'll let me go then?" Rex asked eagerly.

Ferari shook his head. "No, no. That the description is good makes nothing for us. If he were a Nazi and knowing you he could give it just as well. To know if he is good to vouch for you I must see his British passport and then talk with him. But, after all, a fortnight is not so great."

To Rex, at the thought of the Golden Fleece and that at any moment Serzeski might have his car thoroughly cleaned up, a fortnight seemed an appalling time, but he could not possibly mention that, and he had no other reason that he could give for being so desperately anxious to get out.

"Personally," Ferari went on, "this telegram, after our talk yesterday, satisfies me. I think the Poles have raised a mare's-nest into which you have unfortunately got. But officially it is up my duty street to make assurance before I let you go. Still, while you are waiting for your friend we will do all possible to make you comfortable here."

"Thanks," said Rex. "That's decent of you. Perhaps you could spare the time to come and talk to me now and then—tell me the war news and that sort of thing?"

"But certainly. I forget that you cannot read our papers. I must go now as I have other duties to make; but I will come in each day with papers and translate the highlight interesting pieces for you."

It was on the following day, Saturday the 30th of September, that Ferari paid his first social call and brought Rex up to date with the progress of the war, of which he had heard practically nothing for the best part of ten days.

He learned that Germany and Russia had agreed to partition Poland, but that isolated groups of Poles were fighting on and Warsaw still remained uncaptured. A widespread revolt had broken out in Czechoslovakia which the Germans were endeavouring to suppress with all the brutality and vindictiveness of which they were capable. Nothing of any interest had happened on the Western Front, but the Luftwaffe had attacked the Home

Fleet at Scapa, and the R.A.F. had paid a return visit to the Heligoland Bight, neither side scoring any spectacular success.

The major war interest of the week lay in the intense diplomatic activity that continued unabated in Moscow. Having divided the still living corpse of Poland between them, Ribbentrop and Molotov were discussing on the one hand how best Russia could help Germany with warlike supplies, and on the other the formula in which their two countries, 'acting in Military and Economic accord', should 'offer Peace Terms to the Democracies'. In attendance they had both the Turkish and Esthonian Foreign Ministers and, only the day before, Esthonia had agreed to become a Russian 'protectorate'. The Turks were, however, refusing to be browbeaten and had just completed a mutual assistance pact with the British.

None of these goings and comings seemed to Rex to be of any great importance, as it was clear to him that with the war barely a month old most of the nations were still shuffling for position; and, as it turned out, he found the internal Rumanian news of much greater interest.

Although he had been far too occupied, and too cut off from news sources, to learn of it before, it seemed that the Prime Minister's assassination on the 21st had aroused the most furious indignation throughout the country. Far from assisting the Iron Guard to pull off the *coup d'état*, for which this bloody deed was thought by many to be the prelude, it had resulted for them in a *débâcle*. Their organization had been proscribed, thousands of them were being rounded up into concentration camps, and hundreds of them had already been shot, with the full approval of the great majority of Rumanians.

For Rex these were tremendous tidings because, apart from Simon's arrest, inspired by the officious landlord of the Peppercorn, he and his friends had not at any time come into conflict with the Rumanian police. It was the German-inspired Iron Guard organization that had made things too hot for them in Bucharest. The scores of secret agents of this private army who a week before had been hunting for them were now being hunted themselves, so, if only he could secure his release, the likelihood of his running into trouble while searching for Major Serzeski and the Golden Fleece would be immensely lessened.

"I guess the Germans must be pretty sick about their friends in the Iron Guard being beaten up like this," Rex remarked.

"Yes," Ferari agreed. "They are not, as you say, so cock-a-hoop these days. They have never been favourite here. I do not think the German is favourite in any country, really. They have not the manners, and either cringe in time of weakness or become overbearing when they think themselves strong. Lately they had become intolerable quite; but now that their bullies in the Iron Guard are being disarmed our authorities will not sit down any more for their insults. Our police will get some of their own back too. I would make bets that is why they let the two French Communists slip through their fingers."

"What French Communists?" asked Rex.

Ferari turned to an inside sheet of the newspaper that he was holding. "It is an item here that I have not mention because I did not think it would be much interesting to you. Some big-shot Germans were kidnapped and most badly beaten up on the night which follow Calinesco's assassination. These two Frenchmen were suspected. It is now known that they stole two passports and successfully made a get-away on the Athens plane three days ago. It would not surprise me if for them our police winked the eye."

Rex could hardly conceal his excitement, and he had to make a tremendous effort to keep his voice casual as he said :

"That certainly sounds like an exciting story. I'd like to hear the details if you know them."

"Yes. Much excitement is caused by this audacious attack. For some days it had second place in the news to the assassination of our Prime Minister. Two Germans were beaten nearly till they die. One the Commercial Attaché and the other a General von Geisenheim. They have visited one of our big business men, Monsier Teleuescu. While they are in his home their chauffeur is sandbag. The Frenchmen put him in the back of their Chrysler, then when the Germans exit from the house take them for a ride Next morning they are come across out in the country beaten so bad neither can speak."

"How did the police get on to it, then, that it was these French Communists who had attacked them ?"

"They own the car, the Chrysler, in which the Germans' chauffeur is found. He have heart-weakness, so the attack kill him from shock, and he is found dead. The policeman who patrol the beat might have seen something but he is shot dead before he can be questioned in a shoot-up with the Iron Guard outside the British Legation the next day. The Attaché and the General both have had head wounds and so cannot give clear description of their assailants ; but the Attaché makes ravings from which deduction is made that it was a Jew who smash his head in. The Frenchmen are known to be secret agents and already wanted by the police. One of them is a Jew, so that and the car make it most certain that it was they who attack the Germans, perhaps because they hope to take important papers from them."

"It seems a bit surprising, though, that if these guys were wanted on another charge your police should have deliberately let them leave the country."

Ferari shrugged. "I do not say that. It is only my own idea. It may be that there was no charge; only that they were undesirables whom the police would have deported as soon as caught, anyhow. I only suggest that our police have had many insult from the Germans and much trouble from the Iron Guard. Now that the Iron Guard can no longer make pressure on them they probably laugh to themselves about this affair and unofficially are happy that the Frenchmen got away."

"So that's how it goes," said Rex thoughtfully. "Of course, the great majority of Rumanians are pro-Ally, aren't they?"

"Indeed yes," Ferari laughed. "As we are neutrals we must have care to show justice when Allied agents get themselves caught, but in our hearts we do not mind how many Germans they hit on the head."

Folding up his paper, he went on: "I must leave you now, and as to-morrow is Sunday I shall not come. I go this afternoon to spend the week-end at a country house in the mountains."

"Well, thanks a lot for bringing me the news," smiled Rex, standing up. "I hope you have a good time, and I'll look forward to seeing you Monday."

When the Rumanian had gone he sat down again to try to sort out the effect of these surprising new developments on his own situation.

He had naturally supposed that days ago the German Legation would have made a formal charge against the Duke, Simon and himself for the attack on von Geisenheim and that the Rumanian police would be doing their utmost to catch them. But von Geisenheim was the only person who definitely knew the identity of his attackers, and it seemed that he had been too badly koshed to make any statement. Owing to the suddenness of the assault the Attaché would probably never remember more than that two men attacked them as they entered their car and that the one who had struck him down had been a Jew. The only people, therefore, who could have given any lucid description of the occupants of the Chrysler would have been the chauffeur and the patrol man, and, by a strange decree of fate, both of these had died before any statement could be taken from them.

Rex saw that the unexpected turn in the Rumanian political situation, together with the God-sent mistake of the Rumanian police in jumping to the conclusion that the previous owners of the Chrysler were responsible for the attack on von Geisenheim, had changed the whole situation, and that he now had little to fear.

On reaching this conclusion, his first exciting thought was, why should he not now own up to the fact that his real name was van Ryn and ask for one of the members of the American Legation whom he had met in Bucharest to come up and identify him?

He was on his feet now, pacing up and down; but his next thought brought him up with a jerk. How would the Rumanians take that? What reason could he give for having concealed his real name all this time? If someone from the Legation came to Cernauti, it would emerge that he had arrived in Bucharest soon after the war had broken out. The Legation official could do no more than say that he was Mr. van Ryn, and the Rumanians would want to know what he had been up to for the past three weeks. He dared not tell them about the oil barges and the option. To do so was to risk some pro-Nazi hurrying off and securing the Golden Fleece for the Germans before he had a chance to retrieve it himself. If he could not tell the truth, what explanation could he give of all the lies he had told and how could he explain his recent snooping about the Polish frontier under a false name? One did not have to be a German to be a spy and in their pay. The Rumanians would believe that was what he was and keep him a prisoner while still further investigations were made. Even when Richard turned up his evidence would be worse than valueless, and he would probably be held too, as having abetted a suspect by making a false declaration.

The thought was utterly maddening, but the odds were too great on the Rumanians taking umbrage at the way he had lied to them and refusing to let him go until they had checked up all his movements for the whole time he had been in their country. His only hope was to stick to his story and pray that Richard might be able to come and get him out sooner than could at present be expected.

From the heights of exaltation Rex was plunged back into the deepest gloom. But suddenly a new thought struck him. If he no longer had anything to fear from the von Geisenheim affair, then neither had Simon.

In that case, once Simon had got out of that infuriating muddle resulting from his having dressed up in a woman's clothes, the police would have no reason to detain him. He had probably been released the day after his arrest. He would have returned at once to the Peppercorn. By hook or by crook he would have got into their old room and, once there, it was a hundred to one he would have found the message that had been left for him under the china vase on the mantelpiece. Then he would have made his way to Cernauti as quickly as he could. He was probably in the town already and might even have been there for several days nosing round trying to pick up his friend's trail.

On realizing this heartening possibility Rex did a little dance in the middle of the floor; but he soon stopped and sat down again as he considered the implication of this unlooked-for dispensation of Providence. For over half an hour he pondered the problem of how Simon could help to bring about his release, but he could see no daylight there. He saw no way of discovering Simon's whereabouts in Cernauti, and, even if he knew it and asked Ferari to send for him, how could he be primed with the Mr. Mackintosh story before he arrived at the prison?

Yet it now seemed virtually certain that Simon was free, and the thought that he was probably kicking his heels in Cernauti when he might have been getting back the Golden Fleece and taking it out of the country was galling beyond words.

Rex wondered how Simon would set about trying to find him. The obvious first step was to try all the hotels. That was it! Sooner or later he was certain to make enquiries of Levinsky, the Jewish proprietor of the Roebuck, the little place where Rex had stayed. Now, if only a message could be got to Levinsky to be given to Simon when he called!

It was quite possible that Simon had already been there. If he had, on describing Rex he would have learnt that his friend had spent the previous Saturday night there, then paid his bill and departed, but left his suitcase behind.

Rex brought his leg-of-mutton hand down with a resounding slap on his elephantine thigh. His suitcase! What a break that he should have decided to leave it there! When Simon was told about the suitcase he would either make the hotel his headquarters while he cast round for further indications of his friend's later movements or at least pay Levinsky handsomely to report to him immediately the owner of the suitcase reappeared.

Standing up, Rex began to pace the small room again. Surely the suitcase should prove a means of getting into touch with Simon? He could get Ferari to claim it for him. But what then? Simon would trace the suitcase to the prison and might attempt to play Blondin to his Richard Cœur de Lion, but that would not get them very far. It might even lead to dangerous complications, as Levinsky knew him as van Ryn.

No. There was a better way than that. He must leave the suitcase out of it, but find some pretext for getting Ferari to let him send a letter to Levinsky in which he could incorporate a message for him to pass on to Simon.

All through the long quiet afternoon and evening Rex turned the new situation over in his mind, first this way, then that, but he could find no better line for attempting to exploit it.

He was furious now that a day would be lost to him through the fact that Ferari was away for the week-end. The only consolation was that it gave him the whole of Sunday to perfect his plan.

After the most exhaustive analysis of possible repercussions he ruled out any attempt to secure his own release by getting Simon to identify him. It presented so many complications, the most dangerous of which was that Ferari must be shown any communication intended for Levinsky. In consequence, he decided that he would concentrate solely on an endeavour to put Simon wise to the fact that he no longer had the "Fleece" and pass the ball to him, to get it back and safely out of the country.

With this in mind he finally wrote the following letter:

Dear Mr. Levinsky,
         You will no doubt remember me as having stayed at the Roebuck on the night of Saturday the 23rd. Before I left Poland I was recommended

to your hotel by a Jewish friend of mine named Simon Aron. He lent me his car, a Ford V8, number UCZ827, to get away in, and it was agreed that when he crossed the frontier himself he should meet me at the Roebuck. Circumstances prevented me from returning there and in the meantime a Major Serzeski, who is the Polish Assistant Military Attaché in Bucharest, had taken the car from a parking-place in mistake for his own. I had no opportunity to trace Major Serzeski, who left the Polish Internment Camp at Grodek, I think for Bucharest, on the night of Monday the 25th. As Major Serzeski's car was the same model as Mr. Aron's he may not yet have realized that the car he has got is not his own, and the title deeds to the property that Mr. Aron asked me to take out of Poland for him are still in it. So if Mr. Aron has already been to the Roebuck and left an address, or calls there to enquire for me, will you please tell him about his car and the importance of tracing up Major Serzeski immediately, in order to get his property back? You might also tell him that I am very fit and well treated here, and expect to be released in about a fortnight."

He signed it simply:

> *The Big American.*

He pondered this for a long time but did not think that he could improve upon it. There was nothing in it which conflicted with the 'Mr. Mackintosh' story and it would be child's play for a subtle brain like Simon's to pick up the salient facts that, somehow or other, he had been compelled to hide the Golden Fleece in a Ford V8 number UCZ827 that belonged to a Major Serzeski. Once Simon realized that, he would not rest until he had traced the car and, having located it, take it to bits piece by piece if necessary, until he found the packet.

When Ferari came in on Monday morning Rex opened the ball at once by saying: "I've had a real bad attack of conscience over the week-end."

"Oh, how is that?" Ferari asked.

"It's this way. A little Jewish business man I knew in Poland lent me a spare car he had to get out in, and in return he asked me to take some of his family papers over the frontier. It was he who recommended me to go to a little place called the Roebuck, where I spent the one night I was in Cernauti. When I was out at Grodek the car was taken by mistake for his own by a Polish Major named Serzeski. That was only a few hours before I got into trouble, and I've been so mighty concerned about my own position since, I'd forgotten every darned thing about it. Aron, that's the Jew's name, was to settle up a few things and leave Warsaw two days after I did, so he's probably been at the Roebuck for the past week wondering what the hell has happened to me and eating himself up with worry about his title deeds. I've a letter here I've written to Levinsky, the owner of the pub. Would you mind reading it through, and if there's nothing you take exception to, having it posted for me?"

Ferari took the letter and read it carefully.

"Why don't you make use your name as a signature?" he asked after a moment.

"Because he's probably forgotten it by now. I was there only one night, and although I may have registered I don't remember having done so. But signed like that it's bound to ring a bell with him right away."

"This Mr. Aron. For all we know he may be another German agent, and you take this way to communicate to him."

"Hang it all, is that likely—seeing he's a Jew?" laughed Rex.

"There are occasions when the Nazis make use of Jews. And these family papers. They are perhaps secret documents?"

Rex laughed again. "If they'd been anything like that would I have been mutt enough to leave them in the pocket of the car? Come on now. You really are looking for bogeys where none exist."

"Perhaps so," admitted the Rumanian. "But why should I take any risk?"

"I'll tell you," said Rex. "When Richard Eaton turns up here it will be proved that I'm a hundred per cent perfectly innocent American business man; yet you will have been holding me as a prisoner, to my great inconvenience, for the best part of three weeks. You owe me something for that. This little Jew did me a good turn, and I've let him down, largely through your interference, because if you hadn't kept me in the cooler like this I'd have got his car back for him before now. Surely, if you won't let me attend to my own affairs you can oblige me by letting me put things right for him as far as I can?"

"I see the point you make."

Rex waved aside the admission and went on with disarming casualness: "If I wanted any real favours from you I'd ask for something for myself. Sending that letter's not going to do me any good. If you don't care to send it, that's the end of the matter. But I thought on Saturday you'd come to the conclusion that I was just a decent guy who was having a pretty raw deal. If it hadn't been for that I wouldn't have asked you to help me do a good turn to this little pal of mine."

"All right," Ferari smiled. "From my talks with you nothing now persuades me that you are not an American, and there is not one iota of proof that you ever had anything to do with the Nazis. Thousands of Jews, too, these days are sending papers precious to them out of Poland by anyone they can get to carry them over the frontier; so there is nothing of real suspicion about all this. Your letter shall be sent, and as we must keep you here yet for a while I am glad to do this little service."

Rex thanked him, and they then got down to the morning's news. Over the week-end Count Ciano had been summoned to Berlin; President Moscieki of Poland had resigned and a new Polish Government had been formed in France; the Latvian Foreign Minister had been sent for by Moscow, so it looked as if a second Baltic State would soon go the way of Esthonia and be forced to accept Soviet 'protection'.

When Ferari had gone Rex congratulated himself on the result of his strategy and wondered if Simon would find any means of letting him know, should it prove successful. If he were in Cernauti he should receive the letter by the following morning at the latest; that would leave seventeen days for him to retrieve the Golden Fleece and get it to London. The safety margin was narrowing now, as nearly half the time for which it was valid had expired; but Rex felt considerably more hopeful that they might yet pull off their great coup.

He was, however, destined to hear nothing more about his letter, except that Ferari had posted it; so as the days passed he could only hope and pray that Simon had contacted Levinsky and flung himself heart and soul into the game again.

Each morning Ferari came in with the news. That first week in October the only events of military significance were that the Royal Air Force made its first flight over Berlin and that the Germans openly adopted a policy of piracy, both sinking and seizing the ships of several neutrals. Diplomatic activity continued at high pressure, particularly in Moscow, to whom both Latvia and Lithuania in turn lost their independence. The star turn of the week was Hitler's announcement in the Reichstag of his 'Peace' terms, but the statesmen of the Allies had at last learned the folly of placing any faith in the bellowings of this treacherous mountebank, and to the satisfaction of all honest men they now ignored him.

Richard's reply to Ferari's telegram had been despatched on the 29th of September, and in it he had said that it would be at least a fortnight before his doctors would permit him to travel. The actual fortnight would be up on Thursday, the 12th of October, but the journey from Istanbul to Cernauti would take three days, so the earliest date upon which he could be expected was Sunday the 15th.

All the same, from the beginning of his second week in prison Rex began to count the hours until what he judged to be the absolute minimum dead-line if Richard stepped off the night train from Bucharest just before midday. He even went to the length of adopting the old schoolboy end-of-term custom of drawing blocks of squares on paper, as it lessened his frantic impatience to get free, just a little, to be able to cross a few off each morning when he woke and after each meal.

On Wednesday the 11th at four o'clock in the afternoon he still had ninety-three squares uncrossed when Ferari, who had never visited him in the afternoon, entered his cell.

Rex was dozing on his bed. At this unexpected visitation he sat up quickly, full of apprehension that something that boded him no good was the cause of the Intelligence Officer's appearing at such an unusual hour.

Suddenly his anxiety gave place to joy. In the doorway just behind Ferari, supported on a pair of crutches, stood Richard.

Ferari, who had behaved very decently throughout, now wasted no undue time in formalities. He said that Richard had run him to earth in his office at Divisional Headquarters and they had had a long talk together which had fully satisfied him as to his visitor's *bona fides*. Now that he saw these two old friends exchange such hearty greetings there could be no more doubt as to Mr. Mackintosh's identity, and he was free to go.

Rex thanked him for his kindness and accepted an invitation for himself and Richard to dine that night, although he had some doubts which he kept private as to whether they would be able to keep the appointment; then, having packed his few belongings in a brown-paper parcel, he went out to the prison courtyard to a car that Richard had hired.

"Oh boy! It's good to see you," Rex grinned, as soon as they were alone. "How in heck did you manage to get here four whole days ahead of schedule?"

"It was just that we couldn't bear to think of you being in prison for a moment longer than was absolutely necessary," smiled Richard. "And my hip has been mending so well that three nights ago Marie Lou and I decided to bounce the medicos."

"Have you brought her along?"

"No. She wanted to come, but seeing the way we were kicked out of Rumania I wouldn't let her. She agreed to my coming, though, and sent you her fondest love; so did poor Lucretia. Now, tell me what's been going on? We haven't heard a thing since you left us on the train."

"We're in the worst muddle ever," Rex replied seriously. "It's bad, Richard; real bad, and without any good frills attached. But before I spill the beans, where's this fellow taking us?"

"Back to the Royal Bukovina, where I dumped my bags and took rooms for us before I set out to collect you."

Rex leaned forward and spoke in German to the Jewish car-driver, telling him to take them to the Roebuck, then he said:

"I've bad news for you, Richard, just about the worst that could be. We got the thing we left the train to get all right, but all three of us slipped up before we could leave the country. I was pinched trying to get hold of a Polish aircraft; Simon was arrested for wearing women's clothes. That's well over a fortnight ago, and old Greyeyes, well . . ."

"What's happened to him?" asked Richard sharply.

"We don't rightly know. There was a shoot-up outside the British

Legation the day after we got back to Bucharest. I wasn't there, but Simon saw it. He says, well, he says . . ."

"Go on!" said Richard, his voice hard from sudden apprehension.

"He says those Iron Guard boys gave the Duke the works."

"Oh, God!" Richard groaned. "It isn't true! It can't be!"

"I'm hoping so myself," Rex tried to console him. "But as we don't know for certain I try not to think about it. If that's the way it is he left us the legacy of getting the Golden Fleece safely to London. I fell down on the job and had to cache it in a mighty risky place; but I reckon I managed to tip Simon off over a week ago where to pick it up; so by this time he ought to be out of the country with it. That's what I hope we'll learn for certain in a few minutes now."

Richard did not appear to hear. He sat, white-faced and silent, leaning back in his corner of the car. Within a few moments of Rex breaking the awful news to him they pulled up outside the Roebuck.

"Sit tight," said Rex, getting out. "I'll not be long here but I'm hoping to pick up a letter or cable from Simon."

He found Levinsky in his little office, and the Jew rose at once to greet him with a smile.

"Did you get my letter?" Rex asked.

"Oh yes, sir. The letter it comes," replied Levinsky in halting English. "Your friend come too, but till yesterday not; no, I mistaken am, he comes Monday; yesterday the day before."

"What!" Rex gasped. "He didn't come until the day before yesterday! Holy Michael help us! I thought he'd have called here first to enquire for me all of a fortnight ago."

"No, yesterday the day before, it was, and I tell him the car about. Then for you a message he gives. 'Tell my friend,' he says, 'good luck. I go my car to find and will to you telegraph so you news give of me to him when he returns, his suitcase to collect.' "

"Have you had any message?" asked Rex, staring at him.

"No, sir, not yet."

"Hell!" exclaimed Rex. For some reason as yet unexplained Simon had not succeeded in picking up his trail in Cernauti until two days before, so a whole week had been lost. And even now Simon had not got anywhere, otherwise there would have been a telegram from him saying that he had located the car.

It was now sixteen days since Rex had rammed the option under the back seat of the Ford V8, and during that time there seemed every likelihood that Serzeski had come across it. There were now only nine days left to find him, recover the Golden Fleece and get it to London.

Chapter XX

RACE AGAINST TIME

HAVING asked Levinsky to telephone him at the Royal Bukovina if any message from Simon came in, Rex left the Roebuck and told the driver to take them to the larger hotel. On the way he was furiously wondering what could possibly have kept Simon in Bucharest for a whole fortnight.

Richard, knowing as yet practically nothing of the Odyssey of the Golden Fleece, was not giving it a thought. His mind was still numb from Rex's terrible news about de Richleau. All of the Indomitable Four would have found it impossible to list his three friends in the order that he loved them best; yet, if forced to lose one of their number, Richard, Rex and Simon would all have agreed that it must not be the Duke. To Richard his loss meant an almost unendurable grief second only to that he would have felt on the death of his beloved Marie Lou.

The hotel was an old-fashioned place but had installed an American Bar as a concession to the modern industrialization of Cernauti. On their arrival they bought themselves drinks and carried them through to a quiet corner of the raftered lounge.

Richard pulled himself together and strove to bring back his thoughts while for an hour Rex carried on a monologue, giving as full an account as he could of all that had happened to the Duke, Simon and himself since they had left the others on the Bulgarian frontier.

When he had finished Richard stubbed out his cigarette and said:

"You're right, Rex. We must try not to think about Greyeyes. His one wish would be that we should carry on with our mission and see it through. But we've got so little time. That's the devil of it. And we haven't the faintest idea where Simon is, or this Major Serzeski either. What the hell can we do?"

"You're asking me," Rex groaned. "I just hate the thought of sitting still waiting for Simon to send us news."

"What alternative is there?"

"We could light out of here tonight for Bucharest. Serzeski's an Attaché at the Polish Legation, so they should know where he is."

"Simon will have drawn that covert already. He would have taken the night train south on Monday, and been to the Legation yesterday afternoon."

"Why the hell hasn't he wired to me care of Levinsky, then?"

"When did you send your letter to the Roebuck?"

"Last Monday week; that was—let's see—yes, the 2nd."

"Well, in it you said you wouldn't be out of jug for a fortnight, so Simon thinks you wouldn't get any message he might send till the 15th; that's three days ahead, and reason enough for his not feeling that there is any urgency about wiring you yet."

"That's about it. I'll go nuts, though, if we've got to kick our heels in this burg for three solid days."

"We may not have to. Something might come in from Simon at any time. But if we go haring off to Bucharest we've no idea where to pick him up, and by leaving Cernauti we'll be losing touch with Levinsky, so we won't get the wire when it does come in."

"Your smashed hip hasn't cost you your common sense," Rex grinned. "And anyhow, we've accepted to dine with Ferari tonight. It would look pretty fishy if we just cut the party and faded out after they've held me on suspicion all this time. I guess we'll give Simon another twenty-four hours anyhow, then, if nothing comes in from him, we'll talk about going after Serzeski on our own."

Richard nodded. "Ferari won't mind if you make my excuses, will he? I don't think I could face a party after what you've told me about Greyeyes; and, anyway, my exertions today have already been about as much as I'm up to."

"That'll be okay. He knows about your smash and your having got off a sick-bed to come and pull me out. The thing that might get him all hot and bothered would be my doing a fade-out within a few hours of having shaken off the gyves and manacles. I do hope, though, that you're not feeling too done up?"

"No, I'm all right," Richard smiled. "It's just that I have to be a bit careful still. I had a private sleeper right through on the train, but today is the first time that I've been moving about for anything like as long as six hours at a stretch."

"You're going to bed this moment then," said Rex, standing up. "We can *parlé* just as well in your room as we can here, and I'll fix the best dinner the place can offer to be brought up for you before I go out. I owe you a whole packet on top of that."

"Nonsense. If we four had ever paid what we owed one another, we would all have gone broke before now and grown rich again on the spondulics of each other. But we're only three now, aren't we? Oh hell, I think I'll just lie in bed and drink myself stupid tonight."

There was no reply to that heartrending thought of the awful gap which had been torn in the ranks of their little company, and in silence Rex accompanied him up to his room.

When Richard was in bed they ordered some more drinks to be brought up and fitfully discussed the war news; but Poland was now definitely out, and the Western Front seemed to be entering on a stalemate, so there was little of interest to talk over.

At nine o'clock Rex went out to dine. In the past fortnight he had come to know Ferari well and had found him an intelligent and likable fellow. The evening passed very pleasantly for both of them, and the Rumanian now made it quite clear that he thought Rex had had a hard deal in being detained on such insubstantial grounds for so long. They parted a little before one in the morning as the best of friends.

Next day, immediately after breakfast, Rex walked round to see Levinsky. There was still nothing from Simon, but he took the opportunity of collecting his suitcase and used that as an excuse to make the Jew a very handsome present, to consolidate his goodwill.

Richard came downstairs at eleven o'clock, and Rex accompanied him on the short walk that he now took every morning, increasing the distance slightly each day, so as gradually to get back the full use of his legs. On their return they learned that Levinsky had telephoned; consumed with impatience to get news of Simon, Rex jumped into a taxi and drove round to the Roebuck.

A letter had arrived for Levinsky by the ordinary mail, requesting that another enclosed in it should be handed to Rex when he called for his suitcase. With trembling fingers Rex opened the enclosure. It was simply headed Bucharest, 10th Oct., '39, and read:

Mon Vieux,

I gather you've been in a bit of a muddle, but your letter was reassuring, and I felt sure you'd prefer me to get on with the firm's business rather than remain in Cernauti until the 15th or thereabouts.

I've been in a muddle myself, as the beak took an extremely poor view of the fancy dress I wore at that party where last we met. I don't think I'm a malicious chap, but when I learned that you had come unstuck, too, I could cheerfully have crucified our landlord upside down, for, to put it mildly, the "inconvenience" resulting from his unfounded and slanderous inferences concerning my moral character. What a lesson for historians that the Fate of Nations may hang upon the imbecile mentality of a fellow like that!

However, on balance the Fates are behaving generously, as the far more serious threat to our business, connected with the gentleman we met at Lubieszow, has not matured; and for that I gather we owe a lot to the previous owners of the Chrysler. Moreover, the new political situation here opens up quite a number of avenues to the firm that were previously closed.

Your letter came as a bit of a shock to me, as I had been comforting myself with the thought that by this time you would have completed our big deal.

Having read it, I gave one gasp and leapt into the first train for Bucharest. Arrived there I hurtled into the office of Lubieszow, Fils, Aîné et Successeurs, but the partner you wanted me to see had left the capital three days before and, I am told, is now in Ploesti.

*I am proceeding there in the next train, and will either be, or leave word
for you, at the best pub that oil-soaked Rumanian Wigan can boast.*

No news, alas, of Greyeyes.

We'll have to work fast now if we mean to complete that contract.

Yours without frills, or, thank God, petticoats.

"S."

Having returned to the Royal Bukovina, Rex went over the letter again
with Richard. By 'the gentleman we met at Lubieszow' Simon evidently
meant von Geisenheim, and by 'the previous owners of our Chrysler' the
two Communists whom the police believed guilty of the assault ; so he, too,
was no longer worried on that score, and had also realized that the heavy
setback recently sustained by the Iron Guard had removed their gravest
danger. "Lubieszow, Sons, Elders and Successors" was an amusing way
of referring to the Polish Legation, and it was clear that he had adopted
exactly the course that Rex and Richard had foreseen when they had discussed
the matter the previous evening.

"It's cheerful enough on the surface," Richard remarked. "But reading
between the lines one can see that he's really worried stiff."

"Aren't we all?" muttered Rex. "Today's the 12th, and we've got only
eight days to go."

"I know, but Simon's letter is dated the 10th, and he will have been in
Ploesti by yesterday morning, so he should have run Major Serzeski to
earth by now."

"Well, we'd better hit the trail for Ploesti on the first train out."

They found that there was a train leaving Cernauti that afternoon which
arrived in Bucharest at six o'clock in the morning, calling at Ploesti at
4.45. The head porter at the hotel secured them sleepers on it, and they
settled down to the long journey, their anxieties somewhat eased by the
comforting thought that they were at last on the move.

On arriving at Ploesti they got a night-hawk taxi at the station and
asked him to take them to the best hotel. The man drove them to the Hotel
Carol, a new and imposing edifice, but at its desk they drew blank ; Simon
had not been there. The taxi-man then took them to the Boyar Hotel, an
older place, but having an air of expensive comfort, and there the night
porter answered their enquiry by producing a letter for Rex, which had been
left there that evening.

As he tore it open Richard leaned over, and they read :

Mon Vieux,

*That damn' friend of yours has unconsciously given me the slip.
I arrived in Ploesti late on the night of the 10th and located him as staying here,
but he had gone out to dine with friends and not yet returned.*

I sat up in the lounge waiting for him until four o'clock in the morning, but he didn't come in, so I went to bed, having left word to be called at eight. The fool of a porter mucked my call, and I didn't wake till ten. By the time I got downstairs the Major had packed, breakfasted and gone, but not, apparently, to the station.

I questioned scores of servants and garage hands, but it was not until the night porter came on duty last night that I got anywhere. According to him our friend was still in the Ploesti district and had moved from the hotel to stay with friends outside the town, but he couldn't give me the name of the people or the least idea where they lived; so I had to chuck it for the night.

This morning I tried the head waiter again to see if he could give me the names of anyone our quarry might have entertained while staying here. He then recalled that our friend had given a luncheon party for five men on Sunday last, the 8th.

Two of the guests were strangers in the place, but he gave me the names of the other three, all of whom were locals mixed up in the oil game. I got their addresses and spent the rest of the day chasing them up.

Only one lived outside the town, so I naturally went for him first. With him my luck was out as he had not seen the Major since the luncheon party, but he gave me the name of one of the others that the head waiter did not know; he was a chap named Vimeru, a tanker man who lives in Constanta, so the Major couldn't be with him.

On getting back here I gatecrashed the two others, and the second one, a Greek called Zimovobodos, told me that the Major had spent the previous night with him at a week-end chalet that he owns up in the mountains to the north of the town. Our friend had, however, left that morning to go up to Cernauti again on some job connected with the Polish airmen who are interned there.

The next train for Cernauti is the night express, so I've booked a sleeper on it and am writing this after dinner. As the journey takes longer by road than rail I expect to be in Cernauti within an hour or so of our friend arriving there; so with luck I'll have good news for you by the time you're a free man again.

The odds are that you'll never get this letter, as I shall leave another for you with Levinsky; so, if you're not out till the 15th, you'll get this news via him, and I hope more; and of course realize that there's no point now in your coming to Ploesti. I've only written this on the offchance that you might get out earlier than expected and act on a letter I sent you two days ago from Bucharest.

Yours as ever, but quite breathless,

"S."

"Well, thank goodness he did leave a letter here," remarked Richard, "otherwise, we'd be at a dead end again."

"What god-darned awful luck, though," Rex muttered. "Just to think that old Simon and Serzeski were both sleeping in this caravanserai and that Simon missed him in the morning because he wasn't called in time."

"I know, and d'you realize that we must have been within about ten feet of Simon only about three hours ago? Our trains must have passed each other somewhere round half past two this morning."

"Sure! Still, we'll catch up on him tomorrow. There should be a morning train that will get us back to Cernauti before midnight."

It proved that the day express from Bucharest for the north called at Ploesti at 9.25. So, having given the night porter a handsome tip in advance to ensure their being called at 7.30, they went upstairs to get a couple of hours' sleep in comfortable beds.

This extra two hours and hot baths in the morning did much to refresh them after their wearisome night journey and the always unpleasant business of having to turn out of a sleeper in the small hours of the morning.

After breakfast they listened to a French broadcast and learned that Russia was now exerting pressure on the Finns, who were proving much more stubborn than had been the case with the smaller Baltic States.

At a few minutes after nine a taxi that they had ordered to take them to the station was reported at the door by the head porter. Having distributed the usual tips, they went out to it and drove off, thoroughly glad to be leaving so soon this dreary town in which everything smelt and tasted of petroleum.

The taxi had not covered a quarter of a mile and was still in the main street when Rex sat forward with a jerk.

"Hi!" he shouted to the driver, and added in German: "Quick! Turn round and go the other way."

"What the devil's the matter?" exclaimed Richard.

"That car!" gasped Rex. "The one that just passed us. It was the Ford V8! I saw its number."

The driver had slowed down and drawn in to the kerb. Tense with excitement, Rex bellowed fresh directions at him, while craning his neck out of the window so as not to lose sight of the Ford, which was now half-hidden in the stream of traffic.

The taxi banged, rattled and coughed as the elderly Rumanian who was at its wheel hove it round regardless of the indignation of the other drivers of vehicles in the crowded street.

"Go on!" yelled Rex impatiently. "Go on, man! That dark blue, dusty Ford. Triple fare for you if you catch up with it."

The man needed no further urging. He had got the taxi round, and it was now doing twenty miles an hour again as it wove dangerously past a bus and two lorries.

The Ford had a lead of about three hundred yards, and there were still a dozen vehicles separating it from the taxi.

It was well driven and moving fast, but gradually they edged up on it, passing five more cars and vans in the next half-mile. Then it reached the main cross-roads of the town and turned south. For a few minutes they lost sight of it, but it came into view again as they swerved round the corner, and there were now only another bus and two cars between them and it.

They passed the bus and were gaining on the two cars when one of them signalled that it was turning right at the next corner and so forced the taxi to slow up. As their pace increased again, they could catch an occasional glimpse of the Ford's number-plate beyond the one remaining intervening vehicle. It was UCZ827 all right, and Rex and Richard were now both leaning forward, breathless with excitement, as they urged their driver on.

While they were running through the suburbs they neither lost nor gained upon either of the cars ahead. The taxi was now rattling along at thirty-five miles an hour, but its engine was old and worn, so that seemed to be the maximum pace that could be got out of it.

Soon there came gaps between the houses on each side of the road, and through these openings glimpses could be caught of the desolate treeless country and a skyline broken only by oil derricks. They passed an ugly water tower, and Rex, recognizing it from his previous visit to Ploesti, realized that they were on the road to Bucharest.

"We shan't do it," Richard muttered at that moment. "He's gaining on us now."

"Yep!" Rex nodded grimly. "This old tin can will never be able to catch the Ford once we're on the open road."

The car immediately ahead of them was a long low limousine. As it reached a fork where the trunk road to the capital broadened out it put on a burst of speed and passed the Ford.

All unconscious that he was being pursued, the Ford's driver slowed a little to let the bigger car pass, but then he put on speed again and gradually drew ahead at a steady forty to forty-five miles an hour.

Rex and Richard both sat craning forward, wondering how on earth they could attract the attention of the man in the car ahead, or at least keep up with him.

It flashed into Richard's mind to start shouting "Stop, Thief!" as a means of getting him pulled up by some approaching vehicle that, hearing the cry, might slew across the road and block the Ford's path; but he did not know the right words in Rumanian, and, even if he had, his voice would never have carried far enough to be effective.

The gap between the taxi and the Ford had now widened to nearly half a mile. The taxi-man turned round and shouted:

"It is no good! He is too fast."

"Go on!" yelled Rex. "Stick to his tail!"

They were well away from the city on the open road now. On each side of them stretched the hideous waste scarred by the wooden oil towers and ugly tin-roofed hutments. The air was so heavily laden with the horrid reek of petroleum that it seemed as if the lighting of a match would have caused the whole sordid landscape to disappear in one terrific sheet of flame.

The Ford was still gaining, while its pursuers sat with their hands clenched in impotent fury. In the car ahead lay the all-important document for which so much blood had already been shed, or at least the means of tracing it. There in the Ford, which was still moving at no more than a moderate, unhurried pace, lay the means of cutting off four-fifths of Hitler's oil supplies; of permanently grounding two-thirds of the Luftwaffe or rendering the bulk of Germany's Armoured Divisions impotent.

To secure it would be of more value to the Allied cause than the sinking of all Germany's capital ships in a general Fleet action, and be a more far-reaching victory than any the Allied Armies could at present hope to achieve for years to come. For it the Supreme Allied War Council would unhesitatingly have sacrificed fifty thousand lives, knowing that the loss of a mere three divisions was a bagatelle compared with the infinitely greater losses their countries must sustain if the war had to be fought out, as was the 1914–1918 war, until both sides were bled white and rocking from exhaustion.

And the driver of the Ford was not even trying to get away from them. He would have pulled up to see what they wanted if only they could have got close enough to attract his attention by their shouts. Yet they could only sit there watching the Ford draw away from them in a little cloud of dust.

It was now nearly a mile ahead, but they could still see it down the long stretch of flat almost empty road. It was just approaching a solitary building standing on a corner where a side-road branched off up a slight rise in the plain.

As they watched, their eyes glued to the Ford, its pace seemed to slacken.

"My God!" cried Richard. "He's slowing down!"

Rex jumped in his seat. "Holy Michael! You've said it. That place is a service station, and he's pulling up for gas."

On tenterhooks now, they craned still further forward. The Ford was pulling up. There was not a doubt about it. It had stopped now in front of the roadside garage. A man came out to speak to the driver.

Their taxi-man shouted something and crouched over his wheel, striving to get the last ounce out of his aged engine. They had decreased the mile that separated them from the Ford by a quarter; by a half.

The garage man turned and walked back towards the house. It looked as if he was going in to get something. Only a quarter of a mile now lay between them and the Ford.

Suddenly, with an awful sinking feeling, they saw it start to move again. It had not, after all, pulled up for petrol, oil, air or water, but only that its driver might ask some question.

It was moving quite slowly. They were within two hundred yards of it. Rex was leaning out of the taxi window and shouting at the top of his voice; Richard and the taxi-driver joined in. But their voices were drowned for the driver of the Ford by the sound of his own engine, and the garage hand had disappeared into the building.

As they rattled past the garage they were still only two hundred yards behind the Ford, but now it began to draw ahead again. Rex waved frantically to the driver of an oncoming lorry, but in vain, as the man did not understand what he wanted.

The Ford was steadily increasing its lead; a quarter of a mile, half a mile, three-quarters. Richard and Rex sat back glumly staring at the little cloud of dust which half obscured their quarry. They were now leaving the desolate oil country behind and entering the northern fringe of the farm lands that spread right over the rich Wallachian plain. Trees, hedges and isolated homesteads broke the horizon, and the broad road began to wind its way between the cornfields and meadows so that from time to time the Ford disappeared from view.

Suddenly the taxi began to lose speed and crawled to a halt at the side of the road.

Rex swore and leaned forward to ask the driver what had happened.

The game old chap replied in halting German : "I have run out of petrol. I knew we were getting low, but we would have had no hope at all of catching him if I had stopped at that garage for more."

He had done his best for his passengers, so they could not possibly grumble at him ; and they both felt now that even if the petrol had not given out the odds would have been all against their catching the Ford on the open road.

There was no place of importance on the road between Ploesti and the Rumanian capital, so the Ford was obviously on its way there, and Rex asked : "When we get more petrol, can you take us on to Bucharest ?"

The driver shook his head. "No. It is another twenty miles, at least; and I am far outside my limit already."

"We'll make it well worth your while," urged Richard. "It is terribly important to us that we should speak to the man who was driving that Ford, at the earliest possible moment."

But the taxi-man was adamant. To oblige them he had taken a risk as it was in going so far outside the limits of his own town. If he took them to Bucharest it was certain that the police would have him up for contravening the regulations under which licences to ply for hire were issued to taxi-drivers.

"Then we must get back to Ploesti just as soon as we can," said Rex, "and go on to Bucharest by train."

After pulling up several passing cars and lorries in the hope of being able to buy a spare tin of petrol off one of them, they at last got a "bidon" from a

On this sober note they left the *grădină* and drove back to the Polish ation, where they learned that Brigadier Molikinski had now returned. They found him to be a thin, good-looking man with greying hair. received them most courteously, and in reply to their enquiry said at : :

'No. Serzeski is not in Bucharest. He was in Ploesti for some days, I spoke to him there on the telephone—let me see, yes, on Wednesday ; I asked him to go up to Cernauti for us, so he would have left Ploesti erday morning for the north.''

'I think you must be mistaken,'' Richard smiled disarmingly. "We 't actually see him face to face, but we saw his car in Ploesti this morning ; it took the road to Bucharest. We tried to catch him but our taxi wasn't enough, and we ran out of petrol some eight miles outside the town.''

'May I ask why you are so anxious to contact Serzeski?'' enquired the ;adier.

'I'm wanting to get back some private papers that I left with him for keeping during the recent excitement up on the Polish border,'' replied with a substratum of truth.

'I see. Well, I'm sorry I can't help you. I'm sure Serzeski would not e ignored my order to proceed to Cernauti, and if he did go there he could possibly have got back to Ploesti so soon. I think it must have been eone else's car that you mistook for his.''

'No, sir,'' Rex insisted. "I saw his number, UCZ827. It was his all right.''

'Perhaps he left it there and went north by train,'' the Brigadier suggested. : might have lent it to somebody while he was away.''

'That certainly is a plausible explanation,'' agreed Rex, with a swift ce at Richard. Both of them were thinking that, as Simon's information ed with the Brigadier's positive statement that Serzeski had gone to 1auti, that must really be the case, and therefore it could not have been /ho was driving the Ford that morning.

'Can you tell us when Serzeski will be back?'' Richard asked.

'Some time tomorrow, I expect. I sent him to Cernauti on a matter required one personal interview, and there is no reason why he should ain there longer than a day.''

Having thanked the Brigadier, they left the Legation. Immediately were outside, Richard said : "I believe that chap was right. Serzeski regular officer, so he wouldn't flagrantly disobey his orders. If for some ate reason he had felt it absolutely imperative to return to Bucharest, vould at least have let his Chief know. He must have lent his car to ebody or, perhaps, sold it.''

'That's the way it looks,'' Rex nodded. "Now, how in heck are we g to trace that god-darned car?''

furniture van. The taxi then drove them the eight miles or so tha[
had covered in their chase, back to Ploesti; taking them straight [
station.

It was now a quarter past ten, and the next train out for Buchare[
at twenty minutes to twelve, so for an hour and a half they had to kill
in the station buffet. In due course the train came in, and on arriving i[
capital, without giving a thought to lunch, they left their bags in the c[
room and took a taxi straight to the Polish Legation.

The anxiety and frustration which had nearly driven Rex silly du[
the past few weeks had now given place to a feeling of intense excite[
Evidently the information that had sent Simon hurrying off to Cern[
had been ill-founded, and Serzeski had stayed with another friend, or perh[
some woman that he had picked up in the town, for an extra night in Plo[
But, by sheer good luck, they had spotted his car and knew it to have b[
heading for Bucharest only that morning. Within a few moments now th[
was every probability that they would be face to face with him, or at le[
learn quite definitely where they could find him.

With ill-concealed impatience they made their enquiry of two elde[
and seemingly slow-witted clerks in the Legation Office. Both of th[
knew Major Serzeski, but neither had seen him for at least a week.

When Rex insisted that the Major had arrived back in Bucharest a f[
hours ago, one of the clerks went off to consult Serzeski's chief, a Brigad[
Molikinski. He returned to say that the Brigadier had gone out to lu[
and would be back about three o'clock. If they would call again then[
doubt he would see them.

Temporarily baffled but still full of optimism, Rex and Richard we[
the nearest *grădină* and lunched. As they were paying their bill, Ri[
said:

"Now we're back in Bucharest we must, er—find out about Gr[
There are certain things we ought to do."

Rex nodded gloomily. He remembered the job that he and Sim[
undertaken of buying a good plot in the cemetery for poor Jan Lu[
and making certain that he was buried with all the decencies a[
The thought that their splendid friend might be lying in some [
graveyard where unclaimed bodies were sent from the Bucharest mo[
quite unbearable.

"Yes. We'll certainly do that," he agreed. "The fact that[
always said he'd be much too busy to worry what happened t[
once he'd left it makes no difference as far as we're concerned. I'[
he was right about our bodies being only new suits of clothes in [
full of all sorts and colours that we've worn and shed throu[
centuries, but one doesn't throw the cast-off uniforms of the g[
dunghill, and our Duke was a great man if ever there was one."

"We should be able to find out from Serzeski himself tomorrow whom he sold or lent it to. But that means wasting the best part of another day, and it's now the 13th."

"Holy mackerel! So it is. Then we've only a week left and we haven't even got the Golden Fleece back yet. If we don't get a good break soon I'll go crazy."

"We've had a good break already today—spotting the Ford this morning. If we hadn't we'd still be on the train going north to Cernauti. At least we are in the same city as we have every reason to suppose the car to be. I had been hoping to get round some of the hospitals this afternoon to make enquiries about Greyeyes, but it looks as if I'll have to spend it questioning garage hands instead."

"You've said it," agreed Rex.

Having discussed various ways of setting about their new project, they decided that the best would be to go to the Bucharest Automobile Club and seek the assistance of its secretary.

A French-speaking assistant in a Post Office gave them the address of the Club, and when they got there they found the secretary almost too helpful. On their telling him that they had left some valuables in a borrowed car which they wanted his help to trace, he immediately suggested that he should ring up the police and ask them to broadcast for it.

The last thing they wanted was police interference, as they had never borrowed the car at all, and, once the police were involved, they would probably have to enter into endless explanations before the packet, if it were still in the car, was handed over to them.

Richard managed to slide gracefully out of the offer on the grounds that no broadcast could be made until the next news bulletin was issued, and, in the meantime, they might trace the car by ringing up all the largest garages in the city; and it was the secretary's help in securing a list of these with their telephone numbers that they really wanted.

The secretary then turned them over to his clerk with suitable instructions, and they succeeded in borrowing for the evening a trade journal that had a complete list of Bucharest's motor establishments in it.

They next collected their bags from the station. In choosing an hotel to stay at, the Athenée Palace was ruled out on account of the poignant memories of de Richleau, so they took rooms at the Ritz.

Immediately they had been installed in their private suite Richard set about telephoning the garages that had the largest advertisements in the journal they had borrowed; but, after twenty minutes' exasperating cross-talk in a mixture of English, French, German and Italian he gave up, and Rex went downstairs to see if he could find someone to do the job for them.

He returned with a courier that he had hired from the hotel management, and, having explained what they wanted, they sat the man down to say to each garage he rang up : "Are you garaging a blue Ford V8 number UCZ827, or has one of your men serviced such a car today ?"

They had dinner served upstairs in their sitting-room, so that they should hear without the least delay if the courier got an affirmative reply, and, sustaining the man with almost hourly relays of sandwiches and drinks, they kept him at it until one o'clock in the morning ; but they had no luck. As the man pointed out, although he had rung up all the largest garages in Bucharest there were hundreds of little places, and it might quite well be that the car was housed in a private garage or that it had only passed through the city on its way to some destination in the west, south or east.

When he had gone Rex announced his intention of meeting the night train from Cernauti that got in at six in the morning in the hope that Serzeski would return by it, and rang through to the office to have himself called at five.

Richard volunteered to go too, but Rex would not let him, maintaining that he was still an invalid and exerting himself much more than was good for him already.

Rex duly met the train, but Serzeski was not on it. The only other express from Cernauti left there at six in the morning and got in to Bucharest at eight in the evening.

After breakfast they got hold of the courier again, and Richard supervised a continuation of their systematic search while Rex put in some extra sleep. All through the day the monotonous enquiry continued without success ; but when Rex went out to meet the eight o'clock train he was filled with an exasperated confidence that Serzeski must be on it, and his renewed optimism was justified.

He had taken up a position near the ticket-collector where a strong light shone on the faces of the emerging passengers, and after the first half hundred people had squeezed through he suddenly caught sight of the Polish Major.

Stepping back into the shadows, Rex waited for his intended victim to pass the barrier, then followed him outside.

The Major hailed a taxi and, shouting "Polish Legation" at the man, entered it. Rex, hard on his heels, pulled the door open again and jumped in.

The driver looked a little surprised, and Serzeski exclaimed in German : "Here, this taxi is taken !"

"That's all right," said Rex in the same language. "I'm going the same way as you," and turning to the driver he added : "Take us to the Polish Legation, please."

On hearing the interloper give the same address as had his first passenger, the driver slid in his clutch, and the taxi started off. Serzeski's reaction was that the big man must be somebody that he knew, so he made no further immediate protest as Rex plumped down in the seat beside him.

"You don't remember me, do you?" boomed Rex cheerfully.

Serzeski sat forward with a start. "You are—my God, yes! You're the German spy we caught at Grodek."

Rex placed one leg-of-mutton hand flat on the Major's chest and pushed him back into his corner, as he said:

"It's a lucky break for you that I'm not a German spy or this would be about the last ride you'd be taking. Even as it is I've a pretty good reason to tear you up in little pieces and throw the bits out of the window. And, if I weren't mighty sorry for all you Poles, that's just what I'd be doing. Now listen, honey! I'm a perfectly good American citizen. Get that into your stupid head and like it. The Rumanians have gone into my ancestry and examined my birthmarks with microscopes, and you've been proved one hundred per cent a goofy, scaremongering old woman. But all that's over now. What have you done with your car?"

"My car!" repeated the Major in a scared voice.

"Yes, sweetie-pie. The Ford V8." Rex took his arm in an iron grip and shook him.

"Why do you want to know?"

"That's no business of yours. And you'd better tell me the truth. I'll be checking up later; and if I find you've lied to me, next time we meet you'll be wishing that you'd fallen into the hands of Himmler."

"I've sold it," muttered Serzeski.

"Why did you do that?"

"We Poles are in misfortune. Now that our country is overrun, there may not be funds even to keep the Legation open for much longer. I received a good offer for the Ford, and I thought the money would make a nice little reserve for me, so I took it."

"That's fair enough," Rex agreed. "To whom did you sell it?"

"I sold it in Ploesti five days ago to a man named Vimeru."

The name rang a bell in Rex's mind—it was surely one of those mentioned in Simon's letter when he had written of the luncheon party given at Ploesti by Serzeski—so it looked as if the Major were telling the truth.

"What's his address?" Rex went on.

"I don't know. He was in Ploesti on business at the same time as myself. Some mutual friends introduced him to me in the hotel one day, and I asked him to join us for lunch. Afterwards he saw my car and made an offer for it. I got him to increase his offer slightly, and he gave me his cheque. But why do you wish to know all this?"

Rex ignored the question and put another himself. "Did you have the car overhauled at all between the time we last met and when you sold it to this fellow Vimeru?"

"No. It was in constant use. I have been very busy in connection with the evacuation of the Polish Forces."

"Did you have it cleaned up before you handed it over?"

"No. The crankshaft of Vimeru's own car had broken that morning. He wanted another for immediate use. He spent a quarter of an hour looking at the engine, then we drove out to the house of one of our friends in it. He expressed himself as satisfied, and on our return to Ploesti that evening he took it over. But what concern is all this of yours?"

The Major's insistent demand to be told why he was being questioned about his car seemed a fairly certain indication that he had not come across the packet that Rex had pushed under its seat nearly three weeks ago; otherwise, he would have guessed before this the reason for Rex's interest.

"I'll tell you," said Rex, feeling that he must test the matter further. "I told you the truth that night, when I said I was working for the Allies. I had some papers on me that were pretty important, and I didn't want them to fall into the hands of the Rumanians, so on the way to their camp I stuffed them under the back seat of your car. Now, for Mike's sake, let me have the truth. Did you come across them?"

"No. They must still be there, unless Vimeru has found them during the past five days."

"Well, we'll hope to God he hasn't. You can drop me here if you like; and next time you arrest anybody you'll serve your country better if you're not quite so self-opinionated and a little less impetuous."

"You must admit the circumstances were suspicious," growled Serzeski.

"Maybe. But I asked you to take me to your own Commandant and you wouldn't. All you could think of was pacifying the Rumanians. That landed me in prison for over a fortnight, and heaven alone knows what damage may have resulted to the Allied cause."

Rex leaned forward and rapped on the front window of the taxi. It pulled up, and he got out, slamming the door behind him, and cutting short the excuses for his own conduct that the fat Major was still muttering to himself.

Securing another taxi, Rex drove back to the Ritz and told Richard the result of his meeting. The courier had been hard at it all day but had still not succeeded in obtaining any news of the Ford V8. On looking at Simon's letter they saw that Vimeru was the tanker man who lived in Constanta, on the Black Sea; it therefore now seemed probable that he had driven straight through Bucharest on his way back to his home-town.

"We'd better get down to Constanta just as soon as we can make it," said Rex.

"But we haven't got Vimeru's address," objected Richard, "and it might take us the deuce of a time to trace him if we go there without it."

It further emerged from Simon's letter that the man who had given him Vimeru's name was not named himself, and had been the guest of Serzeski who lived outside Ploesti.

They telephoned Serzeski, hoping to get the man's name from him, but he had gone out for the evening and it was not known when he would be back. They then got through to the Boyar Hotel, thinking that the head waiter would be able to help them, but he had gone off duty.

"We could go to Ploesti tonight," Richard suggested, "secure Vimeru's address first thing in the morning, then catch a train for Constanta."

"We'd lose time having to come back through Bucharest."

"No," Richard argued. "Going through Bucharest may be the quickest way by road, but you don't have to come through the capital by rail. There's a direct line to carry the oil down from Ploesti to the port."

"We've only six days now, and every hour counts," Rex demurred. "Still, I guess you're right; by going to Ploesti first we'll make better time in the long run. I'll go down and settle the bill."

They left on the midnight train for the north and soon after one o'clock were back again at the Boyar Hotel in the smelly oil capital.

At breakfast Rex refreshed the head waiter's memory with a generous tip. They learned that the name of the man they wanted was Ramuez; he was a big executive in the Astro-Romano Oil Company and ran one of their largest refineries at a pace called Tirsova. Having hired a car, they set out to see him immediately they had finished their meal.

Tirsova proved to be a grim little township, the whole life and purpose of which revolved round the great refinery. They drove straight up to a fine modern block that housed the main offices, only to find, to their intense consternation, that it was closed.

Owing to the irregular hours they had kept by reason of their journeys during the past few days, they had entirely forgotten that it was Sunday.

After some trouble Rex managed to find a gatekeeper who could speak a little French, and the man directed them to Ramuez's private house. It was a large ostentatious villa set in a garden that had obviously cost a lot of money to lay out, but in which the trees and plants were dwarfed and wilting from the petroleum that saturated the fumy atmosphere.

A further blow awaited them at the house. As it was a Sunday Ramuez had gone off in his car up into the clean air of the mountains to get some fishing. His wife had gone with him, and none of the servants had ever heard of Vimeru.

In a mood of acute depression Richard and Rex debated if they should return to Ploesti and go on to Constanta by train that afternoon without Vimeru's address, or if they should wait until Ramuez got back. The question was decided for them by Ramuez's manservant producing a time-table. Apart from the morning train, which it was already too late for them to catch, there was no other Sunday train to Constanta until eleven o'clock that night.

As there was nowhere for them to go and nothing for them to do in

Tirsova, Ramuez's servant took pity on them and said he felt sure it would be his master's wish that they should make themselves comfortable in the house. In consequence, their day was made slightly less miserable than it would otherwise have been, and they were given an excellent lunch; but they could not throw off the terrible anxiety they now felt at the manner in which time was slipping away.

Ramuez and his wife arrived home soon after six. He told them at once that Vimeru's address was 36, Calea Logothete, Constanta; then insisted that they should stay to dinner, since they would have ample time afterwards to return to Ploesti and catch their train.

When they pulled up at the "Boyar" later that evening, to pay their bill and collect their bags, Richard suddenly said:

"Look. We must send poor old Simon a telegram, to let him know what's been happening. We ought to have done so last night really, but I forgot about it owing to our coming on here."

"Sure!" Rex agreed. "Let's get something out."

The wire they sent ran as follows:

"HAVE SEEN SERZESKI WHO IS BACK IN BUCHAREST STOP HE SOLD CAR WITHOUT OVERHAUL BEFORE LEAVING PLOESTI TO VIMERU OF 36 CALEA LOGOTHETE CONSTANTA STOP REASON TO SUPPOSE CAR THERE SO PROCEEDING CONSTANTA TONIGHT WILL LEAVE MESSAGE BEST HOTEL."

"Simon will get that first thing in the morning," remarked Rex. "But the express doesn't leave Cernauti till four o'clock in the afternoon, so I doubt if he'll make Constanta much before midday the day after tomorrow. With any luck we'll have that god-darned option and be on the way to Turkey by that time."

"Not if we have the sort of luck we've had today," said Richard glumly.

"Yes, I'm feeling that way, too. A whole day wasted, and we've only got five more to go."

They saw nothing of the Dobruja, with its flat, rich farmlands, seemingly endless marshes and sluggish rivers fringed by enormous willow trees, for they made the whole of their hundred-and-seventy-mile journey in darkness, arriving at Constanta at a hideous hour in the early morning. The hotel to which a night-hawk taxi took them was the Sultan Ahmed, a reminder of the days when this Black Sea city was the capital of a Turkish Province.

At such an hour nothing could be done, so they went to bed until eight o'clock; but they hurried over breakfast and were on the doorstep of Vimeru's office in the Calea Logothete when a head clerk arrived to open it at nine.

Their depression of the night before was behind them. They felt confident that they were now in the city to which the Ford V8 had been taken and about to see its owner. From what Serzeski had said it seemed reasonably certain that up to a week ago the packet had remained undisturbed where Rex had hidden it. There was a very good chance that Vimeru had still not discovered it and, if they could only get it back, from Constanta they could yet reach Istanbul in two days.

The head clerk spoke French and received them pleasantly. He said that Monsieur Vimeru lived a little way outside the town and he did not usually get to his office until from ten to half past; but they were most welcome to wait for him, and in the meantime they would, of course, have coffee.

Custom dies hard, and the offering of coffee to all visitors was another survival which continued to give this old city an oriental atmosphere. The brew was very black, sweet and aromatic, and it was served by an old Turk in a tarboosh and baggy trousers, whose sole employment it was to make coffee all day for the frequenters of the establishment.

This pleasant ritual whiled away three-quarters of an hour, and the head clerk furnished them with some illustrated papers to look at; but by half past ten Vimeru had not yet put in an appearance and they were beginning to get distinctly restless. Then at twenty-five to eleven the head clerk bowed himself in to say that he had just received a message to the effect that Monsieur Vimeru would not, after all, be coming to his office that day.

"Why not?" cried Rex angrily, entirely forgetting himself and shouting at the quite harmless little man.

"Madame Vimeru has telephoned to say that her husband has had to go down to Mangalia on urgent family business."

"Where's that?" Richard asked quickly.

"About twenty-five miles down the coast, Monsieur."

"Then there's a chance that he'll be back tonight. I suppose Madame Vimeru didn't say?"

"No, Monsieur, she said only that this morning he had received a letter from his brother on a matter that required immediate attention."

"Could you telephone for us and ask when he is expected back?"

"Certainly, Monsieur. Please to be seated again. I will send Mamoud to you with more coffee."

They accepted Mamoud's further ministrations until the head clerk returned to say that Madame Vimeru expected her husband back to dinner, about nine o'clock. Having obtained Vimeru's address and directions how to get there, they thanked him and left the office.

"This lets us in for another day kicking our heels doing nothing," groaned Rex, as soon as they were outside.

"We've got to arrange about our journey. A coaster would be much quicker than rail if there's one sailing tomorrow. We'll need exit permits too, and, as you've lost your passport, that will mean a visit to the United States Consulate." Richard was every bit as furious as Rex at this new delay,

K*

but he was somewhat better at thinking up ways to take their minds off the terrible baffled urgency they were both feeling.

They lunched early, and while Rex visited the American Consulate Richard went to a travel agency. They met again at the "Sultan Ahmed" at four o'clock. Rex had at first found considerable difficulty over the loss of his passport, but as he was preparing to leave the country forthwith the authorities had been persuaded to give him an exit visa. Richard's was being dealt with through the usual channels by the travel agency. A small steamer with accommodation for six cabin passengers was leaving for Istanbul at three o'clock the following afternoon. The voyage was only one hundred and eighty-eight miles as compared with nearly eight hundred miles by rail, and the steamer was due to dock at the Porte on the evening of the 18th.

At six o'clock they went to a café-restaurant and, not knowing when they would get another meal, had a high tea consisting of an omelette and a bottle of red Cotnar wine.

At a quarter past seven they took a taxi out to the north of the town and left it in the square of the little seaside hamlet in which Vimeru lived, giving the driver a handsome tip and arranging with him to be there to pick them up at ten o'clock. The description they had had of the place from the head clerk made it easy to find. Vimeru's house proved to be an old red-tiled villa standing alone in a small bay.

The lemon-walled house, set among pines, olives and cypress trees, and overlooking the warm blue waters of the Black Sea, made a charming scene in the gentle evening light. The sun was going down in a cloudless sky, and the lengthening shadows lent an air of mystery to the little valley in which Vimeru's property lay. A side road that was hardly more than a track curved down towards it, and, moving off this into the myrtle scrub, Rex and Richard took up a position from which they could watch both the house and the track without being seen.

They had been there about half an hour when a car appeared, but it was not the Ford V8 that they had been expecting so eagerly. It drove down the gradient to the house where its solitary passenger, a middle-aged man, got out and gave some money to the driver, then went inside. The car backed, turned round and drove off up the track again.

"Hell's bells!" exclaimed Rex. "That's a taxi. Vimeru must have decided to go up by train instead of taking the Ford. What mutts we've been! The odds are that the Ford's been sitting in that garage by the side of the house all day."

"If that was Vimeru?" queried Richard. "It's early for him yet."

"Sure, we'd better hang around a bit and see if anyone else turns up."

The sun was setting in the hills behind them now, and the valley was in shadow. Lights went on in the villa, and the sound of a wireless that had just been turned on came faintly up to them. The minutes dragged and they spoke little, but at last it was nine o'clock and no other vehicle had come down the track.

"Let's go," said Rex suddenly. "That must have been Vimeru. God, if only we'd known, we could have gotten through with this by midday and be on our way to Turkey by now."

In the semi-darkness they crunched their way through the *maquis* back to the track and walked down it to the house. The principal rooms faced the sea, and there were no signs of life in the front-door side of the villa at all. They had a story all ready to tell Monsieur Vimeru as a reason for asking his permission to search his car, but as they passed within a few feet of the garage they saw that its double doors were not quite shut.

"Hist!" whispered Richard. "Why waste time talking to Vimeru and risk his wanting proof that the 'Fleece' is ours before he lets us go off with it?"

Rex nodded. "Okay! You stay here and keep cave while I slip inside. I'm a quicker mover, these days, than you." As he spoke he grasped one side of the tall door firmly and drew it steadily open about two feet. It made only a faint grating noise.

Richard had used his legs more during the past two hours than he had at any time since his smash, and he now leaned against the wall of the house to rest himself. A faint glow came from the partly opened garage doors as Rex switched on his torch inside. The wireless was still playing, and for the people in the other side of the house must have drowned the faint sounds that came to Richard of Rex moving about.

While he waited Richard could feel his heart pounding beneath his ribs. This was the culminating point of their long and arduous chase, during which they had met with so many heartbreaking delays and disappointments. Rex seemed a long time, but the Ford V8 must be there, otherwise he would have been out again by now.

Richard fought down a temptation to look inside the garage and kept his head moving from side to side, alternately glancing at the approach from the back of the house and the front door. Would Rex never come? What the devil was he doing in there? He had had time enough to search half a dozen cars.

Suddenly the glow of light disappeared, the grating noise came again, and Rex was standing beside him.

"Well?" whispered Richard.

"It's not there."

"Are you—are you certain?" Richard stammered, aghast at the new misfortune.

"Of course I'm certain." Rex's voice was bitter with disappointment. "I turned the Ford inside out. Vimeru must have found it. Come on, let's tackle him and find out what he's done with the darned thing."

Still furious at having been baulked when they had thought themselves so near their goal, they walked to the front door and rang the bell.

It was answered by a dark, youngish woman whom they took to be Madame Vimeru herself. On their asking to see her husband she replied in very poor French:

"I regret, but he is from home."

Richard swallowed hard and said: "We have important business with him. The people at his office told us that he would be back by nine o'clock tonight."

She nodded. "Yes, I expected him, but my uncle arrived from Mangalia about an hour ago. He has been with my husband there today and brought a message that Monsieur Vimeru will not be back in Constanta till tomorrow morning. If you go to his office then, perhaps . . ."

Lamely they thanked her and turned away. There was nothing else that they could do.

"What God-awful luck!" moaned Richard as they walked slowly back up the track.

"It sure is," Rex agreed, but this time he made an effort to console his friend by adding: "Still, the boat doesn't sail till tomorrow afternoon, so if we can nail Vimeru in the morning maybe we'll have lost nothing."

"That's true, but somehow there seems to have been a hoodoo on us all the time we've been chasing the Golden Fleece. Day after day has been swallowed up in rushing from place to place or waiting for things to happen that never come off."

"You're telling me! And if we don't get our hooks on it in the next twenty-four hours the game will be up."

In moody silence they walked on until they reached their taxi, and having given the man directions they did not speak again before it pulled up outside the "Sultan Ahmed".

"Well," said Richard, as Rex helped him out, "they say the darkest hour is just before the dawn; let's hope the old proverb proves correct in our case."

Rex was about to reply as they passed through the swing doors. Instead, he suddenly grabbed Richard's arm and exclaimed:

"Holy Michael! Look over there!"

Richard followed his glance to the far end of the lounge and gave a cry of delight. Simon was sitting there; before him on a small table were three glasses and beside him in an ice-bucket was a magnum of champagne.

He had already seen them and came hurrying forward, grinning from ear to ear.

"You chaps *have* been a time," was his greeting. "Been awfully thirsty work waiting for you to turn up."

"You old so-an'-so, how did you know we were around?" grinned Rex, clapping him affectionately on the shoulder.

"Yes," smiled Richard. "We didn't expect you till midday tomorrow at the earliest; so we hadn't even left a message for you yet."

Simon wriggled his neck. "They told me at the desk that you were staying here, and that you'd gone out at six o'clock. Hoped you'd be back in time to join me for dinner, but guessed you must be dining out, as it wouldn't have taken you all this time to drive to Vimeru's and back. Knocked off a bottle to my own check while I fed but thought I'd have something on the ice for when you came in. Just thought you might need a spot of cheering up."

Richard's eyes widened. "What the devil d'you mean?" he cried suddenly, grasping Simon by the arm.

"Well, must have been a bit hard for you chaps, missing the boat like that."

Rex grabbed his other arm and shook him. "Come clean, you old sinner. Don't just stand there grinning like an ape. D'you mean you've got it?"

Simon nodded. "Um, it was just where you left it; under the back seat of the car. I fished it out this afternoon."

"Well, can you beat that?" Rex sighed from pure relief and happiness, and Richard echoed his sigh.

A porter took the hats and coats of the newcomers; they went to Simon's table, and a waiter opened the magnum; the band was playing one of those enchanting catchy tunes that are entirely special to Rumania and haunt the cafés for a season without, to the world's loss, ever getting further afield. The glasses were filled and they drank deep of the cool, sparkling wine.

"But how in heck did you hit this dump so quickly?" Rex wanted to know, as soon as he set down his glass.

"Quite simple," Simon smiled. "Soon as I got your wire I chartered a private plane."

"By Jove!" exclaimed Richard. "Then we'll be in Istanbul by lunchtime tomorrow. I tried to get one here this morning but there wasn't a thing to be had."

"Ner." Simon shook his head. "Sorry, Richard, but my chap would only fly me from Cernauti, here. I tried to book him to go on, but his licence doesn't allow him to leave the country. We'll have to go on to Turkey by ship. There's one leaving at three o'clock tomorrow afternoon. I booked on it just before the Travel Office shut, and I learned that you chaps had reserved cabins on her, too."

"But tell us," grinned Rex, "how did you manage to beat us to the Ford?"

"Got in just after midday. Went straight to Vimeru's office. They gave me his address but told me he wouldn't be back till this evening. Thought it worth while to drive out and have a look round. Walked down to the house. No one about, but the garage door was open. Looked in and saw the Ford. Nothing to make a fuss about really, a child could have done it."

"Well, I know two children who didn't," laughed Richard. "Let's have another glass of that wine."

It was the first time all three of them had been together since Simon and Rex had left Richard on the train at Giurgevo, nearly four weeks before, so they had much to tell one another. It was the first time, too, in all those long days and anxious nights of waiting, travelling and scheming, that they had felt really able to relax; so they made a night of it, and a second magnum had gone the way of the first before they eventually sought their beds at half past two.

Next morning they enjoyed the luxury of sleeping late, then at half past ten Richard went into Simon's room. When they had exchanged greetings he said:

"I didn't feel that last night was the time to speak of it, but Rex could only give me a secondhand account of what happened outside the British Legation. All of us realize, I think, that dear Greyeyes was not the man to die in bed. He would have wanted to go down fighting in some desperate encounter for something that he believed to be terribly worthwhile. I'd like to know the details of his last heroic stand to save the Golden Fleece."

"I'll tell you," said Simon. And for some twenty minutes he lived again for Richard that agonizing scene to the last glimpse he had had of the Duke, his gun dropped from his hand, lolling half out of the taxi.

Neither of them looked at the other, and when Simon had done they sat for a little in silence, heavy of heart for the great loss they had sustained. Then, with a word of thanks, Richard went back to his own room to dress.

Two o'clock found the three friends down at the docks and soon after they were settling themselves into their cabins in one of the little cargo steamers that made a twice-weekly trip down to Istanbul. The passenger accommodation was very simple; six cabins, three on each side, which opened on to a small saloon with one central table; the saloon served for lounge, dining-room and bar. The Captain, a bearded Rumanian, made them welcome, and they found that they had only one other fellow passenger, a Turkish tobacco manufacturer. But there was also a motley collection of about a score of cheap-fare passengers who, accompanied by a variety of livestock, were to pass the night on deck.

At a little after three o'clock the ropes were cast off, and the ship left port. The weather was good and the sea calm. The friends spent what was left of the afternoon and the early evening up on the afterdeck, then at seven-thirty they partook of a plain but quite passable dinner at which the Captain and his Chief Engineer joined them. The conversation was scrappy and in many tongues, but it served to pass away the time. At nine o'clock the Captain excused himself to go up to his bridge, as a sea mist had arisen.

The others talked on for a little, then went up on deck for a breath of air before turning in. The mist had increased to a fog. The forepart of the ship was shrouded in it, and the unfortunate deck passengers were now huddling under their wraps, but the ship was proceeding smoothly at only slightly reduced speed, and the chill of the fog soon drove the three friends to their cabins.

All three were asleep when at about one o'clock they were roused by the sounds of excited shouting. Someone was bellowing from the nearby bridge through a megaphone, and there were fainter, but not less urgent, cries coming, it seemed, from seaward to the port side of the ship.

Suddenly there was a dull thud, and the vessel shuddered slightly. The thud was followed by a bumping, scraping sound. There were more shouts, then a creaking and a rending crash as though some great tree had splintered and been brought down in a heavy gale. The shouting continued for a few moments, then ceased; the cries to seaward gradually faded; the silence of the fog-enshrouded ship was broken only by muffled footsteps and subdued cursing.

Rex was first out on deck; Simon went into Richard's cabin to help him get a coat on. As they started up the companionway they met Rex coming down again.

"It's nothing serious," he said at once. "We collided with a poor little fishing-boat, and she got the raw end of the deal. She bumped us on our port bow and scraped along our beam. Her mast got caught in one of our steel boat davits and snapped clean off; but we weren't doing more than six knots, and I wouldn't think we've even sprung a plate."

The silence was now uncanny, and Richard suddenly asked:

"Why have our engines stopped, then?"

"I couldn't say." Rex turned, and they followed him up to the bridge.

The Captain was apparently having a heated argument down the voice-pipe with his Chief Engineer. They could not understand a word he said, but when he had finished he turned to them and spoke in French.

"Some of the gear from the broken mast of that filthy fishing-boat has fouled our propeller. It may mean a slight delay, but there is nothing to worry about; so if you are wise you will go back to your beds."

In view of the urgency of their journey they all felt a little uneasy, but the Captain having said a "slight" delay was reassuring. After all, the consequences of a collision at sea might have been so much worse, and, as Rex pointed out on their return to the saloon, it was the first accident which had caused them any delay at all during the many hundreds of miles that they had travelled on their quest for the Golden Fleece. Disquieted but not seriously alarmed, they returned to their bunks and soon dropped off to sleep.

When they awoke the engines were still silent, and Simon, who was up first, went out to make anxious enquiries of the Captain. On his return he found Rex helping Richard to dress, and they both saw from his face that he had bad news for them.

"We're in a muddle," he announced. "Apparently the propeller was still going when that gear got tangled up in it. Something got twisted and a new propeller will have to be fitted. We can't do anything but lie here until we sight something big enough to tow us in to Varna."

"Shucks!" snapped Rex. "What's the matter with radioing for a tug to come out and tow us in?"

"Small coasters like this are not fitted with wireless yet."

Richard glanced at the porthole. "But the fog!" he cried in quick alarm. "Look! It's as thick as ever. It may be hours before anything comes near enough to spot us in this murk."

"There's our siren," Simon murmured, not very happily. "Anything that gets near enough to hear it will head for us to find out what's wrong."

Even as he spoke the short wailing blasts of the hooter, that had been sounding at intervals of a few moments all night, came again.

In gloomy silence they ate their breakfasts, then went up on deck. The sea was still calm, there was not a breath of wind, and the fog showed no signs of lifting. It was now the 18th, so they had only three days and two nights to go, and even when they reached Istanbul they would have to communicate with London, and London would have to issue instructions in time for Sir Reginald Kent to complete the deal before midnight on the 20th. Now terribly conscious of every wasted moment, they sat up on the afterdeck straining their eyes into the murk for the first sight of any rescuing ship and their ears for a reply to their wailing hooter.

At the first opportunity they spoke to the Captain, and asked him to have them transferred to any ship that appeared in order that they might be landed at Varna at the earliest possible moment, to which he readily agreed; but it was two o'clock in the afternoon before a sudden stir announced that a vessel had at last been sighted.

The vessel proved to be only another fishing-smack, and the friends were faced with the awful question as to whether they should go aboard her or wait until something more speedy and reliable appeared on the scene.

By means of megaphones their Captain and the Master of the fishing-smack held a staccato conversation, after which the Captain reported that the Master said that if the fog lifted he should be able to reach Varna that night, but if it did not it was unlikely that there would be enough wind to enable him to make port until next day.

All suffering the most chronic anxiety and indecision, the friends discussed the matter, and finally, swayed by an intense craving to end their enforced inactivity rather than from any judgment that the soundest brain could have made, they decided to chance a transfer to the smack. A boat was accordingly lowered, they were put aboard, and ten minutes later as the two vessels drifted apart they watched the steamer disappear in the chill grey mist.

The hours that followed were positive torture, and the misery they felt was aggravated by the fact that neither the Master of the smack nor his crew of two spoke a word of any language Simon, Rex or Richard could understand. In consequence they could not enquire how far from Varna they were or what prospects there were of the fog lifting. They could only sit in cramped discomfort weighed down by the appalling responsibility to the Allied Cause which had been placed upon them.

After what seemed an eternity the fog appeared to grow gradually denser, then they realized that this was not actually the case but that darkness was falling; and with breaking hearts they knew that they were condemned to another night at sea.

The fact that their evening meal consisted of steaks cut from a freshly caught white dolphin would normally have provoked their interest; but this passed unnoticed until Rex afterwards examined the fin of the great fish and, having counted its rings, astonished them by remarking that it had been well over two hundred years old, and that some giants of the species were credibly reported to have disported themselves in the Black Sea for eight hundred years before being caught.

When morning came they felt like death from having spent the night huddled together in the one narrow cabin, but the fog had lifted somewhat. Grey wisps of it still obscured the horizon, but there was enough breeze for the fishermen to run up the mainsail.

By eight o'clock the last remnants of the accursed fog had been swept away, and under a blue sky they were lapping along through a slightly choppy sea. But they had been the best part of sixty miles from Varna when the fishing-smack had picked them up and the efforts of the Master had not reduced the distance by as much as half, so it was getting on for two o'clock when they landed at the Bulgarian port.

Another hour went in interviewing the immigration authorities and securing transit visas permitting them to go on as soon as possible to Turkey. They then hurried to the Harbour Hotel and made enquiries as to the quickest means of continuing their journey. When they had learned them it seemed that they were already faced with defeat.

It was Thursday the 19th, and the only passenger-carrying coaster plying between Varna and Istanbul left the former on Wednesdays and Saturdays. To have gone by train would have been equally futile, as the journey was, by comparison, even more roundabout than that from Constanta, necessitating a run inland of nearly one hundred and fifty miles to Tirnovo, then a corkscrew passage south through the Balkan Mountains and a further four hundred and fifty miles as the railway meandered through the south-eastern tip of Europe. It was in fact nearly seven hundred miles by rail as compared with only one hundred and forty-six by sea.

Rex begged the manager and desk clerk, to whom they were talking, to find them a plane, but they clearly thought he was joking, and when persuaded of his seriousness assured him that aircraft rarely came to a little town like Varna.

Simon wanted to hire a car and attempt the three-hundred-mile run round the vast bay, but they were told that most of the coastal roads were little better than tracks and that such a trip would take at least three days.

Richard insisted that some ship or other must be leaving Varna for Istanbul before Saturday, and demanded that the manager should ring up the port authorities to find out. He proved correct. A Soviet cargo vessel was sailing at midnight that night.

It took them three hours to trace the ship's Captain to a little waterside café. They had drinks with him, and after some haggling, through an interpreter, a sum was agreed for which he should take them with him.

The ship did not sail at midnight. It was a filthy tub in which the Captain was far from being the Master and the crew an ill-disciplined set of toughs.

Nearly mad with frustration, the three friends stayed up all night, hardly speaking and alternately tramping the deck or staring over the side as they waited for errant members of the crew. It was five o'clock in the morning before the last drunken Russian seaman was carried aboard and six-thirty before they were clear of the port. When at last the ship was at sea her passengers flopped, despairing and exhausted, onto the filthy bunks that they had been given.

They woke in the early afternoon and, having eaten an unappetizing snack, held a grim council of war. It was the 20th of October, and at midnight the option would become merely a piece of waste paper. The ship was ploughing along at a steady fourteen knots an hour. It had been due to dock at Istanbul at eleven o'clock that morning, but the drunken Russian crew had cost them a good six hours. They could not hope to be in now before five in the afternoon. That left seven hours to explain their mission at the British Embassy, then get a decision taken in London and the requisite instructions telegraphed to Sir Reginald Kent.

Richard was still optimistic, but the other two, who knew much more about cable delays, were of the opinion that the great coup would now misfire by a matter of hours.

Soon after they sighted Fort Kilia they anxiously watched the pilot come aboard. Then they passed Rumeli and entered the narrows of the Bosphorus. Impatiently they walked the deck, their eyes unseeing as they glided by the charming vistas of terraced gardens on either shore and the domed splendour of the old Dolmabatchi Palace, their minds concentrated solely on the flying moments, each one of which now brought them nearer to defeat.

They were at the gangway with their bags waiting for the ship to dock when, to their surprise, she dropped anchor in mid-channel. They then saw a large motor-boat full of uniformed men put off. A few minutes later the usual Customs Officials came on board accompanied by a squad of soldiers. The reason for this soon emerged. Turkey was not at war, but, owing to the war, in a state of advanced preparedness which was causing her to take maximum precautions; particularly with regard to Russia, whose designs she had ample reason to regard with apprehension. The military guard was for the purpose of making certain that no one left the ship unless they had been issued with special permits to do so.

Richard, Rex and Simon argued with the Turkish officials in vain. In no circumstances could the travellers be allowed to land until they had been fully vetted by the immigration authorities, and, as it was now after five o'clock, these would not be visiting the ship until the following morning.

"Well, I guess this is the end," said Rex, as he at last turned miserably away, and they walked to the forward part of the deck.

"Oh, God!" muttered Richard. "Just to think of all those hundreds of Nazi aircraft we could have grounded if only we could get ashore!"

"'Fraid we'd have missed the boat anyway." Simon endeavoured to soften the blow. "As I said earlier today, getting cipher cables through isn't like pressing a button."

Rex was staring at the shore. It was only two hundred yards away.

"I could swim that in no time," he said suddenly. "Give me that option, Simon."

"Ner." Simon shook his head. "If I thought you had a dog's chance, I would. But in broad daylight it would be flat, deliberate suicide; and I saw the Duke shot before my eyes. I'm not going through that again to no purpose. If it was after dark it would be different."

"Come on, ante up," urged Rex. "After dark it'll be too late, for certain. We'd never get our message to London in three hours."

"No." Richard joined the opposition. "Simon's right. You can see by the looks of these Turks that they hate the very guts of the Russians. I've no doubt they think we're Russians too, and they would riddle you with bullets before you could swim a dozen yards. The Golden Fleece would be no good to anybody at the bottom of the Bosphorus."

"Okay," said Rex. "We're sunk then! Jezz, it's tough, though, when you think what we might have done to Hitler. If only we'd had just one more day!"

"If only we'd been crossing the Pacific," Richard sighed, with an attempt lightness, "we'd have made that extra day without knowing anything bout it."

"What on earth d'you mean?" Simon gave him a puzzled stare.

"Why, surely you remember the Jules Verne story *Round the World in Eighty Days*? The hero did it for a bet, and when he got back to London he thought he'd lost his money by a bare twelve hours; but he'd forgotten that when you cross the Pacific from West to East, once you're over the Date Line you have made a day."

"What a grand dénouement," commented Rex. "The only snag is that we haven't crossed the Pacific."

"Wait a minute," said Simon, quickly fumbling in his inner pocket and producing the Golden Fleece. "We haven't crossed the Pacific, but that's given me an idea. Did any of you ever bother to look at the actual date of this option?"

"You're nuts," Rex shrugged. "It was completed by the Rumanian Prime Minister's signature and handed to old von G. on the 21st September, so it must be up today, 20th of October."

"Wait!" gasped Simon. "Wait! It wasn't handed to von Geisenheim until half past ten at night, so if it is dated the 21st he would have lost nearly a whole day. My God! I'm right! I'm right! We're going to win out after all! It is for thirty days as from *midnight* of 21st September. That means the option does not expire until midnight tomorrow."

For a moment they were almost stunned at the thought of this last-minute reprieve from failure, then Rex drew his hand across his brow and muttered: "Holy Jehosaphat! This beats all. Just lead me to a magnum!"

"There isn't one—not in this ship." Richard laughed almost hysterically. "But the Ruskies have got some Vodka. Let's buy a bottle off one of these toughs and drink it to this new Golden Fleece that we've brought out of Rumania."

Hardly knowing what they were doing, so great was their relief, they drifted forrard, and two bottles of Vodka swiftly changed hands for some Rumanian *lei*. They fetched some glasses and taking the bottles up to the afterdeck sat down to savour their victory in advance. The evening sunlight was gilding the domes of the great mosques to the south of the Golden Horn, and the surly wrangling between the Russian crew and the Turkish officials, which was still proceeding in the waist of the ship, no longer held the faintest interest for them.

So great had been their anxiety and distress during the past three days that they had not even thought about their appearance; but now they realized that, owing to their long hours in the fishing-smack and their hectic time securing a passage from Varna, they had not even shaved. So, that evening, they took pains to make themselves presentable for the morrow with all the resources that the Soviet tramp had to offer.

Next morning they were up betimes, and by eight o'clock, freshly shaved once more, they were eagerly awaiting the arrival of the immigration official. But it seemed that the Turks were in no hurry at all to accommodate t'

Russian visitors, and the three friends had to possess their souls in patience as best they could until a new party of Turks boarded the ship at half past ten.

It was eleven o'clock before they were at last allowed to enter the cabin in which the Turks had installed themselves to transact their business. Even then the officials proved far from friendly and showed all the leisurely disinterestedness in time typical of Orientals. They did not seek to disguise the fact that they believed the British passports of Richard and Simon to have been forged in Moscow, and at the sight of Rex's emergency chit from the American Consul in Constanta they showed even more open distrust.

Their questions were endless and often entirely irrelevant; they showed little intelligence and not one spark of imagination. They were typical of the underpaid, low-ranking employees of every Government; just quite harmless men of very limited ability, but having ingrained in them the knowledge that pensions were to be earned only by sticking to the rules and that they had a definite duty to perform.

Time was still marching on. From sanguine confidence, when they had woken up, the friends had gradually once more passed through the stages of uneasiness and worry until, with the flying minutes, they were now acutely anxious again.

At length, as the ship's bell struck for midday, Rex voiced the feelings of his party by saying to the interpreter who was acting for the Turks:

"See here! You'd better tell this bunch of small-time bureaucrats that if they don't let me go ashore right now I'll have their scalps. I'm an American citizen, and I demand to be taken to my Embassy. My old man is Channock van Ryn of the Chesapeake Banking and Trust Corporation. He's done business with Ataturk in person. Ismet Pasha and all the rest of your big shots take off their hats to him. What the hell's it matter who my grandmother was, or any other of your fool questions? I've got urgent business with my Embassy, and if they waste one moment more of my time I'll see your Government have the pants off them and that they're out of their jobs for keeps."

The interpreter gave a, probably, much modified version of this outburst, and almost before he had finished speaking Richard added, with one of the rare spates of cold fury which he so very seldom let go:

"That stands for me too. I'm British, and you can send me to my Embassy under guard if you like. But if I'm not there in half an hour I'll have you people sacked. I'm nobody in particular, just an ordinary English gentleman; but I happen to know our Foreign Secretary, and when I get home I'll see to it that his life is not worth living until I've had redress, if you hold me for another five minutes on this ship."

Again the interpreter muttered; his audience was now visibly scared.

They talked rapidly among themselves, shrugged eloquently and signed permits for the three friends to go ashore.

By a quarter past twelve they were landed at the Galata Bridge, at twenty past they had secured a taxi, by half past it was carrying them swiftly through the traffic in the Gran' Rue de Pera, a couple of minutes later it turned out of Hamal Bachi Street into the courtyard of the British Embassy.

To their consternation they learned that the Ambassador was out and not expected back until four o'clock, but their urgent importunity in the Chancellery Office secured them an interview with one of the Secretaries.

He was a pleasant, youngish man, who insisted on seeing that they were comfortably seated and offering them cigarettes before he would listen to their business.

Richard acted as their spokesman and, once he started, a concise version of the whole story poured from him in an unbroken spate of words that occupied exactly two minutes.

"May I see this, er—somewhat remarkable document?" asked the young man.

Without a second's delay Simon pulled the Golden Fleece from his pocket and pushed it across the desk behind which the Secretary was sitting.

He took it and, putting on a pair of horn-rimmed spectacles, began to read it carefully.

"This is interesting," he murmured quietly, when he had reached the second page. "Yes, it seems that you had quite a useful idea."

"For the Lord's sake . . . !" Rex began, but Simon kicked him into silence.

Ignoring the remark and completely imperturbable, the young man read on to the end of the document, then he laid it carefully down on his desk, removed his spectacles and gave them a charming smile.

"Really, I do take off my hat to you people. You've put up a magnificent show. It would have been a not altogether unprofitable little affair, if we could have pulled it off."

"What d'you mean—'would have been'? grated Rex. "You've got a telephone there, haven't you? For Mike's sake get busy on it!"

The young man glanced at the clock and shook his head. "I'm sorry, but I'm afraid you've missed the bus. If I may say so I am, er—well, not unsympathetic. I gather that you have been at quite some pains to secure this thing. But unfortunately it is invalidated by the time factor. You see, this document and our comments on it could only be sent in 'Most Secret' cipher, and, owing to its length, that would take quite some little time to do . . ."

"Then, for God's sake get down to it!" ejaculated Richard.

"I'm sorry," the young man repeated with his bland smile. "But, regrettable as we may find it, seeing that it is after one, my colleague, who handles that sort of thing, is now out at lunch. But that is entirely immaterial. Even if he began to encipher this here and now, and all we busy people devoted ourselves exclusively to the drafting of a covering despatch, the results of our labours could not possibly reach London much before five o'clock. That, of course, would be with luck and the use of the highest priorities. Then the deciphering would have to be done and the Foreign Secretary collected from wherever he might be. And somehow I have an idea that even the Minister might consider consultation necessary. You see, the expenditure of quite a penny is involved, so no doubt the Treasury would have to be consulted. In fact, in my view, for what it is worth, a meeting of the War Cabinet would have to be called and the P.M.'s views sought. Then, after all that there would be the enciphering of another telegram to His Majesty's Minister in Bucharest, and quite possibly his opinion, as the man on the spot, would be asked for before any final decision was taken. Even in the best case his people would have to spend at least an hour deciphering his instructions, and then he would need a little time to collect such Rumanians as may be involved from their evening occupations, before he could render any action that he desired to take effective.''

As he paused they all stared at him with undisguised disappointment and acute distress.

He went on again, very seriously now and a little hesitantly : "I really *am* sorry. I can guess what this has meant to you. It was a great idea ; really great. But it would need an absolute minimum of twenty-four hours to make the wheels revolve sufficiently to put it across ; and if His Excellency were here he would tell you the same. It was a very gallant effort, but I know beyond all question that it is too late. May I—may I offer all of you some lunch ?''

Chapter XXI

OLD SOLDIERS NEVER DIE

IN spite of the Secretary's passion for understatement, none of his three visitors could doubt that he knew what he was talking about. They had been after game too big for any Foreign Office fund to pay. The Treasury *would* have to be consulted, and before agreeing to the expenditure of the huge sum involved they would rightly require an assessment of the benefits expected to accrue to the Allied war effort. Even if an emergency meeting of the War Cabinet could be called for that evening, or the cautious Mr. Neville Chamberlain took the quite exceptional step of authorizing the expenditure on his personal responsibility as Prime Minister, the delays in getting instructions through to Sir Reginald Kent in time for him to act effectively before midnight were clearly insurmountable.

Their stupendous efforts, their endless journeyings, their plottings, wounds and worries, the frightful strain upon their nerves, had all been in vain. In spite of that last-minute reprieve of the extra day they were still a day too late.

They thanked the young man for his invitation to luncheon but refused it, as they were anxious now to see Marie Lou and Lucretia as soon as possible. Sadly and silently, they left the Embassy and took a taxi round to the Pera Palace Hotel.

"Look!" cried Richard, just as the taxi was pulling up. "Look! There's Lucretia."

The others followed his glance and caught a glimpse of her as she stepped into a waiting car. They shouted to attract her attention, but she did not hear them, and before they could get out of their taxi her car had driven away.

"Gee! I'll say she was looking tops," remarked Rex as Simon paid off their cab.

"Wasn't she?" agreed Richard, and indeed from the brief sight of her they had had she seemed an entirely different woman to the sad-eyed, black-clad girl they had all sorrowed for a month before in Bucharest. Today she had been wearing a gay, sky-blue suit with flimsy ruffles of lace at her wrists and throat, and a dashing little hat cocked at an angle on her burnished golden curls.

"Looks as though she'd got over that awful business of poor Jan," said Simon.

Richard nodded. "Yes. Well, that, at least, is something to be thankful for."

At the desk of the hotel they arranged about rooms and enquired for Marie Lou, but to Richard's intense disappointment she was out.

They had a quick wash and lunched. Over the meal there seemed little to be said. Simon had secured a French newspaper published in Istanbul, and they tried to interest themselves in the war news, but the war seemed to have reached a stalemate, and nothing of sufficient consequence had happened in the past week to take their minds off their own dismal thoughts.

After lunch they went upstairs to unpack and enjoy the luxury of warm baths. Back in his old suite, Richard regretted Marie Lou's absence more than ever. Her perfume was still in the air, and, although he knew it seemed silly, he lovingly fingered some of her things.

At four o'clock they went out to do some shopping, as all of them were sadly in want of new clothes. On their return they found that neither of the girls was yet back, so they went up to their rooms again and changed, into some of their purchases. The psychological effect of feeling really clean and neat once more had restored their morale a little by the time they gathered in the cocktail bar, but all of them were secretly fretting now over a new worry; they had yet to break to the girls the terrible news about the Duke.

When they had sunk three rounds of cocktails Richard suddenly voiced his thoughts. "They both adored him, you know. They're going to take it hellish badly. We'd better hedge till after dinner, then break it to them separately. It's going to be the very devil, but I'll tell Marie Lou."

"Um," Simon nodded his beaky head. "Rex and I will take care of Lucretia."

It was nearly eight o'clock before the girls returned, and they came in together. They had lunched with different friends but joined up afterwards to visit other friends who lived on the lovely little island of Prinkipo. Their delight at seeing their three cavaliers was unbounded, but Richard cleverly forestalled all questions by saying swiftly:

"We've got simply masses to tell you, but we thought it would be best to save our Odyssey till dinner and afterwards. We three are famished, so if you want a wash you'd better run up to your rooms quickly, then we'll be able to get down to it sooner."

Marie Lou gave him a curious glance. She had naturally expected him to go up to their suite with her, but she knew that it could not possibly be indifference. Her quick intuition told her that he was trying to keep some bad news from her for the moment and knew that if they were alone together he would find it impossible to evade her questions.

"Have you come from Bucharest?" asked Lucretia quickly.

"Ner," Simon shook his head. "From Varna and Constanta."

"Oh dear!" she exclaimed. "As Greyeyes isn't with you I'd hoped . . ."

"We'll tell you about him, too, when we've fed," cut in Rex. "Off you go now to powder your noses, while we fix a table."

Both the girls saw that there was something wrong, but they accepted the situation and went up in the lift. Their anxiety to hear what had happened lent speed to their toilets, and they were both down again in fifteen minutes. Rex had secured a corner table away from the band, and they all went in to dinner.

"Now," said Marie Lou, immediately they had ordered. "You are all worried silly about something. I know. That's why Richard wouldn't come upstairs with me just now. He couldn't keep a secret from me for five minutes. It's about Greyeyes, isn't it?"

"Well, in a way," Richard confessed lamely. "But I wasn't there, so Simon and Rex had better tell you what happened."

"Okay," said Rex, taking the plunge. "I'll give you everything up to the time I left the party, then Simon can carry on from there."

While they ate their *hors d'œuvre* and fish Rex talked between mouthfuls, giving a detailed story of the happenings after he, the Duke and Simon had parted from the girls and Richard on the train. He deliberately span out the account of how they had bought the Chrysler and old clothes, and of their interview with Teleuescu, in the hope that they might get through dinner before the point was reached when the hideous blow would have to be delivered; but by the time the pheasant was served he had finished telling of the attack on von Geisenheim and had to hand over to Simon.

The shrewd Simon had at once grasped Rex's tactics and followed suit, dwelling as long as possible on his own fears while he waited to rendezvous with the Duke outside the Cathedral on the following morning; but they had only just finished their bird when he came to the crucial point of the Duke setting him down from the taxi in front of the British Legation.

Suddenly Richard choked and pushed his chair back.

"Sorry," he said, "but I'm feeling ill." And indeed he was looking as white as a sheet. Stretching out a hand, he took Marie Lou's and added: "Come upstairs with me, darling—please."

The two of them left the table and in silence went up in the lift. The moment the door of their private sitting-room had closed behind them, Marie Lou put her arms round his neck and said:

"Richard—darling. What is it? You've had bad news of Greyeyes, haven't you? Is he—is he . . . ?"

"No. Well, yes; but we don't know for certain. That's the devil of it. We haven't heard a thing about him since he was shot."

"I know," Marie Lou murmured. She was crying now but she showed no evidence of shock, as he had expected, and she hurried on: "Lucretia and I have been almost off our heads with worry ever since we heard. This waiting for news is simply killing us. But Jan will be back in two or three days now, and . . ."

"Jan!" gasped Richard, holding her away from him and staring into her tear-stained face. "But Jan was knocked down and killed in the street just before we arrived in Bucharest."

She shook her head. "Knocked down, darling; but not killed."

"But Rex and Simon went to his funeral."

"No," she smiled through her tears. "There were two Polish officers run over in Bucharest that day. I remember thinking it funny at the time that the man at the British Legation should have told us that Jan had died from injuries to his head while Rex said that a lorry had gone right over his body. Both of them were taken to the same hospital. The muddle must have occurred because neither Rex nor Simon could speak Rumanian, and the doctor at the hospital spoke only a little French. It was the poor fellow who was run over by the lorry that Rex and Simon saw buried, while Jan was lying unconscious from wounds to his head."

"Good Lord!" murmured Richard. "And to think we never knew a thing about this. No wonder Lucretia is looking so marvellous. Oh, I'm so glad for her."

"Yes, I think she was just slowly dying of a broken heart before."

"But you spoke of Jan 'getting back'. He's been here, then. How on earth did he know where you were ?"

"He saw Greyeyes in hospital. After Greyeyes was shot he was put into Jan's ward."

"What ! Greyeyes isn't dead then ! Oh, darling ! darling ! This is too wonderful to be true !"

Marie Lou's great violet eyes clouded again. "We don't know. That's what's so terrible. Jan spoke to him only for a moment, a few hours after he was brought in. He was so badly wounded that he fainted from the effort to speak. He got out of bed in the night to say something to Jan. That was absolute madness, of course, and he collapsed across Jan's bed. Next day Greyeyes was moved to another ward, and they didn't see one another again. But Jan got it from him that we were in Istanbul, and as soon as he could get permission from the Polish authorities he came to Turkey to find us. Greyeyes collapsed before he could give Jan the name of this hotel, so he couldn't write or telegraph, and had to hunt for us when he got here. He only arrived the night before last and went straight back to Bucharest yesterday to find out if Greyeyes is recovering or—or if he has died of his wounds."

Suddenly Marie Lou fell forward on Richard's chest and burst into a fresh torrent of tears. He did his best to comfort her. When she had recovered a little she made up her face anew ; then they decided to join the others downstairs.

Rex and Simon had meanwhile heard the same marvellous news of Jan from Lucretia. His head injuries had kept him in hospital for only ten days ; then he had been evacuated from Rumania with many other Polish airmen under a scheme that had been agreed on by the Allies, and had been moved about a lot before he could secure permission to come to Turkey.

The three men related the later stages of their Odyssey right up to the checkmate that had been inflicted on them that morning. Such an ending depressed them all again, but the two girls loyally declared that few men could have done as much, and no one more. They had just struck a vein of incredibly bad luck, and Fate had held all the cards against them.

They talked on until midnight, filling in the gaps ; then sought their beds, comforted greatly by their reunion after these many days, but still in mortal fear of the news that Jan might bring about the Duke.

For the new arrivals the fact of de Richleau's still having been able to stagger across a hospital ward the night after the shooting was stupendous ; as from Simon's account they had all feared that he had been shot dead outside the Legation.

Richard, the ever optimistic, felt convinced that as he had reached hospital alive, however bad his injuries, he would somehow pull through. Rex agreed, recalling his splendid constitution and maintaining that, in spite of his age, he was tougher than any of them. Lucretia, who, as a nurse in Spain, had seen so much of blood and death, feared that his age would tell against him if later he had had to undergo any serious operation to remove the bullets that must have been in his body. Marie Lou had a tremendous belief in the power of the mind to overcome the ills of the flesh, and tried to comfort them with the thought that if any man could cheat death by the sheer will to live it was their beloved Greyeyes. But Simon, who had actually seen the four assassins firing at him, still felt that only a miracle could bring him back to them.

Clocks and watches seemed to remain almost motionless for them all during the next two days, then on the morning of Tuesday the 24th Lucretia received a telegram from Jan ; it read :

"INVALID NOW FIT TO TRAVEL AM LEAVING BUCHAREST WITH HIM TODAY HAVE AMBULANCE AT STATION TO MEET TRAIN ARRIVING SIX-THIRTY WEDNESDAY EVENING FONDEST LOVE."

They could hardly contain themselves for joy and at once set about preparing for the Duke's reception. The management at the "Pera Palace" let them the Royal suite. They filled it with flowers and books and every conceivable thing that they could think of that de Richleau might like to have about him.

At six o'clock on the Wednesday they were all at the station. At half past the long train drew in. For a few frantic moments their eyes searched the crowded platform, then they caught sight of Jan's square shoulders and stalwart back. Running towards him, they poured out a spate of questions.

Jan hugged Lucretia, then smiled round at them. "What a grand surprise for him that you should all be here! He has stood the journey well. I was terrified that he might have a haemorrhage, but he swore that he would die of boredom if he remained in hospital any longer. He must not talk much yet, though, because he had two bullets through his lung."

While he was speaking two attendants had been lifting a stretcher from the train. Under warm coverings the Duke lay on it. Only his head was visible, and round that there were white bandages. His face was very pale, and his aquiline nose stood out from it, seeming thinner than ever ; but his grey eyes were as full of animation as they had ever been, and his smile was wonderful to behold as he saw himself surrounded by all his friends, and the two girls stooped to kiss him, laying great bunches of stephanotis and dahlias on the stretcher.

"What a reception!" he murmured. "To see you all safe and well does me more good than could all the doctors in Christendom."

At the "Pera Palace" an English doctor and nurse, whom Simon had secured the previous day, were waiting to put the invalid to bed. Half an hour later the doctor reported to the rest of the party on his condition.

"He must be kept very quiet for a bit," he said. "Two bullets had to be removed from his right lung, but he should be all right now with careful nursing. Fortunately all his wounds were in the upper part of his body. A third bullet seared his scalp, a fourth took a piece out of his right ear, a fifth went through his right forearm, fracturing the bone, and a sixth got him in the fleshy part of his shoulder; but it is five weeks now since he sustained all these injuries and the arm was well set by the Rumanians, so it is only his lung that we still have to keep an eye on."

"May we see him tonight?" asked Richard.

"Yes. But I think you should limit your visit to five minutes. He needs rest after his journey. So please don't excite him or let him talk much."

De Richleau sent a message out by the nurse that, although he could not join them, he wished them to have a gala dinner in the sitting-room of his suite; so they celebrated there, and at his request the door of his bedroom was left ajar so that he could hear the voices of these younger people that he loved so dearly, and their laughter.

When they had finished dinner they went in to him.

Simon spoke first, as he sat down with a long, happy sigh. "Well, last time I saw you I never thought we'd meet again."

The Duke's firm, sensitive mouth curved into an amused smile. "I foxed them," he said in a low voice. "I knew I stood no chance against all those gunmen. Immediately I had shot the two who were trying to stop you I played Brer Rabbit, dropped my gun, hung half out of the taxi and pretended to be dead. Only two of those brutes continued to fire at me after that and the coachwork of the taxi saved me from the worst. I'd slumped well down into it, so all of me but my head, shoulders and arm were well protected."

"Did you ever get the low-down on what happened to old von G.?" asked Rex.

"Yes. His head wounds were so severe that as soon as he could be moved he was sent back to Germany for special treatment. I imagine he is still too ill to have preferred any charge against us. Anyhow, the fear that he might was one of the reasons why I was so devilish anxious to get out of Rumania."

"Didn't the Rumanians make trouble about your having pinched that taxi, though; and having caused a riot in which several people were killed?" Richard enquired.

De Richleau smiled again. "After they had operated on my lung to remove the bullets I was transferred to the prison hospital. As you will have heard, the Prime Minister's assassination provoked a nation-wide reaction against the Iron Guard. They were blamed for the riot, and several of them were executed for firing on the police."

He paused a moment, and Marie Lou urged him not to talk any more that night, but he shook his head and went on :

"I'm quite all right, provided I talk slowly. After a month in hospital the doctors considered that I was fit enough to answer a charge about the taxi. Sir Reginald Kent gave me every possible help, and the Rumanians behaved very decently. They put me in a private ward, and a magistrate came there with the lawyers and interpreters to enquire into the matter. He was a good chap, and I pleaded the extreme difficulty of getting to my own Legation except by some subterfuge. The case was heard in court the following day, the 21st I think. I was represented by a lawyer and sentenced in my absence to a month's imprisonment. But I had already done my month in the prison hospital, so from last Saturday I was a free man again."

Lucretia poured out for him the second glass from a half-bottle of cham-pagne that the doctor had said that he might have, and supporting his head held it to his lips.

After he had drunk some of the wine, he said : "Now tell me your news. On what date did you manage to inform London about the Golden Fleece ?"

It was the question that they had all been dreading, and before dinner they had anxiously debated as to whether the shock of knowing that they had failed might not be very bad for him in his present state. The men were all anxious to unburden themselves about their tragic defeat, because they felt that they could never be at ease in his presence until they had confessed their failure, but they were equally anxious to carry the unpleasant burden until he was well, if knowledge of it was likely to do him the least harm. Lucretia, whose experience of what would or would not cause a serious setback to an invalid was much greater than that of any of the others, had relieved them of this responsibility by saying that there could be no danger in telling him, because he was only physically ill and his mind had in no way been affected. As the Duke had left the Golden Fleece with Simon it had been decided that he should break the news.

"Er——" he hesitated now and wriggled his neck. "Well, I'll tell you. We got in a bit of a muddle. I was jugged myself for a fortnight for wearing that nun's get-up. I'd passed the 'Fleece' on to Rex, but he got into a muddle, too. He was in prison for even longer than I was. We'll tell you the whole story when we're allowed to get together for a proper session. Anyhow, we came up against one hitch after another and the damn' thing was only good for thirty days."

"Do you mean," interrupted the Duke, "that you didn't manage to get it out after all ?"

"We got it out," gulped Richard suddenly, "but we were beaten on the post. I went back to give what help I could, and Rex and Simon performed absolute marvels, but the luck was dead against us. We didn't get through to Istanbul till the 21st, and when we produced the Golden Fleece at the Embassy they told us that, owing to the time it takes to operate secret cipher cables and so on, we'd missed the boat by a matter of hours."

De Richleau made no remark. He turned his face away from them and lay with it towards the wall.

They sat there in the most frightful silence, as though the bottom had dropped out of the world. The Duke's head was shaking slightly and he gave a kind of sobbing cough, so that they all thought he was crying until Marie Lou suddenly exclaimed :

"Greyeyes ! You're laughing. How can you be so unkind ?"

He turned his face back to them, and two tears were running from the corners of his eyes ; but they could see now that he was shaking through difficulty in controlling his mirth.

"I'm sorry," he whispered, "and I mustn't laugh. It's bad for me. But your woebegone faces were so comic. I imagine you've been through a most devilish time, and I'm certain you did everything that courage and human ingenuity could devise. It was most frightfully bad luck to be beaten by a few hours like that."

"I see nothing about it to laugh at, anyhow, darling," said Lucretia, voicing the thoughts of the rest.

"Forgive me," smiled the Duke. "I couldn't help it, and there is a funny side to the situation. I wasn't thinking of you that night when I saw Jan in hospital. I was too ill to think of anything except the Golden Fleece, and we had hardly exchanged ten words before I collapsed. I knew that all Polish airmen were being evacuated from Rumania to England by the Allies, so that as soon as he was fit enough he would be sent there. I made him swear not to say a single word to anyone and gave him the Golden Fleece to take to London for us."

"You what !" exclaimed Rex, jumping up. "You couldn't have ! We were trailing it through Rumania for a month, and we got it back. Simon's got it in his pocket still."

"Yes, the original," de Richleau breathed, with an effort now. "It will be nice to have that as a souvenir. It was a copy that I gave to Jan. I had three made. One I put in the post on the offchance that it might get through to Sir Reginald, another I left in a secondhand bag that I bought for the purpose, in the cloakroom at the railway station, in case we needed it later, and the third I gave to Jan."

Jan himself took up the story with a broad grin. "I was evacuated from Rumania on the 2nd. They sent us by rail to Athens and then by ship to England. I got there on the 13th. The Duke had written Sir Pellinore Gwain Cust's name and address on the back of the option, so I took it to him.

The British Government completed the deal by taking the option up on the 16th. Sir Pellinore was kind enough to get me an air passage out to Istanbul on a plane leaving that night. But as the Duke had sworn me to secrecy I didn't feel that I could tell even the girls anything, except that, having been evacuated with the Polish Air Force, I'd had to go on a pretty long round trip before I could rejoin them."

"Then we've pulled it off after all!" exclaimed Richard.

"Yes," nodded Jan. "Ninety per cent of Hitler's oil will be cut off now unless he decides to invade Rumania, or there is after all a *coup d'état* and a new Rumanian Government decide to hand their country over to him. They would commandeer the barges then, but as long as Rumania remains free and neutral we have enabled the British Government to stop all the traffic going up the Danube."

"But, er—these copies of the option." Simon stared at the Duke. "How did you get hold of them? When were they made?"

The nurse opened the door of the sitting-room and looked in. "I'm afraid I must ask you to go now," she said. "You've had much more than your five minutes."

As they stood up the Duke gave a little chuckle. "That was the thing I had in my mind when I sent you back to the Peppercorn to get some sleep, Simon. I had no chance to tell you about it the following morning, but I had taken the precaution of digging a photographer out of bed and making him photostat the Golden Fleece for us.

"It's so good that all six of us—no, we're seven now—should be safe and together again. Blessings on you all. Good night."

THE END

AUTHOR'S NOTE

Unless rumour is a "lying jade", the British Government did actually succeed in purchasing a controlling interest in the Danube Oil Barges. But, alas! General Antonescu's *coup d'état* brought this great economic blow against the Nazis to nought, as, after his seizure of power, Rumania, against the will of the great majority of her people, became a partner of the Axis.

Grove Place,
  Lymington,
    Hants.